Just Our Luck

"Williams always writes likable characters who lust wholeheartedly for each other, and this perfectly sweet and spicy novel is no exception."

—#1 *New York Times* bestselling author Ali Hazelwood

"Williams's signature wit, steam, and romance make it impossible not to root for Sybil and Kieran to find their happily ever after."

—*People*

"A fun and flirty ride!" —*Woman's World*

"*Just Our Luck* delivers flirtation, drama, and tender moments alike. . . . Will leave readers craving more." —*BookPage*

"Williams charms in this steamy interracial rom-com."

—*Publishers Weekly*

"*Just Our Luck* is everything I love about Denise Williams's books: incredibly smart, fully realized characters that I'm thrilled to root for, delicious tension, and an abundance of hope. I'm a forever fan."

—Tarah DeWitt, *USA Today* bestselling author of *Left of Forever*

"*Just Our Luck* is sweet and hot in equal measure, just like the best donuts! I adored Kieran and Sybil and their scorching hot chemistry and tenderness with one another as they navigated their fake dating journey. I'll read anything Denise Williams writes!"

—Naina Kumar, *USA Today* bestselling author of *Flirting with Disaster*

"*Just Our Luck* is an opposites-attract rom-com that's delightful from page one. Sybil and Kieran may have been drawn together by luck and fate, but it's their refreshingly raw vulnerability that makes this pairing truly click. I was completely charmed!"

—Myah Ariel, *USA Today* bestselling author of *No Ordinary Love*

"From steamy chemistry to each finding direction and purpose as they support each other, Sybil and Kieran are a fabulous pair."

—*Booklist*

"A sexy fake-dating romance with charm, featuring a protagonist navigating the challenges of family expectations and love."

—*Library Journal*

"*Just Our Luck* is the fun, escapist romantic romp that we need in these very expensive-egg times."

—BookTrib

Praise for *Technically Yours*

"A STEM-focused romance that is as sexy as it is cozy. . . . Williams is a master at crafting relatable characters whose past traumas obstruct their road to happiness, and *Technically Yours* is no different. She writes with the precision and charm of a classic rom-com, innately knowing the code to what makes an irresistible read."

—*Entertainment Weekly*

"If, like me, you love second chances, banter that snaps, and steam that fogs up your windows, do yourself a favor and put *Technically Yours* on your TBR. You'll laugh, you'll swoon, and you'll root for Pearl and Cord's happy ending."

—*New York Times* bestselling author Carley Fortune

"*Technically Yours* is technically flawless: a second-chance romance, a workplace affair, and a love story that will keep you flipping pages until the very end. This book was such a joy to read!"

—Nisha Sharma, author of *Marriage & Masti*

"In Williams's scorching *Technically Yours*, two old flames reignite a passion that defies algorithms. Cord's magnetic charisma, Pearl's breathless yearning. . . . These two are a force to be reckoned with in both the boardroom and the bedroom! This irresistible second-chance romance rewrites the code on rom-coms!"

—Nikki Payne, author of *The Princess and the P.I.*

"Williams uploads her best yet contemporary romance, full of complex characters, the highs and lows of being a Black woman in STEM, and plenty of steam. Recommend to readers who enjoyed Jasmine Guillory and Chloe Liese."

—*Library Journal* (starred review)

"*Technically Yours* is a clever tech-set romance that offers insights into some of the challenges of being a woman, particularly a woman of color, in this industry."

—Bookreporter

"Realistic conflict along with searing emotion and flashbacks to Pearl and Cord's first go-round make for a uniquely terrific romance."

—*Booklist*

"Cord is the kind of caring and supportive hero romance readers will adore." —*Publishers Weekly*

Praise for
Do You Take This Man

"Denise Williams is known for her swoon-worthy tales that celebrate love, and her latest rom-com follows suit!" —*Woman's World*

"If, hypothetically, Denise Williams decided to establish an academy (let's call it the University of DW) and offered courses on how to write pent-up sexual tension, steamy banter, and enemies to lovers, I would burst into the classroom and yell, 'TAKE MY MONEY!!' The writing is unmatched, the chemistry is on fire, and *Do You Take This Man* has one of the steamiest, most addictive, most satisfyingly hard-earned happily ever afters I've read in ages!"
—Ali Hazelwood, #1 *New York Times* bestselling author of *Problematic Summer Romance*

"Denise Williams has mastered the art of writing fun, sexy banter. Smart and witty, with the perfect amount of steam, *Do You Take This Man* is a gift to romance readers."
—Farrah Rochon, *New York Times* bestselling author of *Pugs and Kisses*

"Once again, Denise Williams masterfully blends humor and heart with the perfect amount of steam. *Do You Take This Man* is full of authentic characters with relatable issues, hilarious wedding hijinks, and swoony sexy times. Lear earns a place on my list of favorite heroes, and Williams cements her spot on my list of favorite writers."
—Falon Ballard, *USA Today* bestselling author of *Toe to Toe*

"This annoyances-to-lovers story is steamy like the most luxurious bubble bath! Readers are in for a beautiful ride watching the deliciously prickly RJ learn to let someone care for her body and soul. Denise Williams consistently crafts romances that are so sweetly real. Her voice shines—fullhearted and playful—through every scene."

—Rosie Danan, *USA Today* bestselling author of *Fan Service*

"Denise Williams delivers again with twice the banter, twice the heat, and the best enemies-to-lovers tension. A stellar romance!"

—Jane Igharo, author of *Where We End & Begin*

Praise for
The Fastest Way to Fall

"This entertaining read will have you sweating through your next workout."
—*Good Morning America*

"Warm, fuzzy, and ridiculously cute, *The Fastest Way to Fall* is the perfect feel-good read. Britta is an absolute breath of fresh air, and Wes is everything I love in a romantic lead. It's been weeks since I read this book, and I still smile every time I think about it. If you're looking for a novel that feels like a hug, this is it!"

—Emily Henry, #1 *New York Times* bestselling author of *Great Big Beautiful Life*

"Funny, flirtatious, and full of heart, *The Fastest Way to Fall* is an absolute winner! I loved tagging along with upbeat and utterly relatable Britta as she tries new things, gets strong, and meets her perfect match in Wes. I fell head over heels and never wanted it to end."
—Libby Hubscher, author of *Heart Marks the Spot*

"An addictive romance filled with hilarious banter, sharp and engaging dialogue, heartfelt moments, and a real and empowering heroine worth cheering for. The love between Britta and Wes blooms gradually and realistically and is sure to utterly capture your heart." —Jane Igharo, author of *Where We End & Begin*

"This charming, sexy novel pairs two people who likely would never have connected outside of an app. . . . Their slow-burn romance feels delightfully old-fashioned."
—Washington Independent Review of Books

"Williams follows *How to Fail at Flirting* with another delightfully engaging romance full of humor and surprises. Fans of Jennifer Weiner may like this one." —*Booklist*

"A body-positive, feel-good romance with highly relatable protagonists." —*Library Journal* (starred review)

"There's a lot to like in this romance with its supportive leading man, delightful heroine, and dynamic secondary cast. There's more than just romance going on, and Williams excels at juggling all the parts. . . . An emotionally resonant and thoughtful novel."
—*Kirkus Reviews*

"*The Fastest Way to Fall* is not a story about weight loss, but about learning to love who you are and about falling in love with someone who helps you feel strong. Britta's triumph over her former insecurities concerning her body, her goals, and her job are transcendent moments thanks to Williams's sensitive and masterful storytelling." —*BookPage*

Praise for
How to Fail at Flirting

"In this steamy romance, Naya Turner is an overachieving math professor blowing off work stress with a night on the town, which leads to a night with a dapper stranger. And then another, and another. She's smitten by the time she realizes there's a professional complication, and the relationship could put her job at risk. Williams blends rom-com fun with more weighty topics in her winsome debut." —*The Washington Post*

"Denise Williams's *How to Fail at Flirting* is absolutely SPECTACULAR! Ripe with serious, real-life drama, teeming with playful banter, rich with toe-curling passion, full of heart-melting romance. . . . Her debut grabbed me on page one and held me enthralled until the end, when I promptly started rereading to enjoy the deliciousness again."

—Priscilla Oliveras, *USA Today* bestselling author of *Their Perfect Melody*

"*How to Fail at Flirting* is a charming and compelling debut from Denise Williams that's as moving as it is romantic. Williams brings the banter, heat, and swoons, while also giving us a character who learns that standing up for herself is as important—and terrifying—as allowing herself to fall in love. Put 'Read *How to Fail at Flirting*' at the top of your to-do list!"

—Jen DeLuca, *USA Today* bestselling author of *Ghost Business*

"Naya and Jake's relationship is both sexy and sweet as these two people, who love their work but are not skilled at socializing or

romance, find their way forward. Academia is vividly portrayed, and readers will await the next book from Williams, a talented debut author and a PhD herself."
—*Booklist*

"*How to Fail at Flirting* is a powerhouse romance. Not only is it funny and charming and steamy, but it possesses an emotional depth that touched my heart. Naya is a beautiful and relatable main character who is hardworking, loyal, spirited, and determined to move on from an abusive relationship. It was thrilling to see her find her power in her personal life, in her career, and through her romance with Jake. And I cheered when she claimed the happily ever after she so deserved."
—Sarah Echavarre Smith, author of *Much Ado About Hating You*

"Williams's debut weaves a charming, romantic love story about a heroine rediscovering her voice and standing up for her passions."
—Andie J. Christopher, *USA Today* bestselling author of *Unrealistic Expectations*

"*How to Fail at Flirting* delivers on every level. It's funny, sexy, heartwarming, and emotional. With its engaging, lovable characters, fresh plot, and compelling narrative, I did not want to put it down! It's in my top reads of the year for sure!"
—Samantha Young, *New York Times* bestselling author of *The Love Plot*

"The warmth in Denise Williams's writing is unmistakable, as is her wit. She tackles difficult subjects, difficult emotions, with such empathy and thoughtfulness. Best of all: Jake is just the type of hero I love—sexy, smart, sweet, and smitten."
—Olivia Dade, *USA Today* bestselling author of *Second Chance Romance*

TITLES TO READ BY DENISE WILLIAMS

- ☑ *How to Fail at Flirting*
- ☐ *The Fastest Way to Fall*
- ☐ *Do You Take This Man*
- ☐ *Technically Yours*
- ☐ *Love and Other Flight Delays*
- ☑ *The Love Connection*
- ☐ *The Missed Connection*
- ☐ *The Sweetest Connection*
- ☐ *Just Our Luck*
- ☐ *The Re-Do List*

☐ The
☑ Re-Do
☐ List

DENISE WILLIAMS

Berkley Romance
New York

BERKLEY ROMANCE
Published by Berkley
An imprint of Penguin Random House LLC
1745 Broadway, New York, NY 10019
penguinrandomhouse.com

Copyright © 2026 by Denise Williams
Excerpt from *Just Our Luck* copyright © 2025 by Denise Williams
Penguin Random House values and supports copyright. Copyright fuels creativity, encourages diverse voices, promotes free speech, and creates a vibrant culture. Thank you for buying an authorized edition of this book and for complying with copyright laws by not reproducing, scanning, or distributing any part of it in any form without permission. You are supporting writers and allowing Penguin Random House to continue to publish books for every reader. Please note that no part of this book may be used or reproduced in any manner for the purpose of training artificial intelligence technologies or systems.

BERKLEY and the BERKLEY & B colophon are registered trademarks of Penguin Random House LLC.

Book design by Alison Cnockaert

Library of Congress Cataloging-in-Publication Data

Names: Williams, Denise, 1982– author.
Title: The re-do list / Denise Williams.
Description: First edition. | New York: Berkley Romance, 2026.
Identifiers: LCCN 2025032267 (print) | LCCN 2025032268 (ebook) | ISBN 9780593641453 trade paperback | ISBN 9780593641460 ebook
Subjects: LCGFT: Romance fiction | Novels | Fiction
Classification: LCC PS3623.I556497 R42 2026 (print) | LCC PS3623.I556497 (ebook)
LC record available at https://lccn.loc.gov/2025032267
LC ebook record available at https://lccn.loc.gov/2025032268

First Edition: January 2026

Printed in the United States of America
1st Printing

The authorized representative in the EU for product safety and compliance is Penguin Random House Ireland, Morrison Chambers, 32 Nassau Street, Dublin D02 YH68, Ireland, https://eu-contact.penguin.ie.

This book is dedicated to anyone who's ever had to start over, to put one foot in front of the other as the steady ground of normal and secure crumbled under your feet, giving way to an uncertain future. This is to you and the happily ever after that is patiently waiting with open arms in the distance.
And it is especially dedicated to Sarah.

AUTHOR'S NOTE

When I was sixteen, a tumor compressing my spine was removed in emergency surgery right after my junior prom. For days, I lay in bed awaiting test results to find out what would happen next. Between taking my first steps toward relearning how to walk and watching everything daytime TV had to offer, I spent my days thinking about all the things I might never get a chance to experience. It was my first time considering that I might not have all the time in the world. I was scared, angry, and overwhelmed, and I had a sense there was my life before that moment and everything that would come after. I thought it would redefine who I was.

Since then, I've been lucky to have had twenty-eight years of firsts—a first heartbreak, a first college degree, a first grown-up job, and a first kiss with a guy whose celebrity look-alike, if I had to pick one, was ALF. (If you're unfamiliar with the 1980s sitcom puppet, pause, google it, laugh at my expense, and then come back . . . I'll wait.) I got drunk on tequila and made a fool of myself for the first time, experienced painful loss for the first time, and felt righteous, helpless anger for the first time. In all those years of firsts, I'd take a re-do on a few (I mean, c'mon . . . ALF), but I know that each one shaped a little of who I am, and it wasn't the tumor and the surgery and the recovery that redefined who I was, it was all the moments after when I had the privilege of giving myself permission to grow and change along the way, and that's what this book is ultimately about.

If you've ever stumbled and had to find your footing, this book is for you, but please note it contains references to the unexpected death of a parent (in the past), recollections of injury during battle (brief), and recollections of divorce and the end of a long-term relationship. It also contains references to spinal injury and temporary paralysis. I hope you enjoy Willow and Deacon's story and it gives you the opportunity to think about your own firsts.

PROLOGUE

@ImNoExpertBut YouTube Channel

"I'm no expert, but it's time for a conversation about this generation. I know, I know. You're going to call me a boomer, but did you see that video of the girl losing it during a breakup in the middle of a public park? It's become a pretty popular meme. If you haven't seen it, it's linked in the comments, but basically this girl gets dumped in a park and starts wailing. That's over-the-top in my opinion, but I want to talk about what she's saying. And this girl is probably in her mid to late twenties, okay? She wails about her mom and—it's kind of hard to understand what she's saying, but it's definitely about middle school and something the guy with her told her in middle school. The guy, rightfully embarrassed, walks away. She tries to hold on to him and falls into the fountain nearby, thrashes around like she's drowning, and then seems to realize, 'Oh, I'm fine,' but starts sobbing all over again. It's . . . pathetic, really.

So can we talk about the kids today? I mean, imagine worrying about what your mom would think about a breakup when you're in your twenties and screeching about eighth grade to keep someone with you? This entire generation needs to toughen up.

C'mon. People have actual problems. What do you think? Drop it in the comments and don't forget to follow for more nonexpert opinions."

> JACKEDH2OBOY: Dude is better off without her. You're right! A whole generation of coddled babies!
>
> ZADDYLUVR: Don't blame age—I'm nineteen and I'd never do that. She's clearly got issues. Hope he finds someone better and hotter.
>
> HELEN.APPLESON79: Why would someone film and share this? I feel bad for this girl and what she must be going through with this much negative attention shining on her.
>
> BOATMANOATMAN: This chick lost it in public. Everything is fair game.
>
> SWEETELIZAP: I went to high school with her—she'd just followed that guy around for years. It was kind of pathetic. Better off without him.
>
> JACKEDH2OBOY: She has nice tits in that wet shirt!
>
> BOATMANOATMAN: True—the tits are A+
>
> GRANDMAGG1: ^^^ This is why we need to be worried about this generation
>
> BOATMANOATMAN: 😂 I'm fifty-seven years old.
>
> HELEN.APPLESON79: What happens to these people after they become viral memes?

CHAPTER 1

Willow

> **TO-DO LIST**
> - ☑ Meet Cruz's friend
> - ☑ Find a new coffee order

I STEPPED FORWARD in line, my gaze jumping down the menu, surreptitiously glancing left and right to make sure no one was staring. My hair fell over my shoulders and hopefully obscured my face, but when I glanced up, the blonde waiting for her drink kept looking at me, her brow scrunched as if on the edge of recognition. I tugged on my cardigan hoping for cover.

"Todd!" the barista at the other end of the counter shouted over the rumble of ten conversations and one screaming baby. "Iced chai latte with extra caramel for Todd!"

An iced chai latte might be good. I tried to catch a look at Todd and his drink of choice, but his body was already turned away. The line moved forward again, and my own personal panic percolated as my turn neared and a spark of recognition crossed the face of the blonde. She jabbed a friend next to her, but I looked away quickly before they could see my face.

I just had to decide on a drink order and then I could hide in the back. I'd had this idea that the story hadn't made it to Iowa, like a hearty Midwestern sensibility would make people above the pull of a viral video or catchy meme. Clearly, I was wrong, as the two women were audibly hypothesizing about who I was; so my first big, brave outing in public was going exactly how I'd feared. I would have fled if I wasn't meeting a man my brother had described as a "tall white guy who looks equally likely to rescue you from a burning building as to offer you pot." It wasn't a comforting or helpful description, and I was annoyed all over again that my brother took it upon himself to find me a babysitter while I was in town, as if I was four and not twenty-four. Cruz said it was just so I had someone if I needed anything while house- and dog-sitting for him for a few months, but he was as bad at hiding his concern as he was at describing people.

I didn't see any pot-dealing firefighters in the room, though, and I was next in line.

Decision time. I put my metaphorical fist down in my mind. Time to decide. Just pick something new. New state. New life. New drink. It's easy. *Spencer is probably trying all kinds of new things.* The idea crept in through the crack in my resolve, which led to what he'd said in the park replaying on a loop in my head, the words I thought were the start of a proposal. "Willow, you were my first love . . ." He'd paused and focused his gaze over my shoulder, which should have signaled to me that something bad was coming. And then he'd just said it. "But you won't be my last. This isn't working for me and I need something more. I met someone else." I never got more of an explanation, because after I reacted, I fell in the fountain. Then he was gone. I sucked in a shaky breath and stared again at the menu, willing away the memory. New drink, something that doesn't remind me of Spencer. I could do this.

White mocha? Green tea? A refreshing concoction of fruit and sugar?

The barista by the drive-thru window was looking at me with wide eyes, and I ducked my chin to hide my face the way I'd gotten used to doing.

"What can I get you?" The woman behind the counter smiled brightly, and there was a cat sticker next to her colorfully decorated name tag.

It was a simple question. It was so easy, but my mind whirred. What did I want? For things to go back to how they were, for everything to be different, and mostly to not be recognized.

"Hey, are you that girl?" The two women by the counter, both now holding large iced coffees, approached me. "The Drowning Girl? You look just like her!"

I hated that title. Drowning Girl. Even if I'd felt like I was drowning since that day. I tried to ignore them as if they were talking to someone else, but the taller of the two touched my elbow. "Sorry, aren't you Drowning Girl?" She lowered her voice this time, as if she hadn't already practically shouted it. "From that video?"

I shook my head and pulled my hair forward. "Sorry, not me."

"Would you like to try our Spring-Colada?" The barista looked between me and the taller woman, but motioned to a display featuring a drink stacked with whipped cream and sprinkled with coconut flakes and what looked like shamrock sprinkles.

I might have ordered that if I was someone who spoke up and stood my ground. Then I'd be a totally different person like I needed to be, someone full of life and energy and skin made of Teflon to deflect these kinds of conversations. That wasn't me, though. I watched the clerk's micro expression of frustration form at my hesitation.

"You look just like her! Can we take a selfie anyway?" The tall woman was oblivious to the commotion she was causing. "The Drowning Girl video trend is so hot right now."

I shook my head, panic rising in my chest. I'd seen some of the videos using the filter that could make anyone look like they were living the most embarrassing moment of my life. "Sorry, I'm meeting someone," I mumbled.

"Please?" She held out her phone. "It will just take a second."

"Okay. But I'm not her." My face felt like it was on fire, and I nodded and leaned toward them, needing this little show to end and for them to leave. When I finally looked back to the barista, her smile was gone and her jaw set. "Sorry," I said.

"You do look like her," she said, the skeptical lilt to her voice a clear sign she didn't believe my lie. "What do you want to order?"

"Large dark roast and medium iced caramel latte." I blurted out the familiar, automatic answer in a panic and tapped my credit card.

Old life: one. Willow: zero.

An iced caramel latte was fine. I'd loved them in high school. Spencer said he always appreciated that my order never changed so he could remember it, and back then, I'd wanted to make being with me as easy as possible. So, I let that be my standing order. I looked at the customer behind me deciding to take the barista up on the offer to try the Spring-Colada "for the hell of it," and I was jealous. It turned out I should have tried a lot of things for the hell of it—keeping my coffee order easy to remember didn't keep my relationship intact.

The barista had already moved on to the next customer before I could admit I'd made a mistake and that the person I'd accidentally ordered the dark roast for was fifteen hundred miles away, probably enjoying his new relationship. A dark roast and a caramel latte had been my standard coffee shop order since I was fourteen. Now the paper cup of brewed coffee would sit on the table as a reminder I'd been dumped and left alone, single for the first time since the eighth grade. My first attempt at reinventing myself and I had the same two beverages I'd had in my hands for a decade.

I drummed my fingers on the table and glanced at my phone. Maybe Cruz's friend wouldn't show, and I'd get to go home to sulk in peace where the only one who would recognize me would be my brother's dog. After I got rid of this damn black coffee.

My phone buzzed with an incoming FaceTime request, and I hoped it would be Cruz calling to say his friend couldn't make it, but no such luck.

"Hey," I said, happy to see my best friend's face.

"So," Zoe dove in without preamble. "You promise you're coming back in three months, right? You won't fall in love with Iowa and some beefy farmer, will you?"

I smiled, sipping my iced latte. My best friend, a Denver

native, would never accept that Iowa wasn't all farms. "I'll be back," I said, picturing the boxes I'd hastily stacked in Zoe's second bedroom. "I only promised Cruz I'd take care of his house and his dog while he's overseas, nothing more."

I hadn't needed to tell Cruz I was out of options when Spencer and I split and the video of my "drowning" went viral. It probably wasn't hard to figure out I'd lost my boyfriend and my home in one swoop. Add to that me losing my job once my unfortunate notoriety made me a liability, and he'd known getting out of town was my best option. Our grandpa's old house, the one Cruz had slowly been updating every time he took leave, was a perfect place to escape to.

"Good. I can't wait to help you move on from Spencer! There are so many guys I have to set you up with." I ran a fingertip around the edge of my cup, biting back the automatic defense of my ex that rose in my throat, that despite everything, I missed him being next to me. He'd been my person. Zoe didn't get it, but I'd known Spencer since I was thirteen. We'd seen each other through everything. We'd been a package deal and, as evidenced by the extra coffee, it was hard to remember we weren't even together anymore. Still, I plastered on a smile.

"I know you're sad," she added. "Offer stands to let you cry on my shoulder anytime, but let me first change into something I don't mind getting covered in tears and snot."

I covered my mouth at the chuckle that escaped, not wanting to draw attention from other customers who might notice me. "But eventually, you're going to love being single." Zoe continued listing off her favorite things about being unattached. "No conferring with another human about what to eat for dinner.

Popcorn and vodka or duck à l'orange. That reminds me. I should hit up the farmers market."

She talked more about her cooking plans while I remembered my family's dining room table slowly turning to a storage place for junk mail when we stopped having dinner together. Mom said it reminded her too much of Dad and their old life together after they'd divorced. After dinners together, it was vacations, gardening, seeing family—all of that fell by the wayside, because everything was tied to Dad, so she gave up on everything and pulled further and further into herself. Her life was cut short when a semi lost control on the interstate, but she'd spent her last years in a self-imposed prison.

I'd hated it and vowed that would never be me. I never worried it would be; I believed Spencer and I were forever. I liked thinking of someone else when we were deciding what to have for dinner. I felt so lucky to have met my person when we were young. And now I sat here with an extra coffee in front of me, bitterness creeping in as if it were my first time googling "Drowning Girl" and countless versions of the video appeared, including one with my voice auto-tuned.

Zoe interrupted my trip down memory lane. "Did your brother's hot friend show up yet? They were in the Air Force together, right?"

"Not yet, and yes, they served together. And I have no idea if he's hot. Cruz sent a pic this morning but it never came through—something with the connection. I can't believe I even agreed to meet this guy." I drummed my fingers again and tried to subtly scan the room to check if anyone else had noticed me. "Cruz played the serving-his-country card to guilt me into it."

"Yeah, damn him and his commitment to saving lives." The dogs barked uproariously in the background as she let herself into her boss's condo to walk them. "Do you think nudes would help him see how patriotic I am?"

I coughed, nearly choking on my drink. "Please don't send my brother nudes."

"But . . . it's for America." The dogs kept barking and I held the phone further away, watching a tall and imposing figure stride through the door. His hair was cropped close to the scalp in a severe buzz cut, and he pulled his sunglasses from his eyes, surveying the room.

"I think he's here," I whispered into the phone.

Muscles bulged from the T-shirt with an American flag stamped across the front, and he stepped purposefully toward the counter with a tight nod to the barista.

"He looks way more serious than Cruz described," I said. Across the room, he showed no signs of searching for me. "His neck might be thicker than my thigh."

"You'll have to compare them side by side when his head is between your—" She laughed at my panic in trying to silence her, not bothering to finish the sentence. "You're so easy."

"He's my brother's best friend. There will be no heads between . . . anything." Not that there really ever had been.

"Why not? You're no longer attached at the hip to the Drip."

Out of college, I got a job as a receptionist at a public relations company where Zoe was temping. We'd hit it off immediately and kept in touch after she left—after calling out the manager for sexist behavior. Spencer's dad got me the job, and I didn't want to make family brunch uncomfortable, but I'd been in awe of her power and ability to stand up and say what needed saying. And using that same vocal confidence, she was never hesitant to tell me how boring she found my ex. She was also my only friend who didn't know us as a couple, which meant she was now, post-breakup, my only friend, and I'd abandoned her to move across the country. I prepared myself to convince my brother via his friend that I was fine. "I gotta go, Zo," I said. "I'll talk to you later."

"Hey, Siri," I mumbled to my watch. "Set alarm for fifteen minutes." I sucked in a breath and plastered on a smile. It was refreshing to have someone not recognize me. But as soon as he had his coffee, the guy did an about-face and walked out without a nod to anyone. I wasn't sure if I was relieved it wasn't him or anxious that I might be stood up by this guy and have to spend more time alone in public.

> CRUZ: He'll probably be late.
>
> WILLOW: I don't need a nanny. I'm really fine.
>
> CRUZ: He's more of a friend than nanny.
>
> WILLOW: A friend my brother forced into talking to me.
>
> CRUZ: Best kind of friend. I've vetted him already.
>
> CRUZ: He'll be late but he'll be there.

I flipped my phone screen down on the table where the dark roast still stood sentry. I'd reassure Deacon I was fine, and then I'd get out of here. Cruz was going to be gone for a few months and I didn't need a babysitter. I needed a magic wand to make clear what I was supposed to do now that everything I'd planned for my future—the home, the family, the partner, the security—was all gone. And Deacon Rakes wasn't going to be a magic wand.

CHAPTER 2

"BROTHER," I SAID when the pixelated image of my best friend filled the screen as I waited for the air-conditioning to cool down my truck after hours spent in the school's commuter parking lot. "I'm not going to flake on your sister. I'm on my way, just running a few minutes late."

"I already told her you would be." Cruz didn't even try to hide that he called to remind me, and I looked at the background of the call out of habit, the surroundings so familiar I felt the heat and texture of sand on my skin despite the air-conditioning blowing on my face. "She'll be there early," he said. "Willow is just like that."

"Almost like it runs in the family." The man had never been later than two minutes early to anything the length of our friendship. He was a human Swiss watch. I set the phone in the mounted holder on my dash. "I'm on my way. Don't worry." I put the car in gear and glanced at the clock. "Consider me the sister wrangler."

"Don't wrangle or otherwise fucking touch my baby sister,"

he said with a laugh, the echo of which I remembered from so many late nights and long days on deployment while shooting the shit at the base. "I love you like a brother, but you've wrangled more women than Glenn Ford."

I laughed. "Who the hell is that?"

"He was a famous actor in the forties and fifties. Had affairs with, like, every woman in Hollywood. Even Marilyn Monroe. Also raised illegal chickens in Beverly Hills and secretly recorded all his phone conversations. Fascinating guy."

"Why do you know this?"

His laugh crackled through my phone. "I have lots of time to read now that you're not here to distract me." He paused, maybe catching that I hadn't laughed, too. "Anyway, all that is to say, touch Willow and I'll end you."

Traffic was light, and I nudged the gas to make it through a yellow light. "Man, you saved my life. You can trust me to look out for your baby sister."

"I know," he said, voice dipping in the way it did whenever I reminded him he saved my life. The memory was always in the back of my mind. The lack of sensation in my legs—how I'd been unable to move no matter how hard I tried and how pounding on my own leg might as well have been me pounding on the ground. I'd felt nothing. The memory of bullets whizzing by, the sound of the chopper blades, and the helplessness of seeing my best friend running toward me washed over the conversation like a black cloak, but I pushed it aside and Cruz brought the conversation back to Willow. "She's in a vulnerable place right now. That guy really broke her heart, and it didn't help that meme was everywhere. I just worry about her spending too much time alone. Our cousin invited her to her wedding, but they're not close. She needs someone nearby."

I'd searched for the video of his sister's breakup and resulting meme when he told me about it, and it was brutal. Not only had someone filmed her emotional reaction to being dumped, people added commentary about how it was a testament to the generation's lack of resilience and some other misogynistic bullshit.

"I got you," I said again. I didn't ask where he was—he wouldn't tell me because Cruz was a rule follower, even with me. The fact that we were best friends was a constant source of amazement to anyone who knew us, because I was the guy you came to when you wanted to take chances. Cruz was the guy you found when you wanted a plan. We were oil and water, yet it was hard to remember a time when he wasn't there for me.

"How's school going?" he asked. "Come to think of it, I never knew you could read." His laugh again took me back to being in uniform and I laughed, too.

"They teach you how." With nothing else to do once I was out other than work on my recovery, I'd enrolled in the local community college. Emi, my roommate, had urged me that it was the right next step, and it didn't hurt that my education benefits were sitting there unused. I thought healing, conditioning, and being well enough to request reenlistment would be fast, but so far time was dragging. "It's all right. The courses are kind of interesting." I'd spent the morning preparing for my next econ exam, but the psych classes were good—I'd liked those. I was getting closer to being strong enough to request to reenlist, so it was something to do until I could.

I hadn't told Cruz about my plans to get back in—he would have tried too hard to talk me out of it for all the reasons that probably made sense, but he didn't get it. He was still out there serving, and I was in my truck next to a bag of books. He could still fulfill his duty and make a difference. I was standing still. "I've only seen her photo in the meme and she was all wet. What does she look like? I'm picturing you but with long hair and tits."

He growled. "Don't say tits in reference to my little sister. I'm not fucking kidding."

"Technically, I said tits in reference to you." I flipped my blinker, waiting to pull into the parking lot. "Seriously, what does she look like so I can give her a firm, platonic handshake?"

"She's short. Curly hair, probably in a ponytail. Glasses, I think. She looks young. I want to forget it exists, but you can see her face kind of clearly in that video," he said. "She looks like me a little," he admitted grudgingly. "But don't make another fucking joke," he warned.

"It's too easy." I didn't want to give the video any more views. Cruz had been angrier than I'd ever heard him when he'd first mentioned it. "I'm sure I can spot her."

"I gotta go," he said, as I pulled into a parking space at the back of the parking lot. "Thanks, Rakes, I really appreciate you looking out for her. I wouldn't trust anyone else."

"Look out for yourself, brother," I said. I held up my fist, matching his on the screen. It was strange I'd known him so long and never met his sister, but we were always stationed in other states or overseas. I'd never thought much about what she might look like, and Cruz was many things, but likely to have a photo handy of anyone was not one of them. When the screen went black, I pushed back the shadowy darkness I wanted to sink into, because I'd do anything for Cruz Lewis, and he'd look out for everyone else before himself. That was the job. We were PJs, Pararescue Jumpers, a special operations unit charged with rescue and recovery for the Department of Defense. They were my family, my brothers. Or, they had been. I took in a slow breath the way I'd learned in physical therapy and stepped out of the car, shaking off the conversation, ready to meet my best friend's sister for the first time.

The coffee shop was brightly lit, and as I stepped forward to order, Linda flashed me a grin and sauntered forward with an iced caramel latte. "Hey, sweetie. Looking good today." Linda's flirting was part of my after-school routine—stop for coffee after class, get propositioned by this sixty-year-old woman I adored, study, work, and then proposition someone who wanted me just for my body. Linda handed me the coffee and I surreptitiously scanned the room, first for safety. Old habits die hard. Then, I scouted for the younger feminine version of Cruz sporting glasses and a ponytail.

At the back table, a woman with dark curly hair falling around her face looked up with wide brown eyes. She had two drinks in front of her and must have been waiting for someone. A quick scan for glasses (none) and ponytail (none) alongside her visible curves, and I was certain this was not anyone's baby sister, though I took a second to admire her profile and the roundness of her hips before thanking Linda for the drink and reassuring her I'd be ready if she ever agreed to give me a chance.

Sipping the drink, I looked around again. Over the years I'd taken shit from the guys in my unit for wanting my coffee sweet, but I'd refused to drink it black like they did. The convenient availability of caramel syrup was one of the few things I'd miss about civilian life when I went back. I took another hit from the sweet drink. The woman in the corner waved, giving me a tentative smile that showed a familiar dimple in the right cheek. A dimple I'd recognize in pitch-blackness. The hot woman in the back was Cruz's baby sister. *Oh, shit.*

To be fair, he'd described a kid, and Willow Lewis was not that. Good thing Cruz was on the other side of the world. He would have pummeled me for checking out his sister before I realized who she was.

CHAPTER 3

Willow

"WILLOW, RIGHT?" DEACON strode toward me—I'd always thought the word "stride" was synonymous with "walk," but I was wrong. His steps looked effortless and graceful, like he owned the coffee shop. He was tall and muscular in a way that didn't seem bulging like the first guy I'd seen. He looked taut and strong, and I hadn't expected the long hair and the beard. Zoe was right—he *was* my brother's hot friend.

"I'm Willow. Hi. That's me." I waved because of course I did. What else would one do when approached by a good-looking and supremely confident person? To make matters worse, he'd held out his palm for a handshake as I waved and we met somewhere in the middle with a mismatch of my floppy and his enthusiastic high fives. So, this was going great.

"Hi," I repeated as he sat down.

"I feel like I know you after hearing Cruz talk about you for so long." He pulled the straw to his mouth. "He was bad at describing you, though."

"I didn't think anyone needed my description—my face is pretty widely available on the internet." Even I heard how unconvincing that joke was.

"Yeah, but you're dry now. So that wouldn't have helped."

I'd expected pity, but his comeback made the corners of my lips twitch. "I managed to avoid fountains on my way over. Did Cruz make it sound like you should look for someone around fourteen who might be clutching a teddy bear? He still thinks I look like I did when I was fourteen even though I got LASIK years ago and changed my hair."

Deacon chuckled, the sound low and rich. "He didn't mention a stuffed animal, but yeah, that was the general idea." He set his keys and phone aside, and I noticed how he intentionally flipped it face down. I'd just met the guy, but I was so aware of his attention. His focus seemed to wrap around me, and after avoiding attention for the past couple months, not to mention my whole life, it felt surprisingly . . . nice. He leaned back in his chair and scratched his fingers along his beard. "Which begs the big question, what was your favorite stuffed animal?"

"That's the big question?" I looked at him over the lid on my coffee, trying to get a read on him, but he only looked back at me with bright eyes.

"Sure. Think about it." He settled back in his chair. "They're our first comfort and early confidant. What's bigger than that?

Mine was Mr. Muffin, a giraffe with a blue nose who currently resides in a box of things still in my parents' garage. I really should get him back."

His gaze still hadn't left mine, but not in a creepy way. I tried to remember the last time someone focused on me so intently. "Cruz told me you were kind of different."

"Just kind of? That asshole was underselling me. I'm one in a million, baby." He tipped his cup toward me, the beverage inside looking strikingly familiar to my own, and I tried to read the label. "So, who was your Mr. Muffin?"

"Sylvia," I said, remembering the matted gray fur. "A stuffed walrus in a pink shirt. Cruz got it for me for my birthday when I was four."

He tipped his glass toward me again. "See, now we're getting to know each other." His gaze trailed to the cup between us in the brown sleeve. "Double fisting it or are you expecting another of your brother's friends to show up?"

Heat rose on my cheeks, and I made a grab for the cup, as if I could hide it somewhere on this small tabletop. "No, I just . . . um, ordered it by mistake."

He lifted an eyebrow, the gesture making his eye color look deeper somehow. "Mistake?" I should have just said I ordered it for him not knowing his coffee preferences. Someone with an iota of experience meeting men might have had that wherewithal, or not even ordered it in the first place, but I was beyond out of practice.

"It's embarrassing," I said, hiding my face in my hands. I'd been so determined to order something new, like picking a new coffee drink would mean I'd begun starting over, and then the women wanted a selfie and the barista was annoyed and I reverted to autopilot. I was still focused on that lingering embarrassment when I felt the brush of fingertips by my hand.

"May I?" His voice had dipped, and I looked at him over my fingers.

"May you what?"

"Pull your hands away from your face," he said, nudging my left hand with his knuckles. "We've talked stuffed animals. That's why we start with big questions. Now there's no need to be embarrassed about anything."

"That doesn't make any sense." I pressed my fingers to my lips to cover the smile his words and easy tone brought out. "I hardly know you, and I have lots of reasons to be embarrassed. Millions of shares could corroborate."

"There's an extra shot of caramel in this," he said, swirling his own drink. "And salted caramel cold foam on top, plus Linda wrote her number on the side because we have this ongoing joke." He tapped the side of the drink, attention still on me. "I called her bluff once and asked her out. She laughed at me and told me I could never keep up with her and I wasn't pretty enough. Embarrassing, right?" He looked over his shoulder and gave the barista a wave that she returned with an indulgent smile. "Now you know two things about me that your brother would definitely make fun of me for." He motioned to the bonus coffee again. "So, tell me your embarrassing coffee secret."

The paper cup filled with dark roast coffee looked back at me blankly with nothing to offer. "I'm used to ordering for me and my ex-boyfriend. I got one for him out of habit." Even though I'd thought them in my head already, the words sounded so extremely pathetic as they left my lips. "Which is pretty sad and probably why my brother told you I needed someone to talk to while I'm in town, because who makes friends doing stuff like this?" I'd been shooting for self-deprecating in a charming sort of way, but it had come out sad, and right then I knew this meeting couldn't end fast enough. "It's pathetic."

Deacon swirled his coffee, the ice shifting in the cup, and I was about to change the subject, but he spoke first. "You're right."

I'd been expecting him to say something comforting or placating. That's what I was used to. Maybe awkward silence, but not agreeing with me. "I'm right?"

"Sure. No one makes friends with plain black coffee. C'mon. I'm telling Linda to never serve you this again." He motioned behind him. "I was expecting something way more embarrassing, like you had dropped your retainer or your learner's permit in there and were waiting for me to leave so you could fish it out."

"Because I'm fourteen in this version of events?"

"Exactly." He wrapped his long fingers around the cup and stood, walking the few feet to throw it in the trash, then returning to the table triumphant. "I guess I should have clarified first. Your retainer *wasn't* in there, right?"

I laughed again, pressing fingers to my lips to hide it, and shook my head. "No," I said, fiddling with the label on my cup. "Just my learner's permit."

"Good," he said, sipping from his own drink. "Cruz said you were with your ex for a long time?"

"Since middle school."

"Damn," he said, not adding anything else and just leaning back in his chair as if in invitation for me to keep going. "It's not the first time you ordered that coffee, huh?"

I shook my head from side to side, tears welling in my eyes without my permission. "I'm not used to being alone." I sucked in a breath, the pain of that sentence stealing the oxygen in my lungs. The panic I'd been getting used to crept up my arms like a shadow, but then Deacon's fingers brushed mine again as he handed me a napkin, wordlessly interrupting my thoughts. "Sorry," I said, dabbing my eyes. "I didn't mean to say that. I just . . ."

He ignored my apology, his intense attention still focused on me. "You don't know who you are when you're not part of that thing you thought defined you?" He offered the rest of my sentence casually, just like Zoe had when we'd hashed this out a hundred times before. He sounded like he understood it, though. Like he'd lived it. "I get it."

When I agreed, he gave a tight nod, taking a long drink from his cup before swirling the ice around. "But that's still no excuse for boring coffee."

"Lots of people like good black coffee."

"Not us, though, right?" He shook his head. "We like our drinks sweet and our childhood best friends stuffed."

My eyes still felt wet, but I laughed, the sound unexpected as it escaped my lips. "I'm supposed to go to a wedding tomorrow. I won't really know anyone there—this was a pity invite and I've never been to a wedding alone. It's like every day is more black coffee." I sniffled into the napkin, my neck hot with the mortification of breaking down in front of this stranger in a crowded coffee shop. "I should just skip it."

He gave a quick hum sound and finished his drink. "I'm afraid I can't let you do that."

"Do what?"

"Skip the wedding. Cake and the chance to line dance with total strangers? That's not an opportunity you get every day. I'll be your plus-one."

"What? No," I said, pushing the soggy napkin into my pocket. "You don't need to do that. You only committed to fifteen minutes and coffee."

"I'm a great wedding date." He motioned to his chest. "I look good in a suit, I talk to strangers easily, I'm a great dancer, and I have a decade of combat and medical training in case the 'Cha-Cha Slide' gets out of hand." He held out another napkin. "And I promised Cruz I'd make sure you didn't rebound with someone regrettable, so I can't, in good conscience, let you go it alone and end up with Cousin Rupert."

"Who is Cousin Rupert?"

"Exactly." Deacon ran long fingers through his hair and grinned. "We don't even know this guy. Better stick with me as a plus-one."

My phone buzzed twice on the table. "Shoot," I said, fumbling with the phone and bumping my plastic cup in the process.

Deacon's hand shot out to catch it before it flipped to the ground, and the buzzing finally stopped. "Did you set an alarm to get rid of me quickly?"

"I didn't know if you'd be a weirdo," I admitted, accepting my cup back from him.

"Oh, I am a weirdo." He winked, then offered me a charming smile. "A weirdo who is taking you to a wedding. What time should I pick you up? I assume I'm driving since I threw away your learner's permit with that black coffee?"

I giggled again, but this time I didn't hide my amusement. "You really don't have to."

"Cruz is my brother in all the ways that matter, and you're more important to him than anyone, so consider yourself stuck with me, at least until he gets back."

I nodded. "Okay. I accept." He stood and held out a hand for me as I scooted from behind the table. His hands were rough but his grip gentle, and I caught the scar near his knee I'd somehow missed when he walked toward me. "Thank you."

"See," he said, as we walked toward the exit, with him offering a wave to the staff as we passed. "There's something to my method of starting with the big questions."

The warmth of the sunshine hit my face as we exited, and I squinted against the glare. I'd known Deacon Rakes for all of fifteen minutes and told him about Sylvia, had a meltdown, and secured a wedding date. He held up a palm for a high five, a throwback to our initial greeting. "It's the start of something here, Willow Lewis. The start of something big."

CHAPTER 4

I ADJUSTED MY tie and ran a hand down my stomach to smooth my shirt as I walked from my room toward my two friends sitting on the couch. Emi and Sybil clapped as I strutted into the room. Our other roommate, Marcus, was out of town visiting his girlfriend in Chicago, so I was left with the women's catcalls alone. Having them all plus our fur roommate, Cupcake, as friends the last two years had been the closest I'd come to family since leaving the Air Force. This run-down house on the East Side of Des Moines had been home to a lot of laughs, even though Sybil moved out after winning the lottery the year before.

"Are you going to a job interview?" Emi asked.

"Take it in, E." I held open the jacket and did a spin for my roommate, earning a whoop from both women. "First look is free. Second one will cost you."

She snort-laughed and threw a pillow at me I dodged. "As if it's a first look. I beg you to put on clothes around here all the time." Emi was what I imagined an older sister would be like—she was never happier than when she was in charge, but she kept the house running smoothly. We'd met when I answered her ad for a roommate. After a background check and one of the most intimidating interrogations of my life, she'd invited me to move in. Cupcake jogged into the room, sensing play was happening, but spotted the pillow on the floor and burrowed in for a nap. "I've seen more of that green footprint tattoo on your ass than anyone could want."

Sybil was not at all like a sister given our history of casually hooking up, but all that ended when she met her fiancé. "Why *are* you so dressed up?" she asked. "Hot date? Parole hearing?"

"Remember my friend's little sister is in town for a few months? She lost her plus-one for a wedding, so I said I'd step in." I snagged my keys and wallet from next to the TV. "Definitely *not* a hot date. He'd kill me if I tried anything with her." Willow had been different from what I expected, though. She was beautiful, with those curves and what promised to be thick thighs under the dress she was wearing. But then she'd cried, those big eyes welling with tears. I never handled a woman crying in front of me well—it sent me into problem-solving mode, and it had reminded me I shouldn't have noticed how hot Cruz's little sister was. I had a mission, and it was to support her.

"You look quite dapper," Emi said. "Wait!" She scrambled off the couch and Sybil motioned for me to twirl again, assuring me she'd pay for the second look if needed.

She could afford it. After winning the lottery, Sybil could buy just about anything—or anyone—she wanted, not that she wanted anyone besides her fiancé, the donut shop owner turned medical researcher. "I'm sure she'll love having you on her arm."

"And you can give her this," Emi said, returning with a pink rose. "I bought a dozen since they were on sale at the grocery store, but I can share." She handed over the rose, which was just blooming, and I wrapped an arm around her shoulder.

I gave a little bow of thanks and said goodbye to my friends. On the way to my truck, I waved at the kid next door who was reading on the porch, his leg in a cast propped on a chair nearby. "Looking good, old man," he yelled.

I opened the door to my truck and pointed at his book. "What are the Lannisters up to?"

He shrugged and held up the book. "Mostly just murder and betrayal." Jayden's mom worked a lot, so I'd been hanging with him when I could while he was laid up. "Preparing me for the next time I massacre you at chess!"

"Your trash talk is getting better," I said with another wave. "And you're on."

Cruz's place wasn't far, and the sun was dipping in the sky when I turned into the driveway. As I approached the door, there was one solid bark from the other side, and I smiled. I got Cupcake at the same time Cruz adopted Gus, but one of us was the born dog trainer and it wasn't me. Gus would be silent and waiting until given the release command no matter who was on the other side of the door, and I was glad Willow had that protection. I heard her saying something behind the closed door.

"Damn it, dog, move!" I heard more shuffling. "I can't get to the door!"

"Tell him 'at ease,'" I called through the wood.

"What?"

I chuckled and twisted the rose between my fingers. "At ease. That's the command to stand down."

I heard her say it, and then a breathless Willow swung open the door. Her cheeks were flushed and her lips were painted a dark pink shade that made her features stand out even more than the first time I met her. "Sorry," she said. "He was blocking the door."

I raised one shoulder and did my best not to let my gaze drop to the front of her dress, which dipped low and then hugged her chest and stomach. Willow definitely did not look like anyone's kid sister. "Gus is a force," I said, stepping inside and scratching him behind the ears. The big-ass German shepherd was a beast and looked as intimidating as ever, but right now his tongue lolled out of his mouth and his tail wagged furiously. "Good boy."

"I still feel bad that you're giving up your Saturday night to go to a stranger's wedding with me, and now I've made you wait on the porch."

"Glad Gus is on duty." I handed her the rose. "This is for you."

Her cheeks pinked further. "Oh my gosh. You didn't have to do that." She was cute when she blushed, not kid cute but like I wanted to wrap her up in a hug. "Let me find something to put it in before we leave." She hurried into the kitchen, and I dipped to give Gus a few more pets. She wore heels that had straps around the ankles, and I followed the lines of her calves to the dress's hem while playing with Gus.

"I didn't forget about you, buddy." I pulled a dog treat from inside my pocket and tossed it down the hall for him.

"He didn't chase it," she said, returning to the kitchen and standing next to me, her shin near my sleeve, and I stood before I did something stupid like rub her leg.

"He won't until you tell him he can," I said. The dog looked between us, eager to go find his treat. I leaned down and said near her ear, "Say 'release.'" I regretted the action immediately because, leaning in, I inhaled her scent before backing away.

She smelled like flowers on a beach, and I tried to catch another lingering trace in the air.

"Release!" She said it so excitedly that it almost startled Gus, who only paused for a second before disappearing down the hall. Willow grinned. "How cool is that?"

"I know," I said, holding open the door for her. "Pretty sure that dog is trained to do Cruz's taxes and oversee a multilevel marketing operation."

"Cruz said he meant to leave a list of all the commands, but he forgot and hasn't emailed them to me yet."

I held out a hand to help her into the cab of my truck, feeling how soft her palm was in mine. "I can help you out. I've seen most of them."

She pulled herself into the cab, squeezing my hand in a way I enjoyed. "Is your dog trained like this?"

"No," I said, reluctantly letting her hand go once she was settled in the seat. "We got as far as 'sit' and 'eat' and called it good."

I hit the button to start the engine and flipped the switch to warm her seat.

"Those are the only commands you really need, right?"

"Sit and eat?" My instinct was to make a joke about how those commands were usually a good starting place for me with women, but I bit my tongue. "They get the job done," I said instead. "Now, are you ready to party?"

"No," she admitted. "But there will be cake, right?"

"Exactly," I said, backing out of the driveway. "Sit and eat."

"And dance," she added.

I smiled over at her as we took the exit onto the interstate. "Definitely."

CHAPTER 5

Willow

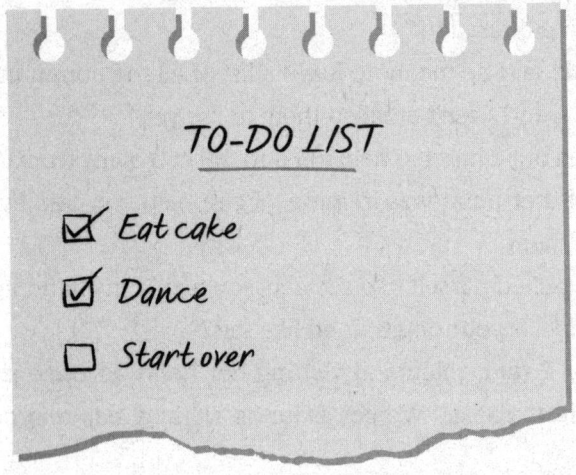

I BRUSHED A few strands of hair off my face, catching my breath after falling into a chair at our table. The ice sloshed in my cup, and I held it to my chest to cool down after leaving my date on the dance floor. Deacon was still in the middle of the crowd, dancing with a group of people he'd become best friends with over the course of the wedding reception. The wedding was more fun than I thought it would be. The music was loud, the food was good, and it was too dark in the hall for anyone to recognize me as Drowning Girl.

Dina approached, pushing her gown aside to take the seat next to me. "I was hoping I'd get a minute to see you!" She wrapped me in an awkward side hug, and I tried to keep my distance and not get her dress sweaty. "It's been years!"

"Congratulations," I said, taking in her wide smile. "It was a beautiful wedding."

"Thank God it's over. I'm telling you, when it's you, just elope!" She laughed and then covered her mouth. "Oh, I'm sorry. I didn't think."

I waved off her apology, wishing I could crawl into a hole in the dance floor, perhaps near where Deacon had talked the groom into doing the worm. "It's okay. No big deal."

"That meme is everywhere. I mean, how could I forget you broke up with your guy? And here I brought it up again. I'm the worst." She took my hand in hers, the light glinting off her engagement ring and wedding band. "But how are you? How is Cruz? How long are you in town?"

"Good," I lied. "Work is good." It was good for the person doing it, anyway, since I'd been let go. "Everything is great." I heard the obvious lie in my voice, but she didn't seem to notice, and her expression softened with relief. People did that. Even if their care was genuine, they visibly let out a breath when you told them their concern was unwarranted.

"Oh, good." She squeezed my hand again and looked over my shoulder. "I think my husband has a crush on your date," she joked, pointing at the two men now sharing a laugh as Deacon helped her husband off the ground. She winked before standing to join him. "He's cute!" She gave me another side hug with a promise to catch up soon. We'd never follow through, though, and I threw back the rest of my drink.

"Save me," Deacon said, approaching the table with an outstretched hand.

"From what?"

"Aunt Gail," he said, motioning over his shoulder. "She's a little handsy and this is a slow one."

He had ditched the jacket, and his shirtsleeves were rolled up over his veined forearms. He shook his outstretched hand again, giving me a puppy dog expression. "Please?"

I accepted his hand and let him lead me to the dance floor. I didn't want to get too close to Deacon, so I kept my distance, making it feel even more like an eighth-grade dance than a wedding, but he pulled me closer. "You seem to attract a lot of older women. The barista, Aunt Gail . . . Cruz mentioned you were a ladies' man, but he didn't mention the ladies had so many years on you."

"Cruz probably exaggerated," he said, resting a palm on my waist, the touch innocent but warm and heavy. "All women have their own kind of grace and sensuality, but I can't fend off Aunt Gail *and* help you avoid Cousin Rupert at the same time."

"I don't think Rupert's going to be a problem. He hasn't even asked me to dance all night."

"Probably lying in wait." A couple nearby called out to Deacon, who returned the greeting without missing a beat.

"I can't believe you've met so many people since we got here."

He shrugged. "Everyone is drinking and dancing. It's easy to make friends."

"For you." I nodded and looked away, hoping he wouldn't notice that no one was greeting me. "You're good at it. I'm awful at these things. At parties or big events, I used to just hang out on the periphery with my . . . with Spencer."

Deacon nodded but then gripped my hand tighter and

twirled me in a circle, interrupting my thoughts. When he pulled me back to him, there was a surprised giggle on my lips, and he winked. "So, you're here for three months. What do you want to do while you're in town?"

"I don't know," I said, shrugging one shoulder. "I guess look for a job. I have a little bit of savings and, of course, I'm not paying rent, but I'll need something when I go home."

"Think bigger." He spun me out and back again, the twirl leaving me disoriented before I was against his chest again. "If you could finish the three months having said you did something, what would it be?"

"This is another big question?"

His hand flexed against my waist and he grinned. "I only do big, Willow."

I rolled my eyes at his cheesy line and traced the seam of his shirt over his shoulder. "Start over, I guess," I said, honestly, blaming the heat of the dance floor and the strength of the mojito. "I'm single and I lost my job. Good a time as any to hit reset, right?"

"I'm single and I lost my job," he mused. "Not the same, but resetting probably isn't that bad. Where will you start?"

I just laughed, looking around us at the couples dancing with their bodies pressed together. "I have no idea. It's like I looked up and everyone seems to have things figured out except for me." I stepped on Deacon's toe with my foot and cringed. "Sorry. I've only ever danced with one other person before."

"Only one dance partner? That's practically criminal." He twirled me again, and though I stumbled, I laughed. "Your ex was your first slow dance?"

I nodded. "First dance. Only dance partner. Once we started

dating and stayed together through college, I assumed he'd be the only."

"No," Deacon said. "None of that." He pressed his hand to my lower back, pulling me closer to lead me around the dance floor. "Consider this a re-do."

"A re-do?"

He nodded, taking my hand and guiding it around his neck. "A re-do on your first slow dance with none of that eighth-grade fumbling. We're adults now." His hand moved down the middle of my back, and he pulled me toward him.

"Where did you learn to do this so well? I know it wasn't in the military."

"My physical therapist made me dance to regain my balance." He laughed near my ear. "I'm gonna dip you now."

"What?" I panicked, clutching his shirt. "No, I'm not ready!"

"Too late!" He held me and dipped us both in what was probably a pretty sad move, but I was already laughing too hard to care. We earned applause from some of the couples around us just as the DJ shifted to a song with a faster tempo.

"Oh my God. I can't believe that just happened," I said as we walked off the dance floor.

"Good re-do?" He nicked his beer bottle from the table and took a swig.

"Definitely," I agreed, nodding when he asked if I wanted another drink. I watched Deacon disappear into the crowd, joining in conversation with that group of Dina's friends by the bar while he waited. A redhead in a tight green dress looked particularly interested and held out her phone, I assumed offering her number. I bit into a piece of ice from my glass when he pulled out his phone as well before reminding myself this wasn't an actual date.

The dance had been amazing, though, and the idea of re-doing my first slow dance was ridiculous, but it sparked something inside me. It had been so freeing to replace that memory with this one that had nothing to do with Spencer and what I thought my life would look like. The life that would include marriage and kids and a happy family. I tapped my fingers on the table, drumming my nails against the linen tablecloth. Deacon was chatting with an older man now, holding both our drinks in his hands. Maybe he was onto something.

Deacon set the drinks down on the table, but as the opening beats to the next song played, he took my hand again. "Another dance, or are you ready to head home?"

I would normally agree to going home, but I accepted his hand again, feeling a boost of bravery from the cocktail I'd had earlier. Everything about tonight had been completely different from what I'd feared—I'd convinced myself that every time I went out in public it would end in disaster.

"Let's dance." I followed him to the floor. "You can teach me some new moves."

CHAPTER 6

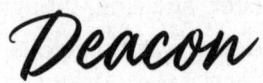

"I DRANK TOO much wine." Willow leaned back against the arm of the couch in Cruz's living room and set her glass aside. "Opening a bottle after the wedding was a mistake."

"Big mistake." My face was warm, as I'd finished far more of the bottle than her. Gus had given up on us and wandered back to his crate after our drunken walk around the block. "Odds are good I'm going to stumble into a bush on my walk home." We sat on either end of the couch and her toes brushed my thigh when she stretched. More drinks at the wedding had led to hours on the dance floor. She'd wanted more practice dancing, and I wasn't going to deny her. Not when she'd been so cute, if clumsy.

Willow snort-laughed, sitting back up.

"Oh, me falling and injuring myself in some shrubbery is funny?"

"I'm just imagining you flailing." She snorted again, the way I was learning she did when she was a little drunk and found something stupid endlessly funny. She wiped a tear from her eye.

"You're mean," I said. "Cruz told me you were nice."

"He doesn't know the real me," she said, still giggling at her own imagination. "Deep down, I'm a cold, calculating bitch." Willow kept laughing, the tone darkening at her self-deprecating joke.

"I don't buy it." I swiveled to catch her eye. "You're a softy. Like a . . ." I struggled for the word. "Like what's the softest thing there is? You're like one of those blankets that only girls have in their house. The ones that feel like a puppy."

She giggled. "Chenille? That was a lot of words to call me a pushover."

"I didn't say pushover. I said puppy blanket." She'd changed out of her dress and into sweatpants when we got back to the house and now sat with her feet propped up on the couch near me. "But in a nice way and not an evil way." I played with her big toe through her thick sock.

She sank into the couch. "We're friends now, right? Cruz gave you to me as a friend?"

"I don't think he gets to give me to people but, yeah. Friends. We bonded over cake."

"I was your wing woman," she said proudly. "I talked you up to the redhead and that dark haired woman when I ran into her in the bathroom."

I dropped a hand to my pocket where the brunette's number was written on a napkin. I'd forgotten about her once I started dancing with Willow, but I reached out my fist for a bump. "And I kept you from hooking up with your cousin."

"Cousin Rupert," she corrected, forgetting the joke for half a second. "He's not even a real person!" She fell into another fit of giggles that made me smile. "Can you do me a favor?"

"Name it, Willis." That wasn't right. "Cruz calls you Willy. What does everyone else call you?"

"Um, just Willow. Why?"

"I'll think of something," I said. I couldn't use the same nickname her brother used. I'd taken too much notice of her body already to make that right. "I can't call you what everyone else uses. What kind of unoriginal friend would that make me?" I tugged on her toe again, a touch that felt safe and platonic and quelled this curiosity and need I'd had to touch her all night. "What's the favor?"

She nibbled on the side of her lip. "Can you look up Spencer on Instagram?"

"No," I said, tipping my head back. "Not my type."

"Seriously," she said. "My best friend won't do it, and I blocked him so I wouldn't be tempted, but I'm dying to know what he's doing."

"Bad idea," I said. "Don't look, Lou." I shook my head. "Lou isn't good."

"Please?" She sat up again and ended up next to me, her eyes big and pleading. "I had such a good night. This is the best possible time to see it."

I shook my head. "I don't know much but I know not to look up an ex. It's never a good idea."

"I'll buy you a coffee."

She looked so hopeful, and maybe she was right about being in the right headspace. What did I know? Maybe seeing the ex's feed would give her the closure she was hoping for. "Extra caramel?"

She nodded and handed me my phone from the coffee table. "I just want to see if he's posted anything interesting."

"Don't tell Cruz I did this for you. It would be almost as bad to him as me taking you to bed."

"I'm decades too young for you to try something. You go for much older women," she said, navigating to IG on my phone and typing his name into the search bar before handing it to me.

I squinted and blinked a few times, forcing the photos to come into focus. "Looks like . . ." I tapped on a photo and read the caption. "Oh."

"What?"

"He got a dog whose name is Annabelle," I said, zooming in on a rat-looking dog snarling at the camera. I scrolled the series of photos all posted within a few days. Him and a brunette in glasses, the same girl and the dog, and a selfie of the girl kissing his cheek at a park. "And is maybe . . . dating someone." Nope. This wouldn't go well. I wished I could pull back the words as soon as they left my mouth.

Willow sat back, her expression crestfallen. "Oh. Wow. That was fast. I knew there was someone else. I just didn't think they'd really get together so soon."

I kept scrolling further back, hoping to catch a photo of him and Willow, but the feed was sparse and mostly photos of birds and landscapes, sometimes with this guy in the foreground.

"But looks like it's new . . ." It was a mistake to look him up, and I needed to course correct. "All of that is posted over the last couple of weeks. No pics of the woman or the dog before then, so you can take solace that he's probably spending all his time cleaning up shit off the carpet."

She sniffed but gave a slight smile. "From the dog or the girlfriend?"

"I meant the dog but maybe both. I don't know what he's into. See? You're better off."

She nodded unconvincingly. "I just can't believe he ended things with me and then, poof, was ready to move on. It's only been a month and a half. We were together for over ten years."

"Hey," I said, rolling to one elbow and tossing my phone aside. "None of this sad face. He's boring black coffee, remember? His feed is full of bird pictures, and you got a re-do on your first dance tonight. You had wasted the original on him, anyway."

She nodded again, blinking back tears I saw welling in her eyes. I'd really fucked this whole thing up.

"And it was way better than your real first slow dance, right?"

"How do you know?" She sniffed again.

"C'mon." I motioned to my body and gave her my best smile. "I'm certain there's no contest."

Her lips tipped up. "It's hard to compare," she admitted. "I was fourteen the first time."

"See? You're moving on, too."

"I guess," she said, wiping away a tear, but her expression quickly changed to a more resolute one. "I got a re-do. That's right." She stood without another word and marched to the back of the house where I heard rummaging noises.

"Willow?" I called down the hall from my spot on the couch. "Low? Can I call you Low? I don't know what's happening here." There was no answer, and I debated following her, but then she reemerged from the hallway holding a notebook and a photo album.

"Are you gonna read me a bedtime story? I like Goldilocks and the three wolves."

"That's . . . very wrong," she said, falling back onto the couch, tossing a pen and pad at me. She'd been flipping through the notebook roughly and I was worried she'd rip the pages.

"Where did that come from?" I pointed to the photo album in her hand. "If that's Cruz's, I need to review what photos he has of me. Lots of potential for blackmail."

"It's mine," she said, tracing a finger of a photo I couldn't see. "I got a ton of digital photos printed when I graduated college."

"Oh, I should not have let you look him up on my phone," I said, making a grab for the album. "Now you've dragged out an album of the guy?"

She shook her head, flipping a page. "Not all him. Look." She held up a page containing photos of her and Cruz, but when she flipped it, there were a lot of shots of the dude from the bird pics. "Not *all*." She waved a hand in the air. "It doesn't matter. We're making a list." She pointed at the legal pad. "You can take notes."

"A list of what? We're both drunk, and you should not assume I understand what you're talking about."

"Firsts." She kept flipping, pausing only momentarily every few pages.

"That doesn't make any sense," I said.

She ignored me, flipping several pages back and forth. "Dancing." She flipped page after page, barely looking at the photos and mumbling between instructions. "Painting, date, brunch."

"Brunch?" I glanced at my handwriting, which was twice the size and half as legible as normal.

"Brunch. Fuck him and his egg white omelets and staying away from religion and politics at the table," she muttered under her breath.

"I don't know what we're doing."

"We're making a list of firsts I want to re-do without him. Brunch. Breaking a rule. Camping. My first concert. We saw Beyoncé. Third row in Dallas."

I stopped writing again. "You want a re-do third row at a Beyoncé concert?"

"No!" She bit the corner of her lip. "Not her. Never her, but now I can't hear 'Formation' without thinking of him."

I glanced at my phone screen and woke it up to see a guy who fairly closely resembled a white version of Steve Urkel from that old *Family Matters* show. "Yeah, you need a re-do on that. This is not the face to associate with 'Formation.'"

She was quiet for a moment. Flip. Flip. Flip. The sound of the pages made me dizzy, like they were swirling around me. She swallowed. "Orgasms."

I dropped my pen at the word. "What?"

"I told you he was the only one I ever danced with."

"Yeah . . ." The dots were coming together, but too slowly.

"Well . . . he was the only one I ever *danced* with. If he gets a new dog and a new girlfriend, then I should get lots of orgasms without him."

I started writing the word to buy myself a little time before responding. "You haven't given yourself one in the time since you split?"

Flip. Flip. Flip. "Just write it down."

I intentionally stared at her face, because my best friend's kid sister had started talking about orgasms and my drunk brain was working on overload. "You have to have given yourself one at some point."

She threw a pillow at me. "I've never been able to do it, okay? I'm aware that makes me a freak, but I haven't, so I've basically just been horny for a decade." Flip. Flip. Flip. "Learn to drive."

I wrote it down, letting her words swim in my head and, if I was honest, my dick.

"Why not add sex, then, if you're so horny?"

She nodded. "Good idea. He's having sex with someone new. So should I."

I shifted, the legal pad hiding my body's initial reaction to this conversation about Willow's orgasms.

Flip. Flip. Flip. "The park," she said quietly.

"Just the park?"

"Just the park." She set the album aside and I put down the pen, leaving the legal pad where it was.

"This is a long list," I said, making a quick count and wondering if I'd caught everything between her mumbles. "You're going to re-do them all? While you're here in Iowa?"

"Yes. That's how I start over." She took the list from me and looked it over. "That's how I make sure I'm ready for the next relationship."

"You're already living your life without him."

She pointed to the list. "Not yet, but I will. If I can make new firsts . . . if I can remind myself who I am without him . . . I know it doesn't make sense, but it's what I need to do to move on and really find my way again. Will you help me?"

I studied her expression and saw a little of Cruz there—the set jaw, the decision to do something that I knew there was no talking her out of. "Can I sober up first?"

She grinned, the smile spreading across her face the way I'd seen earlier in the night when we were dancing. It was a good smile, a friendly smile, and she was a good person. Helping her with this silly project wasn't what Cruz had in mind, but it seemed to be what she needed and might even take my mind off my preoccupation with rushing to reenlist.

"Why not?" I held out a palm for a high five and let my head fall back against the couch again. "We've got three months to make it happen."

CHAPTER 7

Willow

I SHOOK AWAKE to knife blades of sunlight streaming through the living room windows like an attack. Trying to avoid their onslaught, I rolled to my side, coming face-to-face with an imposing black nose, and Gus eyed me curiously over his long snout. "Hey, boy," I said groggily, and he licked my face at the words, which might have been him showing affection and might have been more of Cruz's training to check for signs of life. Wiping the dog slobber from my cheek, I felt the fabric of the couch on my bare legs and realized I wasn't wearing pants. Come to think of it, I wasn't wearing a bra, and a quick inspection of the room found both on the floor next to Gus's front paws. "Oh, this is bad." I squeezed my eyes shut, and Gus gave a quick bark before licking my face again, as if to confirm the badness of the situation.

My head was fuzzy and pounding. I had to pee, and the night before came back to me in pieces. Cracking an eye open, I pulled the blanket with me, looking for Deacon, but he wasn't in the living room. I took a moment to examine the spot where he'd sat the night before—his tall, defined body perched on one end of the couch as if the furniture was built to fit him. We'd had too much wine and I'd massively overshared. It was all I could think about as I stumbled toward the bathroom in search of relief and then ibuprofen.

I finally lumbered toward the back door to let out Gus, but even with the door open, he sat patiently for my hungover ass until I remembered the command. "Go," I said, motioning out the back door, and he took off like a bolt, circling the yard's perimeter before getting to business. The wall was cool against my back, and I leaned against it for a few minutes before deciding that coffee was needed. The night before was a blur, but hopefully I hadn't been drunk enough to do something truly regrettable, like sleeping with Deacon. I started the coffee maker and went in search of my phone where messages waited.

> DEACON: Good morning. You make it up this morning?

He'd sent the message at six forty-five that morning, and if he felt anything like me, I had no idea how he'd been able to even look at the glare of the phone so early in the morning.

> WILLOW: Barely.

I glanced over my shoulder at my little pile of clothes in the living room.

> WILLOW: I wasn't inappropriate last night was I?
>
> DEACON: You talked with our Lyft driver for twenty minutes about his miniature schnauzer, but otherwise no.
>
> WILLOW: Can I ask why I woke up without pants?
>
> DEACON: 😁 You got hot.
>
> WILLOW: Hot?
>
> DEACON: You told me to close my eyes and then you took off your pants and then informed me you would take off your bra.

My face heated. "No," I said to the coffee maker, pushing the memory out of my head. "So cringey."

> WILLOW: Any chance you can forget that happened?
>
> DEACON: No way. But I was a gentleman and looked away.
>
> WILLOW: I'm sorry I drank so much.
>
> DEACON: I had fun, but when a woman gets

me drunk and takes off her pants, it usually ends differently for me.

WILLOW: I'd wager more of those nights end with you stumbling into a bush and passing out than you getting laid.

DEACON: They're not mutually exclusive. 😊 And where did this saucy attitude come from? What happened to the sweet kid sister?

WILLOW: I drowned her in wine.

WILLOW: Drowning. Get it?

    I set my phone aside and poured a cup of coffee before walking back to the living room. The notepad sat on the coffee table, a page filled with Deacon's messy, blocky handwriting. Biting my lip, I reached for it, cheeks warming at the things I'd blurted out before crying on his shoulder. The list was silly. Ridiculous. It wasn't like I could erase my memories of Spencer and the heartbreak he'd caused. Some of them were good memories. I looked around my brother's living room at nothing in particular. The space was too quiet, too empty, and I gingerly picked up the list and glanced at my buzzing phone with an incoming call from Zoe.

    "Can you microwave hot chili peppers?"

    "I don't know," I said, running a finger down the list. "Did you google it?"

    She huffed. "No, why trust weirdos on the internet when I have my science nerd best friend?"

"I'm an unemployed ex-receptionist. I think you'd have better luck with the weirdos." I sipped my coffee and allowed the hot, sweet taste to bring me achingly, slowly back to life. That receptionist job hadn't been great but it had been something. I knew I had to start looking for something else for when I returned home. "And why are you doing anything with chilies? It's eight in the morning for you."

I could picture her waving off my concern. "I haven't gone to bed yet and I wanted to make salsa. I got these great tomatoes at the farmers market."

I glanced longingly at the pillow. Sleep sounded good. "I don't know on the chilies, but don't microwave without some research," I said, giving in and stretching back out on the couch.

"What's up with you? That selfie of you two last night was cute. Please tell me that man bent you over a bed and showed you God."

I sipped from my coffee and let my mind wander to Deacon's strong arms before I pulled myself back. "No. He's my brother's best friend and too old for me." Though our ten-year age difference hadn't seemed significant the night before, when I apparently stripped down with him three feet away. "I drank way too much last night and made this silly list of moments from my life that I wanted to re-do without Spencer." I left out Deacon helping me—I didn't want to add kindling to her fire. "That girl he said he'd met? Turns out they're dating now. I guess I thought he'd wait a while. He's always been so deliberate."

"Oh, Will, I love that! The list. Not the Drip finding someone equally drippy. But it's like a to-do list, but it's a re-do list!"

"You can't get a do-over on memories and experiences."

"Well, of course you can't, but you can make new ones. Even

better ones." I heard the telltale sound of the microwave opening and knew she was ignoring my advice. "Even some sexy ones! And did you break our pact and look him up on social media?"

That had been a mistake, and I felt a pang in my chest at the memory of knowing the person I'd thought would be my forever person was with someone else. Instead of answering, I skirted her question. "Did you decide to microwave those chilies?"

"Of course I did." *Beep. Beep. Beep.* "What's on the list?"

I stared at the notepad. "Just dumb stuff. Going camping, first date, breaking a rule. Learning to drive. That one doesn't even make sense." I kept reading and my eyes snagged on the messy handwriting, my face heating instantly. "Oh, God," I muttered.

"What?"

I remembered. I remembered talking to Deacon about orgasms and I wanted to sink into the couch.

"Oh, shit!" Zoe's panicked tone pulled me momentarily out of my shame sulk.

I sat up immediately. "What's wrong? Are you hurt?"

"Microwave doesn't look good. The pepper might have exploded. I'm fine. I'll call you later." She disconnected before I said anything, but my heart still beat fast in my chest from her exclamation.

> DEACON: I'm ignoring the drowning joke. You're better than that.
>
> DEACON: Hey, you got a re-do on your first hangover.
>
> WILLOW: 👻

WILLOW: Do you happen to know if you can microwave red chili peppers?

DEACON: IDK. That's an interesting hangover cure...

DEACON: Asked my roommate, the chef. He said you can, but you shouldn't. Did you put pants on yet?

WILLOW: Not yet.

DEACON: You probably don't want peppers near your downstairs business. Why are you microwaving peppers?

WILLOW: Friend is. I think she burned them.

DEACON: Marcus said when she opens that microwave the capsaicin is going to be airborne. Your bestie just pepper sprayed herself.

I should have been more concerned about Zoe making her microwave into a pepper spray delivery system, but she hadn't sent me any emergency messages. With her good luck, she'd probably end up getting help from the hottest and kindest member of the Denver Fire Department.

DEACON: She sounds dangerous but fun.

WILLOW: I sent her a picture from last night. She thinks you're cute.

> DEACON: I am cute.

I tossed the notebook aside and walked toward my room in search of the shower after letting Gus back inside. Since Zoe was likely in a lot of pain right now after making the mother of all bad decisions, she was probably the last person I should listen to about this re-do list idea, but she had a point. I could focus on making new memories. I doubled back to pick up the notebook and walked toward my room.

> WILLOW: Are you okay?
>
> ZOE: Mstkes wer madee.
>
> WILLOW: Flush your eyes with water and get outside! Call me later!

The notebook pages were chaotic, and I remembered throwing idea after idea at Deacon. From what I could make out of his handwriting, I'd narrated most of the moments of my life. Did I stumble onto a good idea in my drunken rant? If I could re-do ten years of moments in three months, I could really make a fresh start and be in a better place for the next relationship. Deacon's handwriting was more like a scrawl, and I looked closely at each item. Moving my finger over the lines of each word, the shape of all these firsts in one place. I ripped off the pages in Deacon's handwriting and started copying them onto a fresh list that included a few new items.

Maybe this could really work?

~~TO-DO LIST~~ RE-DO LIST

- [x] First slow dance
- [x] Hangover
- [ ] Painting
- [ ] Romantic date
- [ ] Kiss
- [ ] Holding hands
- [ ] Brunch
- [ ] Breaking a rule
- [ ] Camping
- [ ] Orgasm
- [ ] Sex with someone new
- [ ] Learning to drive
- [ ] Concert
- [ ] Being on stage
- [ ] New look
- [ ] The park

CHAPTER 8

Deacon

HANGOVER OR NOT, I had a date with the gym. Medical discharge be damned, I was determined to reenlist. It was where I belonged and what I was meant to do. After two years of follow-up scans, the growth on my spine that had caused the partial paralysis hadn't returned, and it was unlikely it would. I'd have to show I was medically and physically prepared to get back to the PJs, and for that, the minimum physical requirements wouldn't cut it. I scanned the notes I'd made on my training goals. For the test, I'd have to do a twenty-five-meter underwater swim, a five-hundred-meter swim in nine minutes, a mile-and-a-half run in nine and a half minutes, twenty pull-ups, then eighty sit-ups and push-ups, both in two minutes. I was close.

I pulled my phone from my shorts.

CRUZ: Thanks for taking her to the wedding.

DEACON: Happy to. I like her.

DEACON: Not like that. You warned me.

It had been an unexpectedly enjoyable night. From Willow in that knockout dress to drinking wine with her in Cruz's living room to waking up early this morning next to her wrapped in a blanket and snoring on the other end of the couch, I liked her company. She'd been cute curled up in the pink fuzzy blanket covered in butterflies that she must have brought with her, or I had a lot of shit to give Cruz about his decorating choices. I'd put the glasses in the sink, not wanting to wake her, and snuck out the back, giving Gus a scratch behind the ears. She didn't need to wake up next to me. I liked Willow. She was cool. Really cool, actually. But no need to make things confusing for her.

CRUZ: I trust you.

I strolled through the parking lot, admiring the intricate artwork sketched in the dirt on the back of the semi in front of me. It was a solid depiction of a penis holding an American flag, and I gave silent props to the artist as I flashed my student ID at the desk worker and headed toward the pool. Fitting, since it was in the water where my friendship with Cruz really started.

DEACON: What's your best time for the 500M recently? 🏊

CRUZ: 9:45. Why?

I snapped a photo of the pool and peeled my shirt off, reminded of how Willow had done some maneuver the night before to take off her bra. I'd looked away but there'd been glimpses as she shifted around. She'd done it basically without lifting her T-shirt at all. Not that I'd tell my buddy about that.

> DEACON: About to crush your time.
>
> CRUZ: Doesn't count if the lifeguard is towing you in, dick.

I chuckled and set my phone aside.

WE'D BEEN IN training for five weeks. Five weeks of pushing my body and mind further than I thought possible with hours on hours of calisthenics, deep dive exercises, weight training, and running. So much running. I'd fallen into my bunk one night after a day that included underwater knot tying with my fingers sore and only enough energy left to stare at the ceiling.

"Hey, Rakes," Simms began. "Two guys are walking down the street and come upon a dog licking his balls."

"Simms, your jokes suck," another guy yelled from across the room. We'd started doing this thing during the second week—telling dirty jokes during downtime. Most of us, anyway. We spent all day together, pushing ourselves to the edge and beyond. This was like giving each other a place to land. A few guys like Cruz Lewis never joined in.

Simms ignored the jibe and the boos of our fellow trainees and kept going. "So, they see the dog licking his balls and the one guy says to the other, 'I wish I could do that.' And his friend looks between him and the dog, then replies, 'Maybe try to pet him first.'"

"Horrible," I said, rubbing my shoulder. "You should be ashamed."

"I've got one," Barkley said to the right of my bunk. "What's the difference between a chickpea and a lentil?" Barkley was from Texas, and his heavy Southern drawl always made the jokes sound just a little worse, which was saying something given the terrible jokes. He only paused for a second to finish. "I wouldn't pay fifty dollars to have a lentil on my face!"

"Fucking hell, Bark," I said, laughing along with the guys groaning and booing. "You're on probation."

"Like you could do better," he said, tossing his pillow at my head.

I noticed as I looked around that Cruz was the only one not joining in tonight. He sat with his back to us across the room—I wanted to bring him into the group. I'd spent most of my life on the outside of social groups as the new kid at school every time we moved to a new place and it sucked. "So, Lewis goes to the doctor with a lettuce leaf sticking out of his ass. The doctor says, 'Oh, that's strange.'"

Cruz's posture changed—he heard us but kept ignoring us, and a few of the guys looked over their shoulders at him and rolled their eyes.

"So, Lewis says, 'And that's just the tip of the iceberg.'" The room erupted in laughter. This training was hell, but I loved these guys and the sense of belonging the military had offered me. I'd never been part of a group like this before, and it bugged me seeing someone like him left out.

"Lewis," I said as he stalked past toward the showers. "It was a joke. C'mon. You have one? Impress us!"

"Fuck off," he said. "Wish you morons would shut the fuck up."

"Caesar salad, don't be like that!" Simms called after him, and Barkley acted like he was chasing after him, arms outstretched and calling out, "Cobb, don't go!"

I laughed with everyone else but had a twinge of guilt after lights-out. The nicknames lasted into the night, and he looked at me like I was the instigator of everything. He'd never make it if he couldn't be a team player, though, and I decided it wasn't my job to help him make friends. I had to stay focused on keeping myself going.

And then we got to extended training day, but it was better known as hell night. Twenty hours straight of intense testing. We'd been in and out of the water for hours, exercise after exercise in the dark pool, push-ups, treading water, a reaction drill where they threw every problem they could for us to solve. By the time we trekked toward the reservoir and they ordered us to drop wet suits in the cold water, the finish point seemed so far away I couldn't imagine it. My body revolted, which I would usually ignore, but the lack of sleep and the long day made it harder.

"No arms," the instructors called after we donned scuba fins. There were 1,750 meters to go in frigid water. There was no sign of the jokes—everyone had been pushed well past their limits and there was one singular goal: finish.

Halfway in, my legs and ankles burned, but I willed myself forward. Cruz and I were neck and neck toward the front of the group. It wasn't a race, but no one wanted to be last. I kicked harder, pulling away from Cruz to get closer to the other guys, but a charley horse seized my leg and I gritted my teeth as I slowed, to basically a standstill, and Cruz blew past me as I attempted to stretch the leg, my body sinking down in the cold water. *No. No. Shit. No.*

I stretched but the muscle wouldn't relax and I pressed a hand to my thigh. I was dead last now, and I looked over my shoulder toward the other side, where the guys were beginning to make it to the far edge of the reservoir. My hands shook under the water—I needed to get back to the group. I willed my leg to relax. When it didn't, I tried kicking again anyway, and let out an exasperated growl at the pain.

"Stop it." The voice cut over the water as Cruz neared me. He'd circled back. "Stop or it won't stop cramping."

I stared in disbelief that he'd come back to help me.

"Lean on me for a second," he said, maneuvering so his back was to mine. "Breathe. I know it's hard for you to stop talking for longer than five seconds, but shut the fuck up, breathe, and stretch."

I did what he said, my ankles protesting as I bent my ankle and the cramp finally receded. "I'm good," I said, finally sliding away from him.

The guys yelled for us from the other side, and Cruz gave a tight nod. We both started for the edge of the reservoir, and I called out, "Thanks," but he didn't respond.

A FEW PEOPLE entered the pool area behind me. I'd had a class with one of the women, and I was pretty sure she'd said she'd been Navy. Kelly maybe or Kylie. She had a half sleeve of tattoos up her left arm, and she nodded in my direction—she'd mentioned a couple times about joining the veterans group on campus, but I didn't see the point. I still had the chance to go back. No need to join something new where I'd be reminded the military was in my past.

I slipped into the pool and began a warm-up lap, the mild headache receding as I moved through the water. Goal was 9:35 and I turned when I reached the other side and did a lazy freestyle on my way back across. I liked goals and benchmarks to give order to my days. Then my mind wandered to Willow's frantic, drunken list the night before. It had seemed nonsensical as she was creating the list, but maybe she was onto something.

If there was something I understood, it was reaching goals that seemed impossible. A list of re-dos couldn't be that farfetched.

CHAPTER 9

Willow

- ☑ New look
- ☑ Make new friends

"HEY," SOMEONE CALLED from the neighbor's driveway. "You look familiar. Did you just move in?" She strode across the grass, and I felt the familiar panic of being recognized, pulling my hair forward immediately to hide my face.

"Just house-sitting," I said, dipping my chin and clutching the mail I'd grabbed from the mailbox.

"Oh!" Her voice brightened. "You must be Cruz's sister! That's why you look familiar. God, you guys could be twins, I mean except for him being taller and all muscled and, you know, the facial hair." She paused next to me and held out a hand to shake. "I'm Hollis—I live next door. Well, my parents live next door and I'm staying with them, which I guess is the same thing." She shook my hand without really taking a breath and kept talking. "Anyway, hi!"

"I'm Willow," I said, taking her hand and really looking at her for the first time. Hollis looked about my age, and her blue hair was swept to the side, half of it shaved close to her head and spiky against her pale skin. "I like your hair," I added, tugging self-consciously on my own curls.

"Thanks!" She ran fingers through the blue strands. "I'm kind of bored with the color. About time for a change. Maybe pink or red? Like a real red red." Hollis pulled some blue strands down over her eyes. "What do you think?"

Hollis reminded me a little of Zoe, and her energy eased the need I'd felt to escape quickly. "Red's a good color," I shared. I'd had the same hairstyle for years since Spencer told me I looked really pretty with my hair down. No one had ever called me pretty before him, not like that, like someone who I wasn't related to. I'd felt special, so I kept it the same, and the long curls had been helpful to hide behind lately.

"Red it is," she said brightly. "My brother's in cosmetology school, so he does it for me. I bet he'd do yours if you want!"

"Oh," I said, waving away her offer and pushing my hair off my face. "No, I couldn't."

"Why not?"

I thought about it—even opened my mouth to give an excuse, but I didn't have a good reason.

"I mean, it probably took a long time to get your hair that long." She motioned to the curls falling down my back. "And Blaine's a student, but he's good. Plus he needs the practice, so I usually just pay him in beer and pizza."

I didn't know this woman or Blaine, and I never even cut my hair more than regular trims, but for some reason her offer pulled at me. I slid my fingers through it again, stretching a long curl down in front of my face, assessing.

"At least come over for the beer and pizza." She motioned to the house behind her. "Everyone in this neighborhood is like eighty, and not a fun eighty. I'm bored."

I finally shrugged my shoulders and agreed, perhaps for no other reason than Hollis didn't seem to recognize me from the meme and a new look would mean checking off an item on my list—this was going to be easier than I'd thought.

I'D WATCHED BLAINE work on Hollis's hair all afternoon—stripping the blue and making conversation with me over the sound of the water spray and his sister's chattiness. She was admiring the new red color in the mirror when he turned his gaze to me. "You ready, doll?" In the last few hours, I'd heard about their moms retiring early and embarking on a backpacking trip around the world, Blaine's decision to drop out of law school in favor of cosmetology, and Hollis's recent experience dating a magician who was "dirty sexy" and made her sexual inhibitions disappear. At this, her brother covered his ears with a laugh. Blaine and Hollis both talked to me like they'd known me for years and not hours. How else to explain why I'd voluntarily told them both about Spencer and the Drowning Girl video?

"Yes!" Hollis nudged me forward. "It's time for something new. That's your whole thing now, right? New you? Gotta start with a new look!"

Blaine ran his fingers through my hair once I hesitantly sat in the chair, his touches intimate but professional. "You have a lot of hair. What would you think about shorter?"

I gulped. "How short?"

He looked back at my hair, and I studied his expression in the mirror. "Maybe shoulder-length?"

"Shorter," Hollis chimed in. "Like this?" She held up her phone, and I sucked in a breath at the model whose curls looked like mine but fell around her head loose and light. "With those honey-colored highlights. You'd look so good."

I held her phone and tried to imagine my own face in place of the model's.

"That shape fits your features better than what you have," Blaine offered.

I looked at my face in the mirror again—my mom's eyes, the same dimples as Cruz, and the little scar near my temple I'd gotten after colliding with Spencer during eighth-grade gym class as we both dived for a volleyball. He had a matching scar—he'd always said it was a sign we were forever changed by each other. I traced a finger over the tiny faded line. Forever changed didn't have to mean forever unchanged. If I was going to commit to this idea, I wanted to start big. "Okay. Let's do it now before I change my mind."

Blaine and Hollis had similar smiles—wide and toothy. He gathered my hair into a loose ponytail before holding up a pair of scissors.

"Girl, seriously, it's gonna be hot," Hollis said. "You ready?"

The scissors gleamed in the sunlight shining in through the small window, and I dug my fingers into the cushion of the chair, squeezing my eyes shut. "Yes. Do it."

Hollis cheered and Blaine patted my shoulder. When the scissors sliced through my curls, I felt something even better than the weight of my long hair disappearing. I felt like I'd added two new people to my small circle of friends.

AS I WALKED Gus toward Deacon's place, I couldn't stop touching the curls brushing the back of my neck and moving my head from side to side to feel the bounciness from the shorter cut. A text came through from Hollis, a selfie of both of us in our new styles with Blaine between us. Her new bright red hair color was bold and caught the light of the sinking sun. My own highlights were pretty subtle, but for as different as I felt, it might as well have matched Hollis's color.

As we approached, I saw Deacon on the porch of the house next door with a young teenager with big glasses and a low fade. Both were hunched over a table, and as I approached, I saw it held a chess set.

"Who's winning?" I waved from the sidewalk, pulling Deacon from his concentration.

"Always me," the boy called out. He looked maybe twelve or thirteen and had a walking boot on his left leg. He pushed the glasses up on his nose. "And the ladies love a winner!"

"The *ladies* love an adult," Deacon said, pushing back from the table and standing to meet me. "And you're not winning yet." He wore a T-shirt with a chicken outlined in bright yellow and "Cluck around and find out" printed across his chest. "Jayden, this is my friend Willow. Willow, this is Jayden."

He waved and said, "Hey." Jayden motioned to his side of the board where I saw a number of Deacon's pieces lined up. "Willow, you be the judge. Who is winning here? It's clear, isn't it?"

I chuckled and held up a hand. "I plead the Fifth."

"We can finish this tomorrow," Deacon said, holding out a fist to bump with the kid. "You need anything until your mom gets home?" Jayden shook his head, and they went back and forth in a way that seemed to be normal for them both before Deacon led me down the walkway behind Gus.

"And you're clearly winning," I called out to Jayden over my shoulder as we rounded the front gate.

"Traitor," Deacon said, running a hand through his hair. "His mom works late, and he broke his leg. Try to keep him company when I can," he added. "He's kicking my ass at chess." Deacon's laugh was a low rumble, and I grinned. "And look at you! What's all this?" He motioned to his own hair, which fell thickly over his shoulder, and I tried not to notice how his gaze swept over me. "Looks amazing."

I raised my face, planning to tuck hair behind my ear, but pulled it back, turning from side to side instead. "Long story, but I made some new friends and one of them is kind of a hair genius."

"Cruz will have to update his description of you. Different hair. No glasses. No teenager here." He held out a palm, and I had a wild moment of fantasy that he was going to pull my face to his for a kiss, but he raised it again, motioning for a high five.

"Never thought I'd be arranging dog playdates," he said. "You excited to see your friend, Gus?"

At the sound of his name, Gus's tail wagged furiously. "You ready?" Deacon scratched behind his ears, and the dog barked in response.

I followed Deacon into their backyard, where a wiggling pit bull with white around her snout lumbered toward us.

"Meet Cupcake," he said, as the dog made it to the space next to Gus, who bounced on his feet at the sight of the slow-moving dog, whose own tail wagged furiously. "She's an old girl, but these two are friends." Gus lowered his chest to the ground in his play stance, and Cupcake gave a yip and a shuffle.

Gus sprinted to the middle of the yard then doubled back for his friend who was jogging along, her thick rump wiggling.

"They're pretty cute together," I said as we settled into chairs on the back patio. The sun was sinking in the sky, turning everything a golden color that reminded me of Colorado. But it seemed different here, calmer and quieter somehow.

"I got Cupcake after moving here. Cruz suggested it—I think he just worried I needed something to do besides staring at the wall." He tipped his water bottle to his lips. "She was a rescue, and then my roommates kind of became her other owners. Then when Cruz got Gus a few months later and was out here on leave, we got them playing together. Cup wanted nothing to do with a puppy, but Gus eventually wore her down." The two were rolling in the grass together, nipping and jumping at each other as fireflies dotted the yard.

I'd been wary of watching Gus along with the house for Cruz. I'd never taken care of a dog, but having the gentle beast with me in the house was nice. It was a little like having a bodyguard for a roommate. "He's kind of hard to resist," I said.

"It's one thing that we have in common." Deacon crossed one leg over the other on the patio chair and motioned brushing off his shoulder.

Gus dropped a tennis ball at my feet, and I threw it toward Cupcake, watching them chase after it together. "Do you also sniff the crotches of strangers?"

He froze, obviously taken by surprise at the question, but

shrugged one shoulder. "Sometimes you have to explore to be certain about someone."

I rolled my eyes and laughed. "I should have known. Cruz warned me about you."

"I bet." He tipped the water bottle to his lips again. "I'm gonna fill this up in the kitchen. You want anything?"

I nodded. "Water would be great," I said, bending to retrieve another tennis ball delivered by my nephew to my feet. This time Cupcake blocked his path and got the ball first, though, lumbering back toward me by the time Deacon returned with two water bottles in hand. "I could drink gallons after last night."

"Agreed." He guzzled the water. "Getting to the gym to work out this morning was rough, but hoping to get back tonight for a run."

"Cruz mentioned you'd hurt your back." I'd known he'd been in the hospital and injured badly enough to be medically discharged, but he moved so smoothly and athletically it was hard to remember that an injury had sent him home. "Has that changed your workout routine a lot?"

I wondered what it was like to see him work out, to lift weights and push himself physically. A warmth crept up my neck at the image in my head, but he was busy throwing tennis balls himself now and didn't notice. When he finally spoke, his voice was light again. "It set me back for a while."

We took turns throwing the ball for the dogs, adding a red rubber bone of Cupcake's to the rotation. I didn't want to pry about his injury. I probably shouldn't have asked at all, but when he spoke again, he seemed at ease. "I was in physical therapy for a long time, but I'm getting my strength back." He flexed one of his biceps as if to show me, and I brushed my fingers over the soft skin stretched across the hard muscle. "Gotta be ready to show up your brother during training drills again."

He hurled the ball to the back of the yard, sending Gus off in a sprint while I tossed the bone to Cupcake, who lay on the grass panting after her marathon play session with Gus. "Will you go back to drills? Cruz mentioned you'd retired."

He shrugged one shoulder and bent to scratch Gus behind the ears. "Medical discharge." His demeanor stiffened, and I pulled my lip between my teeth, worried I'd misspoken.

"So, your list." He tapped the table to put brackets around the abrupt topic change. "Now that you're sober, are you still dead set on this?"

I nodded. "I am," I said. "But you don't have to help me. I think I kind of bullied you into it."

"Do I look like the kind of man to be bullied by a woman?"

"I don't know. I get the sense you might be into that."

His laugh boomed across the yard, spilling out of him and punctuated by Gus letting out a quick bark to get him to throw the ball.

"That wasn't bad, Low." Deacon punched my shoulder with a gentle tap. "But what's up next? Obviously, your second first slow dance was epic, so the bar is set high."

"Well," I said, glancing over my shoulder toward the house. "I added a new look, so that's done. Next, I think painting."

"And you need me to pose for you nude? Perhaps with a tastefully placed palm frond to cover myself?"

"No!" I laughed at the idea. "And isn't it supposed to be a fig leaf?"

He motioned to his crotch. "C'mon. For this?"

I rolled my eyes but couldn't help smiling at his ridiculous bravado. "Painting a room. Cruz told me to add some color while he was gone. He's done a great job renovating the place, but it's pretty beige still."

Deacon eyed me but returned to throwing the ball for the dogs.

I toyed with my thumbnail. "Spencer's parents bought a house near campus that they agreed to let us live in if we did some fixing up. They said it was in an investment, but they gave it to him for graduation."

Deacon whistled. "They gifted him a house for graduating college? Damn."

"Yeah." I'd thought the same thing, but after ten years with him, I'd grown a little more used to his family and the way they lived. It was so different from my family, and the money had made me uncomfortable sometimes, but the house was beautiful. "It didn't need anything major, but painting was first on the list, and I was in love with this deep red color for the kitchen. We both liked it, and I was so excited to make the space ours." At the time, I'd imagined the fun we'd have together, the way we'd make mistakes and laugh and build a home. It seemed like a picture-perfect start to what would come next—marriage and kids and making traditions together.

Deacon nodded and tossed the ball for Gus again. "Did you end up making out while covered in red paint? That sounds less romantic and more horror movie, but . . ."

I laughed at the idea, trying to imagine that scene playing out. "No. He actually talked me into a pale gray color in the end. It was nice, I guess. He wanted something neutral."

Deacon's brow arched. "But you didn't like it?"

I shrugged. "I didn't love it."

"And I'm guessing no making out covered in gray paint?"

I laughed and snagged the ball from Gus before Deacon could swipe it. The ball didn't fly anywhere near as far as when Deacon threw it, and I swear the dog gave me a disappointed look before running off to retrieve it. "No making out. We barely talked, honestly. I taped, he edged while listening to some classical music." A wave of rekindled disappointment from that day washed over me. I thought I was compromising, but in retrospect, there was nothing about me in that room, when it was done or while I was standing there. "So, I thought I'd start there. Painting. I know it would be painting Cruz's place and not mine, but I want a re-do on my first time making a space my own, even if just a guest room. It's really satisfying to see the transformation."

Deacon nodded, and he seemed to get my rambling explanation. "Want help?"

"I think I can do it alone," I said, unsure that was true. The room I was staying in had high ceilings, and I wasn't sure how I'd reach them, even with the ladder. But I didn't want to pull Deacon away from his life any more than I already had.

He stood and hurled the ball to the back of the yard. Gus had boundless energy even after playing and our walk there. I'd have to start running soon just to get him tired out. Deacon's hair blew in the breeze, and I watched the muscles of his back while he threw the ball for the dog, wondering why he'd shut down the conversation about his discharge so quickly. I didn't want to push too hard, though. He obviously didn't want to bare his soul to me, even if I already had shared so much with him. He seemed like someone who had things together. He probably had all kinds of plans for what was next.

CHAPTER 10

I LIFTED THE strap on my shoulder, the weight of the books a comfort, like having a pack on my back again. I shifted right to avoid running into two young students, both on their phones. God, they all looked young, and I felt ancient at thirty-four. I took the stairs two at a time. I wasn't in a hurry, but it was a test to see if I could, an inch of progress in what was more like a marathon, but still progress. The second level was mostly empty this time of day, and I cut through the building toward the parking garage. The building was old and in need of renovation, and I kept an eye out around every darkened corner.

From behind me, I heard a burst of laughter, and I glanced over my shoulder to see two guys a little younger than me laughing and walking into the Veterans Center at one end of the floor, a sign above the door advertising the space. I heard more laughter from inside and turned abruptly to keep moving. The laughter reminded me of Cruz and the rest of the unit, and I half expected to hear Simms telling a dirty joke. I sucked in a breath through my nostrils and let it out slowly. Some of the guys used to talk about what they'd do when they got out, imagining the freedom of it. I never did, and everything about it still felt wrong, especially ending things like I did with a freak injury that put others at risk. My body had failed me, and I'd failed my team. I didn't belong in there—I didn't deserve it yet.

I was looking at my phone, scrolling Instagram, when I collided with someone. "Shit," I said, surveying the books that had fallen to the ground. "Sorry."

"No problem," she said, eyes narrowing on me for a moment. It took me a second to recognize her, but then I saw a flash of the tattoos on her arm. "Deacon, right? We have econ together."

"Yeah," I said, handing her a thick math textbook. "Kelly?"

"That's me." She held out a hand to shake and gripped my hand like she was used to dealing with men who underestimated her. She looked me over, not in a sexual way but like she was assessing. "Army?"

"Air Force," I said.

She nodded, looking me over again. "I'm going to the Vet Center to study. You want to join me?"

I shook my head. "Just heading home."

She studied my face intently. Normally, I would have flashed a smile and flirted my way out of the conversation, but I didn't get a sense that would work here. "You been out long?"

"Couple years." I shifted the strap on my shoulder. "You?"

"Three." She shifted her hold on the books and pointed over my shoulder at the center. "It's a good spot. Good people. Come by sometime."

"Yeah," I said with a nod. "Maybe."

She smiled, her demeanor relaxing. "That your polite way of telling me to fuck off and leave you alone?" She laughed, and the sound put me at ease, then she held up a hand before I could correct her. "I get it. But I know from experience it helps to find a group, and I don't give up." She walked around me and called over her shoulder, "You've been given notice!"

I returned the wave and continued toward my truck. I'd been tempted to check out the center, but every time I came close, I'd get this overwhelming sense of wrongness, that everyone in there would know I'd had to stop serving, and not because my contract was up or due to a combat- or service-related injury or trauma. I knew deep down I was a quitter because I let that little growth on my spine put my unit in danger. I didn't want to risk needing to admit that until I knew I was going back and could get a chance at redemption.

I was still thinking about it when I pulled into our driveway. Jayden was out on his porch with a book in front of him, and I walked across the small lawn. "Whatcha reading, kid?"

Jayden held up the book. I read the cover, falling into the seat on the other side of the small table. "*Legendborn* by Tracy Deonn. Fitting. You're a pretty legendary guy."

Jayden rolled his eyes and set the book aside. "Yeah, falling down the stairs on the way to basketball tryouts and then crying was real legendary."

"Memorable." I looked at the chessboard still set from our last game. "That girl you like came to your rescue, though, right? Sophia? Women love a man with a sensitive side. Nothing wrong with crying."

He laughed and motioned to the board. "Your girl give you extra hugs when you cried about losing to me yesterday?"

"Not my girl," I said, moving my first piece. I didn't mind the sound of the words, though. She'd looked really good with her new hairstyle, brighter somehow when she smiled. "My friend," I repeated, more for my benefit than his understanding. "And bring it on."

We went a few rounds without more conversation until Jayden spoke up. "I've read this before," he said. "Read the whole series, actually. I, uh, started writing my own."

"Yeah?" I winced as he captured my knight but sat back in my chair. I'd helped out his mom when he was first in the cast, pitching in if they needed something, but the kid was cool as hell. I wasn't even surprised to hear he'd started writing a novel before he needed to shave. "What's it about?"

"It's an urban fantasy novel. Just something I'm playing around with." He studied the board, his lips tipping in a grin when I moved my bishop, and I knew I'd fucked up—exactly how and why would probably be clear in a few moves. "Kinda always wanted to be a writer."

"That's awesome." I toyed with my rook, looking for a tell on his face. Sometimes I wished he wanted to play basketball or toss a football—I was way out of my depth with chess. "Can't wait to read it."

"What did you want to be?" he asked. "You know, when you were my age. If you can remember that far back." He captured another of my pawns and sipped from his water bottle, a green plastic one covered in stickers. "I know spending time with young people is probably good for keeping your mind sharp."

I barked out a laugh at his audacity—he'd surprise me like that sometimes. "I'm only in my thirties. I oughta kick your butt. This is why people don't like smart-asses." I took advantage of him being distracted and captured his knight.

"Thirty is ancient. And you'd fight a kid in a cast? For shame."

He smiled and moved a pawn into position. "And check. You clearly didn't dream of being a professional chess player as a kid."

I shifted my king to safety. "And spend my life with smug opponents like you? No thanks." I snagged my water bottle from my backpack I'd dropped on the porch. "I wanted to be a firefighter when I was real little, then a doctor, but I didn't think I was smart enough. Once I found the military, that was it for me, though."

"I worry about that," he said, studying the board again. "If I'm smart enough to write a book. If I'm good enough."

"You're going to let this go to your head, but . . ." I said, hearing the uncertainty behind all the bravado in his voice. It reminded me a little of how Willow spoke sometimes. "You're one of the smartest people I've ever met. I'm sure you're smart enough to write a book."

He didn't look up from the board, but his lips tipped up again for a second. "I'm sorry I called you ancient. You're just, like, regular old," he said, but the humble uncertainty was gone, and he just looked cocky again and laughed. "You're not in the military anymore, though. What are you gonna do now? I'm trying to picture you as like a businessman or a teacher or something."

I shook my head. I hated the "what's next" question and I felt it every month when the military disability benefits hit my bank account. It was like a monthly reminder of my failure to continue doing the job. I only spent what I had to and set the rest aside. I didn't want the money, but I couldn't explain all that to Jayden. "Nah," I said, trying to move my king to safety after he put me in check again. "I never want to have to wear a suit, and I couldn't put up with a whole class full of kids like you."

"There's no one like me, son." Jayden's eyes flashed and he actually kind of sounded like me, and he probably was a little cockier since we'd been hanging out. I took some pride in that. "And checkmate."

We talked for another thirty minutes or so until he had to get to his homework. He'd told me the plot of his novel and talked about school. Jayden asked tough questions sometimes, kind of like Willow. I hadn't been ready for hers the night before, the ones that hit too close to home, but I'd been tempted to tell her something real. In the twilight, with the fireflies buzzing around us, being with her felt like being somewhere special. I wondered how her painting plan was going and pulled my phone from my pocket.

> WILLOW: I might have gotten in a little over my head.
>
> DEACON: Did you accidentally paint Gus? Cruz might not notice...
>
> WILLOW: He'd notice and be concerned, given the color I picked. But can you bring the ladder from the basement to the second floor the next time you come by? I've been trying to get it off the wall and up the stairs.

I chuckled and imagined her trying to get the bulky thing up the stairs. I'd told Cruz it was stupid to keep it stored there when the garage was closer, but he insisted on the basement.

> DEACON: Is there any significance to the ladder? You're not re-doing the first time

your ex fell off one and you had to save him or something, are you?

WILLOW: In this case, a ladder is just a ladder.

WILLOW: And at 5'3", I was overconfident.

When I walked in the house to change clothes, Emi was perched on the couch with an e-reader and motioned to the phone in my hands. "Who has you smiling like that?"

"Just a funny TikTok video," I said. I shoved the phone in my pocket, but not before tapping out a quick reply to Willow.

DEACON: **I'll be over soon.**

CHAPTER 11

Willow

☑ Painting
☐ First kiss

I WIGGLED MY hips and rolled a Z shape in paint onto the wall. The dark red against the dusty white made me want to dance, and an old Missy Elliott song filled the room from my workout playlist. The song fit the way the paint transformed the wall, and I was here for it, singing along, mumbling through the parts I didn't know as I started covering the south-facing wall. Cruz had repeatedly told me to make the room my own. He said the walls needed color and he hadn't gotten around to it, but I was certain that this was his way of luring me to move to Iowa and live in his place permanently. I hadn't planned to take him up on it, but with the roller in my hand and the cans of paint at my feet, I wondered if he'd come home to every room in his house painted. I liked how the color looked on the walls, how clear and stark the change was. It's how I wanted to feel about myself—a clear before and after, a new and improved Willow. The next time I dated someone, I'd have a cache of memories that had nothing to do with my ex.

Before the song ended, I gave one last swipe of the roller and stepped back, scanning my work. Spencer had always said that beige and light gray and white were universal, drama-free, and made it easier to cover mistakes. He wasn't wrong, and I'd tried to be beige for a long time, wanting to fit into his world. They were boring colors, though, and if I was going to be alone, I wouldn't be alone and beige. Setting the roller down, I turned to grab a glass of water and screamed in surprise at the hulking form in the doorway.

"Shit, you scared me!" I held my hand over my heart, feeling the splatters of wet paint under my fingertips on my old tank top.

Deacon was leaning one well-developed shoulder against the wood. He was in old sweats, and his arms were crossed over a plain white tank top covering his chest. That damn smirk on his lips.

"Work it," he sang, mirroring my dance moves and going into an exaggerated body roll. "You asked if I could bring the ladder up from the garage. Here to serve."

I swatted his arm. "How long were you spying on me?"

He shrugged, stepping into the bedroom. "Not that long. I knocked, but you probably couldn't hear me over the music." He swung his hips in my direction, mimicking my dance moves. "It looks good in here, Low."

I examined my handiwork again. "It does." Deacon's arm brushed mine when he took a step forward. He'd showered before coming over, and I inhaled the clean scent of his soap. "It's a re-do," I said, putting my hands on my hips.

"Third," he said, setting the ladder up near the partially painted wall. "Dancing with yours truly was number one, and you changed your hair." He motioned to where my new short hair was pushed off my face with a headband.

"True." I bit the corner of my lower lip. "You don't think Cruz will mind the change, do you?"

"Nah," he said. "He needs color in this place, and he's always called this your room. It's quite a red."

"It's my favorite color." I studied a line of blue painting tape along the windowsill. "It makes me feel happy and brave."

"You should wear red more often," he said, crouching to look at the paint along the baseboard. "You'd look really good in red."

My face heated at his comment, and I looked down at my clothes self-consciously. Gray sweats and a light pink tank top. I wasn't sure I owned anything red, and I wasn't sure why. "Thank you," I said, feeling a few butterflies in my stomach that he'd noticed me like that at all.

He didn't seem to pick up on it and stood, clapping his hands together. "I brought the ladder up, so you might as well put me to work. You want me to paint everything higher than . . ." He eyed me up and down. "How high can you reach? Six feet?"

I wanted to say something snarky, but that was exactly what I needed. He pulled the ladder in from the hallway and started taping near the ceiling while I worked on the lower part of the wall. The playlist kept cycling through the hits of the late nineties and early aughts.

"Low, do you like any songs from after 2010?" Deacon had rolled paint onto a good portion of the wall, biceps flexing as he held the roller on a long pole, bringing it back and forth. Every time he did that, his T-shirt revealed a sliver of his back or obliques.

"Yes," I said, hopeful he wouldn't ask too many follow-up questions. "I like these songs, though. I'm an old soul."

"Not that old," he said, recognizing the opening beats of the next song. "This came out my senior year of high school. Between you and Jayden, I'm getting a little tired of being called old."

"You're only ten years older than me," I said. "That's not even half the run of *Grey's Anatomy*!" I grinned, tracing along the baseboard, focusing on keeping my brush moving in a straight line. "That's a show from your era, right?" He'd glanced down from his perch on the ladder, and I paused my painting to look up and avoid the rag he'd tossed at me.

"Sorry!" I yelped and shifted to avoid the paint on the rag. "I was kidding!" I paused my brushwork again, watching him move the roller along the wall, his sweatpants hanging low on his hips. I shot my eyes back down to the wall, focusing on my work. "Thank you for helping me. You really are pretty great."

He stretched over me with the roller, revealing a sliver of taut stomach. "I know."

"And cocky."

"You have no idea. But I would be the man to ask if you wanted to find out about cocky." He waggled his eyebrows suggestively.

I tossed a nearby rag at him and he laughed, dodging the throw. "Just when I think you're so nice, out comes your dick."

"I would never whip it out in front of you. I'm a gentleman." He rolled more paint into the space closest to the window expertly, the line almost exactly straight. "Of course, if I did, you wouldn't need to make this list of things to re-do, because you would immediately forget all other men. It's a dangerous power to have."

"Thank you for sparing me?" I kept my gaze trained on the wall. I didn't want to chance my eyes accidentally falling to his crotch and giving him more ammunition to tease me.

Deacon climbed down the ladder and began painting the middle of the wall, standing closer to me. "Do you think this will need another coat?" His bare arm grazed mine, and I snuck a peek at the tattoo on his shoulder reading "That Others May Live" under a mountain range.

He repeated the question about another coat, and I jumped, knowing for sure he'd caught me looking at his arm. "Um, yeah." I dropped to my knees to examine a few uneven spots and to take myself away from the temptation to look at him. "I think so." I followed my brushstrokes up the wall looking for imperfections I'd need to touch up later. I could get lost in the red color. It was perfect, even without the touch-ups. "Everything I read said this kind of paint needs a few hours between coats."

"Perfect," he said. "How about we make dinner and then finish up?"

At the word "we," I whipped my head up. And, oh wow. What did Julia Roberts say in *Pretty Woman*? *Big mistake. Big. Huge.* I was face-to-face with Deacon's crotch. I shot my eyes from straight ahead up to his face, where he was blessedly not smirking, though he had to see my eyes widen. "What?"

"Food? We could consume it before painting more? I was supposed to meet someone, but we're already covered in paint.

Might as well finish the job, right?" He motioned to the wall as if I'd forgotten what we were doing, which I actually had a little, not that I could admit he was right.

"Oh. Yeah." I covered the brush and positioned the rolling pan and paint can on the tarp. "Sure." I looked up again, though this time he'd stepped back and something other than his penis filled my vision. "But it's okay if you have to go to meet someone. I can finish alone."

"Low, you're like four feet tall. I can't in good conscience leave you alone, plus I want to see the first project come to completion." He held out a hand to me, pulling me to my feet, but instead of pulling me against his chest, he steadied me and offered his palm for a high five. "Third re-do in the books!"

I grinned, looking around. He was right. I returned his high five and pointed my shoulder toward the kitchen. "I probably have stuff to make pasta."

"Sweet." He followed me to the doorway. "Then you can tell me what's next on your list."

CHAPTER 12

EVERY PERSON I served with would have been shocked to see me, the king of takeout, in a kitchen like this, but I stirred the sauce, the aroma of garlic and onion all around us in the small kitchen. Willow was perched with her forearms resting on the kitchen island. She'd handled some chopping but had otherwise been watching me work as we talked.

"Where did you learn to cook like this? On base?"

"No," I said. "I ate at the DFAC on base, like the dining center, and MREs in the field."

"MREs?" Willow held her palm in the air like she was raising her hand. "Let me guess—Meaty rations for everyone?"

I chuckled. "Close. Meals, ready-to-eat. When on my own, I mostly ate like a raccoon, scavenging whatever I could find." I gave the pasta a few quick stirs and set the wooden spoon across the top like Marcus had shown me. "My roommate has been teaching me a few things. He's really good. Opened a restaurant and everything, though he couldn't quite make the business work. Anyway, I figured I should know how to feed myself and new friends in my life, and I've got time now until I go back in."

She shifted into the space to get plates from the cupboard to my left. "Cruz thought you might want to become an EMT with all the medical training you guys got."

I checked the noodles against the side of the pan, still not a hundred percent on what al dente should feel like. "He doesn't know I'm planning to go back." There wasn't a good reason I hadn't told Cruz yet. He was my best friend, and if anyone could understand wanting to be back in, it was him. Except, I'd realized lately he didn't fully understand because he'd never left. No one seemed to understand that. "I need to get around to telling him, but I wouldn't go the EMT route. The medical part wasn't what excited me about the job, anyway," I added, making sure my voice sounded casual before I changed the subject. "Dinner is almost ready," I said with a flourish.

"Remind me, what is this?" She set the plates on the island along with silverware and watched me intently.

"Bolognese." I moved the frying pan from where I'd been preparing it. "When Marcus taught me, we had to let it simmer for like four hours, so this is kind of a bastardized version." I studied the sauce. It looked good, and I was kind of proud of myself.

"This is very impressive." She leaned over and waved her hand over the pot while inhaling deeply, and that simple motion was so incredibly hot. I glanced away. "You didn't have to cook for me," she said, leaning against the counter and sipping from a second glass of wine. "I already put you to work all evening helping me paint."

"I like cooking." I tasted the sauce and added a little more salt.

"Probably helps you impress the women, right?" She held up the bottle to offer me another glass, but I raised my still nearly full one.

I shrugged. "I don't really cook for women other than my friends."

"You should," she said, watching me stir the sauce. "Imagine what would have happened if you made this delicious meal for the woman you were supposed to meet tonight instead of me."

"I never said it was a woman."

"But was it?"

I chuckled. "Okay, it was. But we've only gone out once, and there was no real spark."

Willow punched my arm, and I almost dropped the spoon I was holding. "Deacon! You canceled a date to help me paint? I feel awful!"

I'd truly forgotten all about the date after canceling, especially when my gaze would drag to Willow as she was stretching or bending to reach something in one of the kitchen cabinets. The bending had been distracting more than once. "Nah. I told you. No spark."

"Sometimes sparks come later."

"Not in my experience." I gave the sauce another stir.

"Maybe you're too impatient. Did you kiss her?"

I wondered if Willow was bold because she was comfortable with me or if it was the wine in her hand. "I'm not impatient." I thought back to a few nights earlier when a woman named Mallison and I met for drinks. The most interesting part of the conversation had been talking about her name, a mash-up of her father's sister Allison and her mother's favorite band, Metallica.

I'd walked away from the date thinking her mother would probably be more fun to talk to than her. "Nosy. Why do you ask?"

"No reason." She sipped her wine again, taking a big gulp and looking like she was hiding something. Next she picked up a paperback that was sitting on the counter and thumbed through it, avoiding eye contact. It looked like a romance novel, with the woman on the cover in a low-cut ball gown and the bare-chested man behind her smelling her neck. "I was just curious!"

"Are these spicy books you read making you think of kiiiiiiissing?" I made a grab for the book, but she held it out of my reach and set the book aside. I'd noticed romance books sprinkled all over the house, and I thought it was nice she still liked reading about love. She hadn't given up on the idea of it.

"No," she said. "But this author writes them very well." She held up the cover, the author's name in bold white type across the bottom: D. A. Bennett. "If you ever want to borrow it. The carriage scenes are top-notch."

I lifted one eyebrow.

"Not that you need to read about kissing," she said. "Not that that's why I read the books, either." Willow blushed easily. I noticed the first time we had coffee and at the wedding, but the charm of her blushes was growing on me. I took another appreciative glance as I sipped from my glass of wine.

"Maybe I'll check it out," I said, letting her off the hook. "Very interested in kisses tonight. Is that the next thing on your list?"

She snort-laughed before slapping a hand over her mouth. "No, of course not."

"On one hand, good, because I am honor bound to your brother to look out for you, and I can't help you find random dudes to make out with. But on the other," I said, offering her a taste of the sauce with the edge of a wooden spoon, "why is it so funny?"

"It just is," she said, setting the glass aside. "And, oh my God, this is so good!"

"That's what you should say after a first kiss."

"I haven't had a first kiss in ten years."

I studied her expression and the way the corners of her lips turned down. "How was it?"

"I can't tell you about my first kiss with Spencer," she said, hiding her face in her hands.

"So only *you* can ask about first kisses. Good to know." I opened a few drawers until I found serving utensils.

"It was clumsy and exciting," she said, after a pause. "I felt lucky that someone wanted to kiss me." She toyed with her fingers. "And there was probably too much tongue."

I laughed at her addition, turning back to the stove to stir the sauce. "I didn't kiss the woman the other night." I'd thought about it—she was all curves and had a great smile, but the whole night I'd wanted to check scores from the game or google how to make honey mustard or send Emi a funny meme. "I didn't kiss her because . . . I don't know. I make it a point not to kiss someone unless they're all I can focus on. It's just something I have a good sense about."

"How do you know?"

I always knew. I trusted sparks and chemistry. "I guess you just do." I flicked the dial on the stove, removing the pasta from the burner. "You'll meet someone, and you'll know they're someone who captivates you. That's how it is for me, anyway."

Willow grabbed a small stack of paper napkins from a drawer.

"I wouldn't even know where to begin. I haven't dated someone new in a decade, and I never had to think about a kiss with my ex. How do you even maneuver into that position with someone unfamiliar?"

The steam rose off the sauce and pasta, the scents of garlic, basil, and celery wafting into the air in smooth ribbons, and I gave her a quizzical look.

"What?" She touched her face like maybe I was staring at her because of something on it.

I served pasta onto each of our plates. "How do you maneuver?" I parroted her words back to her in a mechanical voice. "Are you a robot?"

"Shut up. You know what I mean, like how do you naturally get into a position to kiss someone you're not comfortable with yet? That's a valid question."

I chuckled and handed her the canister of Parmesan cheese. Marcus had tried to wean me off it, offering to grate it and extolling the virtues of fresh, but he'd finally given up. I tipped the green plastic tube on its side, watching the cheese sprinkle down. In my family, it was a treat to have it. It was expensive, and having it felt luxurious, even as an adult when I could keep it stocked. I held it out for Willow, who happily accepted it.

"That is not a valid question. You know how to kiss someone."

"What if it's different from with Spencer?"

I shook my head. "You're overthinking it."

She wiped the side of her plate to catch a drip of sauce. She brought it to her lips, and I couldn't help but follow her finger and take in the shape of her lips. I was so focused on watching her, I startled when she spoke again. "I am not overthinking it."

She set her wineglass down and grabbed my arms, pulling me to face her. She was shorter than me, but I let her position me, curious about what her next move would be. "Say we're on a date and I'm like, I think I want to kiss this guy."

"Because he's good-looking, smells nice, and I think his penis might be especially large."

She pushed my shoulder, and I ducked away with a laugh. "Be serious."

"Serious about your inability to maneuver. Roger that."

"Like I was saying, I'm on a date with you and I decide I want to kiss you and think you want it too."

"Then we kiss."

"Yeah, but we just met. How do I go from 'Oh, hey, nice to meet you!' to 'Let my tongue in your mouth, please'? I was thirteen the last time I did this and drunk on Sour Patch Kids."

"Well, I'd say do that again, but I'd have to object to you kissing someone who took you out for Sour Patch Kids."

"Because that's your move?"

I shrugged, making a grab for her plate. "Fine. Tease me. I won't help."

"I'm sorry. I'm sorry," she said, her hand at my biceps to pull me back. Her touch was surprisingly firm, and she looked up at me through her dark lashes, a look in her eyes that showed true hope. "I know this is stupid."

"Low," I said, stepping forward, moving into her space and wanting to reassure her. I could sense her anxiety around this. She smelled like raspberries, and I inhaled the heady scent while I was close to her. "It's not stupid. I mean, it's stupid that you're worried you'll be bad at kissing, because . . ." I paused, inching forward and letting my fingers graze her waist, the lightest dusting of a touch. My gaze fell to her lips, and I swallowed.

"Because why?"

She looked so damn insecure, and I wanted to take that away from her. I let my gaze move in a lazy path from her lips to her eyes. I noticed how she watched me, wide-eyed and intense, but I didn't go any faster. By the time my hand brushed her shoulder, she sucked in a breath. "Because you're . . ." My grip at her waist tightened and our bodies were touching, the heat from her closeness surrounding me. That little intake of breath was sexy as hell, even though that's not what this was about. I wanted her to feel comfortable if she was around someone new.

"What?"

My fingers slid down her arm and circled her wrist, bringing her palm to my chest. "You can put your hand here."

She flattened her palm as instructed, the heat of her touch surprising.

"You can look for signs," I said. "Does he step toward you?" I closed more of the gap between us and heard her soft intake of breath. "And if you tip your chin up, does he lean closer?"

She looked up at me through her thick lashes. "And then?"

It hit me in that moment that I'd made a horrible decision. That insecurity in her voice was gone, but now I was questioning myself left and right. What started out as something playful felt a lot like a spark, growing stronger by the second. Willow's face was near mine, her lips just inches away.

I searched her face, just for a beat, reminding myself what this was before gently cupping the back of her neck, my fingers grazing her curls.

We stood there in that silence, the smell of dinner and raspberry body wash around us and her hand still resting delicately over my heart. She lifted her chin and our breaths were mingling.

My voice was thicker than I planned. "You did it. This is pretty comfortable, right?"

She licked the corner of her lip again, and my gaze flicked to the curve of her mouth. "Yeah, this is comfortable."

I looked back to her eyes, and the hooded expression there forced my gaze back to her lips, and I imagined the possibilities until I remembered about whom I was imagining. "Good," I said, before taking a step back, the disconnection from her jarring. I hadn't expected my hand to fit so well against her neck or for her body to feel so pliant against mine. "Just do something like that. You've passed Maneuvering 101."

She blinked rapidly and finally nodded, a slow smile creeping across her face. "Thanks. I guess it's not so hard."

Oh, it was getting there. I shifted to the island, partially obscuring the effect that lesson had on me.

"I don't mean to sound so insecure. I mean, how cliché to worry no man will want me again." She made the joke, but it fell flat because I saw the fear in her eyes.

"You'll be fine, Low. You're very kissable, and Spencer won't be the only person to ever think so." I pulled the plate toward me and smiled. "Of course," I said, my signature smirk returning, "no one you kiss is going to make better Bolognese than me."

"No kiss could be as good as this tastes," she said, licking a bit of sauce off her finger again. "But maybe something will come close."

I was jealous of the hypothetical man who would be her

re-do on this, but instead of confronting that thought, I shook my head with a laugh and muttered "maneuvering" as I walked toward the table. "I'm certain plenty of men, good men, worthy men, will want you. I honestly have no doubt of it." But I hoped they didn't make themselves known until I was long gone.

CHAPTER 13

Willow

A FLOCK OF geese honked as they passed overhead, and a few monarch butterflies flitted over wildflowers lining someone's front walk. I'd never known my grandfather—he'd died when I was a toddler, but Cruz always described the natural beauty of Iowa when he'd spent time with our grandparents as a kid, and I slowed down to look around and take it in. Gus momentarily pulled me until he caught on to the new pace. He really was the best trained dog. Deacon had said he'd considered training Cupcake the same way, but he'd fallen for her "fuck it is the new hustle" attitude. It was cute to see him doting over her. His soft side always surprised me, like the way his smile got a little wider when he told me about spending time with the neighbor kid. Deacon had a way of always somehow surprising me.

There was red paint on my fingernails from the last touch-up

I'd done that morning. I hoped to show off the finished room, but inviting him to check out my bedroom sounded like something Zoe would encourage me to do. The memory of painting and sharing dinner with Deacon, especially of how it felt to practice getting ready for a kiss with him, had been distracting me for three days. I'd promised him I'd bake for him next time as a thank-you for the help.

Gus gave a single tug on his leash and looked at me expectantly, as if I'd forgotten we were on our way to the park.

> WILLOW: You up?

The dots bounced, showing an incoming reply, and I glanced up to see Gus sniffing around a tree.

> CRUZ: Please never send me that message again.
>
> WILLOW: It's not like I asked what you were wearing.
>
> CRUZ: I should have been an only child.
>
> CRUZ: Everything okay?
>
> WILLOW: All good. You?
>
> CRUZ: Quiet now.

I called out to Gus and then snapped a photo of his face before he returned to the base of the tree. His ears were perked up, tongue lolling out of his mouth. I sent it to Cruz.

WILLOW: I'm taking good care of your boy.

WILLOW: Could you send me Mom's cookie recipe? I want to make them for Deacon as a thank-you.

Cruz never wrote down the recipe. He'd just tap his temple and tell me it's where all the good secrets were, but I always craved chocolate chip cookies when I missed him or missed her. I liked the idea of sharing them with Deacon.

CRUZ: Thank him for what?

WILLOW: He helped me paint your house. Color on the walls!

CRUZ: Send pics—I want to see!

CRUZ: Do NOT send pics after asking "You up?" again, though. I cannot stress this enough.

WILLOW: I know. I know. You only want those kinds of photos from Zoe or G!

He'd been seeing this guy on and off for a couple years, but he never told me much about his love life. I'm not sure I would have even known that he was interested in men at all were it not for a night we got fall-down drunk on what would have been Mom's birthday and he told me how hard it was to keep part of himself from the guys and how Deacon was the only one who knew.

CRUZ: No more G—don't ask.

WILLOW: No! You were so into them. What happened?

CRUZ: I literally just said don't ask (but I'm fine).

There was a symmetry I didn't love in both our relationships ending this year, but my brother would never admit to wanting comforting or even an emoji hug, so I wasn't surprised when he changed the subject.

CRUZ: And I politely declined Zoe's offer.

CRUZ: Tell her the attempt at patriotism is appreciated, though.

I chuckled and sat on a bench, releasing the tethered lock on the leash so Gus could wander relatively freely in the park. I sent back the saluting emoji and waited. I wanted to ask about G, but I had no idea who Cruz was around, so I let it drop for now.

CRUZ: There's a stack of boxes from Mom's place in the basement. Recipe book is in one of them.

CRUZ: Haven't gotten around to going through them yet.

WILLOW: Want me to?

CRUZ: Sure. Most of it's probably junk.

WILLOW: On it. I love you.

CRUZ: Love you, too.

CRUZ: And Gus is adept at finding trouble in that park. Watch out.

WILLOW: I don't believe that. It's like you put him through basic training. He's more of a rule follower than you.

CRUZ: I'm telling you, keep an eye on him.

My head snapped up as I heard a yelp from Gus. I shoved the phone in my pocket, running toward him. I stopped short at the sight of a whining, large-eyed Gus, his mouth and snout covered in spiky quills.

"Oh, shit," I said, approaching and searching for what had stuck him, only to see what looked like a porcupine scampering away. I didn't even know they had those here. Gus whined, and when my hand neared his face, he yelped and I jumped back. "No. No. No," I said to myself. "Please let me help you, boy." How could I have broken Cruz's perfect dog? And despite being pre-vet in college and doing years of undergraduate research with an animal science professor, my knowledge about immunodeficiency in cattle was not helpful here.

"Best not to touch them," a low voice from behind me said, approaching slowly. I turned to see a tall figure with glasses and the jawline of a Greek god approaching—what was it with all these hot men in Des Moines, Iowa? I'd never seen such a steady stream of drool-worthy guys in one stretch.

"It just happened," I said, my focus returning to Gus. "He won't let me near him."

He held out his hand to me. "I'm Theo." He smiled and looked kind and sweet, and then he spoke to Gus and my heart melted a little at how he coaxed the dog forward. "Who do we have here?"

"Willow," I said.

"How'd you get into so much trouble, Willow?" He held out his hand for Gus to sniff as he visually inspected all the quills.

"Oh, no, I'm Willow," I said. "Obviously, you wanted the dog's name. This is Gus. Gus the dog. Willow the human. I shed less." The human who needed a muzzle to stop her from saying stupid things.

"Well, Gus, you're going to be okay." He shifted his smile to me. "And Willow the human who sheds less, if you don't mind some company, I'm a veterinarian." He pointed to the clinic insignia on his jacket. "I would be happy to help." He looked back to Gus, petting and inspecting his paw for quills before cutting his gaze back to me. Was he flirting with me or was I just so out of practice that dog examination could be mistaken for flirting?

"I'd love company," I said. "I mean, the assist. I didn't know who to call. Is he in a lot of pain?"

"I imagine so," he said, checking Gus's body over more thoroughly. "And I'm happy to help. No need to call anyone else." He gently set Gus's paw back down.

"Um, yeah." And I was three for three on intelligent comebacks.

"Let's get Gus taken care of." He lured Gus forward, and I followed, still grasping the leash. "And after he's patched up, you can get my number so if you need someone to call later, you can call me."

CHAPTER 14

"YOU GOT THIS. One more." I clapped my hands together, and Marcus grunted in approval and lifted the weights above his chest. Once the bar was returned to the rack, I stepped back and let him catch his breath and checked my phone.

"What made you want to lift suddenly?" I glanced at the notifications, sliding my thumb up the screen, but there was no message from Willow.

"Lila joined a weight-lifting club in Chicago after her fellow accountant convinced her when they were at pickleball." He wiped the sweat from his brow. "I want to make sure I can keep up with her."

"Fascinating girl you found." I clocked his dreamy expression at the mention of her and rolled my eyes. I was happy for the guy, though. He'd been hung up on Emi since I met him, and she would never give him a shot. I wasn't sure she'd ever given anyone a chance. She'd told me once she'd done all the falling for someone she ever planned to do.

"Lila's amazing," he said, sitting up with a grunt. "Could kick my ass, though. Hence the workouts."

I chuckled and nodded toward the other side of the gym. "Nothing wrong with that. I knew this natural bodybuilder once. Tiffany could kick my ass ten ways to Sunday. We had a lot of fun."

We strode toward the cardio equipment, and he tipped his water bottle up. "Is there any group or category of women where you haven't *known* someone?"

I laughed off the comment and pointed to the treadmills along the back wall. Willow had said something to the same effect, and it wasn't wrong, but it's not like it was the only thing about me. Cruz gave me shit all the time about my history with women. It was probably why he warned me so harshly against trying anything with Willow. "Never been with a pickleball-playing accountant, so you've got me there."

"Don't worry." He patted my shoulder a few times before climbing onto the machine. "I'll help you get your game as good as mine."

I punched him in the arm and fiddled with the settings. "Pretty cocky for first girlfriend."

"She's awesome." He popped in his earbuds, and I did the same, looking away from my roommate to the treadmill settings and adjusting the incline and speed. I was almost back to where I'd been two years ago before the surgery. If I could keep pushing, I'd be in shape to get my old life back. The heavy beat of "Humble" by Kendrick Lamar pounded in my ears, and I hit start. The familiar feel of my feet hitting the belt as my heart rate beat in sync with the song washed over me, and I sank into the oblivion of running and moving, faster and harder. It was what we'd done in basic and then at a higher level when I started training to be a PJ. That's where I had to get back to. A place beyond being in shape, being as close to a machine as a human body could be, because that's the level the job required.

"Damn, man," Marcus mouthed over his own music, pointing at the readout on my screen where I'd lost track of the workout, only now taking stock of my breath coming fast and my calf muscles burning. In my ear, the music stopped, and the phone rang.

When I saw the name on the screen, I hopped to the side of the belt before turning it off and hopping down. "Low, what's up?"

"Sorry to bother you," she said, and I heard a hesitance in her voice that made the hairs on the back of my neck stand up.

I angled between two women on their phones near the ellipticals. "What's wrong?"

"It's probably fine, but can you meet me at the vet clinic? Gus had an accident when we were at the park."

I heard the dog's whining in the background and the sounds of the road.

"What's the address?" She spoke away from the phone, and a deeper voice rumbled the response.

"Who's that?"

"We were lucky and ran into a veterinarian, actually," she said, her voice softening, and I heard the rumbling of the man's voice again, which elicited a giggle from Willow. A fucking giggle. I glanced over my shoulder at Marcus and motioned between my phone and the entrance. "Theo says he'll be okay. Gus had a run-in with the wrong end of a porcupine."

"Though, to be fair, is there a good end of a porcupine?" The joke came from Theo, so I hated it, but Willow laughed, making me dislike the guy even more.

"I'll be there in ten," I said, pushing through the exit doors.

"It's no rush," she said, a lightness returning to her voice, no doubt because of Dr. Helpful's dumb joke. "Theo said it'll take a while. Gus will need to be sedated."

I heard a man's voice saying something, and I bristled. "On my way," I said, ignoring her reassurance.

The address she had repeated back to me was across town, but I still approached the clinic in just under ten minutes. What was she doing getting in a car with a strange guy who claimed to be a vet? I hit the gas to make it through a yellow light. She wasn't a kid, but Cruz would kill me if something happened to her. And what kind of a vet was just lounging around in the park? I gave a derisive chuff to no one and glanced at my GPS. I half expected to see an abandoned warehouse when I turned the corner, but the clinic she'd mentioned was ahead of me. "Doesn't mean he's actually a vet, though," I muttered.

The clinic was bright with sunlight streaming in the front windows, and the receptionist smiled at me next to a cardboard cutout of a fluffy white cat. "Welcome. How can I help you?"

"Yeah," I said, stepping forward and noting how her gaze dipped to my chest. My T-shirt was drenched in sweat and clinging. Another time, though. "My friend came in with, um, Theo?"

"Oh, certainly." She motioned to the seating area. "Have a seat. She and Dr. Johnson are in the back."

Dr. Johnson. Fine. Probably an old nerd. Rolling my shoulders back, I eyed the door as I texted Willow, but I didn't get a reply. Anxious, I tapped my foot and counted the floor tiles—fourteen feet to the exit and nine to the window. I hated the waiting, and my skin felt tight by the time a door opened and Willow emerged, laughing at something a tall, slender, young guy had said with his hand at her lower back. I zeroed in on the placement of that hand.

"No," he said, his hand not moving despite the death glare I sent him from across the room. "Let's avoid that particular park. How about Latin King? Their chicken spiedini is an East Side staple."

"That sounds good," she said, holding out her hand to shake his, and I took in how long his palm lingered against hers. I hated this guy on sight.

"How's Gus?" I asked in a voice that was too loud for the space, and Willow jumped. She jumped closer to him, making every muscle in my body tense.

"Deacon, you scared me!" She finally pulled her hand from the vet's grip and held it to her heart. "He's going to be fine. He probably won't mess with a porcupine again, though."

The vet laughed, like this was their inside joke. "That's for sure."

"We were lucky Theo was there." She gave him an adoring glance again. "I would have had no idea what to do."

"You would have figured it out," he said, which was what I would have said if I wasn't consciously stopping myself from shoving this guy away from Willow so he couldn't touch her again. "And it gave me the opportunity to meet you."

I didn't know it would be so easy to despise a stranger, but Dr. Theo Johnson had made his way onto a short list of people on my bad side. "Was there a lot of blood?" My voice was too loud again, but I said the first thing I could think of to interrupt this little flirt fest. "Does he need medication?"

The vet looked between me and Willow, but he addressed his response to her in the end. "I'll get Gus finished up. The staff at the front desk will get you the medication and a printed version of the care instructions and will bring him out soon." He pointed to the desk. "And you have my number." He grinned at her, and she grinned back. I debated asking about something else to remind her I was there. "But I'll pick you up at seven tomorrow?"

She nodded and they shook hands again, fingers lingering until I coughed into my hand.

"Oh, sorry." She dropped his hand again. "This is my friend, Deacon. He's going to help me get Gus home."

The vet's expression changed when she declared I was a friend, and I'd never hated the word more. There wasn't an elegant way to work into the conversation that I had extensive military and medical training and could make something look like an accident, so I held back. I gripped his hand too hard when he stuck it out for a handshake, but who could blame me? I owed Cruz that much, and that's where this feeling was coming from, not from any misplaced jealousy.

Willow didn't seem to notice and turned to me, her eyes wide with a beaming smile for me after he'd slipped back into the office.

"Seven tomorrow?" I cocked an eyebrow, this time regulating the volume of my voice. "House call?"

She rolled her eyes and pulled her wallet from her purse. "A date. A re-do on a first date! Can you believe it? You were right!"

I followed her to the front desk without responding. The gnawing feeling in my chest was jealousy, but I wasn't someone who got jealous, not about women, and especially not about friends. Willow winced when she pulled the credit card from her wallet, asking what the total was. I'd dropped enough money on Cupcake to know it wouldn't be cheap, and I squeezed her shoulder in support, regretting it immediately when I felt her warmth through the fabric of her T-shirt. And then even more when I was reminded that the vet might touch her on their date.

"Dr. Johnson said there's no charge." She was an older woman with gray at her temples and *Peanuts* characters on her light pink scrubs. "He likes you," she said in a kind voice. "Said he was glad to help out a new friend." She was just finishing up walking Willow through the aftercare instructions when another woman in blue scrubs walked Gus out, my annoyance fading because Gus looked as miserable and embarrassed as a dog could look.

I dropped to my knees and let him trot to me. "Hey, buddy." I hovered my hand near his shoulder, letting him close the distance. "You'll be okay," I said, petting his shoulder again, since that didn't seem to cause him any pain. "But you had to do this when that guy was nearby?" I said low against his ears, which perked up. Gus got it. I gave him one more pet and took the leash to lead him out with Willow walking ahead of us.

She'd repeated the instructions as I hoisted Gus into the back seat. "I need to message Cruz. He's going to be mad—he told me to keep a close eye on him in the park, and I told him he was being ridiculous."

"He won't be mad," I reassured her, pulling out into traffic. "He won't be thrilled about the date, but he won't be mad." In reality, I wasn't sure if Cruz would care about the date. He was protective, but I didn't think he actually wanted her to be alone. The only person I'd ever heard him seriously encourage her to think of as off-limits was me.

CHAPTER 15

"YOU REALLY DON'T have to stay," I said. Deacon sat on the couch with Gus curled up next to him, the gigantic dog snuggled in like a puppy. He wasn't allowed on the couch normally, but I made a command decision that minor surgery and losing the interesting, new, spiky plaything you were hunting meant you got to curl up on a soft blanket and watch Netflix. Deacon stroked the back of Gus's neck, where the quills had missed him. "We're just going to hang out all night."

"He's already got his head on my lap so comfortably," he said. "I can't do Gus like that."

I grinned at the sight of the big, tough dog asleep on Deacon's muscled thigh and grabbed a beer from the fridge for the makeshift cushion.

"Message Cruz?"

I nodded and handed him the bottle. "I sent him a text thread with some photos." By some photos, I meant thirteen, both pre- and post-quilling plus pics of the medicine to make sure he had proof that his baby was okay. "Do you think he'll see it when he wakes up? Or when he gets . . . back?" I'd gotten used to not knowing exactly what my brother's day-to-day was like, especially when he was deployed, but Deacon would know more. He'd been in his shoes.

Deacon nodded. "He'll see it as soon as he can." He didn't say anything more, just kept stroking Gus's fur.

I was young when Cruz joined the Air Force, and I didn't exactly understand what he did as a PJ until later, when I learned how dangerous it could be. I studied Deacon now, his back straight and shoulders square even as he relaxed with the dog. "What made you want to join?"

"The Air Force?"

I nodded and tipped my beer to my lips, taking the sliver of couch not occupied by Gus and sliding my legs along his furry torso. "Yeah. You like big, important questions, right?"

His phone buzzed on the end table near him, and he silenced it. "Like your favorite stuffed animal. Yeah, okay. Big questions." He scratched his jaw and glanced out the window behind me before looking back at me. "Well, I always wanted to be a superhero."

I would have thrown a pillow at him if I wasn't worried about jostling Gus. "You're not a superhero."

He flashed that cocky smile at me and motioned to his chest with his free hand. "You're right. My physique is more godlike now."

"Are you going to give me a real answer?"

He dropped his hand. "I was being serious, actually. I love superhero movies, comics, cartoons. Always have, and I wanted to do that, to save people and be part of a team. My parents weren't around a lot, but I was close with my grandma. She was part of an all-woman firefighting crew in Texas in the sixties before my mom was born. She was a badass and kind of my role model. She never met a problem she didn't throw herself in front of fixing." He shrugged. "We moved around a lot, and I never got to make many friends or really join things before we'd be off to somewhere new. Fighting a good fight with a group like she had always seemed pretty great to me. And I didn't want to go to Texas, so I looked for other ways to be a superhero."

"But the Avengers weren't hiring?"

"The pay is for shit, and you have to bring your own costume! Did you know that?"

I laughed. "Admit it. You were embarrassed to wear that spandex and leather."

"Please," he said, silencing his phone again. "That's my normal Saturday night." He glanced at the screen and then flipped the phone over. "Anyway, I got it in my head that's what I was meant to do, so when I realized Iron Man wasn't an actual job, I looked at other options. And the PJs . . ." He scratched his jaw again and cut his gaze to a photo on Cruz's bookshelf of a group of pararescuemen in fatigues. I recognized Deacon's smile on the right side of the photo, and Cruz was in the middle. "Of all the options, that looked the closest." He ran fingers through his hair and gave me a wan smile. "How much did Cruz tell you about the job?"

"Not a lot of details." I'd done my searching, late-night googling that I regretted and that left me awake at night worried my brother might not make it home. "But I know it's hard to get on the team. Like, the training is intense. Most people don't make it, right?"

He nodded with a distant smile. "Something like five to ten percent of people make it through, and intense is one word for it. If you didn't feel like throwing up at least once a day, you weren't working hard enough."

"That sounds like hell."

"Yeah," he said, his own gaze straying to the photo and then back to the top of Gus's head. "A kind of hell, but kind of heaven, too, if that makes sense."

It didn't to me, but he straightened his back and chuckled. "Never mind. I'm sure that doesn't make sense at all, but it did for us. It's far from perfect, the military. Far, far from perfect. There's still sexism and homophobia and politics are what they are. But the people. My people. They were my community."

"And you saved a lot of people."

He nodded again, though his mouth was set in a line. I hadn't often seen Deacon like that—reflective and somber, and I wasn't sure what to add, but he kept going. When he spoke next, it seemed like it was more to himself than to me. "That's the job. These things we do, that others may live." The words hung in the air for a moment until his phone buzzed again, breaking through the silence.

"Is that why you chose psychology at school? To help people?"

Deacon shrugged one shoulder. "Just sounded interesting," he said and his phone buzzed again.

"It's okay if you need to check that." I pointed to the iPhone sitting on the table, the message senders clearly waiting for a reply. "You're popular today."

He shook off the expression that had painted his face a moment earlier and gave me a cocky smile. "I'm always popular."

As if he'd planned it, his phone buzzed again, and he picked it up to look at the screen before shoving it in his pocket. "There. I'll text back later. Are you done interrogating me with big questions?"

"One more," I said, settling back on the couch. I thought Gus might have cuddled against me, but he was out and Deacon was his only touchpoint.

"Okay. Did you want length in inches or do you prefer metric? Just know that without circumference, you'll be missing the full picture."

I threw a pillow at him, which he snatched from the air before it hit him in the face. "What?" His smile grew wide as he feigned innocence. "You said you had one more *big* question."

I had an actual question, but I also liked the way he'd returned to this version of himself, with humor and life emanating from him, so I dropped my other question about the job and instead asked about something else I'd been wondering. "Okay. Were all those texts from a woman?"

He shrugged and patted his pocket where he'd shoved the phone. "A few women."

"Wanting to go out?"

Gus gave a little whine and stretched his body out along mine before sinking back against Deacon, who shrugged again. "Go out, come over. Say hi. One was just checking in, I think."

"Cruz always told me you saw a lot of women." I hated myself for the comment and wanted to pull the words back immediately. Why did I care if there were a lot of women? It's not like we were a thing.

He gave me that lazy smile again. "Are you slut-shaming me, Willow?"

"I never called you a slut! And I would never." I tugged at the hem of my T-shirt. "Was just curious." I stroked the German shepherd's leg, now pressed to my thigh. "I've never been that popular. I should take lessons from you."

"Nah. You don't want that." He scratched his jawline. "I mean, those women are great. They're fun, smart, kind . . ." He chuckled. "Well, Val isn't *kind*, but she has other positive attributes." He took his phone from his pocket and looked at the screen before handing it over to me.

There were several texts.

> AMBER: Hey—I miss you! Around Saturday?

> EMMA: Roommate is out of town this weekend. Want to come over and wake the neighbors with me?

> VAL 😼: I bought this today. Come over tonight.

The next message was a photo of a complicated-looking sex toy that made me press a hand to my mouth once I turned the phone sideways and realized what it was.

> MEG: I'm in town for a few days. Would love to see you. HMU.

> DJ: Still on for tonight? Looking forward to it. 😊

"Wow." I skimmed the texts again. "You were asked out like five times in the last hour. I really *should* take lessons."

Deacon accepted his phone back, and our fingertips brushed. "You don't want that, though. You want something special." He tapped out a reply to one message, and I was dying to know which.

"They're not special?" I pointed to the phone in his hand.

"They are. They're special and incredible people, but what we have isn't special. It's . . . fun. It's comfort." He shoved the phone in his pocket again. "When I was on active duty, the job could be a lot, and it was hard to have a relationship. I mean, I never tried, but I saw guys try. But it was still nice to have someone to spend time with when you got home."

He kept his voice light, but it sounded false.

"No one wants to be lonely," I offered, thinking about how much time we'd already spent in this house together. When I arrived, I worried I'd be alone all the time.

"Exactly." He shifted in his seat, twisting his shoulders, and I wondered if the angle was hard on his back. "So I met women. I found company. And I guess the habit stuck."

His phone buzzed again in his pocket.

"You must be good company."

He shifted again, and Gus gave a little snort of displeasure at being jostled. "I treat them well. They treat me well. Everyone knows what's what."

"Did you ever want something special?"

"Would never work with the job."

"But when you have a regular job and are done with school? You might enjoy it then."

"Yeah," he said. "That might be nice. 'Hey, honey, I'm home!'" he called out, loosening an imaginary tie. "It was a hard day at the office. A hard day of... businessing." He chuckled. "Kind of falls apart there."

"Wait," I said, making grabby hands for his phone again. "That last woman said you had plans tonight. Like a date? You did this again?"

He shrugged. "I met her at the grocery store. We were both buying apples. I'll tell her we need to rain check."

"Don't cancel on my behalf! Go on your date." I didn't want him to go, but I felt awful being a burden to him. "You told Cruz you'd look out for me, and I appreciate you helping with Gus, but you can't skip a date for me again! This could be your Red Delicious something special!"

"That sounds like a sex position."

I shot him a glare. "Seriously."

"Seriously," he said, tapping on his phone, "it's not a big deal." He shifted in his seat again and grimaced. "It's done."

I let out an exasperated sigh and stood, holding out my hand. "What?"

"Climb out from under Gus. You are clearly uncomfortable."

"What if this is a ruse to kick me out so I go find Red Delicious?" He still took my hand and slid out from under Gus, who whined, groaned, and then stretched to take over the whole couch, his head sinking back down onto the cushion. Deacon's hand wrapped around mine as he pulled up and arched his back.

"Now you can stretch." I reluctantly let my hand fall from his so he had room. "You looked uncomfortable."

He gave me a side smile, but did stretch out more, bending from side to side and then down to touch his toes. And damn,

Deacon's ass was a thing of beauty. "Sorry," he said, looking over his shoulder from his bent state. "My lower back gets weird if I sit at odd angles for too long."

"Can I help?" I stepped closer and pressed my thumbs in circles along his lower back.

The groan he let out startled me and I jumped. "I was going to say no, but damn, Low. You missed your calling as a massage therapist." He groaned again as I pressed my fingers into the muscle of his lower back. "And I'm not even saying that as foreplay."

I chuckled, more to let out the giddy anxious feeling I got from touching Deacon than because it was funny. "I know."

"Thank you," he said, eventually stepping forward and away from my touch. "Still getting things . . . you know, back in order." He eyed Gus and then slumped onto the floor with his back against the couch.

I lowered myself to the floor and sat next to him, nudging my shoulder against him. "I still think you should go on your date."

"I don't date, Lewis. It's not in my programming." He propped one knee up. "But it is in yours. Excited about your night out with the vet?"

My face warmed at the mention of Theo. I hadn't thought about him at all since we left the vet's office. "First date. Well, second first date," I said, making my voice sound bright.

"Nervous?"

I nodded. "A little."

"You'll be good," he said, bumping his fist against the side of my knee. "He'll adore you. Who wouldn't?" Deacon's voice fell lower, and I looked up from the spot on my knee where he'd touched me, the tingles still radiating up my leg. "But if he steps out of line, Gus and I will come for him."

I giggled and knocked my fist against his knee. "Sounds good." Behind us, Gus snored loudly and let out a little bark. "But I think you're going to be doing the heavy lifting."

Deacon chuckled and reached back to scratch Gus behind the ears. The movement pushed him farther from me, and I pulled my hand back to myself. "Thanks for hanging out with me," I said. I'd genuinely felt bad he'd canceled plans for me, but knowing he'd do that, knowing I ranked high enough on his list of people to duck out of a date made me feel warm all over. I pushed some curls off my forehead, still not used to the shorter length. It would be so easy to sink into a crush on Deacon, so it was good I had a date the next day. "I won't keep you from meeting with your Red Delicious something special tomorrow night. I promise."

He chuckled, but not as enthusiastically as usual, and looked down at Gus. "I'm happy where I am." His chocolate-colored eyes caught mine for a moment. "This is plenty special."

CHAPTER 16

Deacon

AFTER WE BELTED out the final lyrics to "Let It Go" from the stage of the bar, Kieran and I took deep bows to the cheering crowd following our encore. He patted me on the back before abandoning my side when Sybil pulled him in for a kiss.

"Get a room, you two," I said as I took my seat.

"We got an entire house," Sybil said, grinning over the rim of her glass before taking a sip from the fruity cocktail. "And we've christened every room."

Marcus returned with a fresh pitcher and some nachos for the table as Emi leaned into Sybil's story. "Every room? Even the back room in the basement where you found all those creepy old dolls?"

"Hot," I said, glancing at my phone to see the reply to my text canceling plans with DJ from the apple aisle, the same woman whose contact name Willow had taken the opportunity to change. She'd sent a message that afternoon, too.

RED DELICIOUS: Hope everything is okay. Maybe tomorrow night? We'd have fun. 😉

I didn't respond and slid the phone back into my pocket. I'd hoped there'd be an update from Willow—that's why I'd looked at my phone in the first place—but she'd been radio silent all evening. A good thing on a date, I guess, but I kept checking.

"So, anyway," Sybil said, finishing a story I'd missed while checking my phone. "I didn't realize there were so many spiders, and I'll never be getting naked in that room again."

Everyone laughed, and Kieran hugged her tighter. The first few times I met him, I wouldn't have been surprised if he chose to hide in the bathroom rather than listen to a sex story, but now he just laughed, kissed her head, and looked relaxed. Besides being my go-to karaoke partner, he was part of our circle now, he and his sister, Lila, who was dating Marcus. I took a sip from my beer as Sybil and Emi started talking with Marcus about the catering menu for the wedding, leaving Kieran and me out of the decision-making.

"Brought down the house as usual," he said, holding out a palm for a high five I gladly returned.

"No doubt." I glanced at the familiar stage with the binder of laminated pages. It was a cheap setup—a machine the owner bought years ago that somehow still did the trick once a week when he'd trot it out. "Safe to say, panties would have been thrown if the bar wasn't full of middle-aged straight dudes and our close friends."

"Sybil threatened to throw some," he offered, motioning to his fiancée, now deep in conversation about cheeses.

"Yeah, but who here hasn't had Sybil's panties thrown at them?"

He threw a cardboard coaster at my face, which I barely ducked and also probably deserved. "Watch it," he said with a laugh, and I tipped my head in apology. I knew Sybil wasn't ashamed of anything in her past, nor was Kieran. I think he was more offended that she would have been impressed enough to throw them at someone else's singing, but I still handed the coaster back to him.

I topped off each of our glasses from the fresh pitcher. "Before our first assignment after apprenticing in the PJs, we trusted this guy named Dougy to pick a spot for us to get a beer. Brother chose this honky-tonk-looking place called Stinky Pete's advertising karaoke."

I chuckled to myself, remembering how we'd about beat his ass, but still went in. They had beer, after all. Not that I'd be enjoying it because I'd drawn the short straw and was driving. Cruz drew the other one, so while our boys got drunker and more off-key, we sat back sipping water. He'd looked different. Still a cocky, quiet asshole but shaky somehow. He kept looking at his watch. "All right, man?" I'd asked, shouting over the sound of Dougy belting out "I Will Always Love You" to loud cheers from the guys.

The guy was a brick wall, and I envied him. I had a hard time imagining him lying in bed at night, exhausted and questioning if he was good enough to make it to the end, like I had done. Other guys occasionally showed cracks, let their worries slip in a moment of weakness, but not him. Not ever.

"Fine." He sounded annoyed, and I'd rolled my eyes, but when I looked back, I saw him clasp one hand in the other, and I noticed the fidgeting and the tight set of his jaw. I studied him over the rim of my water glass.

"You look kinda shaky."

"I can't hear you," he mouthed over Dougy's wailing, the word "love" taking on eighteen syllables.

THE RE-DO LIST

"You can talk to me," I shouted.

"What?"

"Fuck this," I muttered and grabbed his arm, dragging him toward the entrance, where the warm Texas night air hit us as much as the sudden silence did.

"What the hell?" He shook off my hold and glared, but I blocked his way back into the bar. There was a fifty-fifty chance he was going to hit me, and I'd have to go on stage, sober and with a swollen jaw, because I'd already insisted I was the best singer in the group and talked a lot of shit about everyone else's singing talents.

I'd held up my palms, really hoping to avoid the swollen jaw. "We're about to have people's lives in our hands. Without us, people die, and it's not a simulation or a training exercise. This time, it'll be for real. And that's big. I'm checking on you."

"That's the job," he said, back straight, but anyone could tell that his assured tone was a front. "Why do you even care? You're basically the class clown. You don't care about anything."

"I care about you, motherfucker." God, he was a dick. I'd thrown my hands up, reaching for the door, to head back inside. "I'm going to have your back out there no matter what, because you had mine. During hell night. I didn't forget that. I'm trying to have your back here, too. No matter how much you look like you wanna hit me, I'm still trying to have your back. That's why I pulled you outside."

"I *should* hit you for thinking it was okay to touch me, let alone drag me out here."

"I should hit you to knock some sense into your thick head. We're a team. A unit. If you keep this lone wolf thing going, you're not only going to miss out, you're going to hurt the team."

I dropped my arms and stepped back, holding his gaze. "So hit me if you need to." I held out my arms. "But when I hit you back, it's because I care about you, which is why I'm telling you to get it together."

"I told you," he said. "We're not the same. I'm never going to be part of some bro hug circle with you."

"Maybe not. But we're in the same boat. Can you just take a chance on rowing with us?"

Cruz stood silent, fists clenched, and it looked more and more likely he might actually hit me. I held out my arms. "Give it a try if you need to," I said. "To be fair, that's the only thing that gets me to listen sometimes." I thought the joke might break something, but he was the same rock wall as always.

He didn't say anything further, and I gave a mental "fuck it" before waving him off and pulling open the door to get back into Pete's. I'd been certain he wouldn't come around, but maybe he'd talk to someone. When I stepped into the bar, they were announcing the next performer over the loudspeaker.

"Deacon to the stage. Our next performer is Deacon Rakes." I tried to shake off the conversation with Cruz. He was right that we didn't ever admit we were scared, but it felt fucking great to say it out loud, even just to him. I strode toward the stage, but Dougy snagged the mic and his voice boomed through the room. "And joining our DD is my other fellow rookie, Cruz Lewis! Get up here, boys!"

Behind me, Cruz looked horror-struck for a second before his cool mask returned. He was an asshole, but he was one who understood expectations. We were rookies—we did what we were told. And today that meant I was going to sing a duet with the person voted least likely to pull the stick from his own ass.

He walked toward me with a nod to Dougy, who was pretty amused with himself, and hopped onto the stage.

"What are we singing?" I looked toward the screen, waiting for the song to appear, and the guys at the front table whooped with laughter.

"Rakes talked so much shit about his skills. This better be good," a guy named Leo shouted from the front row.

That's when the song title flashed across the screen and the opening chords to "Ain't No Mountain High Enough" played.

"You've got to be kidding me," Cruz said under his breath, and I ignored his sour mood and laughed before I sang the opening lines à la Marvin Gaye.

"Just hum along," I said, holding out the second mic to him. "I'll take the lead."

"I know the song," he said, snatching it from my hand. "I can hold my own."

"Yeah," I said as the song began. "Right."

"Whoever is worse has to take Leo home! He's been eating nothing but refried beans all night!" The guys laughed, and Leo shrugged from his spot on the end of the table.

"That farting motherfucker is not getting in my car," Cruz said under his breath.

"Oh, he is," I said, before singing the opening line. "I had to air out my truck for days last time."

Despite the stakes, I had expected little from my partner, so I was shocked as hell when he joined in, not only on time but with a strong, clear voice for his part. I shouldn't have been surprised. If there was one thing he hated, it was being bested at something. I'd looked at him wide-eyed, but he'd been focused on the screen for a second before belting out a line. Not to be outdone, I matched him line for line. There was no way I was going to let Cruz outshine me. The guys were catcalling our performance, and we joined up for the duet of the chorus, our voices matching as we worked through the song. The ridiculousness of the competition between us to sing a more convincing love song made me laugh, and I was shocked as hell to see Cruz loosening up.

When I sang the word "wind!" everyone pointed at Leo, who bowed, and Cruz sang back, "No rain!" We kept going, and something amazing happened and the guy smiled. We made it mostly through the song, stumbling once over a lyric together, and he actually laughed along with the guys cheering us on. By the time we'd finished the song, he looked different than I'd ever seen him, and when he sang the last lines, he set the mic aside.

"Thanks," he'd said, scratching the back of his neck. "For making me . . . row. For looking out for me," he added quietly, away from the mic. "Even when I didn't ask for it or want your advice."

He hadn't actually shared anything with me. That would still take more time. But it felt like a boulder had shifted, and I liked that feeling. I'd wanted to help, and it seemed like I had. "No wind," I'd said, holding out my fist.

It took a moment, but he bumped his fist with mine. "No rain."

"ANYWAY," I SAID, returning to the story, "I have that squad and Dougy to thank for my prowess at karaoke." I took a sip of my beer as the memory receded and looked around the bar we sat in now, a much nicer one than Stinky Pete's in Texas.

Kieran raised his glass. "To Stinky Pete," he said, and I clinked mine with his, my mind stuck on that first moment when I really met my best friend. My phone buzzed in my pocket with another message from Red Delicious. When Kieran joined Sybil in the cheese plate conversation, I'd turned her down initially because I'd wanted to spend more time with Willow. But Willow was on a date—not to mention I had no business wanting to spend time with Cruz's little sister instead of a hot, interesting woman who was up for some short-term fun. It would lead to all kinds of trouble if I thought of Willow as anything more than a friend.

I lifted my glass to my lips but paused before taking a drink. The sound of a familiar laugh had drawn my attention to a group nearby, where Willow stood in a red dress that fit her in all the right places, and the sight of her made my breath catch.

CHAPTER 17

Willow

☑ First date
☑ Sing on stage

I SCANNED THE crowded bar as I followed Hollis and Blaine and a few of their friends to a table. I walked cautiously in the heels I wasn't used to wearing—taking in the world from a couple inches higher than my normal height. The night hadn't gone exactly as planned, but at least no one had recognized me or asked for a selfie. I touched my fingertips to the ends of my curls, the new style giving me more confidence and Blaine draped an arm across the back of the chair once I sat. "You'll love this place," he reassured, motioning to the crowd and the stage where two women drunkenly stumbled through "Don't Stop Believin'," pulling the crowd into the chorus.

"I don't have to sing, do I?" I scanned the cocktail menu and brushed my fingers along the hem of the red dress under the table, the fabric grazing above my knee. I'd pulled it from the back of my closet—an impulse purchase I'd made right before Spencer broke up with me. I'd never been brave enough to wear it, so my second first date felt like a good time to try. Turned out it was not the good luck charm I hoped for.

"You'll want to after a few of these," Blaine said, pointing at the list of cocktails, all named for karaoke favorites. He pointed to the women on stage. "Exhibit A."

I laughed and scanned the list again, considering the Cruel Summer—a citrusy coconut rum concoction, and the Oops, I Did It Again, which was basically a Long Island iced tea. Theo and I hadn't gotten through ordering drinks when he was called in to a veterinary emergency. I was in a Lyft home alone before I could even call it a date. Luckily, I'd run into Hollis.

"I have never gotten on stage," she said from my other side. "It's the best to just cheer for other people." She knocked her brother's hand away and threw an arm over my shoulder. Her voice rose above the noise in the bar and the music from the stage. "But I am determined that you have a good night!"

I grinned and nodded. "You didn't have to bring me with you," I said. "I hate to intrude."

Hollis laughed. "Karaoke with Blaine's friends is not exactly an RSVP occasion. The more the merrier." She waved to our server, who headed in our direction. "Plus, I like you and you look too hot to be home alone. This dress is killer!"

"Thanks," I said, observing the room again, out of habit looking for cues I'd been spotted, but no one was paying attention to us. I ordered one of the cocktails Blaine had pointed out, the Eye of the Jäger, and then pulled my phone from my purse when I saw Zoe's response to my earlier text.

ZOE: He ditched you?!

WILLOW: He was on call and there was some emergency, I guess.

ZOE: What injured Pekingese is more important than you? This guy is on my list.

WILLOW: It was a Great Dane, and he was very apologetic.

I'd really not known how to feel. He was hopefully saving someone's furry family member at that moment. But my face had also felt hot as I climbed in the car he'd ordered for me, the sting of embarrassment and the feeling of other diners' eyes on us as we hustled out of the restaurant sticking with me. I'd been hopeful about the date and ready for a little awkward conversation and maybe a tentative kiss at the end of the night. Mostly, I'd been looking forward to that feeling of anticipation I'd felt when Deacon had practiced with me. Despite wondering if I was doing it right, if I was laughing enough or touching him enough, when I hung out with Deacon, I was relaxed, and a sense of fun came easily between us. I thought the same would be true with Theo, only maybe with more kissing and less of Cruz's invisible presence in the background.

WILLOW: Don't add him to your list. I'm fine.

"Okay," Hollis said, returning to me. She pointed at the other people around the table, starting with a tall, dark-haired guy sitting on Blaine's other side. "Alex is Blaine's ex, but I think they're going to get back together." She pointed at the two others across the table, a redhead and a blonde. "Sara and Delta went to high school with us," she said, her gaze sweeping to the last person. "And that's Des," Hollis said, her voice dipping low. Des was walking to the table from the pool table and wore a tight button-up with jeans; their gait was pure confidence. "Des is Blaine's bestie, and I've been in love with them since I was about fifteen." Hollis let out a dramatic sigh. "They're in vet school at Iowa State, so I don't see them much anymore."

"Really?" I sat up straighter. "I was pre-vet in college, well, up until my last year."

"Why'd you change?" Hollis accepted her drink from the server and handed mine over. "No judgment. I changed my major like thirteen times."

I shrugged. "Just didn't work out." Really, Spencer convinced me to get a second major in business on top of the pre-vet curriculum, but as we neared graduation, we were talking about getting married and starting a family, and we decided vet school would make that really challenging. Vet school would have taken a lot of my time, and we thought business might provide more flexibility. Sure, Spencer suggested it and I'd been resistant to the idea at first, but we wanted kids, and I hadn't wanted to disappoint him by having to wait. Cruz had urged me to reconsider the decision, reminding me that I could have both things, but I knew Spencer felt strongly about it, and losing him and being alone seemed like the worst possible thing to me at the time.

Hollis waved Des over and took a large sip from her drink. "Think you'd ever go back for vet school?"

"You're in vet school?" Des pulled Hollis into a side hug, and I saw her cheeks pink at the contact.

"No," I said, trying my own drink. "But I was pre-vet in college." Des's gaze drifted back to Hollis, and I sensed my new friend's crush wasn't completely one-sided. "Do you like your program?"

Des's face lit up. "It's better than I could have imagined." Des talked about their classes and lab work, and I was entranced. I'd wanted to be a veterinarian since I was a teenager when I started volunteering at the humane society. I'd taken every science elective in high school and volunteered as a research assistant for three years with a professor studying immunology in cattle. I should have found someone else to talk to, so Hollis could have time alone with her crush, but every word out of their mouth made me feel an actual ache for the career I'd given up. "I could give you a tour sometime if you want," Des offered, and I jumped—literally jumped—in my chair, blurting a yes before they finished. "And if you'd ever want to apply, it never hurts to get more volunteer work with animals under your belt."

"I'd love a tour," I said, keeping in my seat this time. "Thank you." It took every ounce of willpower to not search for the school website. Iowa State had always been at the top of my list of dream schools when I was considering attending, even though the program at Colorado State was awesome and closer to home.

"Hollis can give you my number," they said, turning their attention to Hollis and giving her an easy smile. Oh yeah. There were lots of vibes here. "You still have my number, right? Haven't heard from you in a while."

She nodded eagerly, reaching for her phone, and I looked around for an exit to give them a few minutes without me in the middle. There was a stand by the stage with all the song options that a group had just walked away from, so I walked there, thumbing through the book. I glanced back at the two of them to see they had their heads close together and felt a pang of jealousy for that kind of connection. I missed that, but talking to Des about vet school and thinking about my plans to be ready for my next relationship had me considering that maybe I was thinking too small. Des brushed a red strand from Hollis's shoulder, and the two laughed. For so long, when I pictured my future, it was having those kinds of moments I most looked forward to. I slid my finger down the list of songs, my gaze catching on one. I still wanted those moments, craved what Hollis might be feeling right now—the anticipation and excitement, the sense of being cherished. But I wanted what Des had, too. Their excitement about their career and their experiences in school preparing to be a veterinarian—it was palpable. Maybe I wasn't thinking big enough. I wanted both.

"You wore red." The familiar deep voice from behind me made me whip around, my drink sloshing in my hand. Deacon leaned against the stage in a plain black T-shirt that stretched across his broad chest, and he ran fingers through his hair, moving it off his face so that the light brown strands fell back into place around his chiseled face. I'd never had a thing for men with long hair before, but I fantasized about running my fingers through it. His gaze swept over my dress in a way that made me feel warm and far more exposed than I actually was. "I knew you'd look good in red."

With my cheeks heating, I brushed my hands down the skirt. "Thanks. What are you doing here?"

He pointed a thumb over his shoulder at a table of people. "Night out with the roommates," he said. "You must have missed my flawless performance."

"We just got here." My brain was tripping imagining Deacon on stage.

He looked around, and the muscles around his mouth tensed. "You and the vet?"

I took a sip from my drink and then studied my feet. "Um, no. Some friends. The date didn't quite work out."

Deacon was a big guy—tall and fit but bulky from muscle—so it was something between terrifying and impressive to see him with his posture tense and standing at his full height. "He stood you up? Did he do something?"

"No," I said, dropping a hand to his closed fist at his side and pasting on a smile. "No, nothing like that. He was called out for an emergency. I guess he was on call, so he sent me home in a Lyft." Deacon's hand was warm, and his fingers relaxed slightly under my touch.

"Not a good excuse," he said. "He should have gotten someone to cover."

"It's okay," I said, hoping he believed the fake smile. "I came here with some friends from next door." I nodded toward the table where everyone was laughing and Des was whispering something into Hollis's ear. The same pang of jealousy hit me, and I realized I still had my hand over Deacon's and pulled it back.

He tipped his head to the list of songs. "You looked deep in thought when I came up. Deciding what to sing?"

I laughed. "Oh no. No way. I haven't sung in front of people since high school." I was in the show choir all four years but didn't have time in college. Spencer had talked me into trying out initially, and I'd loved it. The collaboration, the creativity, and the way I'd felt unexpectedly weightless and brave on the stage in a way I didn't feel in real life. It had been years, though. "I couldn't," I added. "I'm too sober and not brave enough."

"Really? I heard you singing lots of songs from twenty years ago when we were painting, and you're pretty good." He reached to my side, his forearm grazing my hip before he tapped two fingers on the list of songs. The move left his body closer to mine, and I felt the heat from his chest against my bare shoulder. Deacon looked down, his gaze seeming to slide to my shoulder where the strap of the red dress rested against my skin. "And, for what it's worth, I think you're pretty damn brave."

"We've got an opening. You want to go again, Deac?" The DJ cut into our conversation, and Deacon took a step back from me.

"I'm good for now, B." Deacon dropped a hand to my shoulder. "But she might."

The weight of his hand felt so grounding, and I looked around the crowded room.

"Everyone would see me," I said, when the DJ shrugged and turned to answer someone else's question. "I can't."

"Low," he said, setting his beer down and dropping a hand on my other shoulder, his gaze intent on mine. "You look incredible in this dress . . . People already see you. I guarantee they're looking." His thumbs moved in tiny circles over my collarbones as his dark eyes bored into mine. "Never do something you don't want to do, but if people seeing you is the only thing stopping you, you can pretend I'm the only one watching." His words sent a shiver through me at the idea of his eyes on me, even in a room full of people.

"I already had one re-do crash and burn tonight," I said. "I guess a second wouldn't be so bad." I shrugged my shoulders, but he didn't move his hands, and the movement momentarily caused his thumbs to drop lower.

"I think the vet not working out was a good thing," he said. "That guy wasn't good enough for you." His thumbs paused for a moment, grazing the tops of my breasts for a split second, before he pulled them away. "And you won't crash and burn." He tipped his head to the right. "I'm at that table," he said, taking a few steps back. "The only one watching."

I was looking at his back when the DJ returned. "You decide?"

I looked at the book and touched my hand to my shoulder where Deacon's hand had been. "Yeah," I said, flipping through the book for the song I wanted. I'd spent a lot of my life comfortable in the background, but I'd liked singing on stage. I liked the confidence I felt with the microphone in my hand. I wondered if it would be the same if I was up there alone, and maybe this was my first opportunity to think a little bigger, to make the re-do list about just me on this stage in my red dress and not about Spencer.

I glanced from the book to the table Deacon had indicated, and his gaze lingered on me. I felt the flutter of butterflies in my stomach, and he gave me a grin, pointing to his eyes and mouthing, "Only one." I tapped my finger on the laminated page and looked back to the DJ. "I think I did."

I stood on stage, clutching the mic as the DJ announced the next performer. "Give it up for our next performer. Her name is Willow and she can buy herself flowers!" He had the kind of voice that was common to DJs, and the opening notes of "Flowers" by Miley Cyrus started as soon as he finished introducing me.

My voice was low and tentative at first, and I felt my knees shake as I immediately regretted the decision to get on stage, let alone to get on stage stone sober. I'd be noticed, and if I was horrible, it would just be more Drowning Girl stories. But it was too late now. Some people were watching me, but mostly, conversations around the room kept going, and my gaze swept to the right, where Deacon was sitting. His arm was propped on the back of a chair, and he nodded with a grin, raising his bottle to me. I felt a sweep of heat over my skin again but then heard whoops and cheers from the other side of the room, and Hollis and Blaine and Des and their friends were cheering for me, making me giggle before I hit the chorus of the song. Their cheers drew attention from others, and by the time I declared I could buy myself flowers, I heard the volume on my voice go up. Other people in the bar were singing along, and there was cheering and clapping. I felt good. I felt strong, and I felt a little bit invincible, like thinking small wasn't an option anymore.

I oscillated between soaking in the attention and wanting to hide my face, and when I looked over to Deacon again, his eyes were still focused on me. That intense way he had of making you feel like you were the only person in the world that mattered wrapped around me, even as I felt the eyes of the crowd on me as they cheered. I flashed a wide smile as the song ended and the applause rang out, and mouthed a "Thank you" to Deacon who had, true to his word, never taken his piercing dark eyes off me.

CHAPTER 18

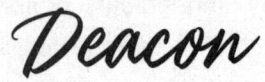
Deacon

I SWAM FOUR or five times a week, always around five in the morning before the pool got crowded. Sleep had eluded me lately, though, and not just because a certain off-limits list-maker had been on my mind. I'd gotten to the pool at 4:30 a.m., thankful for the early hours this gym offered. There was something comforting about the way the light reflected off the water as I did an underwater drill, getting my bearings in the pool. It was where I felt the most like my old self, weightless and in control.

Finally breaking the surface, I sucked in a deep breath and floated on my back, counting the ceiling tiles and resting before I swam some more laps. Underwater, I could block out the world. I could block out most things, but the memory of Willow on that stage kept resurfacing. That red dress accentuated every curve on her body, from her full hips to the swell of her breasts and how her dark eyes sparkled under the stage lights. She'd worn high heels for her date, and I couldn't help considering how I'd have to bend less to kiss her in them. The water lapped at the side of my face, and I pictured the way her expression changed from that tiny grin when she heard the first cheers to the full-watt smile by the time she finished her song. The way the smile transformed her face—that's what I really couldn't shake even though I needed to. When I closed my eyes, I didn't imagine her smiling at Gus or because she did something new; I pictured her smiling up at me, smiling because of how she felt around me.

I reached the other side of the pool and set my watch. I'd gotten my 500M swim down to nine and a half minutes earlier in the week, but I was shooting for nine. I could focus on this—if I pushed hard enough, there wouldn't be any room in my mind for my best friend's baby sister and her smiles. And her soft skin. And the way her legs looked in those heels, the spot right above her knee completely kissable.

"Nope," I mumbled to myself, getting into my start position. As long as she was happy and safe, I was doing what Cruz had asked me to do in looking out for her. And it was for the best her date was a dud. I didn't like the idea of sharing her smiles with some other guy, even if I'd never act on the attraction.

Someone opened the main door to the pool as I started my drill, focusing on the goal, repeating the PJ creed as I moved through the water. When it got hard, the words reminded me why I was putting my body through this and why I avoided considering alternative career paths. *It is my duty as a Pararescueman to save life and to aid the injured. I will be prepared at all times to perform my assigned duties quickly and efficiently, placing these duties before personal desires and comforts. These things we do, that others may live.*

Stroke, stroke, breathe. Stroke, stroke, breathe.

Once, we'd gotten back from a tough mission where we'd

needed to parachute behind enemy lines to extract a pilot who'd gone down in a crash. I wasn't sure the guy would fly again, but he was breathing and conscious. We were at Cruz's place the next day when he asked me if I ever thought about how our best days, the days where we got to do what we trained for, what we had a passion for, were the worst days for someone else.

Stroke, stroke, breathe. Stroke, stroke, breathe.

It was a few months after his mom's car accident, and he hadn't talked much about it, but I handed him a beer and nodded. "Think all first responders feel that way?"

He shrugged and tipped his beer to his lips. "I got the names of the people who responded to the accident." At his words, I sat back in my chair. My instinct was to say something or ask a question to fill the silence, but he seemed to need a moment, and eventually he kept going. "I sent them a note, thanking them. I think I'd hate people thanking me for what we do, but it felt . . . I dunno. Right."

I nodded, unsure of what to say. I'd hate getting a note, too. We all would—there was a common love of the work, but no one felt good taking credit for saving someone.

Stroke, stroke, breathe. Stroke, stroke, breathe.

"I guess I wanted them to know I understood the toll it probably took on them when she didn't make it, even if they're used to it, even if the heaviness didn't last a long time. I guess I wanted them to know I appreciated the sacrifice and that she would have, too."

I nodded again. This was the most he'd said about anything real in months.

"She'd started therapy," he said, breaking the silence again.

"Been in a funk, probably depression after my asshole dad took off, but she'd started therapy and seemed to be coming up for air." He toyed with the label on his beer, peeling at it. "She didn't want Willow to know in case it made her worry—she'd just started college—but, God, Mom seemed happier for the first time in ages." His voice thickened. "I don't know why I shared all that."

"Doesn't matter," I said, finishing my beer. "Glad you did."

"Okay, this is too heavy." He sniffed and took a pull from his beer. "Will you make one of your bad fucking jokes or something?"

I walked into the kitchen to grab two more beers and to give him some privacy to wipe his eyes. I called from the kitchen as I popped the tops on the bottles. "You know who I got a thank-you card from? That waitress in Sarasota, Kiana, and her roommate, Analise." I handed him the bottle. "Oh my, sweet, adventurous Analise."

He laughed, though I heard the emotion he was swallowing. "You're such a fuckboy." He kicked back, his posture relaxing.

"You love me."

Stroke, stroke, breathe. Stroke, stroke, breathe.

Stroke, stroke, breathe. Stroke, stroke, breathe.

I refused to look at my watch but kicked harder and pushed myself to the end of the last lap.

My hand landed on the lip of the pool, and I glanced at my watch. Nine minutes and fifteen seconds. I pumped a tired arm and lay back in the water, floating as my breathing and heart rate regulated.

My smartwatch vibrated against my wrist, and I glanced at it.

CRUZ: Mom's bday is today. Can you check on Willy?

I dropped my arm back to the water and did a lazy backstroke to the other side. There were a few other people in the pool now, and the motion from their strokes made waves that moved against my skin. An excuse to message Willow didn't take any convincing, and I didn't want her sitting at home sad. That night on stage, she seemed like she'd come up for air, too.

DEACON: 'Course. You ok?

CRUZ: Fine.

Same old Cruz, I thought, floating back to the other side. Not that I was much different. Emi told me I should get a tattoo that read "I'm fine," since I said it so often. Maybe it was the job or our personalities, probably a little patriarchy thrown in there for good measure. Saying "I'm fine" was always easier than admitting anything else.

DEACON: Always here if you're not.

He tagged it with a thumbs-up emoji, and I held on to the edge of the pool and used voice-to-text to send her a quick message.

DEACON: Low—wake up!

DEACON: Wake up!

She told me once she never trusted do-not-disturb mode but hated late-night texts because they always woke her up, so I sent a few more.

> DEACON: Good morning!
>
> DEACON: Wake up!
>
> WILLOW: It's not even 6 a.m.

I grinned as I climbed out of the pool. I was pretty sure I had time to pull this off.

> DEACON: Get dressed. I'm picking you up in fifteen minutes.
>
> WILLOW: It's 5:48 a.m.
>
> DEACON: You still have rule breaking on your re-do list, right?

CHAPTER 19

Willow

☑ Break a rule
☑ Holding hands

DEACON KEPT EYEING his watch as we sped toward downtown, the roads speckled with the first stage of morning traffic and the ethereal look of the sky shifting from black to a muted bluish gray ahead of sunrise. I thought I'd spend this day sad and alone, and the unexpected way it was starting left me feeling off-balance.

"Will you tell me what we're doing? Is the rule we're breaking the speed limit on I-235?"

He glanced over after merging into the right lane. "I guess two rules," he said, taking the exit. His hair was damp and he smelled like chlorine. I inhaled the scent—a weird favorite. "And did you just smell me?"

My face flushed. After letting Gus out, I'd had no time for anything other than pulling on a bra and a sweatshirt with some jeans I'd worn the day before. I was suddenly very aware of my messy ponytail and bare face and flip-flops. "No," I lied.

"I was at the pool," he said. "Didn't have time to shower yet."

I bet Deacon looked good wet with his hair slicked back and water sluicing off his taut stomach. I cringed at my own thoughts and looked out the window instead of at his forearm as he turned the steering wheel.

"That makes two of us."

He leaned toward me and inhaled dramatically.

"Ew!" I slid away and against the door, mortified.

He laughed, a low rumble I felt in my belly. "See? Not so nice when someone does it to you, is it?"

It *had been* nice for a second, when he leaned in, before I realized I didn't remember if I'd put on deodorant. "I apologize for sniffing you," I said contritely as he slowed down to stop at a red light on the uncrowded street. "I just really like how chlorine smells."

"Me, too." He nodded like he was cataloging the detail. "So, what was your first rule-breaking experience? Need to know what I'm up against here. Was it a felony-level rule break?"

I laughed at the idea. "It was skipping school one afternoon my senior year to see a movie with Spencer."

"Some real Bonnie and Clyde shit," he said, flashing me a grin.

I chuckled again at the memory of planning how we'd evade detection and how giddy and adult it had felt to forge notes from our parents about excused absences. "So, no felony, but for two kids with perfect attendance and on the honor roll, it felt pretty scandalous." That was a good memory, actually. We'd laughed and spent the afternoon making plans for the future. My smile fell a bit when I backed up to what Deacon had said. "*We're* not heading into a felony this morning, are we?"

"Misdemeanor at worst." He pulled along the sidewalk on Grand in the East Village and cut the engine. "We're here."

"A . . . hotel?" It looked like a nice hotel, and my mind flooded with wildly inappropriate ideas about what he had in mind.

"C'mon!" He climbed out of the cab of the truck, grabbing a duffel bag from the back. He was around to my side before I could get the door open, and he offered his hand as I attempted to climb down. Men and their big trucks—I was too short for this one, and I stumbled into his chest on the way out of the cab.

Deacon didn't let go of my hand as he led me into the main entrance and paused, looking around until a young guy in a vest walked out from behind the check-in counter. "Cutting it close," he said, tossing Deacon a key card. "You don't know me if you get caught."

"Never met you before in my life," Deacon said, catching the card. "Thanks, man." With no more explanation, Deacon hustled me toward the elevator, which opened immediately, and a wave of the card granted us access to the floor he wanted.

"Who was that?"

"TJ. We used to hang together at a bar near the house. I helped him out when he first met his now wife. Like a relationship coach."

"A coach? I've never heard you talk about dating anyone." I really just imagined him standing in a bar and women just appearing beside him ready to hook up. I truly had no idea how that conversation might go—that seemed like advance maneuvering, though. "What was this coaching?"

The bark of laughter filled the slow elevator as we climbed to the top floor. "I gave him date ideas. Just because I don't use the knowledge doesn't mean I don't have it." He still held my hand and gave it a squeeze. Deacon was always warm, and his hand around mine was distractingly nice as we rode to the top floor. The doors opened to a dark floor, and Deacon tugged me forward to what looked like a bar, but it was closed.

"We can't break in here," I said, as he approached the door and looked left and right.

Deacon scanned the card and the door clicked open. "We're not." He nudged me forward and tugged me along a wall toward a door that led to a patio. "We have a key. It's trespassing at worst." His voice was a low whisper, and we pushed through the glass door onto the patio, which offered a clear view of the city below.

"Wow," I said, pausing and looking around. "This is incredible."

"I know." He guided me to a couch near the plexiglass railing and he sat down next to me. "The sun will be up soon."

My heart was doing a two-step. "You brought me to watch the sunrise?"

He shrugged. "It's one of my favorite places in the city, and TJ said no one would be up here for a couple of hours." As he pointed east where the crown of gold was just beginning to fill the sky, I marveled at this entire situation. I didn't have the words, because I'd been dreading how this day would feel, and it was already a hundred miles away from what I expected.

"Will we get in trouble?" A breeze kicked up, and I wrapped my arms around myself, but Deacon was already rubbing his hands up and down my arms. The friction of his touch warmed me all over as his body surrounded me.

"I don't think so," he said. "But if we do, you run for the elevator." He pointed to the door we'd come through, and his thickly muscled arm was solid against me. "I'll take the heat."

"That's chivalrous," I said, leaning in. "And look!" I pointed to the bright spot on the horizon where the sun had crested. It had been a long time since I'd been up early enough to see the sunrise, so I was genuinely excited to watch it, especially from this spot and next to Deacon. "Thank you for bringing me up here."

His hand fell from my shoulder, and he reached for the duffel bag, pulling out a white paper bag and a little plastic bottle of orange juice. "Cruz said it was your mom's birthday today." He handed me the juice and pulled chocolate cupcakes from their plastic packaging, the kind with the little white swirls of icing on top. "It's not much of a cake, but it's the best I could find at the gas station. I thought you might want to celebrate her."

With the golden light of dawn spilling over us both and the city spread out below, tears welled in my eyes, and I nodded, not sure what to say. I missed her. Before everything went down with my dad, she'd loved birthdays. Sitting here, I felt all my feelings toppling down around me. Sadness she was gone. Longing for the happy days. And then there was something else, something I'd had on my mind for days—what she'd say about re-dos.

"Is that okay?" He studied my face. "I can also just stand guard and give you some time to be alone."

I nodded again, still agreeing that it was okay, but then shook my head from side to side.

He tucked a curl over my ear. "I don't know if I know what that means, Low."

I shook my head once more and then wrapped my arms

around him, burying my face in the crook of his neck. "Don't leave. This is perfect," I said against his skin and felt his hand rest on my back. Another breeze kicked up around me, but in Deacon's warm hold, it wasn't cold.

When I finally let go of him, his expression looked a little dazed, and I'd probably made it weird holding on to him for so long, but he handed me a cupcake without commenting. "You know your brother is a man of few details. Tell me about her."

"About my mom?"

"Yeah," he said, cracking open the orange juice and taking a sip before handing it to me. "What were her favorite things?"

I searched the sky and took a sip from the bottle, letting the sweet juice wash over my tongue. I'd spent so much time thinking about how her life ended. I hadn't thought about other things in a long time. "She loved to bake," I said. "And to garden. We used to have these incredible gardens with roses and dahlias and all her favorites. She'd spend hours out there and come inside covered in dirt." I giggled and slapped my hand over my mouth. "She'd track mud into the house all the time. Our carpets would just be filthy." I grinned at the memory, and Deacon leaned back against the couch, his arm stretched behind me.

"Well, who ever worried about a little dirt?"

"Exactly." I nodded, remembering her saying things like that all the time. "Maybe I should plant some flowers, just in pots or something. I never did at our old place."

"Sounds like a good idea." He held out his cupcake to mine for a toast. "To dirt?"

I wiped a tear from my face and tapped my cupcake to his then took a bite of the sugary cake. The boxes Cruz mentioned were still in the basement—I hadn't opened them yet, but I wanted to tackle it. I could take that off Cruz's shoulders—we'd just thrown everything in boxes after she died. I barely remembered even doing it. They were in a neat stack in the corner, and I planned to get to it this week.

"She liked taking action. She'd hate that I'm spinning my wheels," I said before taking another bite of the sweet chocolate in the cupcake. She'd been the one to drive me to my volunteer job at the humane society until I got my license. She loved that I wanted to be a veterinarian. "She'd always tell me if you're bored, you're boring."

"You're not boring." Deacon had a tiny smear of chocolate at the corner of his lip, and I slid my thumb over it on instinct, noticing his eyes widening at the too-familiar touch, but he spoke before I could apologize. "Are you bored?"

"No." I thought about it. "Sometimes. I've always worked, and now my only real responsibility while I'm here is taking care of Gus."

"I feel that way sometimes. I'm doing school full-time and I'm at the gym training, but I miss being busy. Jayden said I should fill my time with some chess lessons." He laughed, and I heard the affection for the kid in his voice. He said he was helping out a neighbor, but I got the sense Deacon really liked spending time with him.

"I was thinking of looking for a volunteer job with animals. It might be nice to have somewhere to go, and I loved working at the humane society when I was a teenager." In the back of my mind, I also thought about Des's recommendation about getting more volunteer hours. "Plus that kind of thing never hurts if I decide to go back to school."

"You should," he said. "Another ex-less re-do?"

I shook my head. I'd always done that one myself. I thought about that. This would have nothing to do with me being ready for my next relationship. It would just be for me, and I could use more of that. I took another bite of the cupcake. That felt like a fitting realization on my mom's birthday.

"I can't believe you did this," I said, looking at the flow of cars along the streets as the city came to life.

"It's nothing," he said, pulling me against him, his hand resting on my shoulder.

It was, though. I took another bite of the cupcake and rested my head against his shoulder, thinking about Mom and what she'd think of this, of this man sneaking me into a rooftop bar to celebrate her. I wiped a tear from my eye. She'd be tickled by it. Completely tickled, and I'd kind of forgotten how her face lit up when she was excited about something. I hadn't seen it a lot since the divorce, and it was nice to picture it. I subtly inhaled the scent of chlorine on his body, then finished my cupcake with the city spread out before us.

"You sniffed me again," he said, the weight of his arm on my shoulder comfortably warm in the morning breeze. "I'll let it slide this time."

I felt his chin on the top of my head. He was wrong. It wasn't nothing. This felt like everything.

CHAPTER 20

I ROLLED MY shoulders and stretched my neck from side to side, glancing at the clock on my phone. I'd pushed myself again at the gym, only this time it wasn't just about the numbers I needed to reach, but a necessary means of distraction. It had been two weeks since I took Willow up to the rooftop bar, since she hugged me and snuggled against me in the cool morning air and told me about her mom. It had all been so . . . intimate, like something special, and I hadn't been able to stop thinking of how much I enjoyed being there for her like that. How good she felt in my arms. I could thank Willow and her big brown eyes for the extra mile I'd run. The extra pull-ups were solely due to how her face fit against my neck and the way her soft breath brushed against the skin there. Even now, sitting in the library in front of my econ book, the memory of those soft breaths made my cock twitch, and that couldn't happen.

The sound of the book closing was a satisfying thud, and I shoved it into my backpack.

"Deacon, hey. Thought that was you." Kelly and a few guys I didn't know approached the table I'd snagged in the library. "Mind if we join you?"

"I'm just leaving," I said, as they filled in around the table.

"Before you go, these are a few of the guys from the center." She pointed to each one. "Bryce, Andre, and Smith." She chuckled to herself. "God, Smith, I don't even know your first name."

They were across the table, so I just gave a nod. I guessed the three of them were Army. Smith shook my hand from nearest me. "Deacon," I said, slinging my bag over my shoulder. I knocked the tabletop with my fist. "It's a good spot. Enjoy."

"We meet every Friday afternoon here," Kelly said, pulling a laptop and books from her bag. "Just to study. You should join us sometime."

I shrugged one shoulder, feeling the sore muscles. "Yeah. Maybe sometime." I gave another wave to her and the other guys. "Thanks for the invite." Walking out of the library, I knew I had no plans to join them. The disability benefit check was an unwelcome, constant reminder of my retirement, and I wasn't ready to hang out with others who were done, too. That felt too permanent.

My body protested when I climbed in the car. I slid a hand across my lower back, feeling the long scar that ran halfway up my back, tracing the familiar bumps and ridges along my spine. An aneurysmal bone cyst compressing my spinal nerve. I learned that was what almost cost us a mission when I'd woken up in the hospital. My phone buzzed with a notification, and I caught sight of the date, not that I needed the reminder. It had been three years to the day since something smaller than a gumball ended my career. The phone buzzed again before I could throw the truck in reverse.

> MARCUS: Lila and I are making a beer run. Negra Modelo?
>
> DEACON: 👍 And limes.
>
> MARCUS: Obviously. You think I just met you or something?

He always remembered shit like that. It was the same way I suspected he or Emi remembered today was the anniversary of the accident and planned a game night in the house just as they'd done the last year. As an only child to busy parents, I didn't grow up with that kind of attention. I'd had it with the PJs, though. Dougy remembered everyone's birthdays and made a big fucking deal about them, and Simms's wife always sent extra cookies, including all our individual favorites, for him to share with everyone when we could get mail.

I scrubbed my hand over my jaw again, shaking away the ache that rose in my chest that had nothing to do with the spinal surgery memories. I slapped a palm against my cheek. I was going back, so I didn't need to get sad about it. And in the interim, I had my people. I'd have limes with the Negra Modelo, and Willow was coming over, too. Once I made it home, I fell onto my bed and picked up the book I'd grabbed from the campus bookstore—*A Beginner's Guide to Chess*. I flipped through the pages. I was tired of Jayden kicking my ass, plus he was a good kid who didn't have a lot of other people he spent time with. I supposed we were kind of alike that way, and I wanted him to know I cared about what he cared about.

"MARVIN GARDENS!" WILLOW squealed as my piece landed on her property, and cheers went up around the table from my traitorous friends. "Rent is due!"

"My God," Kieran said, his arm draped across the back of Sybil's chair. "She's as bad a winner as you are, Deac."

I held up my middle finger in his direction as I counted out the rent due, the amount seriously depleting my stash.

"I'm not a bad winner," Willow mused, bringing the beer bottle to her lips, the same lips that had distracted me all night.

"I'm not, either. Kieran is just a sore loser," I grumbled, handing over the stack of brightly colored bills, my fingers brushing against Willow's, taking away the sting of going broke.

"You literally sang, 'Baby, I own you now' to him when we played at Christmas," Sybil said, defending her fiancé. "Willow, it was impressive. There were verses and choreography."

"*Baby, I Own You Now* . . . as in *Baby, It's Cold Outside*?" Willow looked from me to the group.

"I really can't pay," Marcus and Lila crooned together. "Baby, I own you now."

Emi chimed in. "Is there any other way? Baby, I own you now."

Kieran wrapped an arm around my shoulders and crooned along with them. "Reading Railroad has been . . . so very nice."

Willow's expression was bright as she watched my friends, wide-eyed, before turning back to me. "You did the entire song?"

"Multiple times," Emi said, reaching for the dice. "It's why we all know it so well."

"You really *are* a bad winner," Willow said with a wink and patted my shoulder. The weight of her small hand was an odd comfort, and I didn't want her to stop touching me.

"I've got to pass go," I sang to her, hoping to keep her hand in place, just for a few more seconds, and to hold on to the warmth in the room.

Willow didn't miss a beat and added, "Baby, I own you now." More cheers from my friends went up around the table. Willow's expression was mischievous, and she held up her hands for high fives, pressing her palms against mine like they belonged there. She motioned to her row of properties ahead of my top hat, the hotels and houses crowding the board, but my gaze moved back up to her face and the corner of her lips as she sang, taking in the crinkle by her eyes and how the curls fell over her neck.

Around the table, everyone joined in, the echo bouncing off the walls of the small dining room. Glasses raised toward the ceiling, they finished with a flourish. "Baby, she owns you now!"

"So, what I'm hearing is that you have no room to talk about good and bad winners." Willow giggled, pulling her hands from mine and fanning herself.

"Maybe." I had this feeling like I was where I was supposed to be with my friends around me and Willow so close. At that moment, I felt like I was home. I draped my arm over her shoulders again, my fingertips grazing her skin. "But you could cut me a break?"

"You've met your match, Deac," Sybil said after snuggling back up to Kieran. "I never thought anyone would best you in Corrupt Monopoly."

Lila's phone rang, and Emi asked about refills. Everyone rose from their chairs during the impending break. "House rules!" Emi called over her shoulder, indicating that no one should touch the board during the break.

"Of course," Sybil said as she swiped two fifties from Kieran's organized stacks of bills and slid them to her own messy pile.

"Would never dream of breaking house rules," Marcus added, grabbing those same fifties when Sybil's back was turned.

"Everyone cheats during the no-cheating break time?" Willow raised an eyebrow in my direction and I nodded.

"If you can get away with it." I twirled one of her curls around my finger and waggled my eyebrows. "Helps if you have an accomplice."

"I might help you out," Willow said as the group dispersed. She fanned out a stack of bright pink bills and waved them in front of her chest. *And nope, I won't look at her chest.* "What's in it for me?"

"Are you subtly asking for a bribe?"

Willow tapped the tip of her finger on the top hat. "It wasn't subtle. Quid pro quo is how this thing works, right?" Her impression of the Godfather was god-awful, but I couldn't take my eyes off her.

"How about you let me out of rent until I pass Go, and I take you to brunch tomorrow morning? That's on your list, right? Unless you prefer to eat alone like the robber baron you're revealing yourself to be."

She pressed a fingertip to her lips as if considering, and the red of her nail grazed her lower lip. I'd noticed more red nail polish since we painted her room because the bright shade was a captivating pop of color against her skin tone. She was wearing a red shirt tonight, too—some kind of soft-looking fabric that dipped to a V in the front, showing the roundness of her breasts.

"Tomorrow, I'm going with Hollis to my first protest march. It's against books bans." She curled the end of an imaginary mustache. "I haven't gone full robber baron."

She was so cute, and when she dropped the act and grinned, her dimple popped. "Sunday?"

"Bottomless mimosas and you've got a deal." She held out her hand, and I took it in mine for a shake. Her hands were soft and warm as she squeezed. "But I still own you," she added with a wink.

I gave her hand a gentle squeeze in return and looked away from her face before my gaze dipped to her lips again. I'd never wanted to be possessed by someone so much in my life. "I can live with that."

"Should I put my money in my bra before I go to the bathroom?" She glanced at my friends milling around. Lila had returned and pulled Marcus into a kiss, but was grabbing a property from her place at the table while he was distracted.

"Probably," I said, reluctantly letting go of her hand. "I would, but . . ."

"You don't wear a bra or have any money," she said, patting my cheek. Before heading to the bathroom, she glanced around then shifted the two fifties from Marcus's spot back to Kieran's. My girl was getting the hang of house rules.

No, I thought, *not my girl*. It felt right to have her here, though. I swiped a hand across the scar on my back, but I didn't feel the same pang of loss I normally did. As I took the two fifties from Kieran's stack along with three hundred-dollar bills and shoved them in my pocket, I felt something like contentment. I wandered into the kitchen, lost in my own head. Although I loved spending time with my friends, this connection with Willow felt even deeper as her laugh floated into the kitchen from other room.

"I know that look," Emi said, slicing apples to fill in the fruit plate we'd decimated during the first half of game night. "You've got a thing for the little sister."

I dragged my gaze from the doorway back to Emi before stealing an apple slice from her neat stack. "No way. I've got a thing for you, sweet cheeks." I winked and flexed my arm muscles, earning her eye roll, but another peal of laughter from Willow made me glance over my shoulder.

"Aww, Deac. I've never seen you smitten." When I turned again, she was holding out an apple slice for me, and I took it without comment. It was a Red Delicious apple, which reminded me of the woman I never even texted back. "It's cute."

"I'm not smitten," I huffed, grabbing a few beers from the fridge and snagging the opener from the hook mounted on the wall. "Sure, she's cute and fun."

"Cute and fun is a wonderful combination," she said, pouring blueberries onto the plate. "Almost like the exact combination of qualities that provide a baseline for someone you might be smitten with."

I shot her a narrow-eyed stare and then accepted the fresh apple slice she slid out to me when she relented and held up her palms. "Fine. I give up." Emi studied the fruit plate, looking side to side as if she would present it to a discerning group of foodies and not her best friends who were playing drunken Monopoly with the house rules that made all kinds of capitalism-fueled cheating legal. She always did that—made sure things were perfect from every angle. She plucked a few more strawberries from the clamshell container and placed them on the plate, nudging an apple slice to the side. I loved this woman and her weird quirks. Same for Marcus and Sybil, even though Syb had ditched us to fall in love with a former donut shop owner.

They'd become my people, and my chest felt warm thinking about that. It was the liquor—I wasn't normally that sentimental, but I tugged my friend into a hug, interrupting her fruit checking.

"What's that for?" she asked against my chest, already wriggling to escape my hold. "You're being very affectionate tonight."

"It's not affection. I'm an emotionless womanizer—I'm trying to seduce you." Ignoring the sappy things, I wanted to tell her about what her friendship meant to me. How I thought of her as family. She'd even spotted how I was feeling about Willow in no time. I squeezed her again.

"You couldn't be a womanizer if you tried, and you know I just want you to be happy, Deac. You're a good guy." She patted my chest affectionately and then did some complicated spin, pinning my arm behind my back and pressing me to the counter. Looking at Emi, you wouldn't assume she was a black belt who could take down men my size, but the cool kitchen counter under my cheek was a good reminder, though she let me go almost immediately.

Emi laughed and grabbed the fruit plate with one hand and smacked my ass with the other. "I'm unseducible, Rakes." She looked over her shoulder with a wide, knowing smile as she strode back to the game. "And I love you, too."

I nudged Willow's Park Place card under the board, hiding it from view and hoping to avoid her three hotels, even though we'd made a deal.

She laughed at something Lila said as everyone streamed back in, and I noticed how relaxed Willow looked with my friends. Every day, she seemed a little less scared of being recognized, or at least it seemed like she wasn't letting it stop her anymore. She'd enjoyed knowing that after Sybil and Kieran's relationship started with a social media blowup, our group knew a little something about the public eye. Her laugh, though, seemed to catch my attention no matter where we were in the house.

"I'm an excellent banker," Lila said, taking her seat near the paper money. "I'm the most honest person in the room."

Willow looked around her stack of property cards, no doubt searching for Park Place, and I grinned at my subterfuge. "Didn't Marcus just find three property cards hidden in your bra?"

"Well," Lila said, straightening the money. "He shouldn't have been looking in there." Marcus's cheeks darkened, and the rest of the table laughed except Kieran, who had covered his ears, and I took a sip from my beer. My people.

"So," Marcus said, raising his glass. "I have an announcement."

"Is it about more things you found in Lila's bra?" Sybil accepted the fresh drink from her fiancé, who covered his ears.

"Please stop talking about what's in my little sister's bra!"

Lila lifted an eyebrow at Marcus and ignored her brother's theatrics. "Wait until he hears about what you found in my—"

"La, la, la," Kieran sang loudly, and I noticed Willow's grin widen at the playfulness of the group.

"I promise this isn't sexual," Marcus said above the laughter. "But Lila and I have decided to move in together." Cheers went up from around the table, and I clapped Marcus on the back, happy for the guy.

Lila beamed. "The call I just got was our new landlord confirming we got the apartment. He's coming to Chicago with me!" Another round of cheers and surprise went up from around the table, but those words hit me unexpectedly in the chest. Marcus wasn't just moving out, he was moving away. Chicago wasn't far, but it might as well have been on another continent.

"Wow," I finally said, too late, and I caught Willow's questioning expression from my peripheral vision. "Wow. Congrats, man!" I clapped him on the back again, even as my head swam with the news and trying to picture what this place would be like without him.

"I guess now's as good a time as any to share my news," Emi said, standing to be heard over all the conversation. "I quit my job!"

This time my cheer was right on time. She hated that engineering job, and the guys she worked with were sexist assholes. "All right! Awesome!"

"I've always wanted to get back into watch design, and there's a chance to take this really stellar course with the top designers in the world, so I put in my notice. Time to take a chance."

I stood and wrapped an arm around Emi's shoulder. "So proud of you," I said, dropping a kiss to the side of her head. She had told me designing watches was her dream. She had photos of gears and sketches of her own designs all over her room, but it was a hard field to break into and a competitive industry. Not to mention the best programs were in Europe, but post-pandemic, I guess they'd expanded to online courses.

I hugged her close and caught Willow's thoughtful expression across the table. I wondered if she'd been thinking about what she dreamed of doing next. This whole list thing seemed like what she thought she had to do before she moved on with her life. Her cheeks pinked under my gaze, and I winked at her. I had a renewed energy to help her finish her list. Who knew? Maybe she'd stay around awhile, even after Cruz returned. Marcus was leaving, but with her around, it would still feel like home, like family, until I could get back to my PJ family.

"It's exciting," Emi said, tapping her bottle to Sybil, who had wrapped her in a hug from the other side. "I can't believe I leave for a year in Switzerland in one month."

CHAPTER 21

Willow

☑ First kiss

WITH THE TEMPERATURE dropping, I wished I'd worn more than this thin sweater. Deacon had insisted on walking me home once the game finally ended. That was when I'd discovered my Park Place card shoved under the board, though I still bankrupted the last two players standing in my way. I felt like I was walking on air with how much fun I'd had. "There was so much cheating. I think my breaking rules item has been thoroughly checked off," I said.

I looked to my left at Deacon, who'd been quiet since Marcus and Emi made their announcements. He nodded with a smile, but didn't say anything as we continued along the sidewalk.

"It got cold," I commented to break the silence, and Deacon looked over at me, startled as if I'd interrupted something he was deep in thought about.

"Oh, yeah." He stopped and peeled his gray hoodie over his

head and handed it to me. "Take this." It was heavy and smelled like him. He'd caught me sniffing him on the roof, so I made sure to do my quick inhale when he wasn't looking. "And don't do that girl thing where you pretend you're not cold."

"Are you saying you're not cold?" I smiled and tugged the material over my head, the neck getting momentarily caught on my hair. I felt Deacon's hands through the material, and he tugged it down, adjusting the hood over my hair.

"It's fucking freezing, but I'm doing that boy thing where I hide my shivers so you see me as virile and invincible." His finger brushed my cheek as he helped me adjust the hood, and he flashed a wry grin. A warmth shot through me at the unexpected sensation. The inside of the sweatshirt was cozy from his body heat. "I run hot, anyway."

His hand fell away from my face after a moment, and he nodded toward my house. "I shouldn't have had so much to drink, then I could have driven you home." As it was, Sybil and Kieran took a Lyft back to their place, and everyone else was in the process of passing out at the house.

"You don't have to always take care of me," I reminded him, bumping my shoulder against his, our fingers at our side grazing with the motion. "I'm not actually your responsibility."

"Sure you are." He wrapped an arm around my shoulder and rubbed my arm through the fabric. "I can't let a damsel in distress be cold."

"I'm not a damsel." Ignoring the way his touch sent electricity through my body was a losing battle that had nothing to do with being cold. "And I'm not in distress." I'd felt that more and more recently, actually. "I've actually been thinking more about vet school, and it's so tempting to give it a try."

Deacon's arm felt comforting and heavy on my shoulder. "Why would you not?"

"I should, but . . . you really do need to be the best to get in." I'd never seen a more competitive group of people than my cohort in animal science—everyone who was pre-vet was competing for top of the class, and some of them hadn't gotten in. I swallowed the self-doubt that crept in at my own words.

"Don't do that," he said. "How do you know you're not the best? Real talk, Low?"

A gust of wind whipped around us, and I leaned into Deac, who tightened his hold on me. His touch sent warmth throughout my body that had nothing to do with his body heat. "Of course."

"I think you don't know you're the best because you've spent a long time avoiding situations where you'd have to put yourself out there. I get the sense you were hiding even before the memes. I think you should apply to school if you want to, for what it's worth. It's a re-do, right?"

"Maybe you should take your own advice."

"Apply to vet school? I would look good in the white coat."

"About finding out who you are without your ex. Except your ex is the Air Force. I know you plan to go back in, but while you're here, what are you doing? Your whole focus seems to be on going back—training, keeping your circle tight to not get distracted, biding your time at school." I raised a thumbnail to my lip and paused my steps, pulling away so I could meet his gaze. "I think you're hiding, too."

I couldn't read his expression, but I'd gone too far to back off now, and I reached out to stroke his forearm, his skin still warm despite the cold. "Deac, I hope you get to go back, but what if you don't? I'd hate for you to think your only worth is as a PJ."

"Maybe," he finally said, noncommittal, nudging my shoulder and beginning to stroll again. We walked together in the quiet for a minute or two.

Clouds had rolled in while we played, and it smelled like rain. The night sky was colored a muted dark gray. "Deac, are you okay?"

"I'm fine. Why?"

"Because you haven't made a single sexual innuendo in like two hours." I nudged my shoulder against him again. "Are you sick?"

He chuckled, but it wasn't his usual laugh. "I must be slipping."

"Guess so." I wasn't stumbling drunk, but I felt the lightness in my step and freedom in my words that I enjoyed about being tipsy. "I mean, no allusions to your penis, no subtle suggestions that someone should go to bed with you. You haven't even checked your phone to gently let down the crowd of women sliding into your DMs. Frankly, I'm concerned."

"Wow, you've really got my number, huh?" I thought he'd laugh, but he gave a wan smile. "Makes me sound like kind of an asshole." We both paused for passing cars before crossing the street.

"No," I said, stopping once we'd crossed the street. "I didn't mean it like that. I like the allusions to your penis!" An elderly couple walking their dog gave me dirty looks I tried to ignore. "Seriously, though, what's wrong?"

We started along the sidewalk again. The concrete was crumbling along the path, with patches of grass invading the walkway. "Because you can tell me. Remember?" I paused and sang "Baby, I own you now," with a flourish of my hands still in the sleeve of his hoodie.

He gave another half smile. "You know, that satirical version is actually just as creepy as the original."

"Even more so," I said, snagging the end of his sleeve to tug him forward. The wind was picking up.

"So, will you tell me what's wrong?"

"Why brunch?" he asked, changing the subject with zero subtlety. "What's the significance?"

"Don't think I didn't notice you avoiding my question," I said, but he gave me a one-shoulder shrug and a little smile, and I knew I'd let him get away with it. "Brunch. Well, I told you my ex's parents had a lot of money?"

"Yeah."

"We had brunch with them once a month at their country club. The first time, I was sixteen and terrified I'd use the wrong fork or spill something. They were nice, but it was so stiff and uncomfortable, and I always felt like I was under a microscope. I just wanted something messy to eat, like biscuits and gravy, but that would have made things worse." In retrospect, Spencer never seemed to notice my discomfort, or maybe I just got so used to hiding what I really thought, I never gave him a chance to.

"I will insist you order biscuits and gravy and spill something all over yourself on Sunday," he said. "I'll find the least classy place I can."

I smiled and hugged the hoodie tighter around me. "Thanks, Deac. I can't wait." We continued down the sidewalk toward the house and I added, "And I won't make you tell me what's wrong, but you know you can. Big questions, right?"

We walked in silence for another few moments, and I was resigned to him just being in a mood, but he broke the silence finally. "They're all leaving."

"Marcus and Emi?"

He nodded. "I didn't have people to lean on when I was discharged. Not really." Deacon's voice was low and soft in a way I hadn't heard before. "I had Cruz and the guys, but they were halfway around the world, and I'm not close with my parents. I didn't have anyone for months, and then I had Marcus and Emi and then Sybil, too. This is the anniversary of my . . . of when everything happened with my back. It's a rough reminder, and they always distract me with a party."

I finally understood his mood. "And they're both leaving."

He nodded. "I should just be happy for them, and wow, I sound like a clingy asshole rather than a slutty one."

"Hey, a slutty one with a giant penis, if I've interpreted your allusions correctly."

This time he laughed for real and looked down at me with a wide grin as the wind blew his hair around his face. "Yeah," he said, letting out another chuckle.

"And you still have me," I offered, patting my chest. I was about to say something else when my toe caught on a loose piece of concrete and I stumbled forward, my breath catching until Deacon's arms were around me, one hand at my waist and the other steadying my arm.

"Looks like I'm the one who has you," he said, his lips close enough to mine for me to see his puffs of breath in the cold. When Deacon's hand gripped my waist firmly to steady me, I inhaled the clean scent of him. I expected him to let me go immediately, but he paused with his hands on me, and I tried to memorize the feeling.

"Maybe we've got each other." I placed a palm gently on his biceps, feeling the firm muscle under the soft cotton of his long-sleeved T-shirt and noticing the way he dragged in a breath when I touched him. "I know I'm not as cool as Emi or as good a cook as Marcus, and no one is as fun and pretty as Sybil, but I'm here." I risked another stroke along the definition in his upper arm, and his expression looked pensive.

"You bankrupted me in Monopoly," he said, righting me. His hand remained at my waist, though. "Took all my money."

"That was business," I said, squeezing his arm to get one more feel. "I said I'd be here for you, not let you slide on rent. Just because I do volunteer work doesn't mean this is a charity."

His hand gripped at my waist again and he grinned. The sensation of the squeeze made me imagine him pulling me against him, of all the other ways he might grip me, and I blamed the alcohol because those were wild ideas. "I'm not used to someone else holding me up," he admitted.

"Need me to show you how to maneuver into position?"

He chuckled, the sound a low rumble. "Did you re-do your first time holding hands with the vet?"

"No." I shook my head. As I said it, I remembered Deacon taking my hand up on the hotel roof, comforting me when I was sad, and I debated correcting my answer. I hoped, though, that he might take my hand, not because I was sad but because he wanted to touch me.

Before I decided to say something, Deacon's hand slipped from my waist, but his fingers grazed mine before he interlocked them with my own. "Three birds. One stone. I can keep you from falling. You can get a new first, and I get to hold your hand."

His hands weren't soft, but his fingers felt deliciously warm against mine. "Because I'm a damsel?"

"Because you're my person." His brow creased and he corrected himself. "You're one of my people." He squeezed his fingers with mine. "And I take care of my people."

"I didn't know I signed on for that." He tugged me forward, and we strode along the sidewalk, hand in hand.

"Not optional." His voice was returning to normal, and I wondered if holding hands wasn't just for my benefit, if touching someone, if being touched, might be extra meaningful to him when he felt like he was losing everyone. Again. "Rescuing and access to my exceptionally large penis if you're ever in need."

I laughed and almost stumbled again, but his grip on my hand tightened and I caught myself. "Good to know."

"And you're pretty." Deacon's thumb brushing over my wrist made me feel tingling up my arm and warm between my thighs. I glanced up, confused, and I had to remind myself it was incidental contact, that he was just readjusting his hand after catching me, but I prayed for him to do it again, craving that pulse of sensation. "You said you're not as pretty as Sybil," he said. "That's not true."

We neared a neighborhood park with recent renovations. The new playground equipment glowed in the moonlight, and a gazebo with a picnic table had been constructed in the grassy open area. "Me? No way," I said, picturing her bright smile. She looked like the kind of woman Deacon would go for, not someone like me. "I'm just kind of plain."

"You're beautiful." His thumb brushed my wrist again and this time traced a line up the side of my thumb. I couldn't hide the intake of breath, and he paused his steps to glance at me. "You don't know that?"

The wind picked up, and goose bumps rose on my arms, even under the sweatshirt. "Everyone is beautiful in some way," I said, attempting to dismiss his comment. "I have a beautiful personality, and a lot of internet randos think my boobs look really good in a wet T-shirt."

He shook his head and drew a slow circle on my palm. "Not like that. You're hard to look away from. You're beautiful. You're . . ." He sucked in his own breath when I matched his movements and slid my thumb along his. Seeing his expression change when I did that was like an injection of confidence. Deacon actually liked me touching him. "Goddamn, I shouldn't say this, but you're sexy as hell."

We were only a few houses away from Cruz's, but I slowed down my pace. I wanted this moment to stretch as long as it could, so I slid my fingers back from his and then back down along their length.

"You shouldn't do that," he said, voice low and filled with gravel.

"Why?" I stroked my thumb along his again, and the motion-sensing lights flashed on as we approached the front porch.

"Because I'm not the guy you want your first kiss with, and when you do that, every muscle in my body wants to kiss you."

"You do?" My mouth must have been open like a fish—that's how I felt. My gaze fell to his lips where his tongue peeked out to wet his lower lip. "But you're only hanging out with me because Cruz asked you to."

He shook his head slowly from side to side. "I can't stop thinking about you." Deacon's palm was suddenly along the side of my neck, his fingertips curling into my hair, and his intense gaze met mine. "And I'm only admitting that because I drank too much. I promised Cruz I wouldn't think about you. Not like this."

I couldn't remember anyone ever looking at me the way he was now, like it was taking every ounce of restraint to keep him from pressing his lips to mine. That look vibrated deep in my core. My whole life I'd been timid and shy, a follower, but standing on this darkened street with his fingers in my hair, I wanted something else for myself. A streak of light shot across the sky, and I stood on my tiptoes, dragging Deacon's face down to mine, pressing my lips against his.

I'd never initiated a kiss before, never taken a chance that the other person wouldn't kiss me back, but it was like the lightning we'd seen in the sky the second our mouths connected. He took control of the kiss, an arm moving to my waist and his palm guiding my head to get more purchase on my lips. I'd never fully understood the expression of melting into a kiss. I'd read it hundreds of times in romance novels, but I'd never felt it until I sank against him, losing track of where his body ended and mine began. He slid his tongue along my lower lip, and I felt it between my thighs. My groan inadvertently broke the moment.

We both sucked in a breath and looked at each other as the headlights of a passing car lit the street behind us until the sound of its engine faded away. Creeping doubt slid into my thoughts, even as I marveled at still being in his arms. There were a million reasons I shouldn't have done that—we'd been drinking, he was sad, this whole thing was temporary, and he was Cruz's best friend. I was trying to figure out the best way to put all of that into words, but he tensed as I said, "I'm sorry." I'd spoken too loud trying to be heard over the wind that gusted around us.

He didn't loosen his grip, but sighed as he said, "I'm sorry, too."

"For what?" My voice sounded breathless. I was breathless.

"For stealing your second first kiss." He loosened his grip but didn't let me go.

"You didn't steal it." I touched two fingertips to my lower lip, feeling his gaze there. "I gave it to you."

Another car drove by, the bass of their stereo filling the surrounding air with a heavy beat. Deacon's hand slid away from my waist and grazed my fingertips. "You should get inside. I think it might rain," he said, taking a small step back. The cold that swirled around me had nothing to do with the rain. *What just happened?*

I fiddled with the keypad on the door, but the feel of his lips on mine, of his body, lingered. "Do you want to come in?"

He shoved his hands in his pockets and shook his head. "That's not a good idea."

Gus waited at attention when I opened the door, and I scratched him behind the ears. Deacon's brow furrowed, and I had a sinking feeling in my head. He'd said I was sexy, that he'd wanted to kiss me. The kiss felt like the start of something, not the end. Had I missed something? I dipped my gaze to Gus in hopes of avoiding the pity on Deacon's face. "Okay."

"Low?" He reached for my hand again, now a familiar warmth. "I shouldn't have . . . It's just not a good idea. Cruz . . ."

"Nope. I understand," I said hurriedly, injecting as much sunshine into my voice as I could. "You're right. We're drunk. It never happened." I gave him a wide smile I didn't feel. "Good night."

A pained expression crossed his face as he said good night,

waiting outside until I closed and locked the door. I peeked through the curtains and watched him walk down the driveway with his phone in his hand, and a message buzzed on my phone as he rounded the corner.

>DEACON: Thank you for giving me your second first kiss.

>DEACON: Sleep well.

CHAPTER 22

MY SHOES POUNDED against the wet pavement, the rain, constant since the night before, cutting against my skin. I'd kissed her. I'd pulled Willow against my body and felt the press of her against my chest, I'd relished how her tentative tongue slid against mine, and the way she groaned when I gently tugged her hair to angle her face. "Fuck," I repeated to myself, increasing my speed. I kissed my best friend's little sister. I kissed her while we were drunk. I looked ahead at the steep hill and leaned into the rain, ignoring the ache in my lower back.

The music in my earbuds paused with an incoming call, and I glanced down at my Apple Watch. It was Cruz, and I silenced the notification. He'd called earlier, too, and I couldn't bring myself to answer. Even with the worst video connection in the world, he'd see the fucking guilt on my face. I groaned and started up the hill at full speed, arms and legs pumping at a sprint as my muscles burned in protest. I'd been in a fog since last night, between Emi and Marcus both announcing they were leaving and then kissing Willow. Sweating like this, pushing my body to any limit I could find, was the only way I could think.

I sucked in a breath, inhaling the icy rain as I neared the top of the hill. After lifting that morning, I'd already run several miles, but slowing down meant thinking, and if I did that, things got dark. I skirted around a puddle and slowed at the top of the hill at the red light. My career demanded peak physical conditioning, but I still knew how overtraining felt, and my muscles screamed at me as I slowed, stretching and bouncing on my heels while I waited for the traffic to clear.

I'd always competed with Cruz—in training, we competed with everyone, but once we became friends, he was the person who got the most from me. We motivated each other. My phone buzzed once more against my arm, and I stared at the oncoming traffic with hands on my hips as I paced in small circles, refusing to look at his message.

He'd visited me a week after the surgery, after my parents had flown home with promises to check in periodically. There had been forty-two ceiling tiles in the room, the ones right above me dappled with spots of water damage that looked like a rough rendering of Peter from *Family Guy*.

"You look like shit," Cruz had said, because what else would your best friend say to you after spinal surgery? I wanted to laugh, but I caught sight of the gash over his eye, the one he'd gotten doubling back for me, and I looked away instead.

"Got your own room," he said, glancing at the empty bed on the other side of the divider. "Should make it easier to seduce hot doctors and nurses," he said casually, but his eyes were on the tubes and wires attached to me, studying and inspecting how bad it was. When I didn't say anything, he kept going. "Of course, this whole cutting open your spine thing might slow your game. You might have to date Ms. Rosy Palm like you did back in basic until you're off your back."

I chuckled just once. It wasn't funny, but it was normal. "Women like being on top with me," I said, finally turning my head toward him. "They enjoy looking at my pretty face." My voice croaked—I hadn't been using it other than to tell the physical therapist to fuck off and thanking the nurses for pain meds. Cruz handed me the cup of water sitting near the bed and held it so the straw was near my mouth. When I didn't move, he nudged it forward, adding, "Fucker, I will not beg you to suck on anything, no matter how laid up you are."

I laughed for real then and took a drink of water, feeling the wash of it through my system. I coughed into my shoulder and waved it away. "You dream about begging me to suck," I said finally.

He leaned forward, resting his forearms on the side of the bed. "Told you a thousand times, you arrogant dick, you're not my type. You're too big a motherfucker." I was pretty sure I was the only one he'd told he was bi—even today the military wasn't always a safe place to be out, and it had taken years for him to tell me. "I like my men svelte."

I laughed again at the term and motioned to my body, bulky under the blankets with my size and the equipment and pillows keeping me in place. "You're saying I'm not svelte?"

We laughed until it faded into the ordinary sounds of the room—the monitors and compression device groaning. "You scared the shit out of me," he admitted, looking down at his own hands, and I let my gaze trail to the stitches and bruising down his neck. "I thought you were dead."

I tried to move my toes, and I watched the small shift under the blankets. It took so much effort, completely exhausting me, but I kept doing it. Kept checking. "I thought I was, too," I admitted, not adding that lying in this bed, staring at the ceiling, I'd wondered if I was better off. I didn't want to be dead, but this felt like limbo.

"Rakes?" Someone knocked on the door and walked in, interrupting my spiral. "We need to get you up on your feet." The man was tall and thin and clapped his hands together, plastering on a smile despite my continued attitude. "It's time."

"Respectfully, fuck off," I said, looking up at the ceiling. He technically outranked me, but I couldn't be bothered to care. "Not today."

"Sooner you get back up on your feet, the closer you get to walking again." Instead of backing out of the room, he stepped forward. The tumor suppressing my spine was still being tested, the prognosis up in the air. What I knew was I could barely feel my legs. He held out his hands and spoke in an accent that made me think he'd spent time in the South, just enough to adopt a rounded lilt to his voice. "Just gotta work on taking a step. That's all you need to do today."

"No," I said, crossing my arms over my chest, feeling how that pulled on the staples running up my back. "I said not today."

The physical therapist, the last name on his tag read "Gerald," shot a look at Cruz and down at my form, still under the blankets.

"Can you give us a minute?" Cruz asked, and Gerald nodded.

"But I'll be back in five minutes. It's not optional today, Rakes."

I continued fixing my stare on the ceiling until the door clicked shut.

"What was that?" Cruz stood and walked to the other side of the bed to catch my gaze. "You're scared to try?"

I huffed and stared him in the eyes. "I'm not scared."

"Sure as fuck sounds like it. The Deacon Rakes I know tackles shit head-on, no matter how scary it is."

"I'm not scared," I repeated.

"Bullshit." He snagged my arm when I tried to recross it over my chest. "And you should be. This is scary, but you can't just give up. I'm here to help." He took my hand in both of his. "No wind."

I didn't say anything, looking up at the ceiling instead, tracing the outline of the water spot. It was one step—weeks earlier, I'd scaled the side of a cliff and run for miles. And now I couldn't even walk—Cruz was right; I was scared that I wouldn't be able to do it.

"No wind," he repeated, his voice firm.

When I didn't respond again, he dropped my hand. "Is there any damage to your neck?" The question took me off guard, and I turned toward him.

"No, all lower. T11 and T12."

"Issues with your breathing after extubating?"

"No." I wished I had somewhere to go, because his sharp shift was throwing me off. "Why are you asking?"

And then he'd reached back and punched me in the jaw, not hard enough to knock my teeth out, but it hurt like a motherfucker. "You told me once that's what it takes to get you to listen sometimes." He sucked in a breath and held out his hand again. "No. Wind," he repeated.

I'd fumed, but as I rubbed my jaw, I focused on that pain and the new injury and looked up into my best friend's face. I thought back to the hundreds of times we'd pushed each other, to that night at karaoke when I begged him to trust us, to trust me, and I looked away from the ceiling. "No rain," I said, finally taking his hand.

There was a knock at the door, and Gerald walked in.

"He's ready," Cruz said, clutching my hand still and not looking away. As Gerald gave some instruction, Cruz leaned in to help me out of bed, and I whispered that PT Gerald was kinda svelte. Cruz's laugh filled the room, and I smiled the way I always did when he laughed like that.

"When you take ten steps, I'll ask for his number," he'd said.

I shook my head at the memory, running a hand over my jaw where he'd hit me. I'd threatened to hit him back when he wanted to chicken out of calling the physical therapist. Now, a horn honked, and I noticed the light had changed, and a car was waiting for me to cross. I waved them through and instead walked toward a nearby tree to get some shelter from the rain and checked my phone.

> CRUZ: Get back to me.
>
> CRUZ: Gonna be out of range for a while.

I swallowed. They were sending them out, and if he was giving me a heads-up, I knew what that meant. I looked ahead into the rain and hit the video call icon, walking the short distance back to a neighborhood park where there was a shelter.

"Hey," I said, looking at the pixelated image on the screen. "Sorry, was working out."

"Don't have much time but we're—" The next few words were garbled with the poor connection.

"How long?"

"Unknown," he said as the audio connection cleared. "Take care of Willy. She doesn't always understand our mission and she worries."

I was pretty sure she worried because she understood. I thought it but didn't say it—I'd spent two years on this side of it, being the one at home waiting for news instead of the one out there doing the rescuing, and it sucked. "Sure," I said instead. "I've got her." Then, for no reason, or because the guilt was eating at me and he'd once punched me in the jaw in a hospital, I added, "She's pretty great."

"She is," he said, looking off-screen. "That's why I've warned you to keep your hands off her."

"I'm not that bad," I said, making a joke, even as the urge to confess I'd kissed her climbed up my throat. "I'm actually a pretty decent guy. Even G admitted that once I stopped telling him to fuck off about the physical therapy." The two had a kind of situationship while I was in the hospital and then for a while after. His first name was Antonio, but calling him by his last name or G always felt right to me and kept Cruz's privacy a little safer.

"You're one of the best guys I know," he said. "But you don't stick around. You're not a relationship guy. I'm not, either. I know you and you cut and run. Even if you wanted to stay, you've never had the option." He sighed and looked at his watch. "And Willy deserves someone who is all in."

Those words hit me like that punch in the jaw had two years earlier. He knew me better than anyone. "You're right, man." I looked at the screen, which froze for a moment.

"Shit. I gotta go," he said. "Tell her I love her? She's not answering her phone."

"Roger that," I said, holding up the phone. "Take care of yourself, brother."

"No wi—" he said, the connection freezing again mid-sentence, though this time not coming back.

The downpour around me continued like I needed a visual reminder of the presence of rain. Maybe Willow was my person, but Cruz was my brother, and he was spot-on—I left. I was leaving. I couldn't let her get the wrong idea. I couldn't let *myself* get the wrong idea, considering how motivated I was to leave just like my roommates. Cruz's face was still frozen on the screen, and a drop of water dripped along the surface.

"There's plenty of rain," I said to no one, but hoping the reminder to myself was what I needed.

CHAPTER 23

Willow

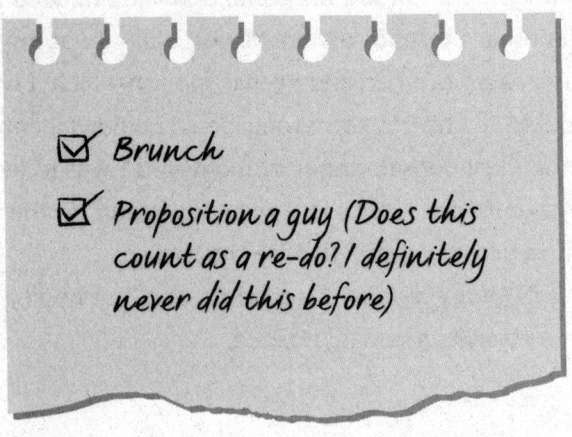

☑ Brunch
☑ Proposition a guy (Does this count as a re-do? I definitely never did this before)

WILLOW: I kissed him.

ZOE: The vet? You went out with him again?

WILLOW: No. 🙈

ZOE: Your keeper?! Tell me everything!

ZOE: And I mean everything. 🍆

    I looked toward the entrance to the diner where Deacon said to meet him for brunch, and I anxiously tapped my nails on the surface of the table, even though I was twenty minutes early and already halfway into a Bloody Mary. Kissing Deacon in the rain had my head spinning. The kiss itself was amazing, and I kept touching my fingers to my lips, remembering the feel of his kiss like I could hold on to the sense memory. But when I arrived home and stood outside with Gus, I had time to think through all the ways it raised more questions I didn't want the answers to. He'd been really shaken by his friends' news, and we'd both been drinking. And it would have been so easy for it to become more than a kiss.

> WILLOW: There was no 🍆. It was just a kiss and we were drunk.
>
> ZOE: I bet there was significant produce still involved.

Deacon had been hard against my stomach; the memory of that rigid length against me was imprinted in my memory. Even as my head spun over the fact that the kiss between us was a bad idea, I felt a pulse deep in my core every time I thought about the way I'd felt in his arms, our bodies aligned. I'd started and deleted more texts to him than I could count, but the day before he'd messaged to confirm brunch and sent this location along with a 👍. I'd expected him to cancel—it would be beyond awkward, but I was also relieved to hear from him. Maybe the kiss meant nothing.

> WILLOW: He's my brother's best friend. We can't get together—if we did and then split, it would put Cruz between us.

Cruz—my brother, my rock, my only family. There's no way I could get into something with his best friend, especially not while he was off saving lives and in danger. He'd left me a message that he'd be unreachable for a while—he'd sent those before. He'd tell me not to worry and then I'd spend the next however long he was gone constantly worrying. If I started something with Deacon like that kiss made me want to, and then it ended, I knew Cruz would choose me and he'd lose his best friend.

> ZOE: So, don't date... No relationship means no breakup.
>
> WILLOW: What do you mean?

The dots bounced, and then a GIF showing a close-up of an animal tongue filled the screen.

> ZOE: And don't say you don't want to... In a moment of weakness, you sent me a picture of page two of your re-do list!

I blushed, realizing she was right. We'd been up late laughing and joking, and I couldn't even blame alcohol because I'd been sipping Diet Coke next to Gus in my bed, wishing there was a human warm body available to keep me company. I'd started jotting down ideas while listening to a really great audiobook by my favorite romance author, and my imagination took over. Page two was never meant for someone else's eyes, a list of the firsts I wanted a re-do on in the bedroom after my lackluster experiences with Spencer. I'd added sex and orgasms to my page one, but there were so many more things. I'd planned to toss the list, but after that kiss, I kept coming back to it. Wondering.

> ZOE: You can tell me I'm right later.
>
> WILLOW: I can't just... proposition him for a friends-with-benefits thing. How do you even do that?

Zoe's audio message came through. "Hey, Captain America, let's see how many times we can make each other come, no strings. You in?"

> WILLOW: !!! I am in public! At brunch! One does not proposition someone over brunch.

I chuckled, picturing the country club crowd and that happening at the table near us between the Fletchers and the Bancrofts.

> ZOE: 😂😂😂 French toast is an aphrodisiac. It could work.

The door pushed open and Deacon strode in, his backpack slung over his shoulder—he'd mentioned he'd be coming from the library. He kept saying how school was just something to do until he could go back into the service, but most days, he seemed to take school as seriously as anyone I'd ever seen. He had glasses perched on his head I hadn't seen him wear before.

WILLOW: Gotta go. He's here.

The dots bounced, but nothing came through, and I set the phone down to wave at Deacon.

"Hey," he said, grabbing the chair across from me. "How's it going?"

I noticed how he met my gaze, but then his eyes skirted across my face and peered over my shoulder toward the bar, then down to my Bloody Mary and the stalk of celery sticking out proudly. I'd planned to talk about the kiss when he arrived, to address it head-on like the badass, assertive woman I was trying to be. But with him sitting here, it was way easier to pretend it never happened.

"I didn't know you wore glasses," I said, motioning to where they were pushed into his hair.

"Oh," he said, snagging them from his head. "For reading. Ignored that advice through school the first time around. Figured I'd try it out this time around."

"Can I see them on you?"

"They're nothing special," he said, sliding the thin black frames onto his face and brushing his hair away from his forehead.

The sharp angles of Deacon's face and the hints of gold in the chocolate of his eyes were only enhanced by the glasses, and my breath caught in my throat before I spoke up. "They look good on you," I finally said, regaining my senses. "Who doesn't love a man in glasses? I bet there are some fans in your study group."

He rubbed a hand over the back of his neck and gave me a wan smile. "Nah. I mostly keep to myself."

"Sure—you're there to learn, not score. Just saying you look good in the glasses. It's a good look for you. And if you wanted to score, I bet the glasses would help." I screamed inside my head to stop talking. My interactions with Deacon had never been awkward until now.

"I'll keep that I mind," he said, pulling them from his face and digging in his bag for a case. He reached for a menu without looking back at me, and the sinking feeling returned. "This place is supposed to have the best biscuits and gravy in town. And I've warned the staff you'll be spilling copiously." His gaze flicked up from over the menu, and he flashed me a real smile, a Deacon smile with a glint of mischief.

"Spilling isn't the goal," I insisted. "I'm not actively trying to be a slob."

"Just unintentional slobbering?" His fingers glided down the back of the plastic menu, and a memory of those fingers sliding along my cheek in the rain flashed through my mind.

"Shut up," I said, swatting him across the table with my menu. "And slobbering is something else."

"Oh," he said with a suggestive wink. "I know."

I laughed. "You're ridiculous," I said, looking at the menu and then back up at him, stealing a surreptitious glance as the server approached to take his drink order. Maybe we didn't need to talk about the kiss or anything else that was more serious. This felt normal again.

Of course, that wasn't my luck.

On the table, my screen lit up with an incoming message from Zoe, and I tapped to mute the thread, but of course hit play on the voice memo instead.

"Ride that man until he can't see and then remind him his sense of taste is enhanced with his lack of vision."

My face flamed, and Deacon looked surprised, his eyebrows moving into his hairline. "How is Zoe? Interesting woman."

I silenced my phone, fumbling with the right icon, and felt his eyes on me. "She is," I said, not meeting his eye.

A server brought over a glass of orange juice and winked at him. Deacon knew all the women in the metro area, and they all liked him, but he nodded kindly and thanked her before turning back to me. I'd been too distracted by his fingers on the menu to notice her recognition of him the first time. "Is she talking about the vet? Haven't heard you talk about him much."

"Who knows? She could be talking about anyone." I shrugged, still embarrassed, but it was beyond time to fess up. "He never asked me out again. There wasn't really a spark, but he did help me get that volunteer gig and lent me his old GRE study prep materials."

"Sparks matter." He looked between me and the menu. "And he was too short for you, anyway."

I snort-laughed at the ridiculous argument to make me feel better. "He's almost as tall as you," I said, not thinking before the words came out, and I realized I'd implied *he* was the right height for me. Implied he was right for me, and that was not the energy I was going for. "Did Cruz ever tell you Zoe has a thing for him?" I tried desperately to change the subject because it felt like my face was on fire.

He chuckled and took a sip of the juice. "He did. Mentioned she'd offered to send photos."

I cringed. "He told me he turned her down. Please don't tell me he accepted her offer!"

"I plead the Fifth." He raised his palms. "I doubt it, though. He's too cautious about things like that. He's nuts about phone privacy."

"What about you?" I wished I could pull the words back into my mouth because they sounded so suggestive and way too flirty. Plus, I didn't want to imagine him exchanging sexy photos with women.

"Not recently." His easy smile had returned, and this was his normal, indiscriminate flirting I'd gotten used to. "And only if she wants to—there's way more at stake for women sending pictures, I think. Why do you ask? Are you offering?"

"No!" I made a grab for my drink and tipped it to my lips, only to realize there were a few drops left, and the ice hit my lips ungracefully. "No," I repeated. "I've never done that."

Deacon shrugged. "I think a photo showing something hidden is sometimes better than showing it all." His gaze looked hooded for a moment, and when he looked up, I thought he glanced at my lips, but then his expression looked neutral, so I was sure I'd imagined it.

"What can I get you, Deacon?" The server smiled brightly, returning to the table with her notepad at the ready.

He motioned to me with a flourish. "I'll let my buddy go first—but I think she's going to want the biscuits and gravy with extra gravy and another Bloody Mary."

I nodded with a fake smile when she looked at me, the sound of the word "buddy" hanging in the air like a lead balloon as

Deacon ordered waffles with eggs and bacon. Buddy. Okay, that's fair. And that was what I wanted to get back to, or at least, what I should have wanted to get back to.

"I'll feel it during my workout later, but who can resist waffles?" He unrolled the paper napkin, and I was distracted by his fingers again with the neatly trimmed nails and calluses. "Bet your country club brunches didn't have napkins this nice, did they?"

I grinned, another fake grin I hoped he couldn't read on my face. "Definitely not." I looked around at the groups of people out for brunch—the diner was busy with old couples and young college students in sweats and kids giggling and joking. It was loud and messy and worlds away from the country club and stiff conversation with Spencer's parents. I nodded again. "It's perfect."

"We can come back—I don't know how many rooms I want to paint with you, but any re-do that involves bacon, count me in."

"Thanks, buddy," I said, focusing on my napkin and ignoring the bitterness of the words in my mouth. Out of the corner of my eye, my phone screen flashed again, and Zoe's text appeared on the silent screen from the spot between us where it rested.

> ZOE: Show him page two!

I was going to block her number or kill her, and I flipped the phone over.

"What's page two?" Deacon casually leaned back in his chair, one elbow slung over the back, and took another sip of his orange juice.

The curve of his biceps and muscular forearms was defined under the compression shirt, and I bit my lower lip, remembering how it felt to be held in those arms. How was I ever going to stop imagining that on a loop in my brain? "It's not polite to read someone else's screen," I chastised, ignoring the loop.

"You've never wanted me to be polite." His smirk, that voice. The loop could not be stopped. "I believe you told two strangers on the street you liked my penis allusions."

"Here you go." The server approached with my refill.

"Thank you," I said, hoping she'd get the hint she could keep moving along.

"Page two?" Deacon raised one eyebrow and ran fingers through his hair. "Did you add more to your list?"

"Um . . . yeah. Kind of."

"You're making progress on the first page. What's next?"

"I don't think these are ones I'll actually do." I pulled the notebook from my bag, holding the scribbled pages to my chest.

"You didn't think you'd do any of them," he said. "But look at you now. You sing on stage. You march in rallies." He motioned down my chest but then stopped his hand. "Let's see." He held out his hand, and his fingers brushed mine, sending a spark up my arm. Our gazes met for a split second, and I felt the same sparks. But of course he didn't. I was his buddy. His buddy's baby sister.

I reluctantly handed over the list, Zoe's suggestion still dancing in my mind. He read over the first page, noting the items I'd crossed off, including hand-holding and a first kiss. I thought his own cheeks grew a little pink when he saw those but didn't comment. He pointed at the page where I'd written learn to drive. "I feel compelled to remind you that you already know how to drive. I've seen you do it."

I chuckled, hoping now he might forget to move to page two. "But I never learned to ride a bike, so I thought I could do that. If there are wheels, it counts, right?"

He laughed. "I never relearned how to ride after my surgery. I could do that one with you. We can ride until we can't see anymore," he added with a wink over his glass.

"Oh, God," I groaned, dropping my face into my palms, again committed to destroying Zoe, but when I looked up, he was flipping to the second page.

"I can take that back," I said, making a grab for the list, but he pulled it toward him and held it out of my reach.

"What's on page two, Low?" he asked, but then his eyes widened.

"Oh, God," I whispered. "I shouldn't have let you read that." I tried to tug the notepad back, and he held it out of reach again.

"Wow," he said, scanning the list, his gaze moving back up to the top of the page. "Dirty talk, hand stuff, oral—giving and receiving, girl on top, against a wall, being tied up . . . Holy shit, Low."

"I know," I said, back into my hands. "I told you, I'll never do them. But you like big questions, so I thought I could share my big, silly list. I was just . . ."

He leaned in when I trailed off, eyes skating over the list again. "Just what?"

"Just . . . imagining. I really liked sex. I mean, the idea of it. Sometimes the real thing was good," I said, lowering my voice. The server set down syrup and ketchup on the table and paused. I saw her feet because I hadn't looked up from my shame spiral, and Deacon finally thanked her and she walked off. Things were quiet for a moment, and I finally looked up to find him studying me intently.

"There's nothing wrong with liking sex," he said, his voice low. "Stop hiding your face. You should do these if you want to."

I took the list and shoved it back in my bag. "There won't be a second date with Theo. I don't have anyone in my life to do these things with."

"It wouldn't be hard to convince someone, Low. I told you, even though I shouldn't have. You're sexy. You're . . . Lots of guys would jump at the chance to be with you." I noticed the set of his jaw tense at the words.

"I don't think I'd be comfortable with a stranger, though, and who knows what will happen in a couple months when Cruz is home and I have to decide what comes next."

"True," he said, some realization coming over his face. "You're not sticking around." He looked thoughtful for a moment and then pushed his empty glass aside so he could take my hand across the table. The warmth of his touch sent tingles through my body. "Maybe when you get home, there's a buddy who might be up for friends with benefits."

I laughed. "I don't have any buddies left back home." Other than Zoe, our friends had been couples, mostly, and a lot of them we knew through Spencer. "As far as men go, you and Blaine are my only buddies. And Blaine is gay and definitely into his ex, and you're . . . you're the only other man in my life."

Dear God. I'd propositioned him over brunch. Commence sinking into the floor.

His eyes met mine again, the gaze intense, and reminded me of how he'd looked in the rain before he kissed me, his irises impossible to look away from as his thumb grazed my wrist and made a little moan escape my lips. And I thought, *Maybe*. I held on to the maybe.

"Low. We kissed the other night after the party, but it was a bad idea." At his words, "maybe" drifted into the air like a runaway balloon. "For a lot of reasons. You're leaving, but I'm not sticking around, either. Also, I'm too old for you *and* I promised your brother. I'd never want you to expect things and be disappointed."

He swept his thumb across my wrist again, the touch barely there but still making my core pulse with need.

"I don't think you could ever disappoint me." I swallowed hard, because every instinct told me to drop this and take the rejection, but then his thumb would shift again and my nerve endings lit up. The old Willow would have dropped it. "I know you're leaving. I know Cruz is your best friend. And the ten years you have on me are filled with experience. You're kind of the perfect person, Deac."

Deacon stroked a thumb over my skin again, and this time, his gaze definitely dipped to where I'd pulled the corner of my lip between my teeth. "Is that what Zoe was referring to?"

I chuckled and slid my thumb along the side of his, testing the waters. I did want those things just for me, and even though asking made me feel nine varieties of anxiety, I pushed forward. "She said I should say, 'Let's see how many times we can make each other come, no strings.'"

His eyes flashed, and I wanted more of that gaze, even for just a few weeks or a couple of months. He'd be the perfect person to help me forget Spencer and move on.

"So," I said, nervously. "Should I ask that way?"

CHAPTER 24

Deacon

NO. NO! THE words screamed in my head at her suggestion even as my dick twitched at hearing her repeat Zoe's direct phrasing. And now I'd memorized how the word "come" sounded on Willow's lips. "No" was an easy word to say, even "no, but thanks." And still, I couldn't make my lips form the word. Willow's eyes were wide and hopeful, the light from over our table catching the warm brown color, and she did that thing again where she pulled her lip between her teeth. Another flash of heat pulsed through me.

I have to say no.

"You're not saying anything," she said, those big brown eyes impossibly wide before she buried her face in her hands again. "Oh my God. I can't believe I asked you that. What is wrong with me? One drunk kiss doesn't mean you want to . . ." She waved one hand toward the list in her bag with her eyes still covered. The image of her hiding and waving was endearing until she caught the edge of her drink and the glass tipped, the red liquid and ice splashing across the table, one celery stalk threatening to glide off the edge. Willow jumped back, but her white top was already sticking to her, and the ice cubes fell to the floor. "Could this get any worse?" she muttered, accepting the napkin I held out, which did little to soak up the spill.

"Here, Deacon," the server said, rushing over with a towel to help clean up. "Saw the spill," she said, flashing me a smile while thrusting a few paper napkins in Willow's direction without looking at her. I didn't remember her name, but I had vague memories of something happening in the back room of a nearby bar one night right after I'd gotten back. I'd been so drunk and still unsteady on my feet despite physical therapy. The memories ran together, and I flushed. Further proof I was not a good choice for Willow's little experiment. Willow, who was dabbing at her shirt, the white fabric clinging to her chest where her nipples stood under the cold fabric. The server had cleaned up our table and stood there batting her eyelashes at me. "You know," she said, "I'm off in an hour."

Willow was still trying to dry herself, but she'd heard the offer in the woman's words, and she looked on the verge of crying, her eyes down and her lower lip quivering, which finally pushed me to action.

"Thanks," I said, glancing down at her name tag. "Addy." I was not the guy who could do this with Willow. I was the guy who couldn't remember the name of the server he'd banged in a bar. "We're good, but have a nice day. Could we get more napkins?" I brushed her fingers away as I stood. "You've been very helpful."

"Are you . . . sure?" She looked doubtfully at Willow and then back to me, the question behind her question making the hairs on the back of my neck stand on end with annoyance.

"Absolutely." I walked around her and handed Willow another napkin. She really had taken the entire large glassful with her body. It looked like she'd butchered her own bacon at the table, and around the room people turned to look. She was trying to hide herself, and I did my best to block her from view of our fellow diners. It cut me to the core to see her hiding again. "Here," I said, making a grab for my backpack. I pulled a T-shirt from inside. "It's clean. I was gonna wear this after my workout. You want to go change in the bathroom?" My gaze dipped to her chest, and I sucked in a breath before I looked back at her expression, which I'd probably classify as dazed mortification.

"Thanks," she said, taking the soft cotton from my hand with tears welling in her eyes. "I'm sorry I'm such a . . . mess." She didn't give me time to respond before she hurried toward the bathroom, arms crossed over her chest as she made her way across the room, head hung low.

I watched her until she disappeared into the bathroom to find that Addy was still standing there. "That was nice of you," she said. "That girl *is* a mess, though. Before you got here, she was just staring at this notepad and talking to herself." She touched my biceps and leaned against our table. "You said she's a friend, right? That's why I asked what you were doing later." She stroked my arm, even as my gaze dragged to the door Willow had run through. "Because I'd really love a repeat of the last time."

I shrugged off her touch, hackles rising again. She was being rude. I was worried about Willow, but also, I could hardly walk the last time from the liquor and nerve damage—why would she want a repeat? "Listen, I think I pretty politely told you I'm not interested." Willow had looked really upset, even before the spilled drink, and I worried what she was telling herself. "I don't remember much about last time—and I don't know you, but you deserve something better than someone so drunk that the whole experience is a blur." I grabbed my bag and Willow's from the table and threw a twenty down.

"You're not drunk now." Addy looked back at me skeptically. "Is she your girlfriend?"

I rolled my eyes to myself and strode toward the bathroom to find Willow. She wasn't my girlfriend. But she was still Willow, and she meant something to me and I hated the idea of her hiding again. "She's the one I'm following."

I hurried my pace when I saw she was still in there, and I knocked on the door of the single stall space. "Low?"

"Gimme a minute," I heard her say through the door, her voice choked. Oh God, she was crying.

"Low?" I knocked again. "Are you okay?" I tested the handle on the door, which gave immediately since she hadn't locked it behind her. "I'm coming in, okay?"

I pushed open the door slowly, giving her time to stop me, but she didn't. Willow stood by the sink in my shirt, wiping at her eyes. "I'm fine," she said. "Just clumsy and awkward. Hey, drowning again, just in tomato juice, so I'm pretty on-brand, right?" She gave a sad, choked laugh, and I had an uncomfortable sense of recognition. I'd told those kinds of bad jokes hundreds of times after saying I was fine. "You don't have to check on me," she added, wiping at her eyes again.

I shut the door behind me, closing us in the small space together. "It's my favorite T-shirt. I was checking on that," I said, rubbing the fabric of the sleeve between my thumb and forefinger. She held the soaked shirt, and I saw the clasp of a bra hanging down with it. When she let out a sad laugh, I ran my thumb over her cheek, brushing away a tear and noticing the way her wet lashes looked when she glanced up at me.

"I'm sorry I asked you that stupid question." She glanced away from my face, looking down. "It was a ridiculous idea. You have girls like that server throwing themselves at you. She's beautiful and you're not interested. You don't need me doing it, too." She looked around and kept her eyes off my face.

I stroked my finger under her chin and tipped it up, bringing her gaze back to mine. "Stop hiding from me."

"I'm embarrassed." Her plain admission was like a punch to the gut. "I had this whole silly hope in my head that you'd be into this idea." She dragged in a shaky breath. "Be into me enough to say yes." She wiped at her eyes. "So stupid. I have no idea what I'm doing."

All I wanted was to chase away the self-doubt that was clear on her face. So I stepped closer to her, continuing to stroke my thumb over her cheek. "I kissed you, Willow. I kissed you because I was very into you."

"We were drunk."

I rubbed my palm up and down the goose bump–pebbled skin of her upper arm. "I kissed you because I wanted you, and I didn't answer your question because I was so damn tempted to say yes."

She jumped in surprise, but I held her face, keeping her gaze on me. "You wanted to say yes?"

"Of course," I said, tucking a strand of hair behind her ear. "But I was being honest. I'm not a guy who sticks around. I'm going back to the service, and I know my life there isn't any good for relationships. I don't want you to get hurt, and that's what would happen if we tried anything."

"I know." She nodded, a bit of hope returning to her face—it was something about how her lips tipped up. "And I would never want Cruz stuck in the middle—he lost as much as I did with my parents' split and when Mom died."

It pained me to say it, especially with her soft skin under my fingertips. "As much as I want you, he's my brother."

Willow's smile widened, a spark of humor through her shaky voice. "Does that make us half-siblings?"

I grinned and stroked a thumb across her cheek again. "Adult half-siblings? Does that make it less weird that I still can't stop looking at your mouth and noticing the way your nipples look through that shirt?"

Her face reddened, and she pulled her lip between her teeth.

"Hey." I slid my thumb there, the pad grazing her supple lower lip. "I asked you to stop hiding from me."

"I know you're leaving, and I know you don't do relationships. That's why I asked you," she said, and her fingers grazed my waist. "You're safe. I'm leaving, you're leaving, and nothing can happen, so it can just be . . . page two. And that's all."

I traced my thumb along the column of her throat, noticing her pulse and stroking the soft skin there. "Are you still doing all this to get over your ex?" Despite this entire conversation, and knowing I couldn't have her, I wanted her to say no.

She shook her head, the curls bouncing around her face and her long lashes dipping before she met my eyes again. "Kind of, but I think . . ." Her tongue brushed over her lower lip, and my cock twitched at the movement. "It's less about being ready for the next relationship. I just want a fuller life, just for me. I don't think I could see that before, but now . . ." Her gaze traced from my eyes to my mouth back to my eyes. "I want to experience everything I wanted but was too afraid to ask for or didn't feel I deserved."

I'd immediately committed that list to memory, imagining Willow under me, on me, and spread out on my bed ready to be devoured in the way she deserved. "Just page two?"

"If you want to," she added, her fingers pausing their brush over my obliques, my body willing her to skirt lower. "And when it's over, it's done. My heart won't get broken. Cruz will never have to know, because there won't be any awkwardness."

I felt torn in two. My mind screamed at the dissonance of knowing this was betraying my friend's trust, but I still wanted to do it, needed to touch her more. And she was right—this was safe if we were both leaving. Her back to Colorado to live her life with her re-dos under her belt, and me back to the only place I'd ever called home.

"I'm not good at relationships, Low."

She nodded. "That's not what I want here." She sounded resolute, self-assured, and stood a little taller, which warmed my heart in a nonsexual way. "I only want to re-do page two so I'm ready for the next relationship and whatever happens next, so I can bring my best self to it and . . . I trust you."

Willow had laid everything bare at my feet—what she wanted and what she needed. I cupped her cheek and slid a thumb over her lower lip. "Cruz can't know," I said. "And we take it slow. I'm not going down on you in a diner bathroom."

She nodded, the warmth from her body radiating over my stomach and chest. "But you would go down on me somewhere else?"

I groaned, and my dick twitched again at the thought of her spread before me, that plump lower lip pulled between her teeth. I nodded and slowed my movements over her lip. "It's on the list."

She swallowed audibly and her smile widened. "So, you'll do it? You'll help?"

"Let's see how many times we can make each other come, no strings," I said, echoing her advice from Zoe. "But first, brunch." I motioned to the door of the bathroom to lead her out. "Page one still matters."

Everything about this was wrong. If I stopped to think about it, we were both betraying Cruz by taking anything further than this. So then why did looking down at Willow's smile—that one that felt like it was just for me—feel so right?

CHAPTER 25

- ☑ Dirty talk
- ☑ Orgasms

GUS PAUSED OUR walk to inspect a fire hydrant, and I scanned the sky, a deep orange with pearlescent sweeps of clouds along with the setting sun, my thoughts returning to yesterday. When we got back to the table, it was clean and dry and our food was waiting. Then despite everything that had happened in the previous ten minutes, we'd fallen right back into normal. Deacon let me try his bacon, and I managed to not dribble any gravy on his favorite shirt. It was delicious on so many levels. I'd gotten home from brunch, legs like jelly from what Deacon and I had agreed to, and that whole moment in the bathroom that had ended with him finally stepping back from me and leaving me alone to wash my face.

Gus tugged me forward when he was done with his inspection, and we moved toward the house. I couldn't help but grin to myself at how the whole thing had turned out, and I couldn't wait to see what happened next. I'd been in a bit of a floaty state all day, and I pulled my phone from my pocket.

> WILLOW: He heard your voice memo. We're no longer friends.
>
> ZOE: Did it give him ideas?
>
> ZOE: I bet it did. We're still friends.
>
> ZOE: Give me deeeeeetails!

I wanted to tell her everything, but I remembered the way his thumb had felt brushing tears from my cheek, the concern and care in his eyes when he came in and the heat in them when he told me he wanted me. That all felt private, like holding on to it would keep the sparks fresh.

I just sent the thumbs-up emoji, and when she replied with the eyes, I laughed. I'd make her wait for a while as punishment for the voice memo.

Gus sat patiently waiting to be unleashed and then took off to do his security scan of the house, his usual routine after our evening walk. I kicked off my shoes by the door and wandered to my bedroom. I wanted to shower after the walk, and I took one more peek at the phone screen where Zoe had sent three middle-finger emojis and a kissing face after my lack of response.

With the hot water sluicing over my skin, I reveled in the steam of the shower and let my mind wander back to Deacon's touch. It had been soft against my cheek, but so firm when he'd kissed me. I wondered how many different kinds of touches Deacon had. At the thought, a pulse made my core flutter, and my breasts felt heavy. I ran a soapy finger over my sensitive nipples and closed my eyes, imagining Deacon touching me there. I rolled them now, eyes still closed and picturing the heat in Deacon's gaze when I'd said the word "come." I'd spent my entire time in Iowa denying myself fantasies about him. He was off-limits, and now, under the hot water, I wanted more than the fantasy.

I dipped my fingers lower, stroking between my thighs and sending a shiver up my spine at the memory of the intensity he possessed, of how it felt when it was focused on me. Getting myself off rarely worked for me, but I stroked again and again, enjoying the warm flutters of sensation the desire sent through my body. I wished I had longer arms or was more flexible because I was so close, but I finally shut off the shower and stepped out into the steamy room. My phone sat on the counter by the sink, and I flipped it over as I strode into the bedroom to find pajamas. I had a message waiting from Deacon.

> DEACON: How's my favorite shirt?

I grinned and sat on the edge of the bed. I snapped a photo of the shirt on the corner of my bed.

> WILLOW: Safe and sound.
>
> DEACON: But no longer wrapped around you.
>
> DEACON: Poor shirt.

I grinned, my stomach swooping, knowing this back-and-forth could lead somewhere now, and my pussy pulsed again, my body unsatisfied with my lackluster shower efforts.

> WILLOW: I just got out of the shower.
>
> DEACON: Tell me about it.

I sucked in a breath when I read his message and looked around as if someone might be watching me, but all I saw were the red walls we'd painted together.

> WILLOW: The shower?

The phone buzzed in my hand, and a request for a video call came through from Deacon.

"You want to know about my shower?"

"I want to hear about how you felt in the shower." His eyes widened as my image came through on the screen. "Low, you're still in a towel." His own hair was wet, and he was shirtless against his wooden headboard. "Get dressed before this conversation."

"Why? You're shirtless. That's not fair." I squeezed my thighs at how naughty this felt. This was exactly what I wanted when I added it to page two, this kind of pleasure-riddled anticipation.

"Okay. Let me see," he said. "Show me the full effect of Willow in a towel." His voice was low and slow, and I swallowed, suddenly nervous, but I propped the phone on the bed and took a few steps back so he could see my full body with the towel wrapped around me. It wasn't a large towel, and a slit over my thigh showed off more of my legs and a hint at my hip and belly.

"Holy shit, Low." I could see his gaze move up and down the length of the phone screen. I stroked a hand self-consciously along the terry cloth and noticed the sliver of thigh he would see where the towel didn't come together. "I've never seen you in so little."

"I took off my pants that night after the wedding." I considered walking back toward the phone but stayed where I was, knowing he was looking at me.

"I was being a gentleman," he said, his voice still in that low, gravelly timbre. "I didn't look."

"You're looking now."

"I don't plan to be very gentlemanly during this conversation." I saw his eyes move, and I wondered where on my body he was looking.

"That should make me nervous," I said, taking the few steps back toward the bed to snag my phone. "But it doesn't. Weird, huh?"

He held the phone away from him, and I saw his hand resting over his taut stomach. I imagined it dipping lower, but he spoke again, the hand unmoving. "But please put on clothes before you tell me about your shower. My head might explode if I know you're naked."

I chuckled and set the phone face down on the comforter, pulling his shirt on over my head and climbing onto my bed, taking the phone with me. "Better?" I asked.

"You're wearing my shirt again," he said, running a hand through his damp hair and pushing it off his face.

"It's soft," I added, stroking the fabric over my belly. The Air Force logo was faded and the fabric worn and lived-in.

"You look good in it." His voice dipped again, the rumble low and delicious. "Tell me about the shower."

I giggled self-consciously. "What do you want to know?"

His palm rubbed across his stomach, and my heartbeat sped, imagining doing the same. Deacon's body was insane, and his abs were ripped and brushed with a smattering of dark hair that disappeared under the waistline of his pants. "You had dirty talk on your list. What do you want to happen? What was the first time like?"

I scrunched my nose and Deacon chuckled. "Uh-oh."

"It's not bad—he was abroad on a trip for a few weeks and I thought it would be fun to try but it felt really awkward. He was uncomfortable using any of the words and kept laughing when I'd say something. I wanted to really try and he couldn't. It was sweet, just not . . ."

"What you wanted."

I giggled, hoping it hid my inexperience, and tucked my hair behind my ear.

His fingers glided across his scruffy jawline, the pad of his thumb trailing over his lower lip. His gaze lowered on the screen, and I had the sense he was imagining looking down my body. I flushed at the feeling. "And then there's . . ."

"What?" My voice sounded breathless, and I squeezed my thighs together.

"Eager?"

My cheeks heated. "Just . . . curious."

He grinned. "Letting the other person control or guide things."

"Oh." I gulped. "So, you'd tell me where to . . . and what to . . ."

"And how to." His voice rumbled through the phone. He rubbed a hand over his lower lip again, and I studied him on the screen. "Anything happen in the shower you want to share?"

I swallowed, remembering the feel of my own fingers brushing between my legs. "Kind of."

"Mmm," he said, the groan low and rumbling. "Did you touch yourself?"

I squeezed my thighs on instinct. My experience with talking about things like this was pretty light, and no one had ever asked me that before. Dampness pooled between my thighs at admitting it to him. I nodded. "I did."

"Where?"

I opened my mouth and then closed it, stuck on what to say and afraid he'd laugh at me. "I'm sorry," I said. "I've never described it to someone. I don't know what words to use."

"It's okay," he said, that hand lazily moving over his stomach. "Use whatever words feel right or you don't have to tell me. It's all up to you."

"No," I said, feeling my nipples pucker under the shirt. "I want to tell you. It's . . . kind of hot."

He nodded again, his smile slowly tipping up.

"I played with my nipples." I looked down at my chest, where they peeked out below the camera's reach. "They were . . . sensitive."

Deacon's expression was unchanged, even as my breath sped. "Are they usually sensitive? Do you like having them touched? Licked?"

I nodded, goose bumps rising all over my body at the sound of his voice. I brushed a thumb against one nipple now to relieve the ache, and I shivered at my touch.

"Are you touching them now?" His question caught me off guard, and I stilled, sucking in a breath at being caught.

"No! Of course not," I said, holding up my hand in front of the camera.

"Liar." Deacon's laugh rumbled through the phone. "How do you like to touch them?"

My embarrassment at being caught faded immediately into a full-body flush at his question. "You really want me to describe it?"

"Tell me."

I shivered at his command, feeling the rumble of his voice through my core. "I stroke them with my thumbs and then kind of roll them." I held up my fingers to show the motion.

Deacon groaned again, and his hand moved lower on his stomach toward the end of the screen. "Put your hand down, Low." God, that voice when he was turned on. Deacon's voice was sexy and irresistible, and the command in his tone sent a quiver down to my core. "I don't need to know what you're doing off-screen."

I swallowed and lowered my fingers, intentionally brushing my nipples as I did. "This feels so . . ."

"Naughty?" he offered.

"Good," I corrected, letting out a little sigh. I leaned back against the pillows and tweaked my nipples again. On the screen, Deacon's eyes flashed and his shoulders tensed, and I liked that I could make him do that.

"Did you touch yourself anywhere else? Did you stroke your pussy?" He chuckled at my reaction to the word I wasn't sure I'd ever heard a man say out loud, at least not in this way. "You like me saying that?"

I nodded and saw his hand dip out of the frame. "Tell me about it," he said.

"I, um, slid my finger along my slit and then around my clit in circles." I grew wetter between my thighs and squeezed them together, watching his eyes flash at my words.

Deacon's breathing sped up, and I wanted to ask him if he was touching himself. Imagining that had me squirming. "Did you come?"

I shook my head. "No. I don't usually get myself there, but it felt good. I can never get the angles right. My orgasms are kind of . . . fickle." A flush rose on my chest—I'd faked it more than once with Spencer, ashamed I couldn't cross the finish line.

Deacon's brows lifted, but then his expression relaxed. "You said it was good. Tell me about it."

I swallowed. "Tingly, and like little sparks of electricity were moving through me. It was hard to stop. It felt really good." I let my eyelids fall closed and my fingers dip lower down my stomach.

"You don't have to tell me what you're doing off-screen, Low," he repeated, voice like gravel. "But if it feels good, don't stop."

I let my fingers move lower, my knees falling apart. Was I really going to do this while on the phone with Deacon?

"And if you don't want to do it with me on the phone, hang up."

I shook my head. "Don't go." I moved my fingers lower and stroked along my slit where I was wet, my motion sending a wave of pleasure as I stroked the already sensitive skin, and I let out a whimper, repeating the motion.

"Fuck, Willow," he said, on a groan, his cool mask disappearing and his muscles tense. "You're killing me."

"It feels good," I said. "But I wish I could come."

His voice was strained. "Do you have a toy?"

"No." I shook my head. "I've never known how to buy one or which to pick." I grazed my finger around my clit, tipping my head back as a flash of sensation rolled through me and then dissipated.

His voice was ragged. "Keep doing what feels good. Are you wet?"

I flushed again, heat running up my neck at the question. "Yes."

"Are you circling your clit?"

I pulsed at his words, the direct, commanding tone I felt in my core. "Yes," I said on a pant.

"Keep going," he said. "Don't stop while it feels good."

"I can't believe I'm doing this," I said, the tension growing in my belly.

"I bet you look beautiful with your legs spread wide."

"Do you want to see?" I bit my lip, focusing on keeping my movements the same, noticing the wave growing and growing, the sensations with each swipe coiling in my belly.

"Don't worry about me," he growled now, his gaze so heated. "Focus on you. Focus on that pretty, slick pussy. Focus on that needy, throbbing clit." His words were like bolts of lightning within my body as they landed, and I bit my lip at the feeling of the elusive build, the tightening and tingling. "You don't need another person to get you this wet and ready. Focus on how good you feel right now and let me imagine what you'll look like right before I slide my tongue over you."

"I'm so close," I said. "I'm never close."

"Put the phone down and play with your nipples while you come, Low."

I was on the razor's edge and tossed the phone down next to me, rubbing my free thumb over my nipple, and the coil snapped. I let out a yelp as tiny points of light appeared behind my eyes and groaned as wave after wave moved through me.

I collapsed against the pillows and remembered to pick up the phone, where I saw Deacon grinning, his gaze hooded. "So fucking hot," he said.

My body was on fire, my cheeks flaming from the embarrassment of doing that in front of him and from the force of the orgasm. "I can almost never make myself do that. You're really good at dirty talk."

He chuckled, his voice strained. "You did most of the talking."

"It's your turn," I said, wondering what his hand was doing off-screen. "I want to turn you on, too."

He laughed and the sound warmed me. "How could I hear that and not be insanely turned on?"

"Proof or it didn't happen." I still felt my pulse race, and I eagerly clutched the phone.

"Bold after coming, huh?" He lowered the camera and I saw his erection bulging under his sweats, his fingers wrapped around it in a long stroke.

I swallowed thickly, feeling anticipation rise at the sight of him thick in his hand. "Can I see you?"

"Slow down, page two. Why don't you go to sleep? I think that's all for tonight."

I was disappointed, but my body felt so languid that I nodded, unsure how to sign this off. Did I say thank you? Was asking what we'd do next too needy?

"You were perfect tonight, Low." His smile was genuine and

warm, and my stomach flipped. "Thank you for being so brave with me. We'll talk tomorrow."

I fell back against the pillows, hugging his soft shirt to me, and watched Gus wander into the room, eyeing me curiously. "This might be the best decision I've ever made, Gus."

CHAPTER 26

THE BARKS OF laughter carried down the hall from the Veterans Center, the sound of four or five voices talking over one another before another peal of laughter filled the otherwise quiet corridor of the student union. It reminded me of the thousands of times I'd had moments like that with my squad, shooting the shit between missions or drills or just because. I quickened my pace to pass the open door, still clocking the group inside, including a few people I recognized from around campus. One raised a hand to wave. I recognized him and slowed. He looked like a Marine, hair still buzzed short, and we'd had some classes together where we were the only people over twenty-five. For the first time, I was tempted to go in, but I kept walking. I looked at my phone intently and scrolled to the thread with Willow, rereading the last few messages from the day before.

WILLOW: I can't believe you sent me ten different ideas for toys!

> DEACON: Just to get you started. The options are vast.
>
> WILLOW: How will I choose?
>
> DEACON: Get them all 😈

There was another burst of laughter from down the hall, and I tapped at my screen, checking the clock. I still had an hour to kill before my next class.

> DEACON: Make a choice?

I waited for her to respond. As it was, I hadn't stopped thinking about her since that night on the phone. I thought it would be a little sexy banter to get her comfortable. I had not expected to coach her through an orgasm or the way it would knock me on my ass when she got there and I saw the way her neck and cheeks reddened. Outside of the many, many ways that turned me on, it was more. She'd trusted me so completely, which filled my chest in a way nothing ever had.

> WILLOW: I picked two.
>
> DEACON: I'm all ears.
>
> WILLOW: Only ears? Disappointing.

I grinned at the surprising response and ran a hand through my hair.

> DEACON: What will you care? You'll have toys.

> WILLOW: I got these.

She pasted in a screenshot of her order confirmation, and I took in a ragged breath. She'd actually bought three items, a rabbit-style vibrator with a pink silicone shaft and a purple clitoral stimulator. Then there was a black satin blindfold.

> DEACON: You definitely found #3 on your own. Interesting.
>
> WILLOW: It was free when I spent enough!

The noise from down the hall drew my gaze away. Cruz had bugged me plenty of times to check out the center, but I'd ignored him, like I'd ignored his warnings to stay away from Willow. I thought things would be fine, though. What was important was that we had an agreement and she wouldn't get hurt. That was his main concern. Plus, there were a ton of things we could do that were only nudging the line without fully crossing it. I hit the icon to call her.

"Blindfolds can be fun," I said when she picked up, and I couldn't see her face, but I knew she'd be adorably flustered. "You keep surprising me."

"I didn't pick it! They just added it to the order." I heard sounds of the road in the background.

"Hmm, but would you have?" I leaned against the wall and crossed my arms over my chest, knowing she was thinking about it. "Never mind. Don't tell me . . . I'll wait to be surprised once it arrives."

"Aren't you supposed to be in class?"

"On a break. I thought you'd be missing me."

The road sounds on her end gave way to barking. "I'm at the dog park with Gus," she said, and I listened as she gave him the "at the ready" command Cruz required before he'd send Gus into the fray with all the other dogs. "And I missed you a little." She paused as I soaked in the words, but corrected herself. "Missed that filthy mouth," she whispered, as if not to offend Gus's delicate sensibilities, and then giggled. It was fucking adorable.

"You have no idea," I said, tucking one ankle over the other. "But you will. When does your shipment arrive?"

"Tomorrow," she said, releasing Gus to play. "What class did you have this morning?"

"English. We had to write a short story. I made mine about a girl who discovered something magical she could do with the right inspiration." I pitched my voice low the way she liked, but she laughed on the other end of the phone.

"Shut up! I'm at the dog park!" She lowered her voice again and whispered, "I can't do dirty talk here."

I laughed again at her concern—that dog park was huge, and I could guarantee no one was nearby. I hadn't wanted to get her going, though; I just wanted to hear her laugh. "Fine," I said, returning to my normal voice. "I did have English, though—ready to be done with that class." I'd picked psychology when I needed to declare a program of study, and I liked it, but spending time with Jayden made me wonder if I should pick up some kind of education class. I wouldn't need it in the PJs, but maybe for after.

"You had that vet school tour this morning, right?"

"It was, wow, incredible. I wished Des had more time, because I would have stayed there all day. They showed me their labs and classrooms and, damn, it all just looked so fantastic." She spoke quickly, like the words and ideas couldn't come out fast enough. "I really didn't want to leave."

"Time to bite the bullet and apply," I said. State was only half an hour away, and the idea of having her nearby made my heart beat faster.

"I've been out of school for so long. It feels too late." I pictured her nibbling on the corner of her thumbnail the way she did when she was thinking about something too hard. I wondered if she'd done that after our call. Before I could fixate on that, she continued. "It was my dream, but I gave it up. It feels hard to turn back to it. And vet programs are all supercompetitive."

"I told you. Competition ain't a thing when you're the best," I said, tipping my head back against the wall. "And is it ever too late to give up on a dream?" I thought of my own goals and the notebook where I was tracking my progress for the fitness test.

She chuckled and paused for a moment where I heard her sweet-talk Gus. "I'm not the best," she said. "Competition is definitely a thing for me."

That flicker of self-doubt in her words would show in the angle of her smile, and I hated to see it. "I think you're the best person I know. I can't imagine someone better." My words were drowned out by barking and Willow's voice.

"Sorry, what did you say?"

What did I say? Rather, why did I say it? I bumped my head against the wall. "Nothing, just that you should think about applying."

"Maybe," she said. "I'll think about it. I'll see Des tomorrow. A group of us are going to go see *Steel Magnolias*. That theater by the airport is doing a special showing."

I grinned and lifted my head at the change of subject. I adopted my best Southern accent and shared my favorite line from the film I'd watched a hundred times with my grandma when I was a kid.

"Oh my God! Yes!" Her voice was back to normal, bouncy and light. "I can't believe you've seen it. It was actually my mom's favorite movie. Feels kind of symbolic to go see it now since she can't, I guess."

"It's a good one."

"Do you want to go with us? I like having you along with me for my re-dos."

I wanted to say yes. I imagined my arm around her and the way she'd snuggle against me in the dark after our hands mingled in the popcorn bucket. "No," I said, bending to pull my textbook from my bag like a prop would help sell the lie. "I should study." I didn't need opportunities to touch her in the dark. I'd already blown past the lines I'd set for myself when it came to Willow. "But what's next on your list?"

"It involves riding and protection," she said playfully.

"Tease." I glanced down the hall toward the center when a few new people walked in and the group called out to them with greetings. "It's bikes, isn't it?"

"Yes." Willow's giggle left me smiling, even if the joke wasn't that funny. "But I thought you'd appreciate the double entendre."

"I did." I snagged my bag from the floor and slung it over my shoulder, deciding to kill time outside. "Tomorrow?"

"I can use Cruz's bike. It's mounted up on the wall in the garage, though." I thought of her struggles to get the ladder up from the basement herself and offered to come over after class when I had a few minutes this afternoon to get it down and fill the tire.

"Fill the tire. That's not a euphemism, is it?"

I grinned. "Not this time."

CHAPTER 27

Willow

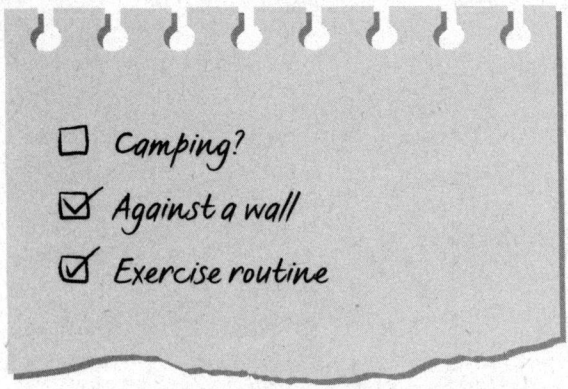

SHORTLY AFTER DISCONNECTING with Deacon, my phone pinged next to me with a text from Zoe that included a link to an airline website.

ZOE: I miss you. Flights to Colorado are cheap now. Come hoooooome!

WILLOW: What would we do?

ZOE: Whatever the hell we want. Maybe ride a Bronco...

ZOE: And by that I mean a football player.

WILLOW: I'm more of a Cowboys fan.

ZOE: Save a horse?

I looked at the flights she'd sent, and she was right—the flights to Denver were cheap. After a couple minutes, my phone flashed with an incoming call.

"I'm just looking at the flights," I began. "But I shouldn't. I'm living on my savings right now. Plus my volunteer job. I'm putting in fifteen to twenty hours a week, and I enrolled in that GRE prep course to prepare for the standardized admission test I'll need for vet school. I've got so many things to figure out."

"Figure them out with me! I'm the smartest person you know."

I clicked through the departure options. "Didn't you pepper spray yourself recently?"

"That notwithstanding. Let's do it!"

"I visited the vet school today," I said, changing the subject. "It was really amazing."

Zoe would always be my cheerleader. "All the more reason to escape now, before you have to study all the time! You'll never have time to escape to the woods with me on a whim when you're a hotly recruited vet student."

"It's not that easy. It's hard to even get into a program. The acceptance rates are lower than most medical schools, and all the materials I had prepared are still at Spencer's place."

She gave an audible grunt of disgust at his name. "After we get back from the trip, I'll break into his house and steal them for you."

I laughed at the idea of her dressed as a cat burglar all in black, especially since everything in the house was so beige and she would stand out. "I can ask him for it like an adult." Unless he had thrown away the things I'd left. I hadn't realized I'd left them until I was moved out, and by then, I couldn't bear the thought of seeing him. "And I don't know about the trip."

"Ooh! A trip. Where are you going?" Hollis appeared at the fence, arms crossed over it.

I twisted the phone toward her. "Zoe, this is Hollis." My neighbor waved, and I walked toward the fence.

"I love your hair!" Zoe said, and Hollis tossed it on her shoulder dramatically. "I'm trying to talk her into a trip back to Colorado to go camping."

"You should!" Hollis exclaimed, "S'mores!"

"That's what I said," Zoe added. "I like her. Hollis, come with us. Any friend of Willow's with such great hair and ideas is someone I want to hang with!"

"It was your idea," I said, with an eye roll, but Hollis was already nodding.

"C'mon, Willow. You can be away from your brother's hot bestie for a few days," Zoe said.

"Oh, we're talking about Deacon. I'm here for this," Hollis added.

"I don't need to see Deacon every day," I threw back, even though we *did* talk every day, and since that night on the phone, I spent a lot of my day and more of my evenings thinking about him than I should. We'd watched three episodes of a medical drama we'd both been wanting to catch the night before over the phone. When he called, I thought he'd want a replay of our dirty talk session, but we'd gotten sucked into the show. He pointed out everything that was inaccurate, and I told him which cast members I thought were hot. I'd always wondered if he planned to use his EMT training outside of the military, and he'd said that he didn't, even when I commented about the average hotness of the EMTs on the show. He really hated talking about any future that didn't involve the military.

My stomach hurt from laughing by the time we hung up. It ended up being even better than a sexy call. I rarely let myself laugh when I was worried about Cruz, but something about Deacon made it okay, made it feel safe, and I knew he was also worrying about my brother.

"Well, then it's a deal. I found a great campsite. Hollis, are you free next weekend? Flights are really cheap. And the airline is . . . questionable, but still . . . cheap flights."

"I didn't agree to go yet," I reminded her.

Hollis ignored my hedge. "Isn't camping on your list, anyway? We'll make s'mores!"

"I have to find someone to take care of Gus," I hedged, watching him run the perimeter of the yard in search of his favorite ball. "Cruz loves no one more than this dog." Mentioning Cruz made the familiar string of worry about him tighten in my chest.

Hollis chimed in. "Hmm . . . If only you knew someone who both loved dogs and would do anything for you . . ."

"It's not like that." I bit my lower lip.

Zoe laughed. "Except that it is . . ." She yelped. "Shit! I just spilled orange soda all over my boss's dog inside her Porsche. I gotta go."

I had so many questions, like why she was driving her boss's Porsche, and how she spilled orange soda on the dog while doing so. But I guess I could ask her while we were camping.

"If he can't, Blaine can," Hollis offered. "Assuming you're actually okay with me coming."

"It would be fun to hang out with you both." It really would be—they were both so enigmatic, and I felt more alive when I was with them. Hollis and I had started walking every morning—it felt good to start my day moving and laughing. I'd never had a regular routine like that before.

She looked at her phone. "Oops. Des is waiting, but text me what you decide!"

I walked toward the house. Spending money on a flight was irresponsible when I was between jobs, but she was right—camping was on my list. I toggled over to Deacon's contact, my finger over the call button once I got back in the house. Before I could hit it, there was a knock at the door.

"Bike mechanic at your service," he said when I opened the door. I fought the urge to greet him with a kiss—every cell in my body wanted to, but that's not what this was, so I held out my hand for a professional handshake.

"You come highly recommended."

"Oh, I come *very* highly recommended," he said with a wink. "All my clients are *very* satisfied."

I nodded toward the garage. "You don't have to convince me," I said as we made our way through the house. I'd gotten a few peeks at how satisfying he could be, but I didn't expect his fingers to close around my wrist and then back me up against the wall. Deacon's big, hard form pressed me forward, and his head dipped to my neck, his nose sliding up along my throat. I let out a whimper. I couldn't help it. His hand steadied my waist, set firmly in place, but it felt like he was touching me everywhere.

"I don't have to convince you?"

"Um," I said, taking in the feel of his breath on my neck. "No," I said, my voice more of a squeak than I planned.

"Hmm." He hummed against my skin and, my God, it was hot in here. "I might still try." Deacon squeezed my waist and his lips brushed the shell of my ear and he spoke low, making my legs feel like jelly. "God, you smell so damn good."

I swallowed hard at his words, but Deacon stepped back after a beat. He looked from my lips to my eyes. "I don't think that counts," he said. "I can do better."

"Counts?" My mind was awhirl, and my body was still making its way back to earth from whatever that was. "Better?"

He grinned and traced a finger down my bare arm. "You had against the wall on your list, but I can do better. I never asked exactly what you wanted against a wall."

"That was . . ." I squeezed my thighs together, needing some kind of friction after that. "You surprised me."

"I'll warn you next time," he said, taking another step toward the garage. I really wondered if Deacon understood how unexpected he was. I'd had the wall on my list because I'd told my ex how sexy the idea of making out against a wall was to me, but he'd insisted it was inefficient and we'd end up knocking down artwork. It wasn't really about the wall in any case—it was about the overpowering need, the craving. I wanted him to feel that way about me. I definitely hadn't been concerned about the artwork on the walls with Deacon.

He was already taking the bike down off the hooks on the

wall when I followed behind him. "What do we have here?" he said, dropping to his knees to inspect the tires. His growly, sexy voice was back to normal, and I did my best to pretend I was, too.

"The tires need air," I said, snagging a hand pump from a shelf nearby. "I can fill them, but could you adjust the seat?" The metal of the pump was cold in my hands, but did little to cool down how heated I felt from the moment in the house. I fiddled with the valve cap and felt his gaze on me.

"I was going to be a gentleman and do it for you," he said, his big body angled against the concrete where he was leaning, toying with a wrench he'd taken from its spot on the wall. "But if a woman insists on pumping something, I won't ever fight her."

I chuckled, his blatant innuendo cutting the tension. "I can do *some* things myself," I mused, not taking the bait on his comments as I pumped air into the tire, conscious of how he was watching me as I stepped onto the footholds and pressed down on the handle with both hands. "And even you can't find a bike pump sexy."

When I looked over my shoulder, his gaze was on my chest where my breasts were pressed together from the motion, causing, from my vantage point, a kind of pornographic level of cleavage.

"Yeah, we can agree to disagree on that," he said, patting the seat as I finished with the second tire, double-checking the air pressure. "Excited to try this out?"

"Yeah," I answered. "Love learning something new."

"So I've seen," he said with an exaggerated wink, and I wished I had something to throw at him, but I still laughed. "Can you hold this?" He handed me a wrench he'd been using on a bolt to lower the seat, and our fingers grazed over the metal of the tool. I admired the muscles of his back under the shirt as he worked the seat down, and when he spoke again, it startled me. "Try this," he said, patting his palm on the seat. "See if it's the right height."

It was awkward to climb onto the bike with him right there, but the height seemed good, and I settled my hands on the handlebars but froze when Deacon's fingertip moved up my calf. "So, was there a big, meaningful significance to the wall?" He asked it as he tightened the seat again. "I mean, anything I should know before the next time?"

I didn't move as his finger moved in circles over my skin. "Um, no," I said. "I always . . . wanted it." I glanced down, watching Deacon's gaze following his fingertip over my leg. "There will be a next time?"

He wrapped his fingers around my ankle and tugged on my leg until I met his eyes. "Definitely."

"I'll be done with my list in no time," I said, climbing off the bike and ignoring how that one word made my heart rate speed up. "Um, speaking of the list. Can I ask another favor of you?"

"Well . . . the last favor you asked was pretty interesting. I'm all ears."

I smiled wide, glad he couldn't see the effect that simple statement had on me. "Could you watch Gus next weekend? Zoe wants to go camping in Colorado. She invited Hollis. I think they're going to be best friends."

"Sure," he said. "Zoe seems a little wild . . . Will you be safe with her and an open flame?"

"Safer than any Denver Broncos who might camp nearby. She has big plans for finding someone besides me to warm up her sleeping bag."

"Be careful," he said, his voice sounding serious. "I mean, I wouldn't trust any guys in the woods, including professional football players."

"Well, I wasn't planning on it," I said. "I'll be focused on the stick holding my marshmallow."

I thought the joke was pretty good, but when Deacon spoke again, his voice was still serious. "I can walk you through some self-defense moves, just in case," he added.

"My older brother is Cruz Lewis. Do you honestly think I don't know self-defense moves? I could take you down."

Deacon chuckled. "Fair enough."

A silence drew between us for a moment at the mention of Cruz, and I could almost feel the weight of one of his bear hugs on my shoulders. I spotted the stack of boxes from Mom's place I'd brought up from the basement but hadn't opened yet. Every time I planned to do it, something held me back. Most recently, worrying about Cruz. "Is it wrong for me to be considering doing something fun while he's out there risking his life in some dangerous situation?"

Deacon was quiet for a few beats and then pressed his thumb into the bike's tire. "If you let that stop you, you'd never consider having fun. It's always risky; there's always the potential for danger." His gaze was focused on the tire, but it looked like his mind was somewhere else. Probably somewhere risky with the potential for danger. A different fear than what I was used to with Cruz clawed into my brain, into my heart. He wanted to go back to those places more than anything, and that terrified me.

"That doesn't make me feel better!"

"Sorry," he said, finally looking up at me sheepishly. "Go camping. Keep Zoe from sexually harassing a football team."

Deacon fiddled with the chain. "I'm sure he's good. Our buddy Dougy is in logistics now, and if something bad happened, he'd give me a heads-up."

I steadied the bike. "I didn't know they did that. I thought it was, you know, classified or need to know only."

He shrugged. "It is."

"You're just so well-connected it doesn't matter?"

"There are the rules," he said, pumping air into the tire with smooth movements, his biceps flexing. "And then there's brotherhood." He shrugged and checked the tire's pressure again. "No word from Dougy means you can go camping, guilt-free."

"Not until we ride, though." I wanted to change the subject. I saw the shadow crossing his face. "I can't in good conscience go camping until I learn to ride." I held out my hand to help him off the floor, and the warmth of his palm against mine sent a shiver down my spine. He gripped my hand but rose to his feet on his own, his body only inches from mine in the garage. "Thanks for looking at the bike."

"Anything for you," he said, not stepping back, his gaze moving over my face.

The way he looked at me was kind of how Spencer had once upon a time, like my face was an endlessly fascinating thing. I wondered if I could ever trust a look like that again. With Spencer, it had ended without warning. With Deacon, it was just . . . Deacon being himself.

ZOE: You're in, right?

In my heart, I knew I shouldn't trust those looks—it was merely physical attraction. It hit me in waves that I'd been waiting for those kinds of looks for years, hoping and craving to see affirmation that I was wanted and loved.

I tapped out a reply to Zoe and added Hollis to the thread before sending. I had to break that habit, and that's what this re-do list was giving me. I glanced back up and caught the tail end of Deacon's assessing gaze, his soft eyes and the quirk of his lips. I had to figure out how to be enough for myself so those kinds of looks didn't hit me so squarely in the chest every time.

WILLOW: I'm in.

CHAPTER 28

"SERIOUSLY?" I EYED the molded plastic Willow held out to me the next day in the park. "A helmet?"

"When you ride a bike, you wear protection." She thrust it at me again. "Those are the rules."

"For children," I said, grudgingly accepting it. I pointed at the lightning bolt on the side. "Wait." I pulled it onto my head, feeling the snug fit. "Is this actually made for a child?"

She laughed, the sound reaching into my chest somehow just before she gave me a light shove. "No! It's adult size, it's just . . ." She giggled when I pointed to the lightning bolt again. "Peppy."

I pointed to her knee pads, which were lime green and reminded me of the ones Margot Robbie and Ryan Gosling wore in the *Barbie* movie. "I'm not wearing those. Or the elbow pads. A man has to have a little pride."

"A man is going to need Band-Aids," she said, ignoring my jibes and squeezing the brakes on the ten-speed bike in front of her.

"Now, knee pads could have other, more fun uses . . ." I raised my eyebrows and earned another shove in the chest. "Fine," I said, reluctantly fastening the helmet and picking my bike—well, Marcus's bike I'd borrowed—off the ground. "How do we do this?"

She shrugged and straddled the bike seat, which we'd had to lower significantly from where Cruz had it. I tried not to watch her legs and how her thighs parted with the movement. "How did you learn when you were a kid?"

"I don't remember," I said. "I probably figured it out on my own—my parents worked a lot." I set Marcus's bike down and strode to her. "C'mon. I'll hold the seat to get you started," I said, making a grab for the molded plastic and not so subtly stroking her butt, though I jumped back in time to avoid the next swat she sent my way.

"I do actually want to learn to ride. Don't distract me." She gave me a cutting look that felt more like she was trying not to laugh. The hot pink bike helmet pushed down on her forehead did little to enhance her intimidation tactics, and I lifted it up and back slightly for her, the tip of my pinky moving along the soft skin over her eyebrows. When I slid a wayward curl out of her face, her expression softened. "I need you to be my drill sergeant."

"Consider me your MTI," I said, placing my hands firmly on her shoulders and catching her confused expression as if she was running through all the possibilities for the acronym. "Military Training Instructor. Drill sergeants are for the Army, and you don't want one of those guys when you have me." I squeezed her shoulders. "Eyes forward and grip the handles." I watched her fingers tighten around the rubber, which I definitely didn't find strangely erotic. That bikes might be a new kink crossed my mind. "Remember that you're in control. If you lean, the bike leans. If you move forward, the bike does as well."

"Got it," she said resolutely, bouncing a bit on the seat. "But . . . you'll still hold on, right?"

"Count on me," I said, gripping the seat, but this time stopping myself from touching her, though I can't say I didn't let my gaze linger a little. The seat was awkward to hold on to, and I realized a little too late I had no idea what I was doing, but that had never stopped me before. "Place one foot on the pedal and then, when you're ready, the other." Her body tensed as she balanced on the bike before slamming her feet back down.

"That is so weird," she said, smiling over her shoulder. The park was mostly empty with a few walkers and a couple parents with strollers, so we mostly had the area of the path to ourselves. "It feels like I'm going to fall."

"You're right . . ." I tapped her neon-colored elbow pads. "Think you need more safety gear? Some Bubble Wrap?"

"You're such a dick," she said with a laugh, once again gripping the handlebars. "Let me try again."

"This time, pedal forward." I leaned closer to her ear. "You've got this. It'll probably feel natural to go slow, but if you go too slow, you'll tip over, so keep going." She was focused on the path ahead of her but gave a sharp inhale when my breath grazed her ear. I never claimed to be a saintly instructor. "Ready?"

She nodded and I patted her back, taking hold of the back of the bike, and she pushed on the pedals in earnest. "Faster," I said, striding along beside her. "Ride like you want to make it hard for me."

"You're a pig," she said over her shoulder as she sped up, the bike wobbling but staying upright.

"Oink, oink, baby." She sped up, though, the bike wobbling less, and I moved into a jog behind her. "Low, you're doing it."

"I'm doing it!" she cheered for herself.

"I'm going to let go."

"No!"

"Yes!"

"No!" She kept pedaling, maybe even faster. "I'm not ready yet. Don't let go." She wobbled forward along the path and then glanced back to see me waving both hands. "You let go!"

"A while ago." I let her ride ahead of me, admiring the lines and curves of her body as she rode, and the way her cheeks looked from this angle as she smiled. "You're a natural!" I called out down the path, earning a smile over her shoulder, before she veered into a bush.

"Shit!" I ran to Willow and helped her climb out of the bush, but she laughed and brushed a hand down her body.

"Good thing I was protected," she said, tapping the elbow pads. "Never mock my safety precautions."

She took my hand and stepped over a root sticking out of the ground. "Can you help me get started again?" She beamed—from her smile to her bright eyes, her whole face lit up. My heart lurched at the overwhelming sensation of being proud of her, excited for her, and I nodded, holding on to the back of the bike again.

"Let's go." I ran behind her for just a few moments this time before I let go. She wobbled again at first, but then moved down the path at a steady speed. "Stay out of the bush!" I called after her and thought about following it up with "That's advice I never take myself," but since a group of women who looked to be young mothers and their toddlers approached from the other direction, I kept my commentary to myself. Willow slowly circled the small section of the park and pulled back around toward me. "Now use the brakes," I instructed, but jumped out of the way when she veered toward me without slowing down, only to pull into the grass. She almost tipped over but caught herself in time.

"Stopping needs a little work," she said with a huff when I approached. "That was kind of a fail."

I opened my mouth to speak, but she held up a palm.

"Let me guess. Are you about to say, 'Don't stop, baby,' or something equally sexual?"

I hadn't even thought about it, actually. "I was going to say you're doing great." I tried to picture the Willow from our first meeting—covering her face in embarrassment and trying to hide behind anything she could. I'd liked her from the jump despite that, but this Willow . . . I couldn't take my eyes off her, and not because of her face or her body. It was her posture—her shoulders were back and her smile was wide and she wasn't hiding anything. She moved like she was in charge of the ground beneath her feet, and I felt like I was witness to her blossoming. "You're amazing." I held out my palm for a high five, and her hand connected with mine. "Again?"

"Yes." Her palm lingered against mine for a moment, and she grinned, that kind of determined grin I noticed she got when she was tackling things on her list. "Let's go again."

CHAPTER 29

Willow

☑ Learning to ~~drive~~ ride

"I DON'T THINK I can hold the bike up with you on it," I said, trying again to get a grip on the seat. The sun was high in the sky. I wiped my brow and pushed my sleeves up on my arms.

"That's okay." Deacon shrugged and straddled the seat. "I used to know how to ride. I assume this will come back to me fast." His shoulders and muscled arms strained the give of his T-shirt, and I allowed myself a few moments to admire the muscles of his back, rationalizing that was within the bounds of our agreement. He had sent me sex toy recommendations between classes, after all.

"You sure?" I looked at the bike with skepticism. I had been shocked how unsteady I felt once both my feet were off the ground. "It was really helpful when you were holding on for me."

"I'm always sure," he said, giving me that cocky fucking smirk that melted me a little more every time. "Watch the magic," he said, propping one foot on the pedal and pushing off.

The bike rolled for a few feet, and then he immediately tipped to the side with a loud and kind of comical "Whoooa!" followed by a louder "Fuck!" that earned glares from a small group of parents nearby watching their toddlers run in circles.

"Sorry," I said with a wave at their disapproving stares. "He's a veteran," I called out, hoping to smooth things over or at least make them feel bad about judging. I reached him in two steps—that big man went down hard and fast—and held out a hand to help him up. "I think we've made some enemies." I'd been gawked at a lot over the past few months, but I'd never been given that particular look of disdain by a stranger before. I kind of liked how it didn't really bother me.

I nodded behind me at the group who'd gone back to focusing on their children, who, to be fair, were just as loud if not as obscene as Deacon. "Are you hurt?"

He grumbled a response I couldn't make out, but begrudgingly took my hand as he untangled himself from the bike.

"I couldn't quite hear you. Did you say, 'Yes, Willow, I'd love the help'?" I tried to pull him up, but he was doing most of the work there, and the pressure on my hand increased, reminding me of the night in the park, of the way his grip had tightened against me.

"Again," he said, lifting the bike and throwing one leg over it and ignoring my taunt. "Just need to get used to it." His jaw was set, and he put one foot on the pedal.

"Wait!" I put a hand on his back to stop him, and the tension in his muscle relaxed under my touch.

"What?"

"Your helmet." I stood to his right and placed both hands on either side of the plastic, adjusting it. "It got knocked to the side when you fell." I glanced down at him as I adjusted it, realizing how close my face was to his as the furrow between his brows lessened. He was watching me, and my face heated at the attention.

"Better?"

The intensity of his gaze on me lingered at the front of my mind. Deacon's looks always felt unique, like no one had looked at me quite that way before. "Perfect," I said, backing away. "Are you sure you don't want a hand?"

"No," he said. "I've gone through some of the most taxing training the US Armed Forces could dream up. I don't need help riding a bike." I heard a little annoyance in his voice, and I held up both hands. "But thank you," he said, gripping the handlebars. "For fixing my helmet."

He pushed off again, the bike wobbling and his legs looking unsteady. "Fuck," he said, loudly, as he pulled himself up from a fall. "Shit!"

"Hey!" a petite blonde in big sunglasses called from the group of parents. "There are kids here!"

I waved in acknowledgment, but it was no use.

"Fuck!" The word boomed around the park as Deacon hit the ground hard again, the bike falling on top of him. For the first time, I wondered if this was bad for his back and if I'd end up with a man bathing in his own wounded sense of masculinity. I'd seen that with Cruz sometimes growing up and even with Spencer when I'd bested him at something he thought was tied to his manhood. I bit my lip and approached Deacon.

"Are you okay?" I braced for another grumble or stream of swearing, but he'd already pulled himself out from under the bike and sat with his forearms resting on his knees. His shoulders shook, and he was laughing.

"Yeah," he said, chuckling again. "Maybe I could use your help." He grinned up at me, and I held out a hand for him.

"You think?"

He gripped my hand again, and I soaked in the familiar heat of him as he stood, his body momentarily so close to mine. His thumb made a slow path up the side of mine where our hands were joined, and I felt the same jolt at his touch as the last time. "You like when I do that," he said, stroking again. "You always take in this kind of surprised breath."

I swallowed and met his gaze. "I guess I do," I said, not wanting to give away the other reaction it elicited.

"How's my helmet?" He stroked my thumb again, still holding me close. "Can you fix it for me?"

His helmet was fine, but I still dropped his hand and reached up to touch the sides, my arms brushing the tops of his shoulders. He didn't do anything right away, and I was second-guessing myself until his fingers grazed over my sides in a smooth stroke.

"Interesting. Same breath," he said, doing it again. "Good to know."

I ignored the shiver running up my spine. "Are you hoping to get out of having to try again?"

"Maybe," he said, giving another stroke. "There are other ways to spend our time that might be more fun."

I lowered my hands and reached for his waist, but instead of matching him, I wiggled my fingers, and he squealed and tried to push me away.

"You tickled me!"

"You're ticklish. Also good to know," I said, mimicking his tone. "Let's go again. This time with my help."

He laughed, a real, deep, rumbling laugh, and reached down to pull the bike up. "Fine," he said. "Maybe you're the drill sergeant."

"MTI," I said, enjoying his grin, the real, non-smirky one. "I'm kind of fond of the Air Force lingo now."

He rolled his hand around the handlebar but then kicked the stand so it stood on its own. "Could I borrow your knee and elbow pads?"

"I thought you'd never ask," I said, beginning to unfasten them. The neon color actually looked good on him, and the Velcro strained as he strapped them around his arms and legs.

"I know you're checking me out," he said, still bent over his left knee.

"It wasn't a secret," I said, feeling bold.

Deacon's movements paused, and I thought he'd say something rumbly and sexy and wildly inappropriate, but he just wiggled a little before standing. "Okay." He didn't quite look at me, which was a little disappointing. "Let's go again. I thought muscle memory would kick in, but it's like I've never been on a bike before." He grumbled under his breath, but I heard him say, "Fucking tumor." I'd hoped for more flirty banter, but his voice was all business, in a problem-solving mode, and my earlier disappointment faded fast. "I know you can't hold the bike while I'm on it. Can you hold on to me?" He patted the side of his stomach, and I let my eyes dip to the flat planes of his abs. "Then I can get the hang of the balance."

"Sure," I said, my voice more of a squeak than before. "Right here?" I stood behind him, awkwardly straddling the wheel, and rested my palms on his sides.

"Yeah." He put one foot on a pedal and looked forward. The elbow and knee pads were blindingly bright, and I smiled, appreciating how he'd asked me to borrow them—the last thing I thought he'd do. I tightened my grip as he slowly pedaled forward, and I struggled to keep hold of him as he wobbled, but we stayed upright.

"You ready?" I yelled. It was hard to stay behind the bike, and my arms ached from holding him, but he seemed to wobble less.

"Is that angry mom still there?"

I glanced to the right. "Yeah."

"You ready to fight with me if I say 'fuck' again?"

"Maybe you won't fall this time," I offered, breath coming fast. "Or you could just watch your language."

"I think the odds of a fight are better." He laughed, and I pulled my hands away from his waist, my arm muscles rejoicing but other parts of me missing the contact.

I watched him wobble again, his pedaling slow, but he stayed upright, and I called after him, "I'll always fight with you!"

He raised a fist into the air. "I got it!"

I giggled at his over-the-top celebration and then slapped my hand over my mouth as he yelled, "Fuck!" and toppled to the ground again.

CHAPTER 30

WE WALKED INTO Cruz's place after stowing the bikes in the garage. "Hobbled" was maybe a more accurate descriptor—my back was killing me. "I really thought it would come back to me faster." I sat on the couch and examined the scrape down my arm from my last fall.

"Let me get something to clean that," Willow said, her face adorably scrunched up. "It looks bad."

I waved her off and ignored the sharp pain with the movement. "I'm tough. Don't worry about it."

I bent to stand, and my lower back protested, but Willow must have seen the wince, as she placed a hand on my chest and gently pushed me back. The move was more commanding than I was used to—and I savored how her hand rested on my chest and the firmness in her voice when she said, "Sit."

"I'm fine," I insisted, but I leaned back on the couch as she disappeared into the hall bathroom. I rubbed the side of my leg where a stick had worked its way under the knee pad. I glanced at the neon fabric that I'd tossed aside. I'd been lucky she had those, even though I'd looked like a clumsy tool.

"Didn't your pride already get in your way once today?" Her voice carried from down the hall, and I heard drawers and cabinets opening and closing.

I scratched Gus behind his ears. He'd trotted over when we entered and now rested his snout on my leg. "It's not pride, it's confidence! I'm a machine, baby." Gus looked up at me, his head tilted to the side as if to convey how un-machinelike I looked after a morning spent getting my ass kicked by a ten-speed bike and one 5'2" angry mother who wanted to police my language. "Maybe not," I said more quietly, just to the dog. Cruz had given me that same look, he and his dog like creepy clones of each other, although Cruz had given it to me when I was in the hospital refusing physical therapy.

"Well," Willow said, walking toward me, the purple fabric of her long-sleeved shirt clinging to her chest as she walked. "You're a machine I don't want getting an infection." She set down the first aid kit next to me, along with a wet cloth.

"I'm a machine with extensive EMT training. I can handle it."

She thrust an ice pack toward me. "For your shoulder," she said, motioning to the spot I'd banged into a light pole. "I feel bad," she said, dropping to her knees and tugging my leg forward so she could see the scrape along my knee. "This little adventure was my idea, and you got hurt." She pulled the wipe from the stack and dabbed at the scrape. "Are you going to do that tough-guy thing where you grin and bear the injury only to wince at the alcohol on the cut?"

"Depends." I adjusted my leg so she didn't have to maneuver as much. "Will that keep you on your knees longer?"

She flashed me a playful smile, and then I yelped at the sudden press of the alcohol wipe on the scrape. The burning sensation surprised me. Willow pressed a palm over her mouth, but her giggle escaped. She had such a great laugh, and she shot me another look before refocusing on my scrapes, applying an antibiotic gel and then pressing a Band-Aid over the cut, her delicate fingers sliding along my skin.

"Thank you," I said, leaning back and pressing the ice pack to my shoulder and ignoring the ache lingering at my lower back.

She looked up at me through her thick lashes, and I flexed my fingers, fighting the urge to stroke the side of her face. "You're welcome." She moved to a minor scrape on my hand that didn't need attention, but I liked the way her touch felt too much to stop her. It had nothing to do with her being on her knees and everything to do with the way warmth spread through my limbs from any spot where she touched me. "I think you were getting it there at the end," she said, her voice managing to pull me out of my head.

"Yeah," I said. "I guess." If Willow hadn't been there with me, urging me to take a break, I would have stayed out there all day, no matter how many times I fell or how my back protested. I'd spent most of my life pushing to go harder, faster. Even before the PJs, I always knew I could do it, no matter what the goal was. There were hundreds of times as a kid when my parents probably should have told me to slow down, but they didn't. It made me good at my job—I didn't quit until the mission was complete. Late at night alone, I thought about whether that was why I ignored the issues with my back for so long, and if it was that inability to stop that ultimately put my team at risk. Now riding a fucking bike had stopped me. They'd warned me in physical therapy that some things would have to be relearned, especially related to balance, but I hadn't expected this kind of a struggle for a physical activity kids could master.

"What's that face?" Willow had paused her inspection, but her fingers still rested against my hand.

"Just my face." I smirked. It was the expression most likely to earn me a glare from Emi, but it was easy. I'd learned it was one of those things that masked any other expression, and I didn't want to get into what I was really thinking with Willow. She didn't need my baggage. "Ignore my broken old ass. You got a new first!"

"I did." She grinned wider and moved her fingers from my hand before scooting to join me on the couch. She stroked along the cut that ran up my arm. It wasn't bad, but I relaxed and let her comfort me. "And I kind of like your broken old ass."

"Feel good?"

She laughed. "I guess." Willow pulled another wipe from the kit and cleaned around the cut on my forearm. "When I learned to drive, I finally had freedom to escape my parents and their fighting, but my first stop was Spencer's place." She looked reflective and patted at my skin with the cool wipe again. "This time, I don't know where I'm driving." She pulled the tube of bacitracin from the box and smeared a bit on the cut. "Well, riding."

To me, I thought. *Ride your bike to me. Steer your whole world toward me.*

I didn't say it, though. That was nuts, both that I'd even think about it and that I felt an ache in my chest when I remembered I didn't get to want that. I should have made a joke about her riding me to cut the moment, but I set the ice pack aside and ran a finger along her cheek. I knew my skin might be cold, but she let me, looking up from where she'd been bent over my arm. "You get to go wherever you want," I said, and then looked into her eyes as I stroked her cheek again. "Anywhere at all." My thumb slid along the constellation of freckles that ran over the bridge of her nose and cheeks.

Her eyes widened, and she leaned into my touch.

Stop, I told myself. *Stop whatever this is.* I stroked her skin again, unable to pull my fingers away. "To anything or anyone," I said. *Else.* She gets to ride to someone else. That finally nudged me to let my hand fall away.

"It's scary," she said, letting her gaze drop from my face after a moment. "To imagine something new."

"Is it?" I'd never imagined something new. I'd imagined nothing when I was discharged, a dark expanse in front of me I didn't like, so I'd imagined being back instead. Even now, when the fantasy of being with her could almost play like a movie in my head, I couldn't imagine a nonmilitary version of myself in that reel. She was nothing like me, though, and she probably had lots of possibilities for her future.

She pressed a Band-Aid onto my skin and walked to the kitchen and threw away the trash from her session of nursing me back to health. Her laugh trailed behind her like a ribbon.

I winced as I adjusted how I sat on the couch. My back felt stiff from my position.

"Advil?" She stood, already on her way to find some before I could wave her off, and I hated the concern on her face.

"I brought you something," I called after her, unzipping the pocket in my shorts and pulling out the bottle. I was glad for the opportunity to change the subject.

Willow handed me two pills along with a glass of water and accepted the bottle from me. "What's this?"

She'd already read the label when I answered, and I grinned at her wide-eyed expression. "It's lube," I said, swallowing the pills. "Luckily, it didn't burst open or fall out during one of my many crashes to the ground. That uppity mom would have had lots to say about that."

Willow pressed the bottle between her hands, as if to hide it from prying eyes. She lowered her voice and sat close to me, which I found hilarious. "Why did you get me lube?" she hissed, voice still low even though we were alone in the house.

I still took advantage and leaned close to her. A few curls fell across it, and I tucked them slowly behind the shell of her ear. "Because you can never have too much. No need to risk discomfort," I said, noticing her shiver as my breath caressed her skin. "And you have a toy to try out now that you've learned to ride." I didn't touch her, but stayed still, my lips close to grazing her ear.

Willow's swallow was audible, and she turned her head, so our lips were inches apart. "Right here?" She bit the corner of her lower lip, and my cock thickened as she unclasped her hands and looked down at the bottle. "With you?"

"Fuck, Willow," I said, tucking my fingers along the shell of her ear again. "No. When you're alone."

"Oh," she let out a nervous laugh. "I thought you meant you wanted to watch me."

"Oh," I said. "I do."

"You do?" She spoke low again, and her eyes snapped to me, wide and surprised, but she didn't pull away. She looked curious. I was going to hell.

I dipped my lips to her ear again, this time letting them graze her lobe before I spoke. "Yes."

"More dirty talk?" Her eyes sparkled above her pink cheeks. "This is way beyond what I ever did before."

I let my fingers drop again to the inside of her knee and traced those same circles. "I'd love to watch you spread your thighs." My circle widened on her knee, grazing her thigh with one finger. "I bet you'd love showing me your pretty pussy."

She gave a little gasp of surprise when I widened my circle more, sweeping a finger higher on her leg. "Oh my God," she murmured.

"But not yet." I lowered my lips and swept them across the skin under her ear. "You use this later alone."

"Can I tell you about it?" She was breathless, and I considered scrapping this entire plan and pressing my fingers to the apex of her thighs, to feel her heat, but I narrowed my circles back to her knee.

"You're getting better at dirty talk," I said in her ear again, but then pulled back. "Very good." I was rock-hard at the visual I'd created for myself with the sound of her breathless voice. "Yes, you can tell me all about it."

She took a steadying breath when I pulled away. "It's not even a re-do. It's an actual first," she said, thumbing the bottle.

"I'll expect a full report," I said, pushing to my feet, glad my truck was right outside so I didn't have to walk home at full staff, imagining my friend's little sister getting herself off.

"You're leaving already?"

"You have plans," I said, motioning to her hand.

She blushed, and I could see how turned on she was. The buds of her nipples poked through her thin shirt. "Thank you," she said, holding up the bottle. "For this and for the support this morning." She followed me to the door. "I can't believe you brought me this," she said, more to herself than to me.

"It'll make it better," I said, reaching for the door and doing nothing to get my dick to calm down. "And you deserve for it to be good," I said. "You deserve all the good things."

Willow's arms wrapped around me from behind, her small hands pressed to my stomach and her full breasts against my back. I dropped my hands over hers. "Thank you," she said.

Her voice was sexy and soft and hit me like a sack of bricks. The moment of silence had nothing to do with my hard-on, the ache in my back and arm, or the press of her body to mine. It had everything to do with the way I longed to turn, take her in my arms, and tell her all the reasons she deserved the best.

CHAPTER 31

Willow

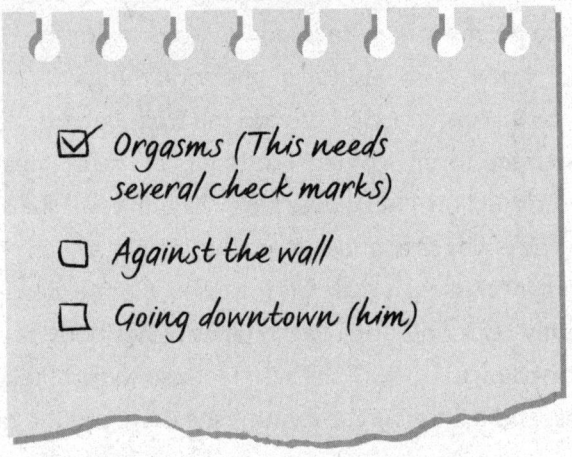

"HOLY SHIT," I said into the empty room, my body shaking from the powerful orgasm and the toy still vibrating between my thighs where I'd dropped it after the second wave hit me. "Holy shit," I said again, fumbling to turn it off. My head spun in the best way, and I tried to calm the trembles running through my body. I stared at the ceiling as if looking for an answer to a question I hadn't asked about the pleasure that was still rippling through me. I'd had a few errands to run after Deacon had left, and then Hollis wanted to get dinner—I felt like I'd been anticipating this all day and it hadn't disappointed.

My phone buzzed on the nightstand, and my heart jumped,

wondering if it was Deacon. If he'd somehow sensed that I'd been imagining him the entire time, picturing his fingers and mouth and . . . everything. I let my head loll to the side against the pillow as the trembling subsided and I sank into it. I pictured his smile, and a warmth spread through my belly.

I finally grabbed the phone, but the message was from Zoe, not Deacon.

> ZOE: I bought the same one you did!

She included a photo of the same toy I'd just tested out, only hers was black.

> ZOE: How is it?
>
> WILLOW: ☆☆☆☆☆
>
> ZOE: Did Captain America use it with you?
>
> WILLOW: No!

I thought about leaving it there, but I felt like magic was still swirling through my body and I was going to explode if I couldn't share.

> WILLOW: He bought me lube, though.
>
> ZOE: No one's ever given me that useful a gift.
> Marry him.

I stretched on the bed, pressing my thighs together and tugging Deacon's shirt I hadn't given back yet across my chest.

I slowly slid my legs off the side of the bed, my skin feeling electric, and I wondered if I'd been missing the feeling the whole time. And I'd done this alone. The release when I'd been on the phone with Deacon had been powerful, but this was something even better, and I imagined what it would be like to feel that way every time, what it would feel like to be next to someone when I did. Next to Deacon. I shivered at the way the thought seemed to slide up my spine, but even through wanting that, I took note of the looseness in my body and the heat on my cheeks. I could make myself feel this way without anyone else.

And there was one person I wanted to tell. Before I could talk myself out of it, I hit the icon to FaceTime Deacon, who picked up immediately. "Hey," I said, tucking a curl behind my ear.

"Look at that smile," he said. His brown eyes kind of danced, and his smirk didn't look smug, but just so Deacon. "You tried out the unicycle, didn't you?"

I burst out a laugh. "The unicycle?"

"We spent the day riding bikes, and I'm in public." I saw the background of the call was a Walgreens and there were rows of medicine behind him. "Appreciate my discreet behavior, babe."

"I tried the unicycle." I lowered my voice, even though I could see the earbuds tucked into his ears.

"And . . . ?" He was walking through the medication aisle, and I saw him pause in front of a bunch of candy. "Will you be riding the unicycle regularly? Did it get you to where you needed to go?"

An older couple paused behind him. They looked to be in their eighties or nineties and the man wore a golf hat and I didn't have time to warn Deacon of his approach before he tapped my big, strapping conversation partner on the shoulder. "Young man, did you say unicycle?"

"I did." Deacon held the phone away, and I could see them both clearly. "My friend is learning to ride one." He winked at the screen and pointed in the man's direction at me.

"I rode unicycles as a young man." He looked wistful, and his wife took his forearm in hers.

"Oh, he did. All the time. Sometimes I had to call down the street for him to get off that dang unicycle and come in for dinner!" She had a kind laugh, and the couple shared a look with each other before turning back to Deacon, who was doing an admirable job hiding his laughter.

"You know, I fear that's what's going to happen to her," he said, nodding at his phone. "Any advice?"

My entire body was red with embarrassment, but Deacon's easy laugh made it feel comfortable, even though I couldn't believe this was happening.

"Well," she said, thoughtfully. "Once, I just told him he'd only get his unicycle back if he'd done all his chores around the house." She patted his arm.

"Took away my toy until I did as she said," her husband said, squeezing her arm.

"Now that sounds like a good idea." He winked again at the phone, and a new flush that had nothing to do with embarrassment moved through my body.

"You never hear anyone talking about unicycles," the man said. "Thank you for that memory, young man." He patted Deacon's shoulder again, and the two started down the aisle.

"And thanks for the suggestion," Deacon replied. When he

looked into the phone, he opened his mouth like he was letting out a silent laugh but paused and looked over his shoulder.

"Did they say something else?"

Deacon looked over his shoulder again before turning back to me. "Nah, just goodbye." He smiled to himself, this quick, tiny grin, then said, "So it was an enjoyable experience?"

"Unicyling?" I nodded. "Very."

His nostrils flared. "I'm really glad you got it," he added, and I saw him move along the aisle. His voice pitched low, and his smirk returned. "Will I have to take it away until you're a good girl?"

I'd never played games like this, and hearing him say that made my skin prickle with enjoyable goose bumps. "Maybe." I didn't know what to say, but I liked him being in the room with me when I felt like this, even if it was just his voice. "It was really intense."

He swallowed and paused as he paid for his purchases at a self-checkout kiosk. "Intense how?" His voice was like gravel moving over my body, like tiny pebbles rolling over my skin as he spoke.

"Um," I said, pressing a hand to my belly, where I still felt butterflies. "I've never had that reaction. I was shaking and could feel the waves for so long. I felt completely out of control in the best way."

Deacon walked outside, and the light from a streetlamp cast shadows over his face. "How did it feel to be out of control?" His car dinged as he climbed inside, and I noticed the wince on his face as he did, but he kept going with his line of questioning. "To be wild."

I grinned. "I don't think I was wild . . . I was in my bedroom alone but felt really good." I pressed a hand to my lips. "It's so weird to tell you this."

"Not so weird," he said, and I heard the engine roar to life. "We have an agreement."

"I imagined . . ."

"Tell me what you imagined, Low." He wasn't moving, and I pictured him there in his big truck, focused on the screen in that parking lot. I wondered if my talking about this turned him on.

"I imagined feeling that out of control but someone else being here, like being next to someone or having them being the one who was making me lose control." Really, I'd imagined him making me lose control, him making me feel that good, but more than anything, being able to cling to him after. But that was too big, too beyond our agreement, so I wasn't going to go there.

"You've never come that hard with another person?"

I shook my head. "I mean, it felt good. And I've finished, but not like . . ." I squeezed my thighs together to remind my body of the sensation. "Not like this."

"Low, you had oral on your list."

I flushed but shook my head. "I asked once and it didn't go well so I never asked again."

"But you wanted it?" The humor was gone from Deacon's voice, and it sounded like a growl, like he was personally affronted at a lack of oral sex.

I nodded. "That's why I tried this kind of toy. It . . ."

"You bought a toy that feels like someone sucking on your clit," he said, and he seemed to put the truck in gear. "And you want someone to do that for you?"

I nodded and eyed the toy, still sitting on my nightstand.

"Guess I just imagined someone else being with me is all I meant to say. It was good, though. It was great. I didn't mean I want you to. I know you want to take things slow, and I monopolized your whole day already."

"Low." He spoke as he drove, and I could only see the side of his head.

"What?"

"I'll be there in ten minutes."

CHAPTER 32

I TOOK A sharp right turn into the neighborhood and forced myself to slow the truck before I hit a mailbox on my quest to reach Willow. Yeah, I'd said we should go slow. I'd told myself, no matter how sexy this whole sex-coaching thing was, I'd put the brakes on at some point. But all that had gone out the window, and now, every muscle in my body moved into action to get to her.

Not just my body. My head was swimming, too. I pulled up to Cruz's house, and the porch light flicked on. I heaved a sigh and cut the engine because she hadn't heard the last thing the old couple at the store had said, but I did. He'd said, "It made me happy, so she always gave it back, no matter what. That's what you do when you're in love."

Love. I wasn't in love. I didn't fall in love. I was the guy you had great sex with in a bar bathroom before he deployed, not the one who talked about love. I'd never really seen love up close until I saw Marcus and Sybil with their partners. Love wasn't a verb in my house growing up.

At the house, the curtains shifted by the door, and I could tell she was standing there waiting for me, eagerly bouncing from foot to foot in nervous excitement. She knew what this was, though, and as I grabbed my bag from the seat, I strode toward the door, ignoring the landscaping I'd helped Cruz with. The judgmental bushes and flower beds said enough all on their own.

"You came," she said, pulling open the door as I approached. She was still in my T-shirt, and the expanse of her thighs below promised what might or might not be underneath.

"You came first," I said, pushing the door shut behind me and backing her against the wall, a hand behind her head to protect it from the hard surface. "I told you there'd be a next time with the wall."

She groaned when my thigh slipped between her legs, and I felt her heat through my track pants. "You're here."

"I told you I would be." I settled my hand at her waist and then lower, teasing under the hem of the shirt. "You wanted someone here."

She wriggled against me and tipped up her chin, her dark eyes hooded as I teased my fingertips along the hemline of the shirt. "I wanted *you* here."

Her words hit me like a hundred tiny punches to the heart. She didn't want a body, she wanted me, and the thought filled me unexpectedly. I wanted nothing more than to take care of her, to keep her happy and warm and safe. And before I could think more about what the couple at the store had said, I lowered my mouth to hers, tasting the sweetness of her lips and tongue as the softness of her body melded into mine. "You took care of me earlier. Let me take care of you this time," I said, lowering my kisses to her neck and letting my hand trace up her ribs.

"Deacon," she said on a pant when my fingertips brushed the underside of her breast, the skin like satin beneath my touch with the promise of those peaked, sensitive nipples. "Please."

I slammed my lips to hers again, and we stumbled toward the bedroom, the Walgreens bag still hooked around my wrist crinkling, which would be funny if I'd taken a break from her lips and her skin to think about it. "I imagined you here," she said, her words breathless as we paused by the bed and I inched her shirt over her head.

"I'm here." I bent to kiss her neck again, inhaling her scent and exhaling all the reasons I shouldn't be doing this. "Let me take care of you." I pushed her back toward the bed and fell to my knees, focused on the apex of her thighs. I tugged my shirt over my head and admired her sweet center, but when I bent forward to kiss her belly, I froze, an eruption of pain taking my breath.

"What's wrong?" Willow's head snapped up, and her fingers moved over my hair. "Deac, are you okay?"

The ache had been there all day after the falls I took off the bike. It's why I'd gone to the store in the first place, but with Willow in front of me and the promise of seeing her fall apart, I'd ignored it. "My back," I said through gritted teeth. Gus must have heard the concern in Willow's voice, because he'd come bounding into the room and was now sniffing at my legs and licking my arm.

Willow scrambled off the bed and helped me get onto the bed from the floor. I tossed an arm over my face as I fell onto the bedding that smelled like her. "You would have been better off with the geriatric unicyclist," I said. "I'm sorry." I'd had bad nights before, I'd suffered from whiskey dick a few times, but this was a different shame. This one reminded me that this wasn't the first time I'd promised to take care of someone only to need caring for myself.

"Hey," she said, lifting my arm from my eyes, and the mattress next to me dipped. "Stop hiding from me." I blinked against the light. She was sitting right next to me, looking down and stroking my hairline. "What can I do?"

"You were supposed to be coming already."

"After one minute? C'mon." She kept stroking my forehead. "I'm sure you're good, but you're not a unicycle."

I chuckled at her bad joke, and a smile tipped her lips. "What can I do?"

"My back seizes up sometimes," I said, wanting to look away, but her comforting touch on my face felt so good. "Since the surgery. I just need to relax and rub some stuff on it. That's what I was grabbing at the store."

"I can help with that." She hopped off the bed and picked up the bag from where it had fallen on the floor. "Condoms, jelly beans, and Icy Hot."

"Devil's three-way," I muttered, and Willow laughed, the sound delicate and inviting. "You don't have to," I added. I tried to roll to the side, determined to handle it myself, but sucked in a breath as my back protested.

"Roll over," she said, returning to the bed and handing me the bag of jelly beans. "I can help." She lifted my shirt and pushed the waist of my pants down an inch. "You eat jelly beans while I work. Doctor's orders."

"You're not a vet yet."

Her hands tentatively worked over my lower back, checking on where it hurt and where was best to spread the ointment.

"Willow's orders, then." As she touched my back I pushed away the worry that I wasn't feeling it fully, that the nerve damage was still impacting me. It was hard to know if the feeling was all the way back, and I focused on the feel of her fingertips instead, the ointment cooling my skin until the warming sensation took over.

Willow got up to wash her hands and then climbed back onto the bed next to me, checking in. "Relax," she said, dragging her nails gently over the middle of my back and between my shoulder blades. "I'm sorry my orgasms led to you sprawled out, immobile."

I chuckled and turned my head toward her, resting it on my crossed forearms. "Plural? You didn't tell me there was more than one."

Willow crossed her hand over her stomach, a guilty smile crossing her lips. "I, uh, went for another unicycle ride when we hung up."

Groaning, I cursed my body. "I'm sorry. I didn't think this would happen."

"Don't be sorry." She shrugged and nudged my side with her hand. "I got mine."

I laughed, wincing at the pain as my body moved. "Who is this cocky girl?"

"I learned from the best." She shifted to her side and slid her nails up and down my biceps. Her gaze fell to my back, where I was sure she saw the scar along my spine. I had other scars, tons of them, and this was just one more, or I wanted to think of it that way. "Does this happen very often?"

"No," I said, closing my eyes as she stroked my arm, sinking into it. "Just if I push it too much."

She kept her stroking moves consistent, and the rhythmic up and down of her nails felt hypnotic.

I'd been thinking about what she'd asked earlier, about how I saw myself as a civilian, and I didn't have a good answer yet. I was lying here immobile, though, and I knew what she must be thinking. "I can handle it," I said, beating her to it.

She traced the tattoo on my biceps. She'd seen it before, I was sure—it was the same as Cruz's. "That Others May Live," she said, reading the words as she moved a finger along them.

"These things we do, that others may live," I said, eyes still closed, repeating the motto of the PJs, the thing I'd lived by my entire career. "I can handle a little pain. I keep thinking about the people who will need us in the future, and what it means." I couldn't imagine doing anything else that meant that much to me.

"What did it mean to you?" She continued the stroke up and down my arm, and her words fell on me like a comforting blanket.

"To me?"

"Yeah." She slid her fingers up my arm and across my shoulders, working into my hair. "To you."

"It meant they lived. Or it meant they were found. It meant I had a hand in someone going home or back to what they loved, to their families. It meant they lived and it meant I . . ."

She kept her rhythm, stroking my scalp.

"I did something that mattered. We did something important."

She worked quietly for a few moments. "You guys were called in when it was bad, right?" I heard the thought she wasn't voicing and knew she was trying to picture what Cruz was doing at that moment.

"We were called in when it was hard," I said, trying to ease her anxiety, but imagining the same scenarios, only I knew what details to fill in.

"When someone was in the middle of the ocean or high in the mountains?" She traced the lines of my tattoo, the peaks of the mountains and the blue lines meant to signify the water. "Behind enemy lines." Her voice softened, and her finger continued over the lines of my tattoo.

"That's the job," I said. She had it right, and I wasn't sure what else I could say to ease her worry. I'd been lucky in that my parents didn't ask a lot of questions—maybe they worried about me, but I never felt the need to ease their minds... I never knew what was on their minds. Cruz, though, was always worried about Willow and their mom when she was alive. "Cruz is good, though." I turned my head so I could meet her eyes. "I'll never admit I said it, but he's the best. Always has been."

She gave a hum of acknowledgment and continued to rub my back.

"My tumor reached the tipping point in compressing my spine in the middle of a mission," I said, gaze locked on the pillow. "It had been bothering me for months, but we were used to abusing our bodies. Everyone had something going on. I kept taking Advil and ignoring the tingling and pain. That night, we'd retrieved injured Marines, and I was providing cover as they got them to the chopper. It was quiet. Still. Too still." For a long time, I heard the chopper blades in the still landscape every time I closed my eyes. "Bullet whizzed by me and I clipped the shooter, but then hell broke loose. They were closing in. I ducked back to take shelter behind a few boulders and to draw the combatants away from Cruz and the others who had the Marines."

Willow gave a sharp inhale above me, her fingers slowing their movements.

"Cruz signaled he had me covered, but I couldn't get up." I shuddered at the memory. I'd been scared thousands of times. I always saw the danger, even if I was determined to rush through it. But that feeling of sudden immobility, of not being able to move, and of my team in danger waiting for me—it was a new kind of fear. The three men we'd rescued would have been strapped down to stretchers and in need of immediate transport. "My legs wouldn't work. I kept looking at them, willing them to move, and nothing. I couldn't stand up."

She flattened her fingers and slid them up over my neck and shoulders. "And he came back to get you?"

"It was heavy fire, and the Marines weren't going to make it if we didn't move fast. One was unconscious already. I told them to get out."

"But they didn't. They saved you? Of course they did. You're here."

"I'm here," I said, the image of Cruz running across the sand, avoiding fire, would be forever burned into my brain, the relief and horror when he reached me and hoisted me onto his shoulders. "Cruz got me back to the chopper." I didn't tell her how close we'd both come to getting hit or about the combatants our team took out with cover fire. I didn't tell her about the hits Cruz took to his body armor. "We got out, but one of the Marines didn't make it." I turned my face away from her. "If we'd gotten out five minutes sooner—if they hadn't had to wait for me—he might have had a chance."

"It's not your fault," she said, sliding her palms in circles over my back.

I nodded. It was what I'd had to agree to with the therapist in the hospital. It was my fault, though. "That's why I need to go back. I need the chance to balance the scales. And I need to have Cruz's back like he had mine."

I cringed at her next touch because of the way her soft, warm skin against mine made me feel like I could melt into the sheets. This was one more thing I'd have to pay penance for. "Anyway," I said, pushing away the thought. "He's the best. The actual Captain America," I added, trying to defuse the tension of the last few minutes of my confession.

"Zoe certainly thinks so."

I chuckled.

"You miss him."

"Him and the team." I nodded and kept my eyes closed. "You know how you described feeling out of control?"

"You were having wild, toe-curling orgasms while doing pararescue work?"

"No." I chuckled at her question and settled against my arms, inhaling her scent. "But without the team, without the work, I feel out of control in kind of the same way. Only there's no big joy, and no comedown. I'm just kind of floating."

Willow's fingers grazed the side of my ear, and I let out a sigh at the touch, my back beginning to feel better. "Do you think there are other ways you might help people? Save people?"

I pictured my document I'd been using to track my progress. "I don't have another plan."

She stroked my head and didn't add anything, but I still kept my eyes closed, not wanting to see her expression.

"Except for helping you finish your list before I go." I flexed my fingers and tried to sit, but I winced at the jolt of pain and fell back to the bed. "And taking the risk I promised you I would."

"Slow down," she said. I finally opened my eyes and took her in, her curls wild around her head and her gaze soft as she studied me. She was beautiful, like the kind of beautiful that made my heart rate speed up in her presence.

"And I will help you with your list, pages one and two, before I go back. I want you to feel like you've really started your new life."

She gave my head another stroke. "And if it's what you want, I want you to get back your old one."

I nodded, and she slipped off the bed, promising to return with a paper towel for the excess ointment. I watched her walk out of the room, Gus following on her heels, and I wondered what it would be like to have my old life back and no longer have her in it. My eyes fell closed, and I inhaled the sweet, heady scent of her lingering on the bed. It meant everything to go back to my team, to my work, to my life.

I had never had to weigh that against someone I loved enough to make me want to stay close to home. Because I wasn't that guy. I was a guy who threw my body in front of problems and who had things to atone for. I was a guy who owed a debt to a friend I could never repay. I was not the right guy for Willow. In my head I knew that. My heart was a different story entirely.

With the ghost of her touch on my arm and the scent of her in my head, I wondered what my life would be like if I was a guy who got to talk about love out loud.

CHAPTER 33

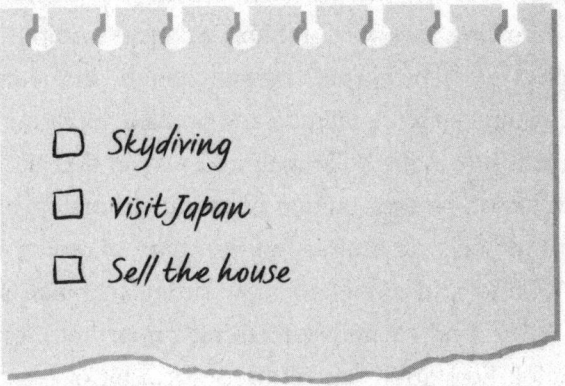

- ☐ Skydiving
- ☐ Visit Japan
- ☐ Sell the house

HOLLIS BRUSHED HER palms down the front of her jeans. After a bike ride across the High Trestle Trail, we'd hauled the boxes from the garage into the house that afternoon. I'd very quickly realized sorting through Mom's things while sitting on a concrete floor was not going to work.

"Sure you don't want help?" She eyed the stack of boxes skeptically, and I followed her gaze, reading the familiar handwriting in black Sharpie. I'd forgotten Spencer helped us box things, but seeing his neatly formed letters didn't send me down a wormhole of memories—not about him, anyway. The ones we'd dragged in were labeled with "Documents/Papers," "Bedroom," and "Kitchen," and I honestly had no idea what I'd find in each one. "Happy to help if you want," she added.

"I think I should at least start on my own." I'd walked by the boxes so many times since Cruz told me to go look for them and finally decided I needed to start. I couldn't say why—maybe it was knowing the trip back to Colorado was in a few days or just that I'd felt braver since starting on the list, but I knew it was time. I thanked Hollis and took the tape off the box labeled "Documents/Papers," finding neatly sealed plastic tubs inside. I smiled, knowing that was probably Spencer's doing, making sure things were protected. Again, though, the feeling that swept through me was gratitude and not longing or hurt.

The first box looked like mail and papers that had probably been tossed on the counter. After thirty minutes, most of it was trash or bills we'd already taken care of, and I reached for my phone and stretched after sitting in place so long. Maybe I'd hoped to find something important, something meaningful. I'd started this re-do list for a lot of reasons, but one of them was definitely wanting to avoid ending up trapped like she was, as someone who gave up on things because they reminded her of the past. Maybe I'd been hoping for something else, some reason to see she wasn't irrevocably changed by heartbreak, but that was probably too much to hope for from old bills and junk mail and receipts. I wasn't learning anything meaningful. I rolled my head from side to side and reached for my phone where I had a message waiting from Deacon.

DEACON: How's it going?

WILLOW: Found a winning lottery ticket in the stack. $3!

THE RE-DO LIST

> WILLOW: What are the odds you'd know two big winners?

It still blew my mind that his friend Sybil had won the lottery and won big. When I met her and her fiancé, they were the most down-to-earth people I could imagine.

> DEACON: I guess I'm a lucky charm. You're heading to Monaco, then?

> WILLOW: Already on the plane. It's been nice knowing you. I'm off to be rich and elusive.

My phone buzzed with an incoming call, and I tapped the green icon. "We're taxiing—it's too late to change my mind."

Deacon's low, easy voice made my heart do a little flutter, even through the phone. "I'll never forget you." It was a joke. I knew it was a joke, but it still made that flutter even more pronounced. "How's it actually going?"

I tapped the speaker button and returned to sorting. Nothing would quell the flutter of an inappropriate crush like sorting through junk mail of the deceased. "Okay, actually. We threw everything we found in boxes, but most of this is trash."

I pulled out a plain-looking white envelope with *For T* scrawled on the front in an unfamiliar handwriting. Inside there was a single folded piece of paper. "Thanks for checking up on me, though. I'm fine." Next to me, the dog stretched, his big paw nudging against my thigh. "Gus is keeping me company."

"You want me to come over tonight? I promised Jayden I'd join him for a game when I got back from the gym, but after?"

"Yeah," I said. I grinned and wondered if he knew how his voice sounded when he talked about spending time with the kid. It was the same way he sounded when he talked about the people he served with. "I'd like it if you came over," I said, already anticipating the way my stomach did a little flip-flop when he walked through the door. Things were so different now, and I remembered the rush of him taking hold of me in the entryway before his back gave out last week. He'd been at the gym a lot lately, and based on the sound of weights clanking in the background, I guessed he was there now.

We hung up, and I still had a grin on my face as I returned to the envelope in my hands. The paper was plain printer paper, and it was a copy of an email confirmation for a skydiving class for two, along with a handwritten note on a Post-it in my mom's loopy handwriting. The note said, *Too late to back out now. We're booked!* I stared at the email—the date for the session had long passed, and I had no idea who T might have been. My mom didn't do things like skydiving, but the date on the email was for only a few weeks before her accident. I set it gingerly aside on top of the small pile of things to save or review and kept digging in the box. More junk mail and bills, a few magazines, and then an official-looking envelope, unopened. I tore at the perforated cardboard and found a crisp new passport inside, the pages stiff and my mom's unsmiling photo at the front. I traced a finger over the stamp. We didn't know she had one—she never enjoyed traveling.

I wished I could message Cruz, but there was only Gus to hear me today. "Where was she going?"

I set it aside as well and kept digging into the box where I found cards from Realtors and a printed confirmation for a flight to Tokyo. I couldn't believe what I was seeing, because the mom I'd known since the divorce would never skydive or need a passport, let alone sell the house she'd fought my dad for. The time had flown while I was digging through things, and the sun was already setting when I looked up again. Question marks and new discoveries were the last things I'd expected to find among my mom's possessions. Had my mom been on her own kind of re-do journey?

CHAPTER 34

MARCUS HANDED ME a towel and looked back at his stopwatch. "Eighteen," he said. "Damn, man."

"Not good enough." I dragged the towel across my forehead, feeling the burn in my arms and shoulders from the pull-ups.

"Isn't the minimum like ten?"

"Eight." I tipped the water bottle to my lips. "But that's the baseline. I could do twenty-six at my peak." I caught his expression before he fixed his face in a neutral nod, the same expression he'd been giving me since he started helping, the one that said, "I don't think you're at your peak anymore."

I shook off my arms. "Let's go again."

"You want to rest your arms for a few minutes?"

"Fine," I said, nodding to the mat. "Sit-ups." Two minutes was the only rest I could take. I'd been more on edge than normal. Having my back pain stop me from giving Willow what she needed really messed with my head and made me want to go even harder to get my body back to where it had been.

"I'll have to warn your next workout buddy how intransigent you are," Marcus said, following me to the mats.

"That's right," I said, settling myself back on the mat. "You leave soon." I hadn't forgotten. The house was full of his boxes and Emi's to-do lists, a constant reminder that they were both shipping out soon. Emi had asked me to stay in the house, adding a few beats too late, "Until you head back to the military." She didn't think I should return at all, even if I was back at peak performance.

"I can't wait," he said, grinning. "It was hard when the restaurant failed." He'd worked with Sybil to buy Kieran and Lila's family donut shop and turn it into a lunch spot. It was good, but ultimately couldn't survive. He'd closed after about a year. "But Lila was always there. Even on the worst days, she makes me feel like I'm the luckiest man on earth. She's the best thing in my life."

"That's hella romantic, bruh," a guy near us doing crunches said between grunts.

His buddy nodded. "Oscar Wilde said to keep love in your heart. A life without it is like a sunless garden when the flowers are dead." He held out a sweaty fist for Marcus, who knocked it with a nod.

"Your gym is very literary," Marcus said, looking back at me.

"He's right, though." Marcus loved Lila like people love someone in a movie. "Hella romantic" was a good way to describe it, but feeling lucky around someone was familiar to me. It was how I felt around Willow even before she asked for my help on page two of her list with those big brown eyes.

I shook the thought away. "You're a lucky guy," I said. "Timer ready?"

Marcus nodded, and I pulled my body into sit-up after sit-up, trying to clear my head of how she'd rested against me and the pillowy softness of her lips. I moved faster, needing to work myself further from that memory. I'd agreed to help her, that no one would get hurt because it was a temporary arrangement. So why was my stomach tightening at the thought of her moving on without me?

"Time," Marcus said, interrupting my thoughts. "Eighty-one. Damn, man." I'd been counting myself, mentally preparing for being alone in the gym again when he moved to Chicago. If I could get my reps up a little higher, the chances of them taking me back had to be better. I kept telling myself that, but sometimes I wasn't sure it was true.

I fell back to the mat and sucked in a breath, hoping to ignore the twinge of pain in my lower back. "Eighty-five next time," I said. "I can do more." This was a good distraction, and I was barely thinking about Willow's lips or the feel of her skin under my fingers or her damn plans to be taken up against a wall. *Fuck.*

"Pull-ups," I said, lifting myself. "I need more pull-ups." Across the room, a woman was mid-lift, her form for the pull-up perfect as she finished her last rep and stood on the mat, reaching for a towel. I recognized her when she turned. "Someone you know?" Marcus raised an eyebrow, and I rolled my eyes.

"Not like that." I approached Kelly after she waved in our direction. "Nice job," I said.

"I know." She wiped her brow with the towel and held out a hand to Marcus to shake. "You want to arm wrestle?" She laughed and took a sip from her water bottle. "You have a life outside of school or the gym? You're here all the time."

"Guess that says something about you," I joked, leaning

against the bar. Kelly had been annoying at first, but I liked her. She was as cocky as me, and it made me relax.

"Probably." She glanced at her watch. "The workouts keep part of the old me, the active-duty me, front and center."

I nodded—I felt that, too.

"But I'm at the center a lot, too. And you never are. Why are you avoiding us?"

Her direct question landed squarely. "I'm not," I finally said. "Just busy."

Kelly gave me a dubious look over her water bottle and shrugged one shoulder. "We look out for one another at school and beyond," she said. "It can be tough getting out and reacclimating. I won't force you," she said, starting toward the machines across the room. She looked over her shoulder and flexed her biceps. "But I could!" she called out, and I chuckled.

"Where does she want you to go?" Marcus stood nearby, and I prepared to begin the reps.

"Veterans Center," I said, gripping the bar and positioning my hands.

"Hmm," he said, watching me do the first couple. "I've never seen you hang out with other veterans. Might be good to be around people who understand some of what you used to do." He offered the casual observation and then returned to counting.

I was hung up on the phrase "used to" and all the things I'd never get to do tied up in the past tense for the rest of the workout.

"HEY," I SAID, holding up a bag from Tasty Tacos, Willow's favorite place in Des Moines. "I brought dinner." She had dust across her forehead and looked like she'd been crying, but she squealed at the sight of the bag, taking my other hand to pull me inside.

"I never ate lunch. You're my hero." She pulled plates from the cupboard and began unpacking the bag. "These flour tacos have no business being this good." She inhaled the scent of the seasoned beef and let out a little groan that sent a jolt through me. She seemed really happy, and not faking it to look fine, but genuinely happy.

"How did it go today?" I glanced around the open-concept main floor. There were stacks of papers and opened boxes strewn around the house like a tornado had touched down, the damage localized to this ten-by-fourteen-foot space. "I can help you . . . clean up?"

She smiled again, brightly, betraying her swollen eyes. "I found so many things," she said. "It was like I was learning about someone totally new through these clues."

I accepted the plate she handed me, and we sat at the kitchen bar, side by side. "She was making plans to travel and go on adventures. I think she might have been dating someone. Lots of notes and references to a 'T.'"

"Wow," I said, taking a bite as she walked me through some of the other things she'd found, the new things she was realizing about her mom's life. "And you guys never knew any of this?"

"I didn't." She took a swig from her water bottle. "She was always scared of flying, even when she and my dad were together, and here she was making reservations to go skydiving and fly halfway around the world." She picked up a tortilla chip, studying it for a second. "She was being pretty brave. I think she was moving forward."

Her dimple popped when she chewed, and there was a crumb from the fried tortilla of the taco on her chin. "You take after her, then," I said, brushing the crumb away with my thumb and stealing a stroke along her cheek. "You're pretty brave yourself."

Willow lifted her eyes to mine, and the depth of the brown of her irises always took me by surprise. "I think I'm getting there."

Braver than me, I thought. I didn't want to think about what Marcus and Kelly said at the gym. It opened too many doors, and I didn't like the sense of imbalance and guilt that still washed over me every time I thought about how I'd let down the unit, how I'd failed, and the increasing uncertainty about getting back in. Willow bit the corner of her lip, and I pushed those thoughts down. She was in front of me, and I knew that wouldn't last. I didn't want to squander any of these moments while I had them, while I had her. I slid off my stool. It felt so natural to nudge her legs apart and stand between them.

"You look like you're going to kiss me," she said, the corner of her lip tipping up.

"Thinking about it." I tucked a curl behind her ear and let my hand slide to her neck, my thumb brushing along her throat down to the hollow at her collarbone. "I like kissing brave women."

"I'm covered in dust, and a spider crawled out of the box and I don't know where it went." She paused, taking in a slow breath when I pressed my lips to her neck. "It might be on me," she added in that sexy, breathy way she talked when she was turned on. "And I taste like tacos," she added.

"And yet," I said, sliding my other hand under her T-shirt,

stroking the skin along her back as I dipped my lips to her, "I still want to kiss you."

Willow wasn't tentative at all around me, and when our lips met, her kisses were equally soft and assertive, letting me control the speed and pace and then gripping the back of my neck when she wanted more. I was breathless when she pushed on my chest, her cheeks flushed.

"Something wrong?" My fingers were in her hair and her legs around my waist. It had been a long time since I'd made out with someone like this, just kissing and touching, and I already wanted more of it. "Do you want to stop?"

She shook her head. "No, but can I ask you something?"

"Of course," I said, dropping my lips to her neck again, needing the way she sucked in a breath when I hit the right spot. "Ask me anything."

"You might say no," she said. "To the thing I want to ask you, which you totally can. I mean, obviously, you should. Not should, just that . . ." She groaned, the sound low in her throat, and I kissed that spot again.

"Willow." I spoke near her ear. "Have I ever told you no?"

She shook her head, and I pulled back to meet her gaze.

"I'm with you one hundred percent. If you asked me to consider a career with you in black market trout dealing, I'd ask how many boats we'd need. If you wanted me to wear hoochie shorts to the bank, I'd ask if you had a color preference, and if you needed two kidneys, I'd get my affairs in order. Whatever you need, just ask."

She nodded and took in a slow, deep breath. "Okay."

"Okay," I said, bracing myself for what might come next. I tried to recall what else was on her list, but all the blood in my brain had moved south, and I had a hard time focusing on anything other than her. "Spit it out. Whatever it is, my answer is yes."

"Okay," she repeated. "Can I blow you?"

I blinked. I'd never been aware of a blink before, but I was aware of this one as her words sank in. "What?"

She spoke quickly, and my legs threatened to give out at her question. "I mean, I'd go first and then maybe you could go down on me. I mean, if you still wanted to. If I did a really good job on you first, maybe you'd want to. Or I could give you a few and then . . ."

My mouth finally caught up to my brain. "Low, slow down." I moved my thumbs in circles over her upper arms. "You kind of short-circuited my brain there for a moment."

"You said to spit it out. And I wouldn't. I'd totally swallow if that . . . I don't know, sweetens the deal. I don't want you to think it's all about me."

I kissed her again, taking her lower lip between mine, and pressed against the heat at the apex of her thighs. "I'm all about you." I wanted everything from this woman, wanted to give her everything. "You seem to think I need convincing to bury my face between your legs, Low." Her eyes were slow to meet mine but widened when our gazes connected. "I thought I'd made this clear." I slid a thumb over her plump lower lip. "I don't."

CHAPTER 35

Willow

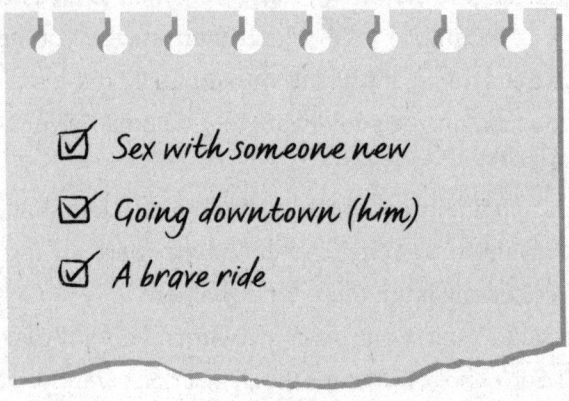

DEACON FINALLY ACQUIESCED to me showering first when I admitted it had nothing to do with how I might smell or taste and everything to do with the possibility of the spider. Now my whole body was on edge, and I looked down at the robe I'd pulled on over my bra and panties. Would he want to undress me? Was it weird to walk in naked? I had no idea what the rules were, and I took in a few quick breaths before gripping the door handle.

He looked me up and down, and my nipples puckered at his inspection before he took a step closer, moving into my space. He circled me, and I felt watched. No, I felt seen, and I grew more and more on edge until he paused behind me. I squirmed when he dropped a hand to my waist and his breath teased the back of my neck. "You smell good and look arachnid-free."

I'd read the phrase "breath mingled" a hundred times, but I'd never really thought of it until that moment when I looked over my shoulder and, somewhere between us, his breath and mine were mixing. Deacon's face was inches from mine, and he stroked my arm. "Are you nervous, Low?"

"No." I shook my head and trailed my palms down my stomach to quell the butterflies there. It was the truth. With anyone else, I'd probably be scared of rejection or maybe worse, something developing and falling into old habits before getting hurt again. I was eager and impatient, but I wasn't nervous. Deacon would make me feel safe, and Deacon would listen to me. I tried to remind my heart that Deacon was the one I trusted to help me with this list because there was no risk of more developing between us. "I'm not nervous."

He was behind me, his chest inches from my back, but I felt the heat of him everywhere. "I am."

"You are? You do this all the time."

"No." His palms slid down my biceps, and I sucked in a breath. "I don't do this all the time." Deacon stepped forward, and his firm chest pressed against my back. "And it's different when it's with you, who is someone who really knows me." My heart pounded, the sound reverberating through my body. His breath teased the nape of my neck before he traced the tip of his nose to my hairline. "Someone I care about. You're important to me, Low, and I want nothing more than to take care of what you need. So, I'm nervous."

"Deac," I said on a shaky exhale and turned to face him. "If you're having second thoughts because of Cruz . . ."

He still searched my face, gaze skittering from one eye to the other.

I worried he'd step back, that I'd feel the loss of his warmth again. I worried he'd have second thoughts about this entire plan, but then his gaze fell to my lips and his eyes seemed to darken.

In an instant, he was pulling me to him, his hand at my waist sure and steady, and he cupped my cheek, a possessive and gentle hold. The red walls receded, and a heady anticipation overtook me. My entire body was on alert, the seconds stretching to fill the infinite chasm of my expectations.

"No second thoughts. Right now, tonight, this is about me and you." His voice was low and filled with gravel, his face so close to mine, I could see the flecks of gold in his eyes. Deacon's other hand slid to the back of my neck slowly, the heat of his touch filling me. His body was stiff against mine, like he was holding himself still, holding himself back. "And you are . . ." His gaze was everywhere—my eyes, the skin above my breasts, my hand resting on his chest. "You're so beautiful I can't think of anything else."

I closed the distance this time, my hand on his shoulder for leverage, and pressed my lips to his. Deacon didn't miss a beat, his lips demanding and needy, tongue grazing the seam of my lips, parting them slowly, his tongue gliding against mine in a way that left me pressing into him. I immediately needed more, and I deepened the kiss, the intensity bruising as his thigh shifted between my legs.

I doggedly chased the friction of that movement, the way his thigh was hard and flexed against me. When I shifted again, intentionally rubbing against him, he groaned against my mouth.

It was intoxicating knowing I did that, knowing I could. It had been so long since I was exciting to someone.

Deacon pulled away from my lips, our foreheads touching, breaths coming fast and heavy as we caught up on the oxygen we'd been denying ourselves. We stood there like that, bodies tangled, heads together, and I waited for him to speak, for the heat building between my legs to dissipate. Neither happened. He brushed my hair away from my ear and kissed me there. "Oh, this is going to be fun." His whisper sent a bolt straight to my clit, and I suppressed the urge to whine as he moved from my head down to my jaw, tipping up my chin and kissing my neck.

I didn't suppress anything when his kiss and tongue reached the spot at my throat where my pulse thrummed. My hips shifted again of their own accord, still seeking the friction of his thigh, the heat and solidity of his body. I was alight, every nerve ending tingling with the pleasure running through my body.

Deacon chuckled against my neck, and my cheeks heated.

"Sorry—"

Without a word, he slid a hand between us, cutting off my apology. His touch on my thighs was a tease, and my panties grew even wetter, my shameless body so ready. "Don't ever apologize for that." He slid his index finger higher, stroking the edge of my underwear, his fingertip sliding just under the material before he was at my ear again. "I want you to feel so good tonight. Do you want that? To come until you can't form full sentences?"

The noise I made wasn't a word. It was barely human, but it was the best I could do. Deacon's finger continued its trail under the fabric, exploring the tops of my thighs, moving over and around them, never quite reaching where I wanted him most. My pussy throbbed, aching for more, aching for his touch or his mouth. I tipped my head back, imagining Deacon's mouth on me, moving over my slick folds the way he was licking and sucking the sensitive flesh below my ear.

"Was that a yes?" He pulled his head back, eyes meeting mine. I expected his smirk, his smug expression, but his gaze was all want and lust. There was no other way to describe it. He wanted me.

"Yes. Please."

His lips crashed down on mine again, and his leg, which had been still between my thighs, nudged me backward. My knees hit the back of the bed, and he held me to him, pressed to his chest before I could fall.

"I thought you wanted me in bed," I said on a pant, clinging to him.

"I want you naked." He reached down with both hands to pull down my panties, the cooler air of the room hitting my heated skin. He tossed them aside without looking, his eyes moving up and down my body, hands skimming over my hips and up my sides. Deacon was exploring me, learning me. I held my breath.

He traced a finger over the top of my breast, along the lacy edge of the fabric. "Fuck, Willow."

The words barely escaped because Deacon's lips were dancing across my collarbone as he reached behind me to unhook my bra. I wanted to toss it aside, but he dragged the straps down my arms, slowly unwrapping me like a present. He stepped back, watching the garment fall. My nipples had been pebbled since we kissed, and I cupped my breast, pinching one nipple myself to ease the tension.

"You're stunning," he added, nudging me back onto the bed and following, his hand replacing mine over my breast, his long fingers squeezing and kneading before rolling my nipple between his finger and thumb. The sparks once again zapped to my clit, and I raised my hips against him. I didn't even worry about how desperate I must have seemed because I *was* desperate.

"Deacon, please."

"What do you need, Low?" He kneeled in front of me. It was surreal. I was watching one of my best friends, ready to explode, and he kept looking at me like I was the only meal he'd ever wanted. He stroked from my knee up the inside of my thigh, then back down. His eyes swept over every inch of me, and I saw want in his gaze with every pass. It was still hard to believe he wanted me, but in that moment I felt like someone who should be wanted. He shifted to his back. "Are you still feeling brave?"

"Yes," I said on an exhale as his fingers moved up the outside of my thigh, awakening every nerve ending.

"I want you to climb over here and sit."

"Sit?" I looked around the bed, trying to make sense of what he was saying. "On the edge of the bed?"

He grinned, beckoning with one finger. "No," he said, tapping his lips. "Right here."

"Is that safe? I mean, will you be able to breathe? Will I—"

I stopped mid-sentence when his fingertip inched up the inside of my thigh, so close to where I wanted him that I trembled.

"You will not crush me, you will not suffocate me." His thumb made an achingly slow circle around my clit, my body on a taut wire from the teasing touches. "You can hold on to the headboard if you want, and then you'll ride my face."

He guided my thigh toward him, and I tentatively placed my knees on either side of him. This felt so beyond anything I'd experienced, but when he slid a finger over my swollen flesh again, I melted a little more. "Are you sure you will be able to breathe?"

"It won't be my last breath, but if it was"—he tipped his head up and ran a flat tongue over my clit, making every inch of me pulse at once—"it would be perfect." He rested his head back on the pillow. "Stop hovering, beautiful." His hand was at my waist, and he guided me down. "Sit."

Holy shit. Holy shit. Holy shit. His lips slid over my swollen flesh, I felt his entire mouth, and my eyes snapped closed.

Any insecurity I had melted away as his tongue worked over me, again and again; the sounds of his lapping filled the room, and I began to rock against him. "Tell me what you want. Use that dirty mouth I know you have," he said. Deacon's tongue and lips moved over me then, the wet heat of his mouth surrounding me. He was playful at first, his tongue flicking and swirling, getting close to the spot where I most wanted him, but not exactly.

"Harder," I moaned.

Deacon immediately pulled my clit between his lips, sucking gently as his tongue swirled. The combination left me throbbing as his finger slid inside me, slowly, making sure I was ready. I'd noticed Deacon's hands a hundred times, the way his fingers looked wrapped around a tool or opening a jar, but I'd never imagined they could feel so good. A second finger slid in alongside the first, and the sensation of being filled, filled by him, was overwhelming and I rocked against him.

"Yes," I groaned as he began thrusting his fingers, moving in and out, nudging my G-spot with each pass and taking my cues.

He moved faster, his mouth giving me more pressure, insistent, like I liked. The tension in my body rose, and I was about to give way.

"Deac!" I couldn't even get his full name out, as the waves of pleasure rolled through me, the electricity reaching every point in my body at once, my center pulsing under his mouth and fingers. I didn't remember sliding off him, but he met my eyes, licking his lower lip, his mouth wet from me, from my pleasure.

"Willow," he said, staring down at me as he propped himself on one elbow.

"I . . ." I'd planned to tell him thank you, to make a joke about his skills, but my body still shook, my muscles somehow languid and loose and ready to tense again. My racing heartbeat stopped my words, stopped the joke, and in its place, I felt like I could break, which made no sense.

He fell to the bed next to me and held me close, our bodies pressing together. "What?" He tipped my chin up, and his gaze met mine.

"I don't know," I said, lost in the gold of his eyes, in the heat of his hands, and the feel of his erection thick against my thigh. "How did you know that would make me feel brave?"

He brushed his lips across mine. "I didn't . . . but I'm glad you did."

"Let me take care of you now," I said, languidly rolling to my side, but his palm slid across my belly, pushing me back on the bed. His lips brushed mine again, the kiss more insistent this time, our tongues mingling. A moment before, it seemed my body would be sated forever, but in an instant, I was needy again. But when I reached for his hand, it was already trailing down my stomach. "Relax," he said. "It's still my turn."

CHAPTER 36

I'D NEVER SLEPT over at a woman's place—it made things confusing—but once I started holding Willow, I couldn't let her go. I woke up to an empty bed, though, shocked I'd slept until seven.

"Good morning," she said, looking over her shoulder from her spot at the stove when I walked into the kitchen.

"How do you feel?" I slid a finger down her arm and kissed the nape of her neck.

"Boneless," she said, stretching again, ironic because the way she was wriggling, I felt the opposite.

"Maybe I should skip this study group I agreed to attend, and we can go for round two."

I'd thought a lot about what Kelly said and then what Marcus mentioned noticing, and they were both right. So yesterday I'd texted Kelly that I'd come to the study group—that was a good compromise. I just wasn't ready to be around a big group who would know the weight of what I'd caused with my injury. I could do a study group, though, and it might get Kelly off my back. But now, this option seemed better.

"You promised you'd take a risk," she said, swatting the spatula in my direction, nearly missing me as I jumped out of the way.

"Going to the library to meet people is not a risk," I said, after snagging plates from the cupboard. Her hair was swept up in some kind of clip, exposing the nape of her neck, the soft skin a temptation I kept eyeing, tracing the way her curls fell over her neck. "I was thinking I'd go parasailing or hide Emi's cleaning supplies."

Willow turned back to the stove and flipped the two pancakes in the pan, movements quick and focused. "Parasailing wouldn't feel risky for you," she said, glancing over her shoulder, her soft brown eyes meeting my gaze. "You jumped out of planes your whole career. And hiding Emi's cleaning solution isn't risky, that's asking to be murdered." She chuckled, and I saw her dimples from the side. Dimples I'd kissed the night before and couldn't stop thinking about. I kept seeing her from new angles, and she didn't look different, but I felt different, like in memorizing these new views of her, I was giving up a piece of myself, little by little. "But I think giving new people a chance, connecting to this veterans group, I think that does feel risky for you," she added, her tone more serious and her words taking residence in my chest.

I was a social guy. I met new people all the time, but she was right. I'd resisted joining this group, and I knew there was probably a reason for that that I wouldn't want to examine too closely. "Maybe." I brushed my lips against the back of her neck, feeling her still under me as my palm rested at her hip. She hadn't asked for stolen kisses in the kitchen—it wasn't on her list, but I wondered if it was on mine. "When did you get to know me so well?"

"Big questions." Her response was a little breathless, and I swept my lips over the same spot on her nape again.

"But if I skip the study session," I said, kissing under her ear, "we can work on page two." Her full hips were luscious under my palms, and I tugged her back against me.

She tipped her head to the side, and I took the invitation to drop my mouth to the crook of her neck. "Deacon," she said, moaning, and I ground against her backside, ready for more of her, but she turned suddenly in my arms and was face-to-face with me. Her hand landed on my biceps for balance, and I took in her face, those dimples from yet a new angle. She slid a confident finger along my hairline, tracing over my beard. "I know you're trying to distract me. Am I right? Is it a risk?"

"No," I said, closing my eyes against her soft touches. I lied because it made sense to me, but it wouldn't to anyone else. If I joined a vets group, if I made military friends here, I felt I was giving up on going back, on this separation from my unit being temporary. And if it was permanent, then I had to give up on the version of me I knew. I didn't know who Deacon Rakes was without the PJs. "Maybe."

"So, you'll go? I can hang out there, too, and work on my vet school application." She drew a circle on my arm. "And then we can get back to page two after." She looked up at me with wide eyes, eyebrows raised, but then her nose scrunched at the smell of burning pancakes.

KELLY WAVED ME over to the table in the corner on the second floor of the library, introducing me to the other four people sitting there, two I'd met once before. "Hey," I said, pulling my econ book from my backpack, noticing the same book in front of the guy to my left, Bryce. "This test is gonna suck," I said, tipping my head toward his book.

He laughed and pointed at my book. "Interesting supplemental reading you've got there."

When I looked down, the romance novel I'd swiped from Willow's nightstand had slipped out with my book, the shirtless hockey player's rippled abs in contrast with the cover of *Principles of Economics*. I laughed, too, after the shock of seeing it there.

"Extra study on supply and *demand*, huh?" Bryce said, picking up the book and scanning the back cover where the goalie's dominant side was hinted at.

"You should read that," Kelly said to Bryce. "I bet your girlfriend would appreciate you brushing up on your skills."

He flipped her off but passed the book to the guy across the table. "My wife reads these nonstop," Milo said, voice thoughtful. "Should read one. She'd be shocked I took an interest."

"It's pretty good," I said, relaxing in my chair as they joked with one another. I don't know what I expected, but it wasn't this. "Took it from my girl's nightstand. Definitely more interesting than this," I said, tapping the cover of the textbook, realizing only after that I'd called Willow my girl.

"Looks like Deacon has inspired a book club," Kelly said with a wink in my direction. I suspected there was going to be an "I told you so" from her in my future, but she pulled her own math textbook from her bag without pressing it further. "I'm pulling rank as peer mentor. Let's tackle these books first, though."

The others groaned good-naturedly, and Kelly leaned over. "Told you it was a good group," she said, elbowing me.

The two hours passed quickly, and at the end of the study

session, Bryce and I made plans to connect to review the study guide next week before the test. My phone buzzed as I stuffed my things back in my bag, letting Milo and another guy, Andre, look at the novel, hypothesizing what "grumpy sunshine" meant and what it had to do with hockey or a praise kink.

> WILLOW: No rush, but I'm on the 4th floor in the northwest corner when you're done.
>
> DEACON: Just wrapping up. What's up there?

She didn't answer, and I waved at the others as I walked toward the stairs to find her. Knowing she was waiting for me had made me eager to finish the work, but I also noticed how much more I enjoyed studying today than I usually did. Today I'd laughed with them and looked up from the task at hand.

The fourth floor was a stark contrast to the second, where tables were filled with groups and individuals studying, talking, laughing, and making the space feel alive. This floor was eerily quiet as I stepped out of the stairwell in search of Willow. I looked at the titles, and there were a lot of research books with titles I didn't understand at first glance. "Low?" I said, into the quiet space. I'd yet to see another person and looked around the corners in search of her. "Willow?"

I was about to text her when I jumped at a hand grabbing my shirt from behind a bookcase and she tugged me into an alcove. "Hey," I said, looking around. "I couldn't find you."

"How was it?"

I ran a hand through my hair. "Kinda fun, actually." I glanced around the abandoned floor. "What's up here?"

She had a glint in her eyes, and she tugged me further into the alcove of books, the smell of old paper mixing with Willow's shampoo in the cramped space. "I had time to explore," she said, finally stopping and looking around. "What's up here is privacy."

I let my backpack fall to the floor and hauled her toward me, my hands on her hips, fingers slipping under the hemline of her T-shirt. I needed to keep convincing myself what I felt was nothing, but I also had only a little time left to touch her like this. "What do we need privacy for? Deep research?"

She giggled and then pressed a hand over her mouth when the sound echoed. "I don't know about deep, but thorough." She leaned in closer and whispered, her body pressed close to mine.

"I'm all for it," I whispered back. "But what did you have in mind?"

She pressed her finger to my lips and grinned before sinking to her knees.

"Low, what are you doing?" She rested her fingers on the button of my jeans, and the sight of her expression—the excitement, the eagerness, the goddamn smile—shattered my heart into tiny pieces even as my cock swelled. "I told you that you don't have to do this."

"I told you to hush," she said, unzipping my jeans and maneuvering her soft hand around my shaft. *Holy shit.* She studied me, her gaze moving up and down my shaft before looking up at me with those big brown eyes. "I know I don't have to." Her gaze dropped to where a drop of pre-cum beaded at the tip and then moved back to mine before sliding her warm, wet tongue over the tip with her eyes locked on mine. "I want to."

I reached behind me to steady my grip on the shelf as Willow's lips slid over me, and I sank into her mouth using every bit of willpower to not groan at the feel of her lips moving over me, her tongue working against my skin and the feel of her soft hands holding me to her. The stillness around us on the fourth floor was alive with what might come next, who might find us, and that made this even hotter.

"Fuck, baby," I said, running my hands over her hair as she circled her fingers over my balls. She shifted position, and I slipped deeper into her mouth, her speed picking up as her fingers worked in tandem with her mouth at the new angle. I gritted my teeth and gave a pump into her mouth, helpless against this unexpected turn of events and the sight of Willow on her knees taking me in her mouth.

My balls tightened, and I tugged on Willow's hair. "Low, I'm close."

In answer, she moved on me faster, her lips tightening around me, and her fingers dug into my thighs. She was incredible, and I couldn't think straight. I gripped the bookcase, unable to hold on, and spilled into her mouth, her lips slowing over me as she drank me down, and everything in my vision went black for a moment.

She dragged her fingers across her lips and looked up at me with a nervous smile as she sat back on her heels. Across the room, a door opened, and her eyes widened in panic.

I hauled her to her feet and pulled her to the end of the alcove where another bookcase jutted out and we hid in a shadowy corner.

"I didn't think anyone would come up here," she said, looking over her shoulder, but I could only look at her. "What?" she said. "Did I get some on my face?"

I pulled her face to mine and kissed her, feeling the slightly swollen give of her lips. "You might have rebooted my brain . . . again," I whispered.

"It was good?"

I kissed her again. "That's not even a real question." The footsteps grew closer, and I tucked myself back into my jeans. "It was incredible," I said softly before kissing her again.

"That's enough, kids," a middle-aged man said. "This is a place for studying, not sucking face."

Willow pressed a hand over her mouth to stifle a giggle and buried her face in my shoulder.

"Sorry," I said to the librarian. "Studying for anatomy just got a little out of hand."

"I'm too old for this," he muttered as he walked away, and Willow laughed against my chest.

"Shh," I said, hugging her to me. "You're going to get me kicked out of school."

I took her hand and tugged her toward the exit, determined to get home and on to step two of whatever this was. Willow gripped my hand and walked with quick steps next to me, even though we'd already been caught.

"I can't believe we did that," she said, glee rolling off her. "I mean . . . that was amazing!"

Sex in public was amazing. The risk of getting caught was exciting, but the thing I couldn't get over as she climbed into my truck was how excited Willow had been to do this with me and how her excitement did funny things to my chest. As I drove to her place, the voice in my head was shouting at full volume, *You love her! Just say it!*

I rushed into the driveway and pulled her face to mine. It had been hell to not kiss her during the short drive, and I swept my tongue over her lower lip. She was going to be leaving for her camping trip in the morning, which meant I had the weekend to figure out how the hell I was going to tell Cruz I was head over heels in love with his baby sister. I knew I needed to come clean with him before I could tell Willow how I felt about her.

CHAPTER 37

Willow

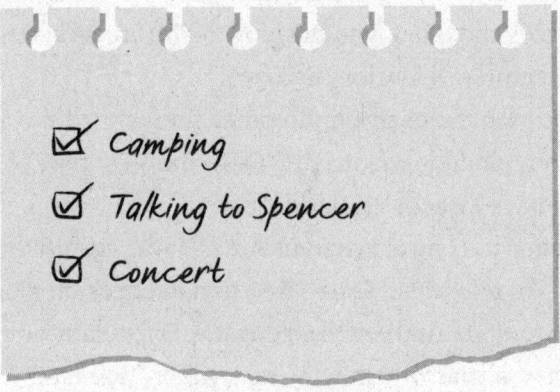

"IT'S NOT MY fault," Zoe said, stepping back from the tent we'd spent the last forty-five minutes figuring out how to erect. Hollis swatted at a bug on her arm and gave Zoe dramatic side-eye.

"You said you wanted a re-do on your first concert. How was I supposed to know the Pius Boys wasn't a cool local band?" Zoe said she had a surprise when she picked us up from the airport—she'd found a concert for us to go to, and it was free.

I wiped my hands on my jeans and fell into a camping chair. "And nothing about the flyer made you question why it was free?"

"In retrospect, there were clues." Zoe toyed with the zipper on the tent and then joined Hollis and me by the fire. "But even though it was the St. Pius X Catholic middle school boys choir, it was technically still a concert."

"And, they kind of rocked," Hollis added.

I laughed and held out my jazz hands, even though my arms were exhausted from hauling gear and then putting the tent up. "I declare it counts," I admitted. "Another re-do in the books!"

Zoe's eyes flashed, and a Cheshire grin spread across her lips. Hollis gave a wolf whistle.

Zoe fell into one of the camping chairs we'd rented, crossing one leg over the other with the glow of the fire flickering across her soft features. "Now for page two!"

Hollis took the chair on the other side of me. She and Zoe had gotten along immediately. "Ooh, the sexy part of the list! Good to have Deacon on hand for that!"

I opened the bag of marshmallows. "I was against the idea at first, but I'm really glad Cruz asked him to check on me."

Zoe grinned. "And you're getting that D regularly now, right?"

I threw a marshmallow at her, which bounced from her chest into her lap where she plucked it, popping it in her mouth. "Is that a yes?" she asked through a mouth full of marshmallow, and I threw another one at her.

"A lady never tells," I said, arranging a stack of sticky, sugary goodness on the metal skewers. I liked mine lightly browned, Zoe preferred hers blackened to a crisp, but we could both agree that adding a peanut butter cup to the top instead of just chocolate was next-level, despite Hollis's protestations about being a purist.

"You told me about the list, and anyone with twenty percent of their vision could see you two are hot for each other," Hollis said. "But you really like him?"

I shrugged, finding a good spot to rest my skewer and rotating it slowly to get an even brown. My face was probably hot because of the fire. Of course I really liked him. No one had ever made me feel like he did, like he'd catch me when I leaped into the air, but maybe more important, he made me feel like I could make the leap in the first place. Deacon, with his dirty jokes and blatant flirting and his big questions, helped me realize I could ask for more in life for myself than just being ready for a new relationship. I wasn't sure he was the kind of guy you could just like—he was the kind of guy you had to fall head over heels for, and I desperately wanted my heels to remain on the ground. "Liking him is a bad idea."

"Someone's in denial," Hollis said in a singsong voice.

"Big denial," Zoe agreed. "But that's okay. You can pretend you're not head over heels for this guy. As long as you're getting over the Drip, I'm happy." She popped another marshmallow in her mouth. "Hollis, imagine someone as dull as watching paint dry but also the paint is bad in bed and very comfortable with you giving up your dreams so you can support him."

Hollis held out her skewer to get a marshmallow from Zoe. "Willow, your ex actually sounds like the worst. Why were you with him so long?"

"He wasn't that bad," I said, checking my skewer again and deciding I wanted them just a touch browner. "He was usually kind, and sometimes he could be funny. He cared about me." I'd spent so long lamenting how Spencer left me, but now I felt like I couldn't think of more words to describe his personality. All the good things, all the things I loved, felt like smoke in my fingers, and I couldn't hold on to them except for one. "He was there for me."

Hollis eyed me skeptically and pointed her skewer in my direction, then tapped her fresh marshmallows against mine. It was by an unspoken agreement that we were having s'mores for dinner. "Like he was your only option? No way."

I chuckled. "I mean, I thought he was the only guy." In middle school and high school, I felt like I was so lucky that I had a boyfriend who was into me. Now that I'd been in front of Deacon, feeling his gaze on me, his lips on mine, all of that felt special in a new way. When Deacon touched me, I felt like it was because I was touchable. When he looked at me, I felt like I was someone who deserved the attention. I knew I just hoped that feeling stuck when he wasn't looking anymore. "But that's not what I meant. I think I stayed with Spencer so long because he was steady. I felt like enough for him."

"Reliability is something," Zoe said begrudgingly. "Not enough. But something."

I lifted one shoulder. "It was all I thought I needed," I said, noticing Zoe straightening. I hurried to cut her off. "But I know I want more now."

"You want someone who's there, but also . . ." Zoe plowed forward and waved in front of her lap. "But also here."

"And here," Hollis said, waving in front of her boobs.

I laughed, covering my mouth to stop the s'more from flying from my lips. Our laughter felt like some kind of cocoon in our clearing along with the warmth of the fire. It felt so good to be here sharing my feelings with my friends. I pointed to my mouth. "And here."

The others whooped and cheered, and I felt heat rise on my cheeks, especially proud to have surprised them a little.

"That's a re-do I can get behind," Zoe said.

"Same. Not sure you'll get much mouth action in the woods, though," Hollis said. "I'm spoken for."

"And I'd ruin you for anyone else," Zoe added. "Plus you're a big fan of equipment we just don't have."

I shook my head and opened the graham crackers. "Camping is on my re-do list." The peanut butter cup was a little melted from being near the fire, and I eased it onto the cracker, licking the melted chocolate from my fingers.

"Okay. Why is that? You had kind of mid sex with the ex in the woods?" Hollis held out her hand for a wrapped peanut butter cup, and I tossed one to her, more gently than I did the marshmallows.

I chuckled. "No." I pressed my s'more together, the middle squishing satisfyingly between the graham crackers. Spencer and I had never gone camping—he didn't really like the idea of sleeping outside and using campground bathrooms. He hated smelling like smoke from the fire. As I thought about it, I inhaled the scents of the fire and the woods. "We never camped."

"So, why re-do it?"

"I was actually camping with my family. It was right before my parents decided to divorce, and they thought it would be good for us to get out of town and spend time together as a family. Cruz was already in the Air Force, so just me and them." I couldn't even remember what the argument was about, but they went from sniping at each other, to hurling barbs back and forth when they thought I had my headphones on, to just being cruel to each other. I didn't remember what they said, but the way they sounded—so angry, so injured, so full of regrets—did stay with me. "They were fighting a lot, and I snuck off to sit by the lake."

"And Spencer was there? Probably wearing khakis, loafers, and an oxford shirt?" Zoe asked, her grin crooked, and I appreciated the attempt to keep the story light.

I shook my head with a smile. "We were already friends, and

I needed someone to talk to." I remembered the feel of my heart pounding in my chest, of how nervous I'd been to text him. We were friends, but I had a huge crush on him. Still, if I didn't talk to someone, I'd just focus on my parents and their issues. "He replied to my text, and then we talked on the phone for a couple hours."

"That's kind of sweet," Hollis said, before taking a bite of her s'more. "He was there for you."

"My flabbers are gasted. Do I need to have a new respect for the Drip?" Zoe motioned with her skewer and the overbooked marshmallow fell off the tip and into the dirt.

"You're never going to get to eat any of your marshmallows," I said, motioning to the bag next to her.

"Who cares? More. What happened next?"

I laughed and took another bite of my treat. "We talked for a long time, and he made me feel better." I remembered staring at the stars as we spoke, and it felt meaningful. "He asked me if I was okay before we said good night. If I needed him to call me the next day. I said no, but he did, anyway." He'd called me a few times a day for the three days we were in the woods. "He really always was kind of like that."

"He was there," Hollis said, sitting back in her chair. "Okay. I get it a little."

Zoe clapped, the skewer still in her hand. "Fine. He isn't all bad, but to be clear, he still wasn't *here* for you, though, right?" She spread her thighs and pointed between them.

I laughed and took a bite of a peanut butter cup to avoid answering.

She dropped her hands. "Boo!"

"He said the idea kind of grossed him out."

"Drip strikes again. What a tool."

Hollis was proving to be the more measured friend tonight. "I mean, everyone has their own sexual green lights and red lights, right? He didn't expect you to go down, did he?"

I winced.

Zoe clapped again. "My assessment stands. Tool."

"Anyway," I said. "My parents fought the whole weekend when they thought I wasn't listening, and he was my solace. My dad moved out shortly after that trip, and my mom was depressed and distant after that. I thought I needed him, and he was always there. Now, I think I never really took the chance to see if I could be strong without him." I toyed with the end of my skewer, debating if I wanted one more toasted marshmallow. "And now I'm realizing I don't need him anymore. So, I thought a re-do on the camping was . . . fitting. I can be my own solace, I think."

I finished my s'more, grateful it kept me from having to say more. It's hard to tear up when your mouth is full of chocolate and marshmallow. Life hack.

Hollis wrapped an arm around me, and Zoe hopped up from her chair to join us, wrapping me in her arms. "But you know we're here, right?"

I hugged them back. I did. I was surrounded by love and care, and there was probably melted chocolate and graham cracker crumbs in my hair, but I didn't mind.

Zoe pulled back but sat on the ground next to me, checking her marshmallows and furrowing her brow when they were only a little browned. "I'm proud of you for realizing you can want more than someone who is just reliable."

I laughed, a few crumbs landing on my jeans. "Thank you," I said, looking up.

"You can look for someone who gives you butterflies," Hollis said. "That's how I feel about Des," she added. "They're reliable, too, but they give me the butterflies."

As Zoe asked about how they'd met, I felt my phone buzz inside my hoodie. I had emailed Spencer asking him to mail me my vet school materials, and I was anxious it might be a reply from him, but when I dug it from the front pocket of my hoodie, I felt something else. Something a lot like butterflies.

> DEACON: Gus misses you but Cupcake is keeping him company.

There was a picture of the big guy snuggled up in the pink blanket I'd left on the couch, his snout tucked under one big paw. Cupcake was stretched out next to him.

> DEACON: How is the great outdoors?

I snapped a photo of Zoe's blackening marshmallows.

> WILLOW: S'mores for dinner!
>
> DEACON: You three really do camping right.

He sent a photo of a hockey romance from my nightstand I was about to start.

> DEACON: I'm bored and started reading another one of your hockey romance novels. Not bad. You're not going to abandon me for a goalie, are you?

WILLOW: No. Maybe a D-man, but not a goalie.

DEACON: Good. I'd miss you.

He sent a selfie of his forearm tucked over his nose like Gus, and I giggled, showing my screen to Zoe and Hollis.

"I'm not going to point out that silly little grin on your face," Zoe said. "But what a sweet little grin it is," she said, studying her marshmallows.

"Caused by Deacon, I'm guessing?" Hollis had walked toward our rented cooler and returned with beers.

"Kind of," I said, trying to wipe the grin from my face. "I'm happy."

I thought about Deacon letting go of the bike and how it felt to go forward on my own, knowing he was behind me but also appreciating the breeze on my face and the comfort that I could handle the bike beneath me. He was becoming such a big part of moving forward for me, but sitting there by the fire with my friends, I realized he was part of it because I wanted him to be and not because I needed him to be. "I'm re-doing all these things, but it's about me, not Spencer. Not Deacon. About how I feel, and I feel . . . good."

Zoe set her skewer down so it was propped in the firepit and wrapped me in another big hug. "I love that for you."

"Your marshmallows are going to fall off again!" I said from inside her hold.

"I don't care." She hugged me again, and I breathed in her familiar scent. She pulled back and placed both palms on my biceps. "Good is how you should feel."

"I know," I said. "It's a relief that I can enjoy these things again. I'm going to be so ready for what comes next, like I can move on from having my heart broken in a way my mom didn't get to."

Zoe hugged me again.

"I think being apart from Spencer has really . . ." I weighed my words, because I had no s'more in my mouth, so I was tearing up. "It's helped me to see myself differently. For so long, I was just waiting for him to call me and tell me he wanted me back. I thought that I'd have a chance to go back to how things were."

"And now?"

"Now . . . I am starting to imagine how things could be."

Zoe nodded and gave me another squeeze before grabbing her skewer from the ground. It was empty, and I offered to toast hers for her the next time. The look she shot me could cut through glass.

"The marshmallow of my dreams will find me, and I'm going to kick ass at vet school and not worry about relationships."

She motioned to the fire where her lost treats were already ash. "The perfect one is worth the wait."

"But sometimes the one right in front of you is good enough for now," Hollis said, holding up a charred marshmallow. "You know, until whatever and whoever is out there for you shows up."

"Hear! Hear!" Zoe said.

Deacon's grin, the real one and not the smirk, floated through my mind, except I knew he wasn't an option for several reasons. He didn't want to be anyone's option long term, but for now he was there and willing and wonderful.

"Because what's out there are partners who are down to go down," Zoe said.

Hollis's expression was indignant. "He really said 'gross'? You're going to be so gloriously impressed when it's your first time with someone good."

I bit my lower lip and studied my marshmallow. "Yeah," I said noncommittally, holding back the grin that threatened to spread across my face and spill my secret. "Maybe someday."

Zoe took a pull from her beer. "Maybe we can find someone talented when we go looking for mountain men for me."

"Stop trying to offer me to strange men in the woods!" I laughed.

"Strange men in the woods are eighty-nine percent more likely to be excellent lovers than known men in the city."

I giggled and pulled my skewer from the fire. "Did you read that in *Strange Man in the Woods Weekly*?"

We were laughing when my phone buzzed again in my pocket.

"Another dog photo?" Zoe pulled her marshmallow from the fire, the flames licking up the side of her blackened treat. "Another man photo?"

I flipped the phone over and froze at the name flashing across the screen.

Zoe blew on her marshmallow, and her brow furrowed when she caught my expression. "Is Gus okay? Is it Cruz?"

"No." I looked at the phone screen.

> SPENCER: I'll send the materials tomorrow. How are you?
>
> SPENCER: Maybe we could catch up sometime?

My hands had shaken when I'd sent the message earlier in the day, and I expected a wave of something when I saw his name, but it never came. A notification that I had another message from Deacon flashed on my screen, and I sent a thumbs-up reply to Spencer and toggled over to the thread with Deacon.

DEACON: Will you save me a s'more?

"Before Zoe ends up on the news or married to a sexy mountain man, can we take a picture?" I motioned for the girls to pull in close to me and took a selfie, marshmallows and beers in our hands. The firelight cast a warm glow on our faces. I tapped to send the photo to Deacon, and he hearted it almost immediately.

I laughed with Hollis as Zoe recounted a story about her boss and waited for Deacon's reply. I felt loose enough that I was ready for some flirtatious banter over text, but when I looked at my phone, I didn't know how to reply to what he'd sent.

DEACON: You look really happy, Low.

DEACON: You really shine when you're happy.

CHAPTER 38

WILLOW CAUGHT MY eye from across the room, flashing a grin before looking back to Marcus, who was describing the kitchen in his and Lila's new place. I saw his hand make a wide arc, and I'd heard about this kitchen enough times to know he'd moved on to the descriptive tour where he talked about the pot-filler faucet.

"We had a bet about how long this would take," Emi said, falling onto the couch next to me and handing over a beer bottle as Sybil sank into the cushion on my other side. "I thought you'd hold out a little longer, so now I'm out twenty bucks."

"I'd like it in ones," Sybil said from my other side where Cupcake was snuggled next to her. "I'm considering taking Kieran to a strip club tonight." Across the room from his spot next to Willow, he heard his name, and Sybil blew him a kiss.

Emi's laugh shook the couch, and I wrapped an arm around Sybil's shoulders. "I cannot think of a single person who would be more uncomfortable at a strip club than your fiancé." The man in question shot us a curious look but shrugged and returned to the conversation with Marcus and Willow, who cut her eyes to me, just for a second, like we had a secret to share.

Maybe we did. I'd slept over at her place since she'd returned from her camping trip, and I was hoarding the secrets of how her breathing slowed right before she fell asleep and how Willow loved my arms wrapped around her first thing in the morning. It had been one of the best weeks of my life, and sometimes I wondered if she was putting off finishing her list because of what it might mean. We'd spent hours and hours in the library the week before, mostly behaving, while she worked on her vet school application after receiving the things she'd asked for from her ex.

"He'd do anything for me," Sybil said, pulling me back into the conversation. "Much like Deac would do for Willooooooow," she said, dragging out the vowel sound while poking me in the side. "I knew it wouldn't take long."

Emi handed Sybil a twenty-dollar bill across my chest. "All I have. Kieran will have to find a dancer willing to make change." She elbowed me in the side. "I really thought you'd wait until her brother came back from his deployment."

Every time I kissed Willow or she sent me a suggestive text—her dirty talk was top-tier now—I had to convince myself this wasn't a true betrayal of our friendship. It never worked, though. Sitting here on the couch at my friends' farewell barbecue the anxiety made me want to run laps. I didn't have an answer to Emi, but Sybil jumped in.

"No. Deacon's never been in love, and he's not patient."

"I never said I was in love," I said, my gaze dragging to Willow as she tipped her head back and laughed at something one of the guys said. "I never actually said anything. You two are having this entire conversation without me." It had been two weeks of falling asleep with Willow and waking up to her bed-hogging beside me, two weeks of hot kisses and breathless murmurs. And laughing. We laughed a lot.

"You didn't *say* anything," Emi pointed out. "But it's written all over your face." Emi laughed and crossed her feet on the coffee table in front of us. "And that's me saying it. Your rational, purposefully single, thinks cute rom-coms are pointless, friend."

"If Emi sees hearts in your eyes, they're clearly there."

"Yeah, well . . ." I watched Willow intently as she looked at her phone and then stepped out to answer. "She's . . ." I stared at the spot where she'd been standing, trying to think of the right words. "It's complicated."

"Because you're reenlisting?" Sybil's question squeezed that lingering anxiety until it pulsed.

I skirted the question. "Plus, she's probably going back to Colorado. There's some stuff to figure out." And then there was Cruz. He'd be flying back soon and would have some time here. I'd have to tell him something, but I still had no idea what.

Sybil patted the arm of the couch for Kieran to sit next to her. "So you'll tell him you've been debauching his baby sister, he'll give you a black eye, and then you'll move on. That's how men's friendships work, right?"

I shook my head and tipped the beer to my lips. "Not really." Though I hoped it could go that way.

"If Lila was hooking up with Deacon," she said, patting Kieran's knee, "it wouldn't bother you, would it?"

Her fiancé tipped his head. "I think Marcus might be more bothered since they're moving in together."

Sybil waved her hands toward Marcus, who'd joined us. "I

mean, if Marcus was no longer in the picture. Like he was taken out by a pastry accident or something."

Marcus looked between us. "Um, why are you killing me off in this scenario?"

"To find out Kieran's reaction to Deacon hooking up with his little sister."

Marcus threw a pretzel at her, which bounced off her shoulder and landed on my lap. I glanced around for Willow, not wanting her to overhear this conversation. "To be clear, this scenario exists only in Syb's head," I said, holding up two palms, both to Marcus and Kieran.

"I haven't told Lila what to do since she was about eight," Kieran said, shrugging. Sybil poked him in the side and gave him one of those you-know-what-I-mean looks people seemed to adopt in relationships. Kieran mouthed a "sorry," and added, "But, uh, no offense, man, I wouldn't be happy about it. You kind of . . . you know, have a track record with women."

Sybil gave him a wide-eyed look that felt scathing to me, but I appreciated his honesty. He was right. It was why Cruz wouldn't just hit me and get over it.

"But," Kieran said, abruptly, straightening at his fiancée's sharp glare, "if she liked and trusted you, I'd be happy for her."

"My traumatic pastry-related death has not affected things, apparently," Marcus added, crossing his arms over his chest. "What kind of friends are you?"

"She never said it was traumatic," Emi said from her spot. "Maybe you just over-laminated some puff pastry and it enveloped you while baking. You'd go peacefully in a sea of croissant."

"You think that wouldn't be traumatic?!" Marcus choked out a laugh. "Also, I would *never* over-laminate." Marcus launched into a lecture about dough technique, and I slipped off the couch, checking who needed refills so that I could escape the rest of Sybil's point. As an added bonus, Willow was coming out of the bathroom and met me in the kitchen.

An eruption of laughter filled the adjoining room, and I glanced away from Willow toward my friends. My friends who were leaving and moving on. She wanted to finish her list, and it was me I worried would take sex with her for more than it was. I'd memorized every inch of her body, the sounds of her groans, and how she tasted, but I hadn't been inside her yet. I told her I wanted to go slow, to give her time to think about this step, but really, I needed time. "You missed my best friends discussing candidly why no brother should want their sister anywhere near me."

"Well," she said, playfully wrapping her arms around me. "They're wrong, and we've already decided we're not going to tell my brother, so it doesn't matter, anyway."

She was cute like this—relaxed, comfortable, and most importantly, she trusted me. It was written all over her face—her perfect, freckled face—and I swallowed audibly, repeating the last step of the plan. "And then we walk away from each other."

"We've got a little more time," she said. "Anyway, you might be bored with me after we . . ." She looked over her shoulder as if someone might overhear. "F."

"F? Like for forage? Fly? Flail?" I grinned and tipped her chin up. "And I could never be bored with you." Because I was unequivocally in love with this woman. She was set on finishing her list, on checking off all the items so she could move on, and I could help her do that. And then, I'd offer that she move on . . . with me. I dropped a kiss on her lips again. "You want to get out of here now to forage?"

She nodded eagerly. "Yes!"

I took her hand and tugged her toward the door. I'd had my reasons for waiting, but it didn't mean it hadn't been torture every time I put on the brakes.

"Don't you want to say goodbye?"

I yelled into the other room, "We're leaving!" and was met with a raucous cheer from my friends. Willow giggled, but it was exactly how I felt inside. I didn't know what I wanted to happen next in my life, but I knew I wanted her, unequivocally and no matter the consequences.

The drive to her place was short, and I hustled out of my truck, unwilling to lose contact with Willow for a moment longer than necessary. I was so eager, I stumbled on the uneven section of concrete and my phone fell out of my hand, and Willow giggled as she hurried toward me, her hand on mine as I caught myself. "Who knew clumsy could look so hot?" she teased, but her touch was warm through my shirt, and it snapped something in my self-control. I'd spent too many hours not kissing this woman, and I had her backed against the truck in an instant, my lips on hers in a searing kiss, a preview to everything I planned on doing that night. When we broke apart, she stared up at me with a wide-eyed, dreamy expression. "I was going to tell you to be careful," she said.

"Careful isn't who I am." I dragged a thumb down her neck and kissed her again as I guided her up the walk, unwilling to let her go.

"Wait!" She pushed gently back as we reached the front steps. "Don't forget your phone!"

It lay on the concrete across the driveway, and I briefly debated leaving it, but instead dropped a kiss to her lips and jogged the short distance to retrieve it. The screen was undamaged, and I was about to slide it in my pocket when it buzzed in my hand. Ice ran through my veins when I saw the notification pop up.

Willow looked at me quizzically from the bottom step, realizing I'd stopped short. "What? Did you forget something at the house?"

I heard her, but I was too focused on the message to answer.

"Deac," Willow said. "What's up?"

I looked up from my phone, seeing the light expression on Willow's face dim. I tried calling on a career of training in detaching my emotions, but it wasn't working, and an anxious cold sensation overtook my whole body.

"It's a message from Dougy."

CHAPTER 39

Willow

MEMORIES OF MY brother laughing flew through my head as every other thought blinked out while I registered the stricken expression on Deacon's face and leaned back against the truck. "What does it say?"

"Not much." He seemed to reread it again anyway, his brow furrowed and the humor that always etched the lines and features on his face gone.

"But it's . . ." I wanted to reach for his hand, but he gripped the phone so intently, I was frightened to distract him.

"Not good," was all he said. "I don't have any details."

The dread that had crept along the edge of everything for weeks crowded into my head. "He didn't say he's dead, though?" I grabbed for him this time, his forearm, which felt like an anchor. "Right?"

He shook his head and reread the text. "Missing."

The words did not warm the chill in my veins, and Deacon's eyes narrowed as he tapped out a reply. I saw only a series of nonsense words and acronyms I assumed were a code. My brother was the only real family I had left. He had to be okay.

Deacon stared at his phone and then shoved it in his pocket when there was no immediate reply. "Missing," he repeated, more to himself than to me as he stared somewhere over my shoulder. "Missing."

"Deac," I said, squeezing his arm because it felt like he'd gone somewhere else in his head. "What do we do?"

Deacon's arm flexed under my touch, and he looked at me, meeting my gaze for the first time since he'd gotten the message. The brown of his irises caught the light from the porch, in contrast to the tension in his features. There was more he wasn't saying—more he knew or assumed—and my hands started to shake.

"Deac?"

His big arms wrapped around me and pulled me into a tight hug, where the wall of his chest was solid under my cheek. "I don't know," he said near my ear, squeezing me just a little tighter, pulling me just a little closer. "But I've got you."

"I've got you, too," I said, wrapping my arms around his middle, and I meant it. I knew I wasn't clinging to him because I had to or because he was the only one I had; I was holding him the same way he was holding me. I'd realized I could move on from Spencer. But holding him now, sharing shock and grief with him . . . this felt like the only place I was supposed to be and an impossible place to be all at the same time. "I've got you, too," I repeated against his chest, and his lips brushed against the side of my head.

"That can't happen," he mumbled, his voice just above a

whisper, and I didn't know if he was talking to me or himself. Deacon let me go and took a big step back. He glanced at his watch and seemed to make a decision. He took two quick strides and unlocked the truck. "I gotta go," he said. "They should still be open."

"What should be open?"

"I gotta try. I'm sorry. I can't just stand here."

"I know," I said. "But there's nothing we can do."

"I can try." He pulled open the driver's side door, and the engine roared to life.

"Where are you going?" The look on Deacon's face was the same one he'd had when we were riding bikes. This serious, focused expression transformed his face. This was determination, and he called out the window as he backed out of the driveway.

"Recruitment office."

CHAPTER 40

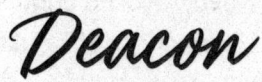

I'D WANTED TO slam the door of my truck after leaving the recruitment office, wanted to rip it from the frame and throw it across the sparsely populated parking lot until I felt less useless. But by the time I gripped the handle to the door, I saw the futility in it as the recruiter's words played back in my head. He said a lot, but "highly unlikely" was a phrase he repeated. Code 4 on the DD 214 meant not eligible for reenlistment without a waiver, and that waiver was, in his professional opinion, never going to be approved.

That had been two days ago. Now, my stomach growled and I eyed the clock on the dash—it was nearly six and I wasn't sure I'd had anything more than a protein bar all day. My body ached after two grueling workouts and a six-mile run. The recruiter's voice repeating "highly unlikely" over and over in my mind was its own kind of workout mix, as if I could prove him wrong then and there.

I'd still hoped I'd made enough progress to rely on the waiver, that there was a chance. Cruz would have rolled his eyes, called me a dipshit, and taken me out for a drink, reminding me of all the things I could do instead. I didn't even have to imagine it, because when I'd joked about getting back out with the unit right when I started PT and could barely take ten steps on my own, he'd done exactly that.

"You're a hardheaded fucking dipshit," he'd said, handing me a beer when I'd told him about my plan to get back to the PJs after the discharge was final. "They told you you're never going to be back to a hundred percent. But you're making progress. That's a good thing."

I'd huffed. It didn't feel like progress. "I'm good at proving people wrong." I'd taken a longer pull on the beer than I planned. "I can do it."

"Even if you could," he said, "you shouldn't. You're going to fuck your back up permanently, more than it already is."

"Everyone we know is hurt somehow," I said, taking another long pull. "That's the job. You're going to go until you can't anymore." I nodded my chin toward him. "You know I'm right."

"You're not." He shook his head. "When it's time, when I can't do it anymore, I'm out."

"Liar," I said. "You love the work more than anything. It's who you are."

"Nah," he said, taking a measured sip of his beer. "I love it. It's part of who I am, but not all I am."

I grunted and took another pull, the bottle nearly empty.

"I missed a lot at home," he said. "I was gone during my parents' divorce, couldn't really be there for my sister, and then when my mom died, we were deployed." He looked pensive, the lines on his forehead creasing. "Doing important work," he added, even though I didn't need him to. "But I want time to be there for Willy when I'm done. You're my brothers, but she's my sister, so yeah . . . the job isn't the only thing I am."

He'd looked down at his hands and then back at me with that implacable stare. "It's not the only thing you are, either."

Now, I swiped wet eyes with the back of my hand. I still didn't know who else I was without the unit, and I wasn't going back.

I stopped at a red light and glanced at my phone. My most recent reply to Dougy asking for an update was unanswered. I tried to reassure myself that meant nothing. There was a time difference. He was busy with the search or the next mission. But if it was really bad, if Cruz was gone, he'd wait. He was a softy under all that muscle and bravado. I let out a frustrated growl and slammed my palms onto the steering wheel as the sun dipped lower in the sky.

There was nothing from Dougy, but I had several messages from Emi.

> EMI: I'm taking Cupcake for a walk. Want to come with?
>
> EMI: Are you okay? Willow said you weren't at her place.
>
> EMI: I'm not in Switzerland yet. If you're just purposefully ignoring me, I'll hunt you down.
>
> EMI: Please let me know you're okay. I'm worried.

I marked the last with a thumbs-up and pulled out of the parking lot. I was a dick for leaving Willow alone. She didn't have anyone to turn to. That was why I'd hugged her, why I'd pulled her into my arms. I had needed a hug, too, and that's why I'd pulled back. Looking at her was a reminder of the promises I was breaking, of the promises I'd already broken to the man to whom I owed my life.

I flipped my blinker to make a right turn onto a random street and past rows of small houses with neat lawns, probably originally built in the forties. The trees lining the street filtered the dimming sunlight, and dappled shadows spread across the front seat. I'd asked for the review anyway, despite the recruiter's doubts, but he was right. It was probably hopeless. I scanned the road ahead where the neighborhood gave way to a business district and people walked along streets dotted with local shops and restaurants.

I pulled into the parking lot for a strip mall with a sports bar to the right and a coffee shop to the left next to a pet supply store. I studied the display in the pet shop window with materials for dog training. If Cruz were here, he would spend an hour perusing and weighing out what challenges Gus was ready for. Before I could sink into another memory that would circle back to the guilt I felt, I caught movement from the corner of my eye where one of the guys from the vets study group was standing, a backpack over his shoulder.

"Hey," Bryce said, holding out a fist to pound when I stepped out of the truck. "My girlfriend was impressed when I came home talking about romance novels. We gotta keep you around."

"Yeah," I said, "maybe." I ran a hand through my hair.

"No pressure." He held up a hand. "Kel is great, but she doesn't give up. Hounded me until I became a regular."

"Yeah," I said with a nod.

"You want to grab a drink?" He pointed between the bar and the coffee shop. "I was gonna meet a study group from my poli-sci class, but they bailed." He chuckled. "I'm the oldest guy in the group by at least fifteen years," he added. "And damn, do I feel it at moments like this when my gut instinct is to shake my fist and curse about these irresponsible kids."

I chuckled. I'd had that gut reaction more than once and nodded toward the bar. I wanted a beer, anyway. Driving had just made me more and more agitated.

The place wasn't crowded, and we were able to get seats at the bar. Bryce was a good guy to sit with. We mostly just watched the game on the TVs behind the bar. Bryce finally spoke, his gaze still trained on the TV. "If you tell Kelly to back off, she will," he said. "I don't think she'd mind me telling you she was in a dark place when she got out, and finding other vets and having a place, well, she talks a lot about how it saved her." He shrugged. "She doesn't want to see anyone else struggle, but I know not everyone wants that. Wants the group."

I took a pull from my beer and looked intently at the screen where they were showing a replay of a questionable foul call. My silence had nothing to do with what he'd said and everything to do with how what he said touched a nerve. I'd enjoyed being around them at the study group. Kelly was a badass, and Bryce was cool from what I could tell, but they didn't know what I'd done and how I'd let down my team. Especially with Cruz still missing during a mission I knew nothing about. That Marine's death was partly my fault, and my roommates, even Willow, didn't get how heavy that burden was to carry, but Kelly and everyone else would. Only I wasn't sure if talking about it would make me feel better or worse. I tapped my fingers on the bar to the beat of "Ain't No Mountain High Enough" playing in my head. At this point, I probably couldn't feel worse.

"Okay," Bryce said, tapping his bottle on the bar when I'd been silent for a while. "Message received. I can take a hint. You ready for that next econ test?"

He'd given me an out, another excuse to tell someone I was fine. I tapped my hand on the bar again. I wasn't fine, though, and I felt like a pressure valve had to be opened or I'd explode. "I was a PJ," I said, still looking at the TV. "53rd Rescue Squadron."

He whistled. "You've been in some shit, then."

I nodded. "Something happened, and my best buddy is in trouble. I still haven't figured out how to be okay with knowing there's nothing I can do. How to just be here when they're out there doing the work." I tapped my fingers on the bar again, hearing the notes in my head. "I feel useless and guilty I'm not on the mission with them, and I don't know what to do about it." I hadn't meant to say all of that, especially that last part. I'd stopped before admitting to the other emotion, the guilt that had never really gone away. I hardly knew this guy, and I didn't want his reassurances or platitudes.

But he didn't offer any. "That sucks," he said, instead. "Hope your friend comes through it." We both looked toward the screen just as the people scattered at a few other tables erupted in cheers when Caitlin Clark scored at the buzzer before the half. "I'm no one to give advice, and ignore me if you want to, but I had those moments of feeling disconnected and useless. Still do sometimes. I finally had to find another way to be useful and meet other people I wanted to look out for. The only way I could make myself move was knowing I had somewhere to go."

The game cut away from the arena to a commercial for a wings restaurant.

Bryce glanced at me. "It's not the same, but it's something. I met my girlfriend on a Habitat for Humanity build after I got involved there. Kind of scored a two for one there."

"I recommend you never tell her you referred to her as a two-for-one deal," I said, thinking about Willow and how much I didn't want to let her go even though it was the right thing to do. I wondered if there would ever be someone like her who I'd feel like was mine.

"You're right." Bryce laughed. "But between her and the work and the center . . . well, it felt right to have people again like I did with my unit. People who . . . get it, who understand, at least a little. And a place you can go. It helps. I have to give Kelly credit for harassing me into getting involved."

I nodded, still tapping on the bar. "Yeah, that makes sense."

"But don't tell her I said that. She's insufferable when there's an 'I told you so' at play."

Bryce looked at his phone and responded to an incoming text. "I gotta get going," he said, signaling for the bartender. "But, stop by or not, and here's my number if you ever need it." He signed his credit card receipt and then jotted down the ten digits on a napkin. Underneath he wrote an email address. "And if you do want to come by or just need anything, JC and Rita are the center's full-time staff. They're good and really fight for what we need. Both Navy, but we can't all be perfect." He laughed at his own joke and held out a fist. "Keep your head up, man. Guilt's a helluva drug." He motioned to my phone on the counter. "Hit me up if you need to."

I wanted to ask him how he figured it out, the part about

finding somewhere new to go, but I didn't want to admit I still didn't know.

Alone at the bar, I stared blankly at the commercials and halftime commentary on the game, too many thoughts swirling in my head. About Cruz, about the PJs, about what I was going to do, and about Willow. Willow's infectious laugh and the way she sighed against my neck after I kissed her. I felt so whole in those moments, like I really was a superhero for her. The second half started on the TV, and I took another sip from my beer. I reminded myself she didn't want a superhero. She didn't even want a boyfriend—she wanted a fresh start, and she was going places. I had no idea where I was going, and that made me all wrong for her.

My message to Dougy shifted from unread to read, but there was no response, and Emi had sent three heart emojis and a plea to come home since I'd left early that morning before dawn. I had to go check on Willow before I did that. No matter how much I'd fucked up this whole thing, I'd sworn I'd take care of her and keep an eye out for her, and leaving her alone with this news probably didn't make everything else that had happened any better. Further proof this whole thing between us was a bad idea. I had to take care of Willow, and then I had to get the hell away from her.

CHAPTER 41

Willow

- ☐ Grieving
- ☐ Planning for the future

I'D BEEN IN a haze and then Hollis and Blaine had come over, surrounding me. They'd both slept over, the three of us camped out in the living room with Gus. Cruz was missing—my only real family, the one constant in my life was missing, and I'd tried to prepare myself over the years to hear that, especially since I'd initially researched what the PJs did, but the reality was different. I'd wanted to curl into myself and hide from everything, but I couldn't do that with my friends there. That's how it had been when Mom died—those were the closest emotions I could link this to. I didn't want this re-do, but it felt like I was getting it all the same. And I hadn't heard from Deacon since the morning prior. He'd read my texts and told me that there was no update, but nothing substantive. I thought we'd be in this together, but we weren't. I'd finally insisted Hollis and Blaine go home—their moms were returning from their trip that evening, and I didn't want them to miss meeting them at the airport. The house felt big and empty without them, though.

Alone, I'd realized I didn't want to hide, not like I'd done in the past, even when things felt this dark.

That's when I'd pulled out my laptop. The application materials were ready to go, and I read through my personal statement again. I'd gone through ten drafts, trying to think of the right things to say. I'd described my experiences volunteering and researching, what I'd learned from mentors and professors, and then there was the last paragraph, the one I was still debating.

> There is a gap between earning my bachelor's degree and applying. You'll see my work experience was as a receptionist, and my degree, in the end, was in Business. This may look as if my interest in and commitment to studying Veterinary Medicine has wavered. It never did, and I am beyond excited to begin studying to achieve my dreams of becoming a veterinarian.

I reread the last two sentences with my cursor hovering over the save-and-submit button, but I still wasn't sure if it was enough. I sent a quiet hope into the universe that I could show it to Cruz and get his opinion. God, I hoped I could.

Gus nudged his snout against my hand, pushing me out of the fog. I needed to move, and this wasn't due yet. I hit the save button, then a second time for good measure, and closed my laptop. I pulled his leash from the hook by the door, and my phone buzzed as we stepped outside. I fumbled with getting

Gus's leash attached as I hurried to read the message, anxious for an update from Deacon.

My stomach sank—it was only a reminder about my upcoming student loan payment. Nothing about Cruz. Nothing from Deacon. I looked down and realized the leash was on the ground unattached to Gus, but just then two cats shot out from a bush, and Gus was off in a flash after them, his powerful body in motion and too focused to listen to my commands. He disappeared from view in what felt like an instant.

I CLAPPED MY hands, my palms sore from all the times I'd already tried to call Gus back over the last fifteen minutes. I'd hoped he'd doubled back to get home, but I saw no sign of him. First, Cruz went missing in action, and then I lost his dog. I called for Gus again, imagining the worst, and my stomach sank as every minute passed when he didn't respond.

"Low!" I hadn't seen Deacon pull into the driveway, but he was climbing out of the truck, his long legs eating up the pavement as the streetlights kicked on in the fading daylight. "What's going on? What are you doing out here? It's going to storm soon."

"Gus ran away," I said, frantically searching back and forth around the neighborhood. "I was clipping his leash on and two cats ran by and he just . . . took off." I wrung my hands. "I was so distracted. I should have put the leash on inside the house." I looked over his shoulder at the Gus-less neighborhood, avoiding his face. Deacon always saw everything, and he'd see my panic—it was so stupid to not check the leash. Somehow, he'd see how I really felt, too. How much I needed him.

"Okay," he said, his voice low and calm. "I can help. How long ago did he run off?"

"Fifteen minutes." Tears pricked behind my eyes, and I finally met his gaze. "What if I can't find him?"

"We will," he said. He sounded almost detached, like he could control this situation through sheer force of will. "Which way did he run?"

I pointed west with a shaky finger. "I ran after him, but he's so fast."

"Okay." He reached for my outstretched hand, and I thought he might pull me in for a hug, but he only nudged my arm down to my side. "Take a few deep breaths and give me a sec." He ran to his truck and pulled a flashlight from the glove compartment, jogging back with the light bobbing along the concrete. "We'll find him. C'mon—we'll head back that way." He nodded back in the direction I'd come and stepped away from me. A gust of wind picked up, and I hugged my arms around myself, feeling a hundred miles from him and everyone else, even though he was right by my side.

We called out as we walked, "Gus!"

"Gus!" My call followed his, and he gave a loud whistle, explaining he'd seen Cruz do that while training him. I could picture that, Cruz whistling repeatedly until the dog picked it up. He was patient like that. My head was jumping thirteen steps ahead of itself and always in the worst possible direction.

We followed the street to the path that led to the park Gus liked and wordlessly turned down the road. The wind had picked up, and a drop of rain grazed my cheek.

"Gus!" I yelled into the trees on either side of the path, listening intently for the rustle of leaves or brush or Gus's loud, imposing bark. Nothing. On the other side of the path, Deacon ventured into the brush, calling out.

"You went to the recruitment office?" As I spoke, another drop of rain dotted my hand, and I shivered against the cool breeze. It was dark now, and the flashlight lit our path, leaving Deacon's face shadowed when he answered.

"Yeah."

"You're going back, then? Back in?" I'd known that was his plan—I was even counting on us both leaving. That was why my page two plan seemed like it could work, but lately I'd secretly hoped he wouldn't. Maybe he'd stay. Maybe I'd stay. I couldn't imagine feeling this way if he went missing one day, too. I hugged my arms again and studied his body language as he looked over my shoulder and called for the dog, flicking the light into the trees.

"Deac," I said, reaching for his forearm, only to pull back when he flinched at my touch. "You're going back?"

He shrugged and started down the path. "That was the goal." The flashlight swept across the path in front of us and into the trees.

"So you can find him?" My voice was hard to hear as thunder rumbled nearby and a bolt of lightning shot across the sky. I jumped at the crack and flash of light. Gus hated thunder, and the idea of him cowering somewhere alone at the sound made my stomach clench. "So you can find him?" I repeated. "Because I don't think it works like that."

He bristled, his posture stiffening as we approached the clearing leading into the park. A few more raindrops landed on my forehead, and I heard what sounded like a dog bark in the distance, but the sound was hidden beneath another roll of thunder, so it was hard to tell if it was real or just wishful thinking. Deacon clapped his hands together, the echo bounding off the trees around us, and the *tap tap tap* of the raindrops hitting the leaves above us intensified.

He clapped his hands again and swept the light across the empty park. "I thought I heard barking." He whistled for Gus again.

"Deac," I said, hurrying to catch him. "Are you going to answer me?"

A clap of thunder shook the ground, and I jumped as the sky seemed to open up and sheets of rain fell all around us. The rain was so intense, I could barely see beyond where we stood, and I jumped again when the next thunderclap was met with a flash of light that momentarily lit the sky in a ghostly white.

"C'mon." Deacon grabbed my hand and tugged me forward. The grass and mud of the park was slick with the onslaught of rain, and my foot sank into a few puddles. The water squished between my toes until we reached the gazebo that sat in the middle of the park, where I could catch my breath from the run. Deacon's hand was still wrapped around mine, as we were both soaked through from the icy rain, his T-shirt clinging to him and hair dripping until he pushed it off his face. He looked down at our joined hands, a pained expression passing over his face before he pulled away and fell onto the bench in the middle of the space. He shone the light into the park, but it was no use. We couldn't see a thing until the rain let up. "Fuck," he muttered. "Fuck, fuck, fuck."

I sat on the other end of the bench—we were only a few feet apart, but it might as well have been miles. Deacon seemed miles away from everyone in a way that worried me. "Deacon." I had to yell to be heard over the rain. "Are you trying to get back in so you can find Cruz? So you can save him? Because you can't. And he doesn't expect you to."

"I'm just trying to help you find the dog," he said, pushing his wet hair from his face again. "That's all I'm trying to do."

"I know," I said. "I know, but you seem . . ." I searched for the right words and ventured another touch on his arm. He didn't flinch this time or shrug away. "I'm worried about you."

He gave a humorless laugh, more of a huff. "I'm not the one who is lost."

"I think we're all a little lost," I offered. "I am, or I was."

"I'm not lost," he said, standing, my hand falling from his arm. "I'm here. I'm standing still, right here. Not going anywhere. Standing right here while everyone else is moving." He paced back and forth in the small space. This was a version of Deacon I'd never seen before.

"Deac," I said, a hedge in my voice as a gust of cold wind blew raindrops toward us. "I didn't mean to . . ."

He swept the light across the park and hollered for the dog again. "I'm not going back so I can find him. I'm just trying to find the dog," he said, walking out into the rain. His voice roared through the rain, and the flashlight fell to his side, lighting the puddles around his feet. "And I can't find him." Deacon's voice seemed to crack, and I ran out into the rain, where his shoulders shook. "He's my best friend, my brother, and I can't find him."

I wrapped my arms around him, and Deacon finally let me touch him, his own arms around me. The rain washed away what I was certain were tears, all of it flowing in streams and rivulets through the grass. "I'm not there. I've betrayed his trust, and I can't do anything to help him." He clung to me as he spoke, tightly like he could stop me from getting lost, too.

"You didn't betray him," I said into his chest. "Don't say that. What happened was between us. Surely, you see it has nothing to do with Cruz. He doesn't get to decide what's right for us."

"I've spent most of my life bending the rules and deciding which ones I wanted to follow. I see how special you are. I see what's right in front of my face, but I don't deserve you." His lips twisted into a grimace, and I knew he was thinking about Cruz. "He asked me to look out for you, and all I can think about is kissing you again, touching you again. It was bad before he went missing. It's unforgivable now."

I didn't have any words for him. Every nerve in my body was raw, and every thought was one part worry, one part fear, and one part warmth when I realized Deacon might be confessing his feelings to me.

"I betrayed him," he said. "An hour ago I planned to walk away from you because I told him I'd keep my distance, and now, holding you, I know I can't. What kind of person does that make me?"

The words sounded pained, but they landed on me like something soft. "Human." I pulled back so I could look up into his face, the furrowed brow and the rain running down his defined cheekbones. "It makes you human."

Around us, the sheets of rain ebbed as suddenly as they'd begun, and the onslaught turned back to a steady, light rain. Deacon brushed the hair from my forehead and stared into my eyes. "I should . . . but I can't," he repeated, the brush of his rough hands against my skin comforting some of my panic.

The park was eerily quiet with the sudden easing of the storm, and Deacon's fingers still traced along my hairline. I felt the pull and push between us, the tension like one of those bolts of lightning, but a loud bark from the west end of the park pulled our attention, and a soaking wet Gus flew toward us from the tree line.

He reached us in seconds, and I dropped to my knees to run my hands over his big head, pulling him to me. "Good boy," I said over and over again, so intent on holding on to the dog that I didn't notice Deacon falling to his knees beside me. "He found us," I said into Gus's neck, running my hands over his ears. "He came back," I said, meeting Deacon's eyes over the dog's. "Cruz will, too." Deacon smiled weakly but then looked away.

"The rain is letting up. We should head back." He said it so stiffly, like he hadn't just exploded my heart into a hundred pieces.

I pulled the leash from where I'd stashed it in my hoodie and clipped it to Gus's collar. The little asshole already seemed to have shaken off the fear of being lost and now trotted happily between us. We walked in silence, our hands brushing once in a while. Finally, I spoke up. The old me would have waited for Deacon to bring it back up, and I pushed away that instinct. "It's not betrayal," I said, finally.

"It is." He shook his head. "On so many levels. He saved my life. And not only can I not save his right now, I did the one thing he asked me not to do."

Gus picked up his pace as we neared the house, his tail wagging at the sight of home. "To touch me?"

Deacon shook his head. The light from the front porch made his skin look golden as we stood in front of the door. He brushed my forehead again, where wet curls clung to my skin, and I held my breath, waiting for his next words. "No," he said. "To—"

His phone rang in his pocket. I'd never heard it ring before—it always buzzed, and he hurried to dig it out, fumbling with the screen. He must have enabled the speaker, because I heard the best sound I could imagine from his phone.

"Dougy has a big mouth," Cruz said, his voice breaking up with the bad connection. "I'm safe."

CHAPTER 42

WILLOW SCREAMED, PRESSING her palms to her mouth. "Cruz! You're okay!"

"Oh, shit. You told Willow? I'm gonna fucking kill Dougy." I listened for labored breathing and other signs of injury through the phone but heard none.

"Shut up!" she said, snatching the phone from me, hugging it like she wanted to hug him. "You're okay, though. You're okay!" She was crying, tears rolling down her face.

He said he was safe, not okay, but I'd take safe for now. "Don't hurt Dougy." I heard the thickness in my voice and my blood rushing to my head. "He owes me fifty bucks," I added, hoping to break the tension.

"I'm safe," he repeated. "Willy, I can't talk long, but I'm safe. I promise. Give me a sec with just Deac, okay?" The end of his sentence faded out with the bad connection, and I turned off speaker. I motioned to Willow to get Gus inside, that I'd be right behind her.

"How bad?" I asked once she was out of earshot. Bryce's

advice rang hollow to me in this moment. Nothing was like this work.

"I'm banged up." That could mean anything from he was missing an arm to he had stubbed his toe. I would have said the same. "Good news is my dick was unharmed."

"Hard for anyone to aim at such a small target."

"Fucker," he said, a laugh and then a groan. "Take care of my sister until I get home, will you?" I knew from his voice it certainly wasn't a stubbed toe.

"Of course." I remembered feeling like a shell of myself in the hospital, the dark thoughts that came in waves. "How's your head?"

"Attached, so that's good." I heard the shrug in his voice. "Simms was with me. Kept saying how his wife was begging him to get out and go be an accountant or something. Can you imagine Simms an accountant? That's as funny as you being an accountant."

"I could get into calculators."

"No, you'll do something with kids. You're a big kid. But Simms. It threw me. Hell, could I choose this if I had someone I was in love with? I'd have to choose the mission over them, right?" He coughed into his hand. "Least you don't have to choose between us and love anymore." Cruz was rambling, and I wondered how strong a dose of pain meds they had him on. His last statement was a kick to the chest, though. "Love. Choose love. It changes everything," he said, his voice dreamy.

"They gave you the good drugs, huh?"

"Hooked a boy up," he said. "I know I'm not making any sense."

He was, though, at least to me. I watched Willow's shadow

cross the front room. "I get it," I said, and as fucking elated as I was that he was safe, a shadow fell across me, even in the dark, because he was making sense. He'd choose the person he loved—it was the guy he was. And it seemed I was that kind of guy, too. Only I had no idea how to choose between the brother I'd die for and the woman who had my heart in a vise grip. I was going to hell—this was the worst thing I could do to him, but I'd been honest when we were looking for Gus. I couldn't let Willow go, at least not yet.

Cruz cut into my thoughts again, and I knew the drugs were fully kicking in. "Did I tell you my dick's okay already?"

"Yeah, buddy." He'd be pissed he was so uncensored when the painkillers wore off. "I wouldn't want the future love of your life to miss out on those two inches."

He laughed, and it was a sound I'd missed. "Inches of steel, baby."

Willow peeked out from the front door and raised her eyebrows as if to question if everything was okay. "Take care of Willy. I'll tell you more when I'm home."

Willow gave me a shy smile, and I didn't mean to return it, but I felt my cheeks rise at the sight of her. I'd never reacted that way to anyone before—wet and cold and emotionally raw. I couldn't stop from returning her smile. And I knew exactly what I was risking to keep the warmth of those smiles in my life. "Yeah. I gotta tell you a few things when you get home, too."

"Sounds good," he said, the connection cracking between us.

I waited for him to disconnect and let the words hang between us. I had a feeling he wouldn't want me as a ride or die when he knew about me and his sister. But when I looked up and Willow was still smiling as she walked toward me, arms outstretched, I didn't regret my decision at all. I had a little more time with her before I had to blow everything up.

"I've never been so scared in my whole life," she said, wrapping her arms around me. She'd peeled off her hoodie and was in a yellow T-shirt that hugged her curves. "Can we just forget today ever happened?"

I swallowed and leaned back, looking into her soft brown eyes. "He's safe," I said, feeling her arms wrap around my neck, her warm body against mine. "You can stop worrying."

"Never, but I'm worried about you," she said. "That you're going to run away from me again." She wrapped her arms around my neck more tightly, and I slid a hand up her back as she spoke into the crook of my neck. "And I understand you think whatever this is is a betrayal. Nothing needs to happen, but . . . I don't want you to go."

I cupped the back of her neck, my fingers crushing the wet curls at her nape. "Okay," I said against the shell of her ear.

She pulled her head back and tipped her chin up. "Okay?"

I brushed my lips over her cheek. "Okay." I dropped another kiss on her cheek, feeling the softness of her skin. "I'll stay."

Her eyes widened as if she expected me to deny her. I guess I'd attempted to. "With me?"

"And Gus," I said, stroking the back of her neck and tugging her body closer to mine. She opened her mouth, no doubt to throw something back at me, but I stopped her comeback, pressing my lips against hers. The connection between us felt like it had grown even stronger than the first time we kissed, her mouth yielding to mine as our lips slid together and tongues danced. Willow pulled herself against me, her body a delicious pressure against my own. I'd never kissed someone like that before, like my whole life hung in the balance if I didn't get one more touch, one more feel of her lips, one more stroke of her skin as I walked us clumsily toward the open front door. "My God, Low," I said when we broke the kiss, both catching our breath. I swung the door shut behind us once we made it inside.

"I don't expect anything," she panted. "If helping me with my list, especially page two, feels like a betrayal to you, it's okay. Nothing else needs to happen."

I nodded and stepped closer, letting one hand slip to her back and the other behind her neck. "I want to help you finish your list." I cupped the back of her neck and tipped her chin up to mine. "I've always wanted to. Just not fighting it anymore."

"Really?"

I nodded and crashed my mouth against hers again. I was also done fighting how I felt about her, how she made me feel whole. I didn't know how to tell her that yet, though, but I would tell her soon.

CHAPTER 43

Willow

DEACON'S KISSES WERE hungry, and each one fed into another, like we couldn't get enough of each other. There was another and another until I had to pull away to suck in a breath as my back hit the wall of the living room. His body pressed me against it as his wide palm cradled the back of my head, that protective hold shifting to a mind-scattering stroke of his fingers when his mouth dipped lower to skate down my neck, and my body grew hot at the contact.

"We did the wall already," I said on a pant.

"I guess we're doing it again." When he kissed me just under the neckline of my T-shirt, where my neck met my collarbone, my knees weakened at the roll of pleasure through my lower belly the kiss elicited. His fingers worked their way from my waist to the skin just under the hem of my shirt, and I groaned. "Are you sure you want to stay?"

He chuckled against my neck and pressed his hips forward, the hard length of him pressing against my belly. "Very."

"Oh," was all I could think to say. Deacon's fingers sliding up my side and over my ribs fried my brain. "Oh! You want to . . . you know . . . F me."

Deacon chuckled against my neck again, raising his head to meet my gaze, his brown eyes soft, his hair still damp from the rain. "Did you just use the letter F as a verb again?" A grin spread across his face, and the slow path of his fingers over my ribs stilled, instead making small circles there. His touches were so comfortable, like he'd been touching me for years.

"We only practiced dirty talk a few times . . ." Despite my brain moving in nine different directions, most of them toward the storm of potential energy between my thighs, I returned his grin. "You knew what I meant."

Deacon's smile continued to spread, and he cupped both of my cheeks and kissed me on the lips—it was a peck, soft and sweet, and nothing like the demanding, insistent connection of a few minutes earlier. I liked this kiss, though. I liked the idea that I got to know what Deacon's kisses were like. "I knew what you meant," he said, hands still holding my face. "And yes." He kissed me again, softly on the lips, for a few beats longer this time. "I want that when you're ready." His gaze moved over my face—to my eyes and then to my lips and back. "You're so beautiful."

"I'm all wet," I said, wanting to touch a hand to my hair to fix it but not wanting to move from where my hands rested low on Deacon's waist.

"That's good when it comes to F'ing," he said, face straight for a minute before his grin returned.

"It sounds silly when you say it." But I couldn't stop grinning back up at his familiar, handsome, chiseled face.

"I'll tell you a secret." He lowered his head, and his teeth brushed my earlobe. The sharp, scraping sensation made that same wave of pleasure roll through my body.

"Oh my God," I said on an exhale when he did it again, leaving me squirming. "What's the secret?" Because if it was how he learned about all these places on my body, I didn't want to know.

He nipped my earlobe once more and then kissed me there. "It sounds silly when you say it, too."

"Shut up." I pushed at his shoulders, and he had his playful smile on his face when he took a step back, holding a hand to his shoulder as if I'd injured him. "If you don't like me talking about F'ing, you won't get to do it to me."

"With you." He reached for my hands and took them in each of his, tugging me forward from the wall. "Not to you." He lifted my hands to his lips and dropped soft kisses on each of my knuckles. "When that happens, it's you and me together, Low."

He kissed each knuckle again and guided my hands behind his neck.

"But I think we should wait," he said, hands falling to my waist.

"To fu . . ." It was on the tip of my tongue. I'd wanted to impress him with my boldness, but I felt flustered by this sudden change of events. "To have sex?"

"You were so close!" He brushed his lips against mine.

"I need more practice," I said, taking in the feel of his hair through my fingers.

"That can be arranged." Deacon's grip on my waist loosened, but I loved the weight of his hands there. "We both had a lot going on the last few days." He swayed with me, like we were dancing or something. "We don't need to dive in tonight."

"You're probably right," I admitted, warring with myself. Every nerve in my body cried out for Deacon—for his touch and his body, for his strength and his tenderness—but in the back of my mind was still the doubt and worry that it would go wrong, that I would be wrong. I recognized the insecurities immediately because I'd internalized them so often with Spencer. "Will you leave, then?"

"Do you want me to?"

"Hell no," I said into his chest. I'd peeled off my wet sweatshirt earlier, but I still shivered from the chill of my soaked jeans. When I wasn't being nailed to the wall by my personal heater, it was much chillier, and I pressed closer to him.

"You should get a hot shower," he offered, moving one of his hands in lazy circles over my lower back.

"Is that an offer to join me?"

He let out a bark of laughter. "No. I don't think that's a good idea."

"Because you'd want to F me in the shower?"

He laughed again. "When you were naked and soapy in front of me in that small shower stall? When I could see and touch you everywhere? Yeah, F'ing would be on my mind."

I pulled his face down so our lips were a breath apart and kissed him.

"What was that for?"

"For using the letter so I don't feel silly." I slid my fingers down his neck and across his broad shoulders, marveling at being able to touch him like this, knowing he wouldn't shy away. "And for agreeing to stay tonight. I don't want to be alone."

"It's been a really bad few days until tonight." He kissed me this time, his lips gentle enough that it made my silly heart wish for more. "I don't want to be alone, either."

I stood on my tiptoes and wrapped my arms around his neck again, this time to hug him. He'd had a rough few days, too, probably rougher than me, and we stood in each other's arms for a minute or two. Deacon was fun and flirty and put up a good front, but he didn't like being alone. Lots of things about him clicked into place with his arms around me.

"Deac?" I said, against his neck.

"Yeah?"

"Your, um . . ." I motioned to where his rather imposing erection was wedged against me. "I feel bad leaving you worked up."

"I'm fine. Go get your shower. He and my hand are foraging buddies from way back." He kissed the side of my head when I did an involuntary shiver, even while laughing. "Shoo," he said, nudging me toward the stairs. I climbed then, looking over my shoulder to see him watching me, following me with his gaze until I rounded the corner.

Cruz is safe. I'm over Spencer.

Deacon wants to be with me.

I'm moving forward.

I repeated the statements in my head as I stripped down and steam filled the bathroom, repeated them to make sure I was reminded that things were starting to feel good again. As I stepped under the spray, the worry that another shoe was about to drop lasted only a second before I chased it away.

CHAPTER 44

THE EARLY-MORNING LIGHT filtered through Willow's window, the sheer white curtains in sharp contrast to the dark red walls. Falling asleep with her in my arms the last few days, her warm body pressed to mine and her curls tickling my chin, had felt surreal. Her hand fell across my obliques, and I grinned as I slowly opened my eyes.

"Holy shit!" A long snout and two accusing eyes were inches from my face. I jerked back, and Willow stirred behind me, mumbling in her sleep before rolling to her side. Gus was unyielding as he studied me. *Guilty*, he seemed to say. *How could you do this to my human?* The dog would have made a good MP—his expression was cold and implacable like military police, but when I reached out to scratch behind his ears and said, "Food?" I was off the hook, and he barreled toward the door, pausing to look back at me.

I shuffled toward the door, glancing over my shoulder at Willow, who'd thrown the blankets off herself and was sprawled on the bed in shorts and a tiny tank that she'd come out of the shower wearing, the fabric so delicate and thin I'd had to bite back a groan and harness all the willpower I'd stored up, especially when she asked if she could kiss me again, looking up at me with those big eyes as if I might deny her. She gave a little snore and buried her face in the pillow, and I followed Gus through the house to let him outside.

Gus took off for the back of the yard, peeing and then doing an inspection of the perimeter. The morning air was chilly, and I regretted not putting on a shirt, but after Willow peeled it off me the night before when that one kiss led to us spread out on the bed together, I'd never put it back on. That would have meant taking a break from holding her, something I wasn't sure I'd ever be able to do now that I'd gotten used to it. Gus loped toward me, tongue out once his inspection was done, and I scratched him behind the ear again. "Cruz will be back soon," I said, leading him into the house and filling his bowl with kibble.

The dog's ears perked up at his owner's name, and he looked up eagerly waiting for the eat command. "Okay," I said, pointing at the bowl. Cruz really should open a dog training school when he got home. I pictured Cupcake, who we'd given up on after the sit command. I left the dog to eat. Gus seemed to have forgiven me for my transgressions, but this morning, walking through Cruz's house, I wondered if his owner would. Willow had become like oxygen to me, but Cruz had been my rock for a decade.

I left a note on the nightstand, not wanting to wake Willow. I needed to move and luckily had a gym bag in my truck. I tapped out a message to Cruz on my way into the rec center asking how he was feeling. He'd let Willow know he'd be home soon and hopefully the drugs were on tap for a few more days, and I wanted to find out when he was going to be stateside.

"You following me around or what?" Bryce's voice startled me as he spoke from behind me, a basketball under one arm.

"Seems the other way around," I said, extending a hand.

"Where are you heading? I'm meeting some folks for a basketball game—nothing too serious, but we could always use another body. Want to join?"

I opened my mouth to decline—I'd planned to swim and then run. That was where I could think, but I'd spent so much time sinking into my own thoughts the last few days. I used to play all the time with the guys in the unit and the other folks on base, but it had been ages since I'd done anything with a team. It struck me then how much I missed it. "Yeah," I said. "I have a little time."

He nodded toward the courts, where I saw Kelly and a few other people warming up. There was a running track on the level above, and we passed a few people on their way to the pool, but we were the only ones on the basketball courts so early in the morning. "Now, do I want you on my team or Kelly's?"

I laughed, following him to the courts. "Depends. Do you like winning?"

"My team it is," he said.

I PULLED INTO the parking lot for the flower shop on the way over to Willow's. After basketball where my team narrowly eked out a win and then lost the second game, a few of us had gone out for breakfast at a greasy spoon near campus. The bacon was burned, the eggs were too runny, and it was the best time I'd had outside of hanging with Willow or my roommates in ages. So, when Bryce asked if I wanted to study for econ—we had a test on Monday—I bit back my knee-jerk response to decline and agreed.

> DEACON: There in a few.
>
> WILLOW: I'll be there at the same time—took an extra volunteer shift at the clinic. I have all this extra time now that I've taken the admissions test. Poor Gus has been alone all day.
>
> WILLOW: Dr. Theo says hi. 😊

I scowled at my phone, just for a moment, remembering him flirting with her. But, he'd hooked her up with this volunteer gig and she said he'd been really helpful with her vet school application. I probably needed to let it go. She'd told me jealousy was not a good look on me.

> DEACON: I'm sure he misses me. 😊

I jogged into the store, looking around for red flowers. We didn't have anything in particular to celebrate, but I also felt like we had everything to celebrate. And she'd been pushing me to get out there and meet some new people. I wanted to show her how much I appreciated it. Appreciated her. Loved her. I reached for a bouquet of red roses sitting in a black bucket but paused. There was a rose plant nearby, a picture of big red blooms on the label, which also read "bare root." It looked like a collection of cut stems, but the clerk assured me it would produce blooms within a few weeks. I handed her my credit card—something told me Willow would like planting something herself, like her mom had done.

"Hey," she said, hopping down from the bike right behind my truck once I'd pulled into the driveaway. "What's this?"

"I brought you roses," I said, handing over the plant. "I think. Or I bought you sticks. Either way, it'll grow and bloom kind of like you."

She smiled. That one that lit up her face. She admired the plant before setting it down and said, "Kind of like us." Her arms went around my neck and I loved the way my hand fit perfectly on her lower back. "It's perfect."

"You're perfect," I said, dropping a kiss on her lips. It was cheesy as hell, but I wanted that smile every day. I needed those kisses.

"Will you help me plant it?"

"Sure." I trailed a few fingers up her neck and unhooked her bike helmet. "I'll play in the dirt with you."

"Including lots of dirty talk?"

I laughed and stepped back so we could walk the bike into the backyard. I carried the plant while we walked her bike in a way that felt like we were completely in sync. She wore the scrubs the clinic had volunteers wear, and even that professional clothing made her look completely devourable. "Talk about dirt or actual dirty talk? I'm good either way. Just want to prepare myself."

She unlocked the gate, then grinned over her shoulder and

beckoned me forward with one finger. The action was so playful and sweet in concert with her grin, but the second I reached her, her lips grazed my ear. "The kind of talk where I beg you to fuck me."

My body went suddenly hot and tense at her words, and I pulled her body flush to mine. "You didn't use the letter."

"I've been practicing," she said, letting out a gasp when my hand lowered to palm her backside through her scrub bottoms. Willow's body was lush, and I imagined all the different ways I wanted to explore her. "I'm pretty good with the word now."

"Say it again," I growled against her neck in the doorway, not giving her time to speak before I was searching out the spot that made her squirm.

"Fuck me," she whispered.

"Low." I guided her inside the house, quickly pushing the door closed behind us. "There's nothing I want more."

CHAPTER 45

Willow

- ☐ Gardening
- ☐ Sex with someone new (F'ing!)

THERE'S A THING no one warns you about regarding pet ownership. When you crash through the front door in the arms of your smoking-hot, absurdly strong guy and he's hoisted you up against the wall like you weigh nothing at all, you're going to feel ready for everything with each rub and thrust. And with his body pressed to yours and his big palms gripping your ass, your groans of pleasure will be met with . . . whining.

Gus whined from behind us, and Deacon jumped when the dog pressed his nose against his butt. "I forgot about Gus," I said on a pant, feeling the flush ride up my chest and the wall hard at my back. Deacon was hard and hot against me, and I squirmed against him on instinct, even as I caught my breath from the harried kiss.

Deacon's lips dropped to my neck, finding the spot he'd learned drove me wild. "I'll let him out." He gently lowered me to the ground, his hands still firmly on me. "Don't go anywhere," he groaned near my ear.

"You want me to stand still?"

He took a hesitant step back, his gaze raking over me. "I don't want to miss a single squirm." He clapped for Gus to follow him and hurried toward the back door, casting a glance over his shoulder at me. Gus trotted after him obediently, but my eyes were locked on Deacon, the curve of his taut ass and the muscles in his arms. I squeezed my thighs together in anticipation of his return.

When I heard the back door slam, I slipped through the entryway and into the kitchen, pulling off my scrubs as I crept toward the stairs, hanging the top on the edge of the counter so it would be the first thing he saw when he came back in, and I hurried up the stairs to my room.

I shimmied out of my underwear and bra and left them in the hall outside my room before climbing onto the bed. I was going for a certain look and paused on the bed to get the pillows arranged just so, when Deacon pushed through the door to find me on my hands and knees.

"I told you not to move."

Embarrassment should have been my primary reaction. I was on full display for him, but I looked over my shoulder and couldn't help but grin as I watched his gaze scan me from head to foot.

"I needed another minute to get everything perfect."

He tossed aside my scrubs and the red underwear—the new

set I'd bought with him in mind—and stalked toward the bed. "This looks pretty fucking perfect."

"I thought you'd want me on my back," I said, wriggling under the feel of his fingertips grazing over my lower back.

"I want you in every position." Deacon shuffled behind me, and I saw his shirt fly to the floor.

"I can't see you in this position." There was something so erotic about the limited visibility, and I trusted him. I trusted him to take care of me, but I trusted he'd like me at this angle because he seemed to like me at every angle. In the past, I always felt like I had to disguise my belly or make sure my thighs were hidden under sheets unless the lights were out. I'd never given my ex the chance to see me. With Deacon, I wanted his gaze. I'd never felt anything close to this sense of trust and comfort before.

"I can see all of you," he said, his voice low and gravelly. I heard Deacon's belt slide through the loops, and a shiver ran up my spine. "My God, Low." The bed dipped behind me before his fingers trailed along my spine and then his palms slid up my thighs and hips, over the sides of my belly and back down. "You're so beautiful."

"You can't see my face," I said, unsure how to respond to his comment.

"I know your face is beautiful. I've memorized every freckle." He inched closer on the bed, and his cock pressed against my ass, hard and tempting, as his hands slid along my ribs and he pulled me up on my knees and against his chest. His palms cupped both breasts and rolled the nipples between his fingers, and his breath caressed my neck. "When I tell you that you're beautiful, it's not because I'm just realizing it. It's because it bears repeating." He kissed down my neck, and one hand slid lower, stroking my belly, and I widened my knees to invite him between my thighs. "I've known all along," he said against my ear, and his middle finger moved along my slit and then circled my clit. "You were the most beautiful woman I'd ever seen from the second I met you."

I let out a whimper at his touch, the deft way he circled me, spreading my wetness with his soft, purposeful touches. "I didn't know that."

"I'll never let you forget," he said, circling my clit again before sliding a finger into me, followed by a second. He pumped into me, the pressure and friction matched only in intensity by his words. "Never." I reached back to run my fingers through his hair, tugging on the strands. One of Deacon's hands kneaded my breast deliciously, and the other worked his fingers in and out of me. I felt like a cat stretched against him.

"I'll always remember this," I said, feeling my lower belly tense as I rolled my hips against his fingers. I sucked in a few ragged breaths, as he stroked my G-spot deep inside and the sensation wound out to every nerve ending. "Always," I repeated as the wave overtook me and I crashed through an orgasm, pulsing around his fingers. "Will you take me like this?" I'd only ever done missionary sex, and this was worlds away, so new, and I craved more of that with Deacon.

"From behind?" He slipped his fingers from between my thighs and sucked them clean, the sounds of his mouth so close to my ear making another shiver run through me. He kissed my shoulder and then pulled my chin to the side to capture a kiss. Deacon's kisses felt so permanent to me, like the imprint of his lips was indelible, like the press of his mouth tattooed something on me I'd never lose.

When we broke the kiss, his eyes locked with mine, just for a moment, but I had to blink away everything I was sure he could see on my face. I was so desperate to keep this man I knew I couldn't. "Are you sure?" he asked, dropping his lips to my shoulder, still rolling my nipple between his thumb and forefinger. "You want to do this?"

"Positive," I murmured, already eager for more, and I wriggled back against him.

"I should make you wait," he said, his hand trailing from my nape to the base of my spine as he eased me down on the bed. I barely recognized his voice—Deacon felt like a live wire behind me, and I could hear in his voice how much he was holding himself back. It was so hot, so primal, and I had the feeling again that this was a true first. He held my hips in both hands, squeezing and stroking me. "I told you not to move earlier."

"You don't want to wait," I said, resting my forearms on the sheets and feeling the weight of him behind me, the heat of his hands. "Do you?"

He chuckled, and I heard the foil of the condom ripping. "No," he said, nudging against my entrance with the wide head. I squirmed against him. "I don't want to wait." He held my hips steady and pushed forward just an inch, making me suck in a breath. He was thick, and I squirmed against his hard flesh, acclimating to the feeling as he moved in deeper. "I couldn't if I tried," he said, pushing in deeper.

"Maybe you can punish me later," I joked, gripping the sheets in front of me as he filled me deeper. "A little spanking?"

At my words, he thrust forward, hitting the sensitive spot

deep inside and making me moan. "You're going to kill me," he said, pulling back out and in with slow, measured thrusts.

"More," I said, backing against him, seeking more friction, more momentum. "Please."

He shifted inside me faster, his thrusts more powerful, and I held on to the bed, meeting him thrust for thrust. My heart rate sped. Sweat dripped down my neck from the exertion, and I cried out as he reached deeper. We moved in sync, and he'd been right—he wasn't doing this to me. We were together and we felt so together. I cried out again and lowered my fingers to circle my clit, my body rising and tense.

"Come around me, baby," he said, breathless, and I imagined him as untethered as I was.

"You're fucking incredible." He spoke in broken sentences between thrusting in and out of my body, and I was hot and needy everywhere.

"Mine," he said, his voice feeling far away and all over me as the tension uncoiled and I bucked against him, giving in to the pleasure as my orgasm erupted from me.

Mine. He said I was his, and I groaned as his thrusts became more erratic, and then he pushed in deep, letting out a guttural cry as he pulsed inside me.

"You're mine," I repeated, an aftershock of pleasure moving through me. "You're mine, too."

We stilled, and I felt like I'd taken off and was floating back to earth, only floating with Deacon's solid, purposeful hands still holding me. I wasn't going to float off into space. "Deac," I said, finding my voice.

"C'mere," he said, his voice hoarse as he fell beside me and pulled me to him, my face against his shoulder and his arms wrapped around me. Deacon's breath came heavy, and he kissed my forehead as we settled against each other. "I am, you know."

I blinked, my eyelids heavy as I tried to snuggle closer to him, our legs tangling. He was warm, and I wanted to sleep in his arms like this. "You are what?"

"Yours." His lips brushed my forehead again. "I'm yours." His palms slid up and down my arms, and too many emotions were battling for control, too many thoughts. I let him hold me, his words wrapping around me. "I never belonged anywhere until I was a PJ. I never had a strong civilian group of friends until I met those weirdos I live with. And," he said, his hands stilling and his body pulling away from mine enough for his chin to tip down. He'd see everything on my face—I couldn't hide it, but I also didn't want to avoid his gaze, and our eyes locked. It was like a hundred lanterns flying off into the air—that's how I felt when he looked at me like that. "And I've never been in love with someone until you." He brushed a curl from my forehead. "I'm a mess. My head's not on straight, and I don't know where I'm going. In a lot of ways, I'm lost, but with you, I feel found. If you'll have me, I'm yours."

I pressed my palm to his cheek, the soft hair of his beard under my palm. "Of course I'll have you."

The grin spread across his face, his eyes lighting. "Really?"

I pulled his lips to mine, sinking into another kiss, knowing on some level, the mark it left was indelible and I didn't have to worry about what came next because this was permanent.

We broke the kiss when we heard Gus downstairs barking. I giggled at the timing. "I guess the dog is supportive."

"Pretty sure it's at the neighbor on his nightly walk with the schnauzer. Gus hates that thing."

"Maybe that's how he communicates he really loves her," I offered. "Like a little kid pulling someone's pigtails."

Deacon met my gaze again and tugged gently on my hair. "I like you." He tugged again and brushed his lips against mine, his dark eyes boring into mine when we pulled apart, like the eye contact was an extension of his touch. "I love you, Low."

I stroked his face again, loving how he leaned into my hand. And then I made a barking sound, twice, and a third was stopped when a laughing Deacon rolled me to my back and kissed me again, his lips playfully moving from my lower lip to my chin and my neck.

"I know you're going to vet school and I don't know what's next and we have a lot to figure out, but right now I'd really like to . . ."

I ran my nails over his head and sucked in a breath when his lips met that sensitive spot on my neck. "F me again?"

He chuckled against my skin, his hand pausing on my hip.

"And we'll figure it out. If I need to, I can put vet school on hold and wait to apply until you know what's next."

Deacon's head lifted, and he opened his mouth to answer me, but he halted.

Cruz stood in the door, and my heart jumped at the sight of him before sinking into my stomach at the chilling quality of his words when he spoke. "What the fuck are you doing?"

CHAPTER 46

HIS VOICE, THE one I'd prayed to hear again, hit me like a gallon of ice water. I flipped to my back, immediately shielding Willow's body.

"I didn't think you'd be home for at least a few days!" Willow yelped from behind me, scurrying under the blankets to hide herself. But his icy stare was locked on me like I was an enemy combatant.

"I called from our stateside layover. Thought I'd surprise you."

I reached around the bed, needing to not be naked, and I snagged my boxers and pulled them on. Cruz's glare didn't leave me for a second. "I didn't think you'd be taking this as a last chance to fuck my sister." He stepped forward, leaning heavily on a crutch, and I stepped between him and Willow again.

"It's not like that, man." I held up my palms as he advanced, and I stepped back, tripping on something on the floor that was probably Willow's bra, but in the split second I looked down and saw a flash of red, Cruz's fist hit my jaw, and it wasn't the gentle get-moving tap he'd given me in the hospital. This one hurt and knocked me back onto the bed.

Cruz hovered over me, fist cocked, but I shifted and the hit glanced off my arm.

"No!" Willow cried out from behind me. "Cruz, get out of my room!" she screamed, panic coloring her voice.

"I asked you to take care of my sister, and instead you treated her like just one of the hundreds of girls you've used and tossed aside." He raised his fist again and landed a blow against the arm I'd raised in front of my face. He stumbled with the motion, but landed another blow that had pain radiating across my face.

"I'm not gonna fight you," I said, noticing the wince of pain when he cocked his arm back. I pushed an arm out to make sure Willow was clear of me in case he did swing again. "Hit me again if you need to. I'm not fighting you."

Cruz glared at me with a coldness I hadn't seen anything close to since training, but he dropped his fist. "I thought we were brothers." He sucked in a breath, rebalancing on his uninjured right leg. "I can't stand to even look at you."

Cruz rubbed his hand and leaned back on his crutch. In another setting, I would have commended him for being able to throw such a good punch while on crutches. "Get him out of my fucking house," he said, pointing at Willow and hobbling out of the room. I suddenly missed the glare—he wouldn't even look at me now. "Before I throw him out myself."

"Are you okay?" Willow touched her delicate fingers to my cheek, where a bruise was surely forming. Her eyes were wide with shock and indignation, and she stroked my face over and over again. "He had no right."

I nodded, guiding her fingers from my face and kissing her

fingertips, despite the pain. "He had every right," I said, resigned. I'd deserved it—even as I stilled and made sure my teeth were intact and my jaw wasn't broken. And I deserved him not being able to look at me, even though it hurt worse than I thought it would. I nodded, reassuring myself I'd been prepared for this, that I knew he'd react that way, that I'd chosen this, because I had. But the way he'd looked at me played on repeat in my head.

"No," she said, searching for her own clothes on the floor as I hunted for mine. "I'm not a child, and he gets no say in who I sleep with."

Adding Cruz hating me to the hazy future ahead made it that much darker. The only bright spot was Willow was still here, with me, and I lowered my chin and kissed her lips, just a peck, but needing the connection. "Not the first time someone's hit me. I'm okay." I wasn't sure that was true—I wouldn't be okay if things between me and Cruz were as bad as they seemed—but I didn't want to worry her unnecessarily. "Me and you need to talk more," I said, taking her hand. "Despite everything, I'm not ready to let you go. Do you want to come back home with me?"

She shook her head. "No. My brother and I need to have a conversation." She stood tall, shoulders back, and despite everything about this situation being fucked, I was proud of her. When I met her, I wasn't sure she'd have had that reaction. I suspected she'd have gone with the easier option and do what I wanted.

I opened the door, and Willow took my hand, leading me down the stairs. To where Cruz stood in the kitchen, ice on his hand and Gus at his feet as if he knew, too, what I'd done and he needed me to know he was cleanly on Team Cruz. I held up my palm, but Willow held tight to the other. "Cruz," I said, backing toward the door with eyes on my friend. "I can explain."

"Fuck your explanation. You go on and on about how I saved your life, how we're brothers. You never let me forget it, and given a few months alone, you lure my baby sister into bed, the most important person in the world to me. I asked you to look out for her! We're done with everything," he said, avoiding my gaze, and once again, I had the sense there was a nail in the coffin of my oldest friendship. "Done."

But Willow took both sides of my face in her hands, and the warmth of her hands grounded me, especially when she forced my gaze to meet hers. "*We're* not done." She was protecting me, I realized, holding me close so I didn't feel lost. I lowered my chin to kiss her, but caught Cruz's glare over her shoulder and paused. "We still have to finish my list," she said. "We have a lot to talk about. I want you to go to the park with me."

"Are you sure you don't want to come home with me?" Cruz would never hurt her in a million years, but every protective instinct in me rallied to keep her close. I accepted her decision when she said no again, and I nodded and took both of her hands in mine, raising them to my lips. "I'll call you."

"The fuck you will!" Cruz yelled from the kitchen.

Willow mouthed, "It'll be okay," but when she closed the door and I walked toward my truck, I had a sinking feeling it wouldn't ever be the same.

I only hoped that whatever came next would still include her.

CHAPTER 47

AS SOON AS the door clicked shut, I whirled on my brother.

"Don't look at me like that," he said, holding a dish towel filled with ice to his hand. "He had it coming."

I could have strangled him, for his smug tone and for hitting Deacon and treating me like I was a child. He had an effective cold stare, but I had the same damn one, and I leveled it on him until he looked away, muttering, "He did."

I planned to strangle him as I stalked forward, but first I threw my arms around his neck. "I might knee you in the balls in a minute, but I am so relieved you're home," I said, clutching him to me. "You're home and you're alive and you're safe." I buried my face in his shoulder and felt his arms, the ones I'd found safety in since I was a kid, wrap around me.

"I'm all right, Willy," he said, pulling me closer, the edge in his voice disappearing.

The roller coaster of worry and fear I'd felt on this deployment came back to me all at once, and we stood embracing in the kitchen, for I don't know how long. "I thought you were dead," I said, against him, the tears I thought I'd tucked away flowing freely. "I thought you wouldn't come home."

"I did, though." He rubbed circles at the top of my back. "I'm fine."

I finally loosened my hold on him and stepped away, nearly tripping on Gus, who hadn't left his side.

"Until you knee me in the balls, but I'm going to ask you not to do that because it's already hard enough for me to walk." He motioned to the boot on his left leg and gave me a tiny grin.

"You had no right to hit him," I repeated. "Are you a fucking Neanderthal?"

Cruz looked slightly chastened and picked up the dish towel again. "Since when do you drop f-bombs?"

"I've done a lot of growing these last few months. I promise not to knee you . . . for now. Come in the living room and let's talk."

"I'm sorry you had to see me hit him," he said, falling onto the couch. Gus leaped up and dropped his head on his lap, earning me a raised eyebrow from my brother, who never let the dog on the couch.

I shrugged. "He does that now."

Wisely picking his battles, Cruz scratched the dog behind the ears.

"And 'sorry you saw me do it' isn't an apology. You could have really hurt him, Cruz."

"Rakes isn't made of glass." He scratched behind his neck. "He's not good for you, Willy."

"You've never seen us together!" I flushed. "Well, except for upstairs," I added. "How can you even say he's not good for me? You know better than anyone he's a good man."

"Because I heard what you said about putting school on hold. He's not good for you if he's another guy you put your plans on hold for. If he's a guy who stands by while you do that."

I opened my mouth to speak, to deny it, but I remembered saying I could wait on vet school until we figured things out together.

"I'm so pissed at him for touching you when I told him to keep his distance, but I'm more angry at you."

"At me?" This turn of events had thrown me enough that I needed to sit back in the chair to hear his explanation. "Why?"

"Because you spent this whole time here trying to move on from Spencer and be your own person. To distance yourself from everything you saw in that stupid drowning meme." His voice was back to normal and not the cold, sharp tone he'd used with Deacon. "And at the first chance you got, you offered to give up your goals and independence for a guy." He crossed his arms over his chest. "That's not what I want for you."

"I . . ." I hadn't even seen myself doing it. I'd offered it up because being with Deacon felt like the most important thing I could do, but in retrospect, it felt so wrong. I thought about the application for school waiting for me to submit it. Suddenly, I knew I was going to include that last paragraph. Maybe with a few more lines I would add. "I don't want that, either."

"And Deacon's like me, Willy. We're not good for other people. We're too focused on the mission, on what's next, and we can't give someone else what they need. That's why Antonio left me." His gaze flicked down to his hands at the mention of G. He almost never used his first name with me.

I sat up straighter, needing to come to his defense. "Deacon's not like that with me."

"Was he going to let you give up vet school for him?" Cruz matched my stance and recrossed his arms over his chest.

"I . . . don't know," I said, rising to my feet and grabbing the dripping dish towel from him to make him a fresh ice pack. "You cockblocked us before he could answer."

Cruz laughed, the first genuine laugh I'd heard from him. The sound made me smile. "Please don't say 'cock' after I had to see my best friend's already tonight."

I handed him the ice pack. "At least you still called him your best friend."

Cruz pressed the ice pack to his hand. "I told him not to touch you because I didn't want you to get hurt. Rakes will hurt you. He'll leave."

"He loves me," I admitted, and in that moment, I realized I could never forget how the words sounded coming from Deacon's lips. His declaration of love was etched in my mind. "He knew you'd be furious, and that it might end your friendship, but he loves me. That counts for something, doesn't it?"

His eyes widened. "He told you that?"

I nodded. "I made this list of things I wanted to re-do, firsts I had with Spencer, and he helped me."

"Just a blanket statement. I don't want to hear about Deacon's re-doing anything with you."

I took the spot on the other side of Gus and threw a pillow at my injured brother. "Not sexual, well, not all sexual," I added sheepishly. "He helped me realize my life wasn't over after Spencer and I broke up. Helped me see more in the mirror than that stupid meme. Helped me see I was still somebody, even when I was alone."

"Willy," he said, leaning forward over the dog, "I didn't know you felt that way."

"Well, I did." I brushed my hands down the front of my robe. "While you were away, I learned to ride a bike, and I went camping, and I kissed a boy who kissed me back, and none of it was tainted by memories of Spencer and who I was when we were dating. For a long time, I felt like all I'd ever be was the person he dumped, the one who was drowning. Now, it's like I can see myself as so much more than that. I'm worth so much more than the role I play in a relationship."

Cruz looked between me and his dog with a contemplative expression. "Mom gave up on everything because it was tainted by the memory of Dad," he added. "Did you think that would happen to you, too?"

"I did at first." My heart ached hearing him talk about her, about normal everyday things about her, because we never did that. "But I went through a few of the boxes. Did you know she planned to go skydiving and travel to Japan? I found the ticket, and I think she was seeing someone."

He grinned, and I saw the brother I'd known my whole life, the one behind the guarded facade he put on for others. "Yeah?"

"Who knew, right?" I wiped my tears on the sleeve of my robe, unsure what words to put to what I was feeling because it was sadness and relief and a little bit of joy. "She was planning adventures. I thought she'd been drowning the whole time, but it turns out that she wasn't. She had found her strength." Cruz held out his free arm, and I shifted to squeeze in next to my brother. We sat in silence for a few minutes.

"Do you love him back?"

I nodded. "I didn't get to tell him yet. You busted in like a G.I. Joe on crutches and broke up our party, and maybe his nose."

"That party involved my baby sister fucking my best friend in *my* house. Don't get too high and mighty."

"Fair enough." I smiled against his chest. "I wanted to tell him I loved him at the park . . . my final re-do," I said. "With Spencer, I said it the first time at the park, and I want this time to be with him."

Cruz rested his chin on my head and wrapped his arm around me. "I just want to keep you safe."

"I know." I patted his chest and sat up so I could meet his gaze. "But I'm an adult. And it turns out, a pretty capable one." I looked at Gus and waved my hand in the way we'd practiced. "Sparkle princess spin," I said, and his ears perked up. He jumped off the couch, spun twice, and then sat at Cruz's feet, resting his head on my brother's knee to receive more pets.

"Sparkle princess? He's a German shepherd."

I reached across and stroked behind Gus's ears. "The prettiest German shepherd there is," I cooed, earning a brief bit of attention from Gus before he refocused on Cruz. "He's very well-trained. Get used to saying it if you want him off the couch."

"Sparkle princess spin," he repeated, disbelief in his voice. "I was gone for three months, and you turned my dog into a princess and my best friend into a lovesick fool."

"I never said he was lovesick," I corrected.

"He'd never betray me," Cruz said. "Not in a hundred years, so if he did this . . . he's more than just into you. He's all in."

I nodded because I knew it was true.

"So, I guess I have to forgive him?"

"It's that or get kneed in the balls," I said with a shrug before wrapping him in another giant hug.

CHAPTER 48

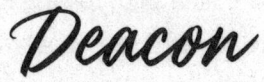

EMI LOOKED AROUND the kitchen and pointed out for a third time that she and Marcus had both left food for me in the freezer, all portioned out.

"I do actually know how to adult all on my own," I said, putting my arm around her. "But thank you." I'd decided to stay in the house alone for the year she would be away. I could have always afforded it, but I wanted people around. Now, I tried to adjust to the idea of being in the house with only Cupcake.

Marcus and Lila had taken off early that morning, and everything Emi was taking to Europe with her was packed into her car for her drive to visit her brother before flying out of the Minneapolis airport. "I'm going to miss you," she said, squeezing me. "No one is going to proposition me when I'm in Europe."

"Give yourself some credit," I said. "Someone will. I'll put in a request."

"Through the vast network of man whores?"

"It's the International Brotherhood of Freelance Pleasure

Delivery Experts. Thank you very much." I walked her toward the car. "And my membership has been revoked."

"I'm happy for you," she said, tossing her purse on the front seat. "You deserve to be with someone who makes you feel all gooey inside."

I opened my mouth, but she held a finger over it.

"No." Emi was so surprisingly strong and held her finger in place. "No. Your membership was revoked. No disgusting jokes about the word 'gooey.'"

I laughed against her finger. "I was actually going to say you do, too."

She climbed into her car and spoke out the open window, her nose scrunched. "I would prefer a goo joke to that. You know I am allergic to relationships." The engine revved to life, and she patted my arm. "But you've found a good one, I think."

I stepped back. "Text me when you get there?"

She nodded and waved before backing out of the driveway and leaving me alone there. My roommates were gone, and it was just me and Cupcake. I took a step toward the house but paused when my phone buzzed in my pocket.

> WILLOW: Cruz is on his way over.

I sent her a GIF of a kid wrapped in Bubble Wrap and added, "I'll be ready."

> WILLOW: Will you let me know when you're done? I want to meet you at the park.

I had no idea why the park was such a big deal for her, but I sent a thumbs-up emoji. I wanted to add more. I wanted to ask if we could skip the park and be done with these re-dos and just start fresh together.

"Check it out!" Jayden jogged from his yard to ours.

"Flip-flops!" I motioned to his boot-free leg and offered a high five. "Congratulations on getting out of the boot. Guess you won't need me anymore." I'd meant it, but the thought of not hanging out with him any longer made me feel a little sad.

"Nah, I'll probably keep you around. Maybe we could still hang out sometime. You know, so I can keep beating you at chess, and maybe you can read my book when it's done."

I ran fingers through my hair, partially obscuring my face so he didn't notice my cheesy-ass grin. Maybe Cruz was onto something about me doing work with kids.

A car pulled into the driveway, and Cruz climbed out of the driver's seat, balancing on his crutches.

Jayden spoke from next to me. "Damn, man. Do you just keep a rotation of people with broken legs around?"

"Got a few minutes?" Cruz approached us, and his expression still looked stony.

I nodded. "Jayden, Cruz and I served together. Jayden is our neighbor."

The teenager waved and then pulled his phone from his pocket as he jogged back to his own house, calling over his shoulder he'd crush me later.

"Your protégé?" Cruz followed me inside the house.

"Something like that." I braced myself for what might come next with Cruz. Gus had loyally stood next to his owner, but

Cupcake gave me a grunt as I stood, and then she curled back in to take a nap. I was left to my own devices.

"Are you gonna hit me again?" I stepped aside to give him room to get through the door with his crutches.

"I should."

"You want a beer first?"

He nodded, and I motioned to the worn couch, grabbing two bottles from the fridge and returning to the room.

"Your face looks like shit," he said, gaze skating over the bruised jaw and swollen eye.

"So does your hand." I pointed at the bruises over his knuckles. "Guess both our dates will be disappointed." I took a swig from the bottle and sat back on the couch next to my dog, who'd ceased giving a damn about me.

"I'm still too damn mad at you to laugh at that," he said, raising his bottle. "But not bad."

"For what it's worth, I'm sorry," I said, leaning forward, forearms on my knees. "I didn't mean for any of this to happen."

"She said you love her. That true?"

I nodded. "I've never felt like this before. And you have to know I fought it. Even when things got . . . physical." I started the sentence before I realized what I was copping to, but he was eyeing me warily and not angrily, so maybe Willow had told him some things. I rushed forward. "Even then, I tried to stop feeling so . . ." I searched for the right word, and Emi's came back to me. "Gooey about her."

"Gooey? Who are you and what have you done with my best friend?" Cruz took a long pull from his beer. "I heard her offer to give up vet school for you."

I'd been ready to tell her in no uncertain terms I didn't want that, but then Cruz had walked in and everything fell apart. I shook my head. "She offered."

"And you told her not to?"

"I was going to *ask* her not to, because she makes her own decisions." I bristled at the idea of her giving up anything for me, of being even an iota like her ex, but I knew she'd hate the idea that we were sitting here discussing her future.

"She showed me her vet school application. Said you'd helped her with her statement."

"I could probably recite it from memory," I said. "She did a good job, I think. It's almost done."

Cruz nodded. "She added something to it this morning. Said she hit submit."

I was relieved, mostly because I could picture her look of accomplishment after she submitted. I hoped she had "plan for the future" on her re-do list, because she was doing just that, regardless of what I wanted or Cruz thought. "Good," I said. "Hope I get to see the final product."

Cruz didn't respond but rather switched topics. "If you hurt her, even a little, all the guys would help me take you out. Dougy, Simms, even that guy who got kicked out because he kept showing up hungover. The one with the worst jokes."

I laughed. "Barkley," I said, remembering the guy who was never sober until 9 a.m. After that, he'd crush every expectation and leave us all behind in any competition. "He's actually good now. Got some help. He's selling cars out in Tucson."

"Well, I'm sure he'd drive over to help kick your ass, too, then."

I raised my glass. "I would never, man. She's . . ." I thought about her smile and her laugh and the way she looked when she talked about going to school. "She's everything to me. If I ever let her down, please bring in the cavalry."

Cruz nodded and took a pull from his bottle. "I guess that's what we had to sort out, then." He set it aside and let out a sigh. "We had a good run. You and me."

A panic I thought I'd come to terms with rose in me, because being here with him, laughing, and shooting the shit and knowing the next thing that would come out of his mouth . . . Willow was everything to me, but so was his friendship. I thought I could sacrifice it, but I realized in that moment, I couldn't let it go without a fight.

"You remember you once told me going back for me wasn't a choice? It's when I first moved back here and you were pretending I wasn't blackout drunk every night."

He snorted. "Who could pretend? I spent my entire leave driving your ass home after you disappointed half the women in the Des Moines metro area."

"I don't remember any complaints," I said.

"That's a testament to how drunk you were," he said.

I laughed and relaxed into the couch. "You remember saying it, though? About going back?"

He sighed. "It wasn't a choice. Going back is what we do. It's especially what we do for each other. You know that. You've gone back a hundred times. Even when it's not smart. Even when it's not safe. It's not a choice, it's just . . . I don't know. Part of who we are."

"Exactly." I tried to think about how to explain this to him. "I knew this was a betrayal of our friendship. Willow tried to convince me it wasn't, and I told myself you'd understand, or since she and I were both going our separate ways, it wouldn't matter . . . but in my heart, I knew I was betraying you because you'd asked me to make sure she was okay."

He looked at me levelly without speaking, and I pushed on.

"Falling in love with Willow wasn't a choice, man. If it was, I wouldn't have made it. It wasn't the smart thing to do or the safe thing to do, but it was the only option I had." I set my bottle aside and leaned forward. "For ten years you've seen me sidestep even a whiff of anything serious, and you want better for her. I'm sorry I didn't tell you, but it wasn't a choice." I let out a slow breath, knowing the next words on my tongue could change so much. "And if I have to lose you to keep her, I will, but I don't want that, man. I'm a selfish bastard, and I want you both in my life."

"Well," he said, pausing with another long pull from his bottle. "I hope you get to read her full personal statement."

I stood to take his bottle. "Another?" He nodded, but held on to the bottle when I grabbed it. He lifted his other fist.

"You decide to clock me after all?"

He shook his head. "No wind."

I bumped mine against his—and the action had never felt so good in the entire time I'd known him. "No rain."

WILLOW'S RE-DO LIST

- ☑ First slow dance
- ☑ Hangover
- ☑ Painting
- ☑ Handling an emergency
- ☑ First crush
- ☑ Date
- ☑ Kiss
- ☑ Holding hands
- ☑ Brunch
- ☑ Proposition a guy (Does this count? I definitely never did this before)
- ☑ Breaking a rule
- ☑ Talking to Spencer
- ☑ Concert
- ☑ Camping
- ☑ Exercise routine
- ☑ Protest march

- ☑ Orgasms
- ☑ Sex with someone new (F'ing!)
- ☑ Going downtown (him)
- ☑ Going downtown (me)
- ☑ Learning to ~~drive~~ ride
- ☑ Being on stage
- ☑ A brave ride
- ☑ Grieving
- ☑ New look
- ☑ Make new friends
- ☑ Gardening
- ☑ Dirty talk
- ☑ Against a wall
- ☑ Planning for the future
- ☑ Apply to vet school
- ☐ The park

CHAPTER 49

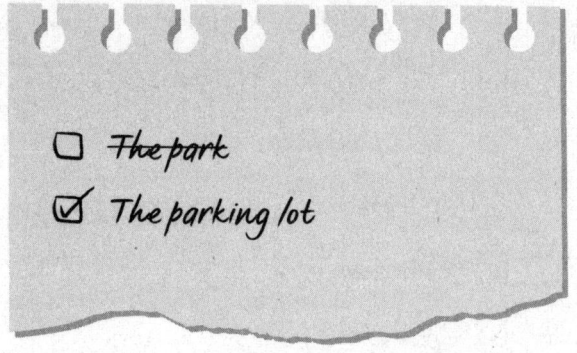

DEACON: Cruz just left.

WILLOW: Do either of you need medical attention?

DEACON: Negative. We managed not to use our fists.

DEACON: Thanks for making him come over.

WILLOW: Will you meet me here?

I sent a pin and glanced around the lush surroundings—it was a different park from the one we'd learned to ride bikes in and across town from where Gus escaped. I'd looked for somewhere new, somewhere bright and open and, most importantly, one that had a fountain.

I sat on the edge, took in a breath, and searched for "Drowning Girl" in the browser while I waited for Deacon to reply. The wide variety of meme options featuring me in the fountain stared back at me, from the original viral video to one with a pretty solid joke about climate change deniers to ones in other languages I couldn't understand. I remembered my embarrassment when I realized that someone had filmed me getting dumped, remembered wanting to crawl into a hole and die twice—first because I thought my life was over without Spencer and again because everyone in the world could bear witness to it. But now, looking at the image, and sitting next to the fountain, it was different. I still was embarrassed and hoped no one recognized me, but it seemed further away, and I didn't even attempt to pull my hair forward. Instead, I clicked on the original video that had blown up.

I'd watched the video again and again, unable to look away, internalizing every word. Maybe I was immature and it was silly to worry about what my mom would have thought, but after talking to Cruz, I watched it again. I watched Spencer and me standing by the fountain where we'd first said I love you, where he'd told me he'd never leave me. I watched my reaction, the crying and hysterics, with a cringey recollection but with a sense of empathy, too. That breakup had happened on the anniversary of my mom's accident, and he hadn't remembered. I'd been emotional all day and then that moment had been a tipping point.

I rested a palm on the fountain's cool concrete ledge and kept watching as I grabbed for Spencer's arm when he'd told me

I needed to calm down, when he'd started to walk away, and I paused the video there. I was curious how he'd looked when I grabbed him—I'd always been too caught up in the next frame where I went in the water, but I zoomed in and saw that he didn't look at me at all. He looked away when I touched him. I'd always given him so much credit for always being there, but in that moment, he'd looked away.

The dots were bouncing on Deacon's text, and I toggled back to the browser window containing the video. I touched my face on the video, wishing I could tell that version of myself how much better I deserved than a man who didn't even look at me. I hit play and watched myself fall into the fountain and flail before realizing I could sit up in the shallow water. And I grinned. It was a little funny, and I wouldn't wish on anyone the experience of being a meme, but I still backed out of the video and took a screenshot of the climate change denier one—it was good.

I scrolled through the other search results, pausing on the YouTube video that was the straw that finally sent me to Iowa. I tapped it.

"I'm no expert," the host began, but I scrolled down through the comments instead of listening to him.

I paused on a comment I'd never read before, one asking: *What happens to these people after they become viral memes?* Someone had replied with, *They probably always live in the shadow of it somehow.* There were several responses to it, and one from someone named AirmanCupcakeWrangler caught my eye.

Comment: *I don't know how others move out of the shadow, but this one brings light wherever she goes, even if she doesn't know it.*

He'd posted a second one, adding, *And OP is an expert on one thing, which is posting bullshit about other people because there's nothing interesting in their own life.*

I grinned, and what I knew now was a Deacon-related heartbeat took hold.

I closed the browser and looked around for Deacon—I'd assumed he was close by when I sent the pin, but maybe there was traffic.

WILLOW: Are you close by?

DEACON: I'm not coming to the park.

WILLOW: Are you breaking up with me? We're not officially even a couple yet.

DEACON: We're not?

DEACON: Do you want to be my girlfriend?

WILLOW: Yes.

DEACON: Good. I love you.

DEACON: But I'm still not coming to the park.

DEACON: No more re-dos.

I grinned and tucked the phone away in my cross-body bag before standing. The sunlight dappled the surface of the fountain, and I sent out another bit of grace to my past self, sending it into the water with some idea it might reach her cosmically, but Deacon was right. I was done with re-dos, too. It was time to start fresh.

I walked toward where I'd parked my bike near the parking lot, thumbing through my phone for a song to listen to on the ride home to meet Deacon, but when I looked up, his bike was parked next to mine. "You said you weren't coming to the park."

"I came to the parking lot," he said, motioning around.

"Same difference." I grinned at the helmet on his head and the knee pads, though he'd found dark gray ones and not my Barbie-inspired pair.

"Big difference," he said, pulling me into his arms. "Now, a big question for you."

I looked up into his brown eyes, flecks of gold catching the sunlight. "We love big questions."

"We do." He settled his hands at my waist, and it was almost like we were dancing under the clear blue sky. "What's the significance of the park?"

"It's where I wanted to re-do saying 'I love you' for the first time," I said. "Thought the grass and the flowers and the water would make it romantic."

He gave a slight head nod. "Well, we've got concrete, a Toyota Camry, and some kid dropped an ice cream cone over there, which is now covered in ants."

"Good enough." I slid my fingers through his hair and pulled his face down to mine. "I love you," I said. "And I love how you've helped me love myself."

"Hey, Low," he said, our lips a breath apart. "Two more big questions."

"Please don't make an allusion to your penis right now."

He laughed before dropping his lips to mine in a sweet kiss. "Then just one more big question." His expression grew a bit

THE RE-DO LIST

more serious. "You won't put your plans on hold for me, will you?"

I shook my head. "I thought I would, but I don't want that for myself. I submitted my application."

His smile widened. "Cruz told me. Said you added something to your epic personal statement. Will I get to read it?"

I nodded, grinning. "I changed the last paragraph." And I held up my phone for him to read. I knew the words by heart and watched his expression as he scrolled.

> This may look as if my interest in and commitment to studying Veterinary Medicine has wavered. And if you made that assumption, you would be correct. But it wasn't my interest in the field that changed; it was my commitment to following my own dreams that wavered. A variety of personal circumstances left me choosing others' needs over my own commitment to become a veterinarian. I don't regret those years of uncertainty, because they brought me back to this moment, when I am certain I will excel in your Veterinary Medicine program. I figured out how to commit to my own goals and to prioritize what matters most to me, which is succeeding in this field and making positive change. This is the second veterinary school application I've prepared, and I can honestly say this re-do is a stronger application for a much more prepared and committed candidate.

"It's submitted. Fingers crossed, but I'd still love for us to talk about what's next for us both."

"Good," he said. "Me, too."

"Any other big questions?"

"Can I now make an allusion to my penis?"

"No!" I said, trying to shove him away, despite the security of his firm grip.

"Fine," he said. "Can I kiss you now?"

I nodded, grinning as his lips dropped to mine again. With Deacon, every kiss felt like it was the first time.

EPILOGUE

THE GROUP CHAT

DEACON: [photo] First day of school!

SYBIL: Willow! You look so good!

DEACON: What about me?

EMI: She makes you look good.

WILLOW: Be nice—it's his first day as a peer mentor at the Veterans Center.

WILLOW: But I do look good.

SYBIL: 👋 🧥 🐶

CRUZ: Who let Deacon mentor anyone? Kidding (sort of)

MARCUS: He was a good fitness coach and he's going to be a great guidance counselor. He'll be a great mentor, too. [photo] 💪

SYBIL: Look at those guns! Chicago is treating you well.

LILA: [photo]

KIERAN: Damn! My little sister is jacked.

SYBIL: I've got you all beat. [photo]

EMI: The baby bump! So glad I'll be back in the country in time to meet this little donut hole.

CRUZ: I don't know how I feel about being added to this group chat—there's a lot of body part sharing.

EMI: You'll get used to it. When we're in person, we also cheat at Monopoly.

KIERAN: Some of us cheat.

WILLOW: No. We all do.

SYBIL: Don't you two need to get to class?

SYBIL: I've never encouraged anyone to go to class in my entire life. Who am I?

EMI: Good luck on your first say of vet school, Willow!

CRUZ: Mentor the hell out of them, Deac.

JUST THE GUYS GROUP CHAT

DEACON: [photo]

MARCUS: I'm blinded by the light. That's a helluva ring!

KIERAN: Damn. Nice. When are you going to ask?

DEACON: Thinking after she gets back from her first day of class.

MARCUS: She'll be exhausted—might want to wait until morning?

KIERAN: In my limited experience, the proposal is followed by a lot of selfies and phone calls—might be hard to squeeze it in before class.

DEACON: Yeah, and Willow is never late.

CRUZ: Keep it that way. I'm not ready to be an uncle yet.

EX PJS GROUP CHAT

DEACON: Morning.

CRUZ: I hate this group name—I'm still in.

DEACON: For three more months. I'm preparing you for your future as a civilian.

CRUZ: 🖕

DEACON: The brothers will be okay without you. I promise.

CRUZ: The siblings. Two women in the unit now.

DEACON: About damn time.

CRUZ: It's early. Why are you up?

[Deacon Rakes changed the group name]

BROTHER-IN-LAW CHAT

DEACON: [photo]

DEACON: Kieran was right—lots of selfies, but you were the first one I wanted to tell.

DEACON: You're not ready to be an uncle, but how about a best man?

CRUZ: Never done that before.

DEACON: I always wanted to be your first.

ACKNOWLEDGMENTS

Denise's List of People to Have in My Corner

The following is a list of people to whom I am endlessly thankful. Unlike the first kiss with ALF, I wouldn't want a re-do on anything that led to me being lucky enough to have them as part of my bookish (and life) journey.

- ☑ Readers who make this all worth it. C'mon . . . what can I say other than thank you, thank you, THANK YOU for making room on your shelf and in your heart for my imaginary friends. Hearing from you, meeting you, and seeing you share the book means the absolute world to me. A special shout-out to the Juicy Readers. Thank you to all the book influencers, not only for shouting about my books but for shouting about romance and making my TBR so endlessly long.

- ☑ My incredible husband, Travis, and my phenomenally smart, creative, thoughtful, and hilarious kid—I love you two squirrels to the moon and back.

ACKNOWLEDGMENTS

☑ Family who would not only be exceptional Corrupt Monopoly opponents but who are endlessly kind and compassionate, and from whom I learned to be funny. Thank you, Mom, Dad, Jay, Amanda, Bruce, Jean, Mike, Melissa, Barb, Tim, Allison, Kaitlin, the best niece and nephews in the world, and the entire beloved collection of aunts, uncles, and cousins.

☑ An agent, who, much like Batman, will always be there when needed and whose tool belt seems endlessly full of solutions. Thank you to Sharon Pelletier—I say it every time, but I'm more thankful for you each time I write acknowledgments. Thank you also to Lauren Abramo, Nataly Gruender, Masie Ibrahim, and Gracie Freeman Lifschutz at Dystel, Goderich & Bourret and Kristina Moore at UTA.

☑ An editor who sees the beauty of a to-do list as much as me. Thank you, Kerry Donovan, for always making my words so much better and pushing my stories to make them great.

☑ A publishing team that is as creative as they are delightful. Thank you to Genni Eccles, Ariana Abad, and Kalie Barnes-Young at Penguin Random House and Kristin Dwyer, Molly Mitchell, and the Leo PR Team! In addition to doing five-star work, all of you made me feel so special, cared for, and seen through this entire process.

ACKNOWLEDGMENTS

☑ A cover artist dreams are made of. Liz Parkes, I will DM you heart-eye emojis until this book goes out of print and probably even after that. This cover is stunning, and you, without fail, always capture exactly the energy I've imagined. I adore you.

☑ Brilliant minds to make the book shine—thank you to Lindsey Tulloch and Alaina Christensen, production editors; Alison Cnockaert, book designer; Marianne Aguiar, my copyeditor; and Karen Dziekonski, the PRH Audio team, and the talented narrators bringing this book to life.

☑ Friends—the ride-or-die, share-your-Cheetos, keep-it-in-the-group-chat kind. Thank you, Emily, Sarah, Jessica, Bethany, Tera, Jen, Rachel, Rita, Janine, Beth, Jae, Allie, Nat, Alexa, and Suzanne for your support while I wrote this book, and hugs, Starbursts, and long, uninterrupted coffee dates to all of my people—I hope you know who you are.

☑ Colleagues who feel like they belong in the last category—thank you to Molly, Anette, Jennifer, Taylor, Jacque, Dynette, and everyone at ISUF for being a joy to work with and so incredibly supportive of your romance-writing coworker!

☑ Booksellers and librarians who are superheroes. Thank you especially to the teams at my local libraries and indie bookstores—Dog-Eared Books, Storyhouse Bookpub, Reading in Public, Shelf Love DSM, Beaverdale Books, and Wandering Raccoon Books—and to Steamy Lit,

Tropes and Trifles, Love's Sweet Arrow, Grand Gesture Bookstore, the New Romantics, and all the other bookstores hyping romance with the fervor and gusto the genre deserves.

☑ A dog who, as I write this, is digesting a frosted sugar cookie she stole from my plate. I still love you, even though you are the worst.

Keep reading for an excerpt from

Just Our Luck

1

Sybil

"SYBIL, IT'S ALREADY seven forty-five." My mom stood in the open garage door with her coffee mug in hand, waiting for me to free up her driveway. It was a little game we played every morning—me losing track of time in the shower and her tapping her foot and dressed for the occasion in her signature slacks and sweater set from Ann Taylor Loft. "We need to go. What are you doing?" Her tone was the one that communicated "you are the child who tests me" versus the one reserved for my sister, which sounded like "thank you for being exceptional, Grace." I'd really tried to be on time that morning—set an alarm and everything. It just . . . didn't work out.

"I found a penny!" I bent to wedge the coin from where I'd seen it peeking between the grass and the sidewalk under the last few layers of melting snow. My fingertips were chilled, but one didn't just leave a penny on the ground—at least, I never did. "Got it!" I held it out like a gold medal toward my mother before shoving it in my pocket.

This was a good sign. Today was going to be lucky. I rubbed

my palms together against the cold, then waved through the windshield. Turning the key, I rubbed the dashboard to coax my old girl to life, and she sputtered but didn't turn over. My stepdad insisted she was a pile of junk, but I knew she just needed a soft touch. "C'mon, girl." I turned the key again and got the same result. "C'mon," I said, an edge in my voice. She *was* a pile of junk, but since I hadn't ever held on to a job for more than six months and was currently living with my parents after getting kicked out of my apartment, she was the only pile of junk I had. "It's my lucky day," I said, petting the dash again and hoping my mom didn't see me doing this dance with my car. She'd side with Paul, which would lead to a long lecture about responsibility, none of which I had time for today.

The engine roared to life, and I cheered, throwing the car into reverse and speeding toward the donut shop. Traffic was light, and I picked up my phone to dial Emi as I drove.

"It's my lucky day," I said into the phone as soon as I heard her answer, her breaths coming heavy as she talked during her run. I imagined her ponytail bouncing as she paused at a red light while we spoke. We were unlikely friends in high school—she was studious and captain of the debate team, and I was everyone's favorite invite to a party, but we discovered a shared love of gelato and the Channel 8 meteorologist we had to watch for a class project. With spoons in hand and an intensely inappropriate interest in barometric pressure, the rest was history.

"You always think it's your lucky day."

"I'm always right." I waved at ancient Mr. Edwards, who clutched his bathrobe closed and waved his newspaper at me. Lucky again. No peek at his stretched-out briefs and everything sagging out of them this morning.

"Marcus and I are going to be at the bar tonight, so if your date is a dud and you want to hang with us . . ."

"No need." I'd been talking to Carl through the app for a few days, and he checked all the boxes. "I'll see you there, but I have total confidence he's going to be a ten. Plus, he has the most amazing eyebrows." He also had a real grown-up job in finance, liked dogs, and didn't make me cringe politically. Since I'd stretched the truth and told my mom and sister I was seeing someone kind and responsible to get them both off my back, it would be great if this worked out.

And it would.

Sure, my last several boyfriends had left a few things to be desired, and one had stolen all my forks before ghosting, but good things happened to me, and Carl was the next good thing. And if that good thing could help me convince my family I was more than just the fun sister, that I could be taken seriously, too, well, that would be a bonus. Grace had Warren, and if I could find a guy that was serious and motivated and . . . well, a little boring, I could show them they didn't have to keep worrying about me. "It's going to go great tonight," I repeated.

"Just in case. You know where we'll be."

I whipped my car into a parking spot. There were signs indicating it was backup-only parking, but I knew I'd only be a minute, and whose bright idea was backup only, anyway? With a quick glance up and down the street for parking enforcement, I closed my door. "I told my boss I'd pick up donuts for the office," I said, hurrying toward the entrance. "She ordered them from this place, and today's the day I ask to be considered for that full-time event planning job."

"Good luck," Emi said as we hung up. The bell above the

door to Joe's Donuts chimed as I walked in, the scent of sugar and fried dough making me want to stop and take a longer inhale. I rolled the lucky penny in my pocket and searched for the cashier. "Hello?"

There was a crash, and a man's harried voice from the back of the store called out to give him a minute. I imagined myself surrounded by the contents of a shelf I'd bumped into in the stockroom at my last job and sent out good vibes to whoever was in the back. Everyone had those kinds of mornings, and I had a couple of minutes, so I looked around. There was a bulletin board to my left covered in thank-you notes from young kids with large, uneven handwriting and donuts colored in with crayons and markers. A couple tacked at the bottom read "Get Well Soon, Mr. Joe!" next to a flyer and a collection box for the Pennsylvania Street shelter, asking for donations to support their programming. I slid a finger along the flyer and continued my visual inspection. The drink case gave a low hum, and the coffee urns were labeled with regular and decaf on handwritten note cards.

The pink frosting and brightly colored sprinkles covering the donuts at the front of the display case made my mouth water. I imagined tapping donuts in celebration with my boss when she applauded my gusto to ask for the job and offered it to me on the spot. I grinned and glanced down at my watch. She probably wouldn't care that I was a *few* minutes late. After all, I couldn't help there being a delay at the shop. Although the donuts and pastries were for a meeting with big potential clients. I tried to peek into the back again. "Hello?"

On the counter, two pink boxes sat, labeled "Josefina." I reached for my wallet, where I'd carefully stashed the petty cash before leaving the office. The total, $36.38, was written under

Josefina's name in black Sharpie, the handwriting small and blocky. "Hello?" I said again, more quietly. It was 8:05 and the meeting started at 8:30. The shop was still, save the faint voices I heard in the back of the store. I could just leave the money with a note. "Here for Josefina," I called out. "I'm just leaving the money!" I thought I heard a grunt of acknowledgment from the back, and I flashed some side-eye to the closed swinging door. We all made messes, but the clerk still hadn't returned. Customer service at this place definitely left something to be desired, but I wasn't letting it get me down. "Keep the change," I added.

I rummaged through my purse for my wallet. If I broke a few traffic laws, which, let's be honest, I was going to break anyway, I could get to the office in fifteen minutes. My fingers landed on my keys, my phone, three ChapStick tubes, and a few loose condoms, but no wallet. "Shit, shit, shit," I muttered to myself. "No, no, no." I tossed it back on the counter and looked inside. On visual inspection, there was a fourth ChapStick rolling around but no wallet. My watch brightly shone 8:07 a.m., and I looked through the door to the back, seeing no one. I searched my purse one more time, as if the wallet would magically appear, and made a snap decision.

I snatched a napkin from a stack nearby, pulled a pen from the cup next to the register, and wrote a quick note and dropped it on the counter. There was a smiley face drawn in the corner of the top box of donuts, and I imagined the owner happily packing up the treats. I traced the smiley face, glancing around for the clerk again, and debated whether I should do this. But I *would* come back with the money and I *did* need to get going. I hurried out to my car with the boxes, tossing them into my passenger seat before peeling out. This was just a speed bump. I could make it there in time. It was my lucky day, after all.

2

Kieran

"WHAT WERE YOU doing on the stairs alone?" I asked, my voice sounding more panicked than intended. I looked my grandfather over for more injuries. "I would have helped you." There was a red spot on his arm, and he rubbed his thigh where I was sure a bruise would form, but I was most concerned about his head and ran my fingers across his scalp, checking for bumps or tenderness.

"Don't fuss. I'm fine." He waved off my hand and sank into the office chair.

"Granddad, you're not fine." I tipped my head to the side to check his left temple. "You just fell down the stairs."

"And lived to tell the tale," he said, offering me a wistful smile, the left side affected after his stroke, but the right the same smile I'd grown up with. "I've started my day at four in the morning for fifty years, and I'm ready to get back to work." He looked around the office, from the ancient desktop computer to the aging photos of my little sister, Lila, and me as kids.

I glanced toward the front, where I'd heard a customer call

out. They'd probably left, and losing customers was the last thing this shop needed. Business hadn't been great for a while, but it was worse now. I hadn't given him the full scope of how bad things really were since I took over tending the store. He needed to heal following his stroke, and the stress would only make everything worse. I shifted so my body would block the stack of medical bills and second notices arranged on the corner of the desk, along with the letter from my medical school informing me that the deadline was nearing for me to accept or decline my deferral. Three months to make a decision and pay the outstanding bill.

I placed a hand on his shoulder. "The doctors told you that you need to rest."

"You can't run this place by yourself, and Lila's still in school. And I'm not the one who looks like he's heading for an early grave." He waved away my touch again and pointed to my face, as if he could see the evidence of my exhaustion written there. "Admittedly, you didn't like *how* I made my way down the stairs, but I'm here now. Put me to work." He stood but wobbled before straightening, and I caught his elbows as I took in the sheepish and frustrated expression on his face. "Fine," he said with resignation. "But this conversation isn't over."

"No, sir." I settled him in the chair, ran to the front, and placed the "Back in Ten Minutes" sign on the locked door. The shop was empty, so as predicted, that customer had given up on me. Jogging back to Granddad, I wondered if giving up was the right call.

I'd planned to be a doctor since I was eight years old, when I learned what it looked like for someone to make things better, for someone to have the power to see a problem and fix it. I decided then that I was a person who would fix things. Now, despite my best attempts to take care of everything, it was all still broken, and the man who raised me needed me to be better. I let out a slow breath. He was right, and I wasn't sleeping enough. If I could get a full night's sleep, I'd stop feeling sorry for myself and could figure out what seemed impossible—how to get us out of debt and how I could return to medical school.

"We hired a teenager to help a little," I reassured him as we walked. I didn't mention that Chad was unreliable, that he listened to only half the things we said, and that we couldn't afford him, but that seemed to give Granddad some comfort. "We're figuring it out." I was careful to make sure my voice sounded positive and optimistic. "We got an order from a new business client, and it's on the counter right now for pickup."

"I hate that it's all on your shoulders, son." He paused, gripping the railing and meeting my eyes. We'd lived with him and my grandmother since social services took us from our mom, so he was the closest thing I had to a parent, and I knew that look. It was the same one he'd given me when I'd quit music in high school after my grandma died and I wanted more hours to work in the shop. It was the same look he'd given me when I'd skipped parties and going out with friends in college to stay in and study, and it was the same look he'd given me when he'd woken up after his stroke and learned I'd left school to help. It was the same look I'd pretended to ignore all those other times. "I don't want that for you. Burdens can be shared."

I nodded and motioned with my chin toward the landing. "You ready to keep going?"

He nodded, and we took it one step at a time up to the apartment over the shop. "Hey," he said as I unlocked the door. He pointed a shaky finger at the dingy linoleum. "There's a penny on the ground. Why don't ya pick it up? You know, for luck."

"Sure," I said, opening the door. "I'll grab it on my way out." I helped him inside, getting him settled on the couch and making sure he had what he needed. "Tom is gonna come by later, I think," I said before leaving. His best friend was a staple in our lives, and I was glad Granddad had some company during the day. He and Tom got up to all kinds of trouble in their lives, but at least he'd have a hand down the stairs if need be.

"Don't forget the penny," he said, and I noticed how he was still breathing heavier from the exertion of the stairs. Still, he flashed me a smile, began humming "Luck Be a Lady" by Frank Sinatra, and nudged me with his elbow until I sang a line with him. "You could use the penny! And sometimes luck looks different than you thought it would."

I closed the door behind me and swiped the penny from the floor. It was hard to imagine this coin had ever been shiny and new. It looked like it had spent its life forgotten at the bottom of a garbage can. "But I *could* use a penny," I said, picturing the mounting pile of bills, the notice that property taxes were going up, and the amount due for medical school before I could reenroll. Jogging down the stairs, singing the Frank Sinatra song under my breath, I unlocked the front door and tossed the penny in the tip jar Chad would probably pilfer later in the day. I settled behind the counter, only then noticing the note scribbled on a napkin by the register. "I forgot my wallet. Will bring money later. Sorry!"

The two boxes of pastries were gone, and because Chad had taken the order, we had no phone number, last name, or credit card information, so were probably just out another thirty dollars. The audacity of someone to just take them and leave a note like this. They must have been the person who called out while I was helping Granddad after he fell. That was the kind of irresponsible, selfish thing my mom would have done, assuming it was fine as long as her needs were met.

As I stewed, it felt like the penny was taunting me from inside the jar. I pressed my thumb to the spot between my brows. Luck wasn't real—good things didn't just happen to people, at least not to people like us.

Author Photo by Destri Andorf

DENISE WILLIAMS wrote her first book in the second grade. *I Hate You* and its sequel, *I Still Hate You*, featured a tough, funny heroine; a quirky hero; witty banter; and a dragon. Minus the dragons, these are still the books she likes to write. After penning those early works, she finished second grade and eventually earned a PhD in education. When she's not writing, reading, and thinking about love stories, she spends her days working in university administration. After growing up a military brat around the world and across the country, Denise now lives in Des Moines, Iowa, with her husband, son, and a dog so quirky, she really needs to end up in a book.

VISIT DENISE WILLIAMS ONLINE

DeniseWilliamsWrites.com
NicWillWrites
AuthorDeniseWilliams
NicWillWrites

Ready to find
your next great read?

Let us help.

Visit prh.com/nextread

Penguin
Random
House